NOT ALL

WIDOWS

WEAR

BLACK

Other works by Dianne Palovcik:

In Trouble – 2019
0-978-1-77354-169-3 Paperback
0-978-1-77354-185-3 eBook

NOT ALL
WIDOWS
WEAR
BLACK

DIANNE PALOVCIK

Enjoy the read!

Dianne

NOT ALL WIDOWS WEAR BLACK

Published by Dianne Palovcik, Edmonton, Canada

sleeping garden – Poem by Kathie Sutherland

Author photo by Carlyle Art

ISBN:
Softcover   0-978-1-77354-374-1
ebook   978-1-77354-375-8

Publication assistance and digital printing in Canada by

PUBLISHING
PageMaster.ca

ACKNOWLEDGEMENTS

First of all, I want to acknowledge the support of my husband, Rudy as I challenged myself to write a second novel.

To my beta readers, I truly value the help you have given me. Your time and talent is much appreciated. "Thank you" John Ashton, Barbara Baker, Carol Rachul, Maria Roach and Kathie Sutherland.

I also want to acknowledge my readers. Thank you for reading my work and sharing your thoughts. I am grateful for your ongoing support.

Finally, I also want to extend my thanks to the team at PageMaster Publishing who made it easy for me to collaborate with the staff while maintaining creative ownership of my work.

CHAPTER ONE

Margaret Bell grew up with no intention of being defined by the rules of Victorian society. When she met and married Thomas Bishop in 1894, she entered the marriage confident her relationship with Thomas would replicate that of her parents, loving and thoughtful. Within months, the truth about her own marriage became clear. Thomas was more complicated than she ever imagined a man could be. Her life was soon filled with indifference, secrets and lies.

Thomas Bishop arrived in Halifax in the fall of 1893. The following January, his attention was drawn to the auburn-haired Margaret during a Saturday evening indoor skating party. Observing closely, he guessed the young man with her was not her admirer. When Margaret and her older brother James purchased ice cream and sat at a table to enjoy the band music, Thomas made his move. He boldly sat beside Margaret and engaged her in conversation, completely disregarding James.

During the following days, Thomas made it his business to find out everything he could about Margaret and her family, including their church activity. He'd never been religious but discovered church attendance provided opportunities to further his personal motives. Within a few weeks, he contrived to meet Doctor and Mrs. Bell, James and Margaret as they exited St. George's Church. And so his pursuit of Margaret began in earnest.

Margaret was in awe of the gifts and attention given to her by the older Thomas. To Margaret and her family, he described himself as a successful orphan raised by an aunt and uncle now deceased, inferring their wealth was considerable.

Thomas was well-mannered, charming and most importantly for Margaret's parents, besotted with their daughter. Margaret's headstrong nature increased her parents' desire to settle her into a good marriage sooner rather than later. They were convinced Margaret's future well-being and happiness would be secure with Thomas Bishop.

From the beginning of the courtship James did not take a liking to Thomas and quietly made a few local inquires regarding his wealth and background. He discovered Thomas owned a business and belonged to the Halifax Club, a social club for prominent Halifax business people.

At the time, James was more interested in enjoying life and finishing his medical training than his soon-to-be brother in-law's credentials. He was a smart fellow with a quick wit and charming smile plus a hankering for risky behaviour. It came in the form of gambling and drew him to the backrooms of pubs on the wharf side of the city. None of his fellow medical students saw the fun or benefit of gambling, so James often kept company with a few men who worked on the docks, fellas he'd known from his early school days.

During the fall Margaret became increasingly troubled by Thomas' unpredictable behaviour. At times he was pleasant but could also be cold and overbearing. He was quick to anger, shunned most social events and preferred to stay at home in his study, leaving Margaret to crochet or read in the sitting room. While popular romantic novels were entertaining diversions, Margaret fully expected an affectionate, intimate relationship with her husband. She intended to do something about it.

One evening in early November, Margaret made up her mind to approach the problem. She entered the study to find Thomas at his desk sipping Rémy Martin. Two red accounting ledgers sat open on the desk. He held a fountain pen in his right hand but hurriedly placed it in the ink pot and snapped the ledgers closed as she approached.

"May I join you? It's quite lonely in the sitting room." She poured a small amount of cognac in a snifter and sat in the brocade wing chair closest to Thomas.

"Drinking is not becoming to women of your class, Margaret." He paused. "I suppose I can overlook it in our home but only on the rare occasion."

Margaret dove right in. "You appear content to be on your own or are you not happy?" She smiled disarmingly, took a sizable sip of cognac.

"I've always been happy with my own company. I don't see why that should change now."

The hot rush of brandy flushed Margaret's face, leaving her emboldened and eager to challenge Thomas' stern look. "And a need for social contact and enjoyment of my company, is that not something you desire? Perhaps we could spend more time together alone, get to know each other better. Maybe now?"

Thomas avoided her intent. "You are at liberty to socialize without me. I'm sure your brother or parents would welcome more of your company. Perhaps a friend? Perhaps that girl who was your bridesmaid?"

Agitated, Margaret raised her voice. "Are you ashamed of me or already bored of me?"

Thomas didn't intend to tolerate her queries nor intrusions. "Is that you or the brandy talking?"

"A bit of both." She waited for a sharp retort. When none came, she went on. "I don't understand why you are so short with me at times. Is there something at work bothering you?" She breathed deeply, fearing she'd lost her way in the conversation. Being at odds with Thomas and his work had not been her intention but she found herself there.

Thomas sent her a smug smile. "Work is none of your affair and I do not appreciate you judging my treatment of you in those terms."

"But that's how it seems to me. Do you not want to know how I feel about our life together?"

"What I know is, you need to become less emotional about day to day interactions between a man and his wife. You're reading far too much into this. Perhaps another year or two will mature your perspective and reasoning." His gaze returned to the ledgers, dismissing her and the questions outright.

"I'll leave you to your work." She rose and left the room, taking the glass of Rémy with her.

* * *

In mid December Thomas arrived home from his club in a more pleasant mood than usual. "I see you have the Christmas decorating underway. Quite appealing."

"Thank you. My eyes are crossed! Cookie and I have been stringing popcorn and cranberries all afternoon."

"Cookie?"

"Mrs. Gilmore. She told me everybody calls her Cookie."

"Sounds unseemly for a woman in your social position to do so but if that's her preference, so be it."

Margaret followed him to the study. "Good evening at the Club?"

"Very. New contract coming from Montreal." He turned his back, walked toward the liquor cabinet.

Margaret kept the exchange positive. "That is good news. You'll be able to hire more people."

Thomas turned quickly. "Why would you make that comment? Business is not your strong point." He paused. "Did you want something?"

"I do. I would like us to attend the fancy dress ball later this month and speak of my wish for more family conversations with you, about the two of us." She held her breath.

Thomas put his glass down. "That again? A conversation as you call it, is a 'no'. You're far too emotional, too often. I see it in your daily demeanour, how you carry yourself around the house.

Perhaps you need to see a doctor, take some pills. Maybe new clothes would make you feel better. Ask that dressmaker woman, whatever her name is to come and stay with us for a few weeks. She can make as many day dresses and gowns as you want. She'll be someone new to talk to. That's what you need to fix this, a woman in the house." He took a deep breath, clenched his fists and moved close to tower over her.

Fearful, Margaret inched back keeping her eyes on Thomas' face. She braced for a slap or punch.

The storm passed but he maintained control. "If you want to attend the ball, then yes, we'll go." He fixed his eyes on Margarets'. "You need to get out more and stop blaming me for the problem you think we have." Smoothly changing his tone, he asked, "Are you happy with your cook? Any complaints from her about her room?"

"Everything is fine." Margaret turned on her heel and stormed out.

"Fine." Thomas said to himself, smirked and returned his attention to the new contract.

* * *

On the evening of the Winter Ball, Margaret descended the stairs, closely followed by Cookie.

"You look lovely, my dear. The carriage is waiting."

"Thank you, Thomas. Mama's dressmaker made a beautiful gown for me." Reaching the bottom of the stairs, she twirled around slowly. The bodice of her dress was cornflower blue crepe over silk with a low-cut square front. Two wide bands of navy silk ribbon encircled the hem of the long skirt. A navy silk belt with short sash completed the look. Her white opera gloves were trimmed with pearl buttons.

The Ball was an elegant affair. A floral embroidery lace tablecloth covered the long banquet table in a room adjoining the ballroom. At one end of the table, coffee and tea were served. At the other, guests could choose from ices in the shape of flowers and fruit, cracker-bonbons, biscuits, cakes, cold tongues and sandwiches.

Thomas roamed the banquet room, leaving Margaret alone to engage in her own conversations while he button-holed men to discuss business, first and foremost, Bishop Import Export.

Robert Fraser caught sight of Margaret and rushed across the room. "Margaret, I haven't seen you for ages! How are you?" He clasped her gloved hands, grinning from ear to ear.

Margaret chuckled. "Don't say ages. You make us sound like we're old already!" She eased her hands free.

"Well, it has been since the summer of '82. By the way, you look lovely, so elegant."

Margaret felt heat spread across her cheeks. "Thank you."

"Using our dance class lessons this evening?" Robert's usual easy smile relayed his natural warmth.

Margaret's fleeting wariness gave way to comfort with her old friend. "Not really. James and I had one waltz. I think he felt sorry for me." She hastened to add. "While you were away, I married."

"Who'd you marry? One of my friends from school? Thought you'd wait for me." He winked.

Margaret ignored his flirty comment. "Thomas Bishop. He's older, moved here from Montreal. He has a business on the wharf."

"Got to be a great fella to catch you. Care to dance?"

Thomas moved close to Margaret, grabbed her arm.

"Good evening. I'm Thomas Bishop, Margaret's husband and you are?"

"Good evening, Thomas." Robert extended his hand which Thomas reluctantly shook. "I'm Margaret's school friend and old dance class partner, Robert Fraser. Pleased to meet you."

Margaret prevented Thomas from quizzing Robert by asking her own question. "Where have you been living all this time?" She kept her eyes on Robert's face, despite Thomas' increasing pressure on her arm, knowing she would have a bruise.

"Montreal. Stayed with Uncle Everett and Aunt Myrtle while

training in the bank since the fall of '93. I've been home a couple of times in the past year, only for a few days."

Thomas turned to walk off. "Excuse me. I see a man I must speak with."

"Fair warning, Thomas. I'm going to dance with Margaret while you're gone."

Margaret 's heart was beating much faster than usual. "Thank you. A dance sounds lovely. But aren't you here with someone?"

"No. I'm on my own. The orphanage is a good cause to support. Mother and Father are also here."

Margaret felt safe gliding across the floor in Robert's embrace. Their bodies fit together so easily, it was as though they'd never been apart. Robert's collar held a refreshing blend of citrus cologne. She breathed deeply, intending to remember the scent long after the dance ended.

Robert's old habit of softly humming in Margaret's ear while they danced soon returned. She whispered, "Miss Dubois could never break you of that habit!" They both laughed out loud, drawing smiles from several couples nearby. Across the room, Robert's mother Regena also heard their laughter.

"Thank you for the dance, Robert. More than one dance with a man not one's husband would certainly set tongues wagging. Let's have some refreshment."

"Sounds perfect. By the way, you'll see more of me in the future. My new work brings me to Halifax once a month, beginning in June."

"That is wonderful news. Your parents must be pleased."

"I hope you will be too. It'll be good to resume our friendship." His smile found its way to his eyes.

Margaret returned a quick grin but refrained from commenting. Apparently, Robert did not understand society's rules for married women.

* * *

At home, Margaret had barely reached the front hall when

Thomas grabbed her arm. "Before you go any further, who was that fellow you were smiling at in the reception room this evening?"

Before Margaret could respond, he continued. "Come on, the one who held your hand far longer than necessary. He didn't appear to have a lady with him."

Margaret kept her response light. "You can't be referring to Robert. You met him and he wasn't holding my hand."

"Not that Robert fella. The red-haired one."

"Oh, that was Arthur Taylor. His wife Eleanor had a baby girl three days ago. Her name is Flora. Arthur was so excited, he came to tell everyone. He's a lovely man who..."

Thomas cut her off, his words took a softer tone. "Very well." He took Margaret's hand and led her upstairs."

Lying awake after Thomas had satisfied his own needs, Margaret's thoughts turned to Robert's kind manner and easy laughter. She looked forward to June, then fell asleep remembering the scent of his lemongrass cologne.

* * *

At the Fraser home, Regena was quick to remind Robert of Margaret's marital status.

"Don't worry, Mother. She's a great sport. I'm sure she enjoyed our little chat and dance as any old friend would."

Lying in bed, Robert realized the evening had given him the enjoyment and sense of well-being he'd been missing. He was looking forward to spending time with Margaret in June.

CHAPTER TWO

HALIFAX, NOVA SCOTIA
JANUARY, 1895

Margaret was naturally curious about Thomas' earlier life, thinking it would offer an explanation for his moods. But despite her casual questions about life and work in Montreal, she was repeatedly thwarted by his vague replies. She concluded he was a superficial man, lacking warmth, simply consumed by work and enraged by his disappointments.

Thomas came home angry on several occasions in early January. He grumbled about late deliveries and lazy workers, often slamming the study door and cursing to himself. Margaret referred to these episodes as his 'tempers', let him rant but never engaged him in dialogue. Instead, she read to avoid his anger and her own growing fearfulness.

While Thomas could see little reason to socialize, Margaret understood that Halifax society expected the Bishops to fulfill their social obligations. She forged ahead with plans for one city event during January and one in February, counting on Thomas to discover the benefits for himself.

Halifax had opened an indoor skating rink in 1880. In short order, ice carnivals were a regular occurrence with up to three thousand spectators watching hundreds of costumed skaters. The upcoming carnival was January nineteenth. As she'd met Thomas at the rink, it seemed an appropriate suggestion.

"Skating? I can't skate. Why on earth would we go? It has nothing of interest to me."

Her heart sank. "We don't have to skate but we can watch the others in costumes, circulate in the crowd. You never know who we'll meet." She avoided mentioning the new business opportunities approach, fearing it would unleash another lecture about her place in the marriage.

Silence followed as Thomas finished his scotch. "Well, the carnival may be a good idea for my business, my dear. Do you need a new wool cape? Can't let you look shabby in society."

Margaret smiled but made no comment in case Thomas changed his mind again.

* * *

After the ice carnival success, Margaret set her sights on an art exhibit at the Victoria School of Art and Design. Thomas balked at any suggestion that he stand around looking at pictures on a wall. She went anyway. Her defiance marked the beginning of a days-long silence.

At dinner a few evenings later, Thomas put his wine glass down. "That art evening. Who did you meet there?"

"No one in particular." After three days of being ignored, she expected to be berated or at least belittled.

"You don't recall Francis Allen, the shipbuilder?"

Margaret couldn't recall a man by the name of Allen. "No." She waited for the explosion.

"Perhaps you should think again about your answer. Allen came to see me today and said he spoke at length with you."

"I honestly don't recall the man." She leaned away. Her heart thudded.

"He wants to do business with me. You must have said something to earn that kind of attention. It's best I attend further outings with you."

* * *

The usual Sunday lunches with her parents and James had become tedious. Thomas used his work to leave after the meal.

Margaret stayed on and played the role of a contented newlywed, spoke of social events and joined her mother to cross-stitch or embroider.

Margaret increased her church committee involvement in March and April thinking it would lessen Thomas' critical comments. He was pleased and frequently complimented her 'good work'. He took particular satisfaction in her biddable nature, while never failing to quell her interest in his business, insisting she simply sit by his side and read.

The quarrels lessened but Margaret knew she was paying a terrible cost. She seriously questioned her own behaviour. Do I deserve this cruelty, these cutting remarks and insinuations? Am I not thoughtful or caring enough myself?

One evening in late May, Thomas asked Margaret to join him in the study. She couldn't pinpoint any reason for him to be critical of her. Dinner had been without incident. She entered the study uneasily.

"Come sit beside me." Thomas patted the red brocade sofa facing the fireplace. "I have a delicate question to ask."

Margaret sat, arranged her skirts, placed her hands on her lap and waited for a 'temper'.

"My dear, don't you think it's past time you should be expecting a child? Is there some reason why not?"

Margaret muttered a response which later, she could not recall. It must have satisfied Thomas as he quietly nodded, held her hand and led her to their bed.

* * *

Nineteenth century society held fast to its rules. Margaret had been reared with them and knew the outcome for those who broke them. Being shunned by your peers for a lifetime was not something to take lightly. Revealing intimate details of marital life to family or friends was simply not done. Her grandmother's comments were gospel. "Don't feel sorry for yourself, keep a stiff upper lip and carry on." If someone made a poor marital choice, she had the answer. "She's made her bed, now she can lie in it."

Margaret's head was reeling. The reality of having a child with Thomas alarmed her so deeply she went to see her mother the next morning. She would no longer keep quiet, smile, suffer, endure.

Margaret began to cry as soon as she was seated in her parent's drawing room. She sobbed her way through Thomas' verbal abuses ending with, "Work is his great passion. What I think doesn't matter. I don't matter."

Grace was momentarily unable to speak. "Have your tea, dear. Then we'll continue."

Margaret nodded. After the hastily consumed cup of tea, she lowered her head and spoke quietly. "There's more, Mama." She rubbed her hands over her face. "I don't know how to say this, it's so horrible. I don't think I can say the words. He's cruel, even when I try to push him away. He forces me to…"

"I understand what you're saying." She rubbed Margaret's hand. "There's no need to speak of that any further."

By the time Margaret spoke of Thomas' expectation of a child, her words were scarcely audible. "I'm frightened sometimes. How can I have a child grow up being frightened its whole life." She wept as her mother held her in her arms. She grabbed her mother's hands. "How did I not know, Mama?"

"He's fooled us all. He's a master of deception."

"I'm a fool. How can I get away from him?"

Grace shook her head. "You're no fool, Margaret. Remember that. You are clever and capable." She paused. "We will help you. I don't know how right now but we will help. Are you in imminent danger?"

"I don't think so, as long as I'm agreeable." She wiped her eyes.

The front door closed then William appeared in the room. "Well, well. It's lovely to see you but why are you here?"

"Sit down, William. Margaret needs our help."

A deep frown furrowed William's brows as he leaned toward Margaret. "What's happened?"

As Margaret briefly told her story, his expression moved from concern to anger. "Are you in danger?"

"No, I've learned how to keep myself safe by being submissive." She clenched her fists, twisting the handkerchief. "I don't plan to spend my life being under his thumb. I'm more angry with myself than afraid." She took a deep breath. "I'm here this morning because Thomas wants a child. I will not raise a child with him. Can you help?"

"I will but I'm afraid there's no quick answer, my dear. "

"I understand, Papa." She sighed. "Can I ask you about work?"

He looked puzzled. "Of course."

"How does work make you feel?"

"Feel?" He carefully weighed the answer. "Fulfilled. I'm helping others. And being happy with my family, of course. Why do you ask?"

"Thomas' greatest interest is work. Why does he excuse his anger by saying it's all about work? There must be another reason. When I ask about life in Montreal, he puts me off."

"Montreal. Perhaps there's a way I can find out."

Margaret let out a deep sigh and sank back into the chair. "What should I do now? Continue humouring him?" She dropped her hands in her lap. "Give up?"

William replied. "Don't give up but you should not openly challenge him. I believe that's the safe thing for now. Come for lunch a week tomorrow. I'll have more ideas by then." It's time to speak with Samuel, he thought.

* * *

During lunch at home on Sunday, Thomas opened a door of opportunity for Margaret to get an answer to her question. "I'm going to the office this afternoon. I shouldn't be long."

Margaret stepped over the threshold. "Your work must be very interesting to go in on Sunday. Does work make you happy?"

"I love my work. I love the fun of it." His voice became animated. "It's like a game. I convince men to buy my ideas, give me their money. I get what I want. Win."

"What happens when you don't get what you want?"

"I play the game harder." His eyes held Margaret's in a head-on stare. "I push them." He leaned forward.

She felt herself getting to the core of this man, not the one on public display. Hungry for more, wagering against his possible rage, she maintained eye contact and asked her questions. "How do you push them? Doesn't that make them angry, stop playing the game?"

Silence. Then, "Trying to find my deep secrets, huh?" Thomas' eyes narrowed. "When the game starts, I know more about them than they realize or know about me. I win. Remember that, Margaret. I win."

A shiver shot through Margaret's body. She knew she'd gone too far but it was too late.

CHAPTER THREE

HALIFAX, NOVA SCOTIA
JUNE 3, 1895

Every day Margaret gave way to Thomas she felt more helpless and worn out. It was not normal for a young woman to need a sleep most afternoons simply to prepare for what might happen in the evening. She was sound asleep when she heard her name being called.

"Margaret, are you there?" Thomas called up the stairwell as Cookie came out of the kitchen.

"Mr. Bishop, you're home! Dinner's not near ready. What's happened to your arm?"

Thomas ignored Cookie and kept his arm hidden behind his back.

Margaret peered from the top of the stairs. Her stomach clenched. "You're home!"

"Come down, Margaret. I finished work early and came home to see you. Can't a husband surprise his wife?"

As Margaret reached the bottom step, Thomas swung his arm from behind his back and thrust a bouquet of flowers toward her. She flinched.

Cookie read Margaret's look. "You and Mr. Bishop go have a chat in the study. I'll put the flowers in water."

Margaret pulled herself together and muttered, "Thank you."

Thomas pranced about in the study rubbing his hands together. "I found a new opportunity for business. First thing tomorrow, I'm knocking on the door."

"What's this new store selling?"

He shrugged. "I don't know but I'm going after their business." He walked toward the drinks cabinet. "A small glass of wine, my dear?"

During dinner Thomas' conversation focused on his business plan for the store. In bed, he had another interest in mind. He took Margaret's hand in his. "Won't it be grand. A boy in the house. He'll go to the office with me, learn the business and be company president one day. Bishop and Son Enterprises sounds right. What will we name him?"

Margaret's stomach churned as Thomas' fantasy carried on.

"How about Thomas Bishop Junior? I like the sound of it." He pulled Margaret to his side of the bed.

When Margaret heard Thomas snore, she slipped out of the room and paced the hallway. No amount of walking eased her concern for a child in a home with a bully.

The following day, Thomas came home early again. "Hello, Mrs. Gilmore. Is my dear wife about?"

Margaret came from the drawing room to find Thomas holding a gold watch. She exaggerated her appreciation, fearing anything else would bring on a tirade.

On Thursday morning Margaret found a cameo broach, inlaid with pearls and diamonds from Birks beside her tea cup. She immediately left for her parent's home.

"You're here early, dear."

"Look at this broach, Mama! It was beside my cup this morning. It's the third gift this week." She paced the floor.

"I'll see if your father can leave the office."

William followed Grace into the room. "Hello, my girl."

"I can't take much more, Papa." Margaret ran her hands over her face. "He's coming home early with gifts. The night before last he talked about our child being a boy, calling him Thomas Junior."

"I have a few minutes before my next patient. I've spoken with someone who will help us. The plan has started. In the meantime you need to keep up what you're doing. Do you keep a diary?"

"I have one but don't write every day and it's usually poetry."

"Time to change that. Write daily. Note what sets him off or what he talks about. Don't push for details. Just let him talk and you listen. The diary will be your witness." He took Margaret's hands. "Think of your writing as your path to freedom. Now, I need to go back to the office. We can talk again during lunch. In the meantime, try to be calm. Things will happen."

Grace stood, crossed the room then returned to her chair.

"What's the matter. Is there something you need to tell me?"

"Your first anniversary is this month. A party will be expected."

Margaret shook her head. "Why would I want a party? I don't want to talk about a party today."

"We'll leave it today but we must talk soon."

* * *

On Friday Thomas went to lunch at his club, a quick carriage ride from the office. On his way back, a poorly-dressed version of himself crossed in front of the carriage. He jumped up and yelled at the driver. "Stop. Drop me off here."

"Right you are, sir."

Thomas raced down the cross street to the wharf. When his look-alike couldn't be found, he returned to the office. "Miss Elgin. I'll be away the remainder of the day."

"Wait a moment. I put an envelope on your desk. It looks important." A smug smile crossed her face as Thomas retreated to his desk and ripped open the envelope.

Monday morning. Outside door at seven.
Two hundred dollars cash.
T.

Thomas waved the envelope in Maude Elgin's face. "Who left this envelope?"

"A man wearing shabby clothes. He delivered it right after you left for lunch."

Thomas stuffed the envelope in his pocket and returned to the wharf but all his ferreting about resulted in nothing.

The wharf was not Thomas' usual haunt during the day. At night though, he sought out illegal games of chance or off the books business deals with the underbelly of society. Thwarted in his afternoon efforts, he returned after dark, pulled his hat low over his forehead and took a seat on a bench near Sailors Hotel. After an hour he took a stroll on the wharf and returned for a second hour on the bench. He noticed a stocky woman standing outside the hotel and guessed she worked there. Unsuccessful in a third search, he took a carriage home.

At breakfast the following morning, Thomas spoke to Margaret without lowering the paper. "I'll be at the office all day tomorrow. Enjoy Sunday lunch with your family." As an after-thought, he added, "We have an anniversary later this month. You should plan something."

* * *

Margaret loved Cookie's stories and she was far better company than Thomas so she decided to miss church, enjoy breakfast with Cookie then go for lunch with her parents and James.

* * *

"Come in my dear. Lunch is almost ready. I missed you at church this morning. Everything alright?"

"No worse than usual. Thomas went to the office and I enjoyed breakfast with Cookie. She talked about her husband. She misses him terribly. He died in a factory accident a few years ago."

"Yes, I recall. Terrible day. A piece of equipment fell onto the work floor." She paused. "James is in the garden and your father will be back shortly. He went across the street to the Hastings' home. Their daughter Kathleen is three months pregnant and having a terrible time with nausea."

"Don't mention my problems with Thomas to James. It's humiliating enough that you and Papa know."

"James knows. It didn't seem right he be left in the dark. After all, he lives here."

"He might tell his friends!"

"He wouldn't do that, dear. Here he comes now."

"Hi, Margaret. Mama says you're in a spot of trouble." He held her closely. "Come sit beside me. Anything I can do? I'll be discrete."

"Thank you but I've no idea what you could do."

"You might be surprised. Thomas not here?"

"At the office. Sometimes I think he really goes to his club or other places."

"Could be." James drew on his pipe and exhaled a stream of smoke, smiled to himself.

"The gifts and attention are not the real Thomas." She exhaled loudly. "I'm not myself either."

"Hello, girls and James." William called out from the hall as he threw his hat on the hall closet shelf and hung up his suit jacket.

"Girls! I'm no girl, William."

"You'll always be a girl to me, Grace. How are the studies going, James?"

"Challenging. The best part is cutting up bodies in the laboratory."

"Oh, for heavens sake, James! Must you, right before we eat!"

"Sounds like you want to be a surgeon, son."

"Hope so, Papa."

"I'll wash my hands then we can get to that roast. Bring your diary, Margaret? We can talk about it after we eat. A meal is for pleasant conversation, not troubles."

James knew a little something about trouble himself but he

decided to keep quiet. Telling his family where he saw Thomas would raise questions he didn't want to answer, at least for now.

"That was a great roast. Hazel outdid herself today. Now I must be off to the university. I have cutting work to do."

"James, really!" Grace gave him a stern look. "Take off your good suit."

"Yes, Mama."

"Ladies, I have a patient to see. Can you give me a quick update on Thomas?" He looked in Margaret's direction.

Grace interrupted. "A patient? It's Sunday!"

"Samuel's sister. Just a quick check on her foot. Seems she tripped over the dog last evening. I won't be long, dear. Margaret?"

"He's up to new tricks, Papa."

"Well, well. Fill me in when I'm back." William needed to check up on their Thomas plan with Samuel, including his own surprise visit to Bishop Import Export in the morning.

* * *

James told his family the truth, up to a point. He did go to the university but at dusk he was on his way to the wharf area to find and follow Thomas. Shortly before giving up the hunt at midnight, he noticed a woman on a bench near Sailors Hotel. It struck him as strange why a prostitute would be wearing a black dress and veil.

CHAPTER FOUR

HALIFAX, NOVA SCOTIA
JUNE 10, 1895

On Monday morning William left home early and positioned himself across the street from Thomas' office. As Thomas reached for the office door, a man wearing shabby clothes appeared from the side of the building. William's jaw dropped. The man was Thomas' double. Following a brief exchange of words, the double grabbed an envelope from Thomas and scurried toward the wharf. Pursuing the look alike was tempting but William chose to follow his own plan. Margaret's welfare came first. He walked across the street and into Bishop's office.

"Good morning, Thomas."

"What are you doing here?" The tone was blatantly accusatory.

"There may certainly be something very wrong. Let's go into your office."

"You can ask me anything right here. My secretary won't be here for at least half an hour."

"My concerns may take longer than you think. Let's move into your office."

Thomas nodded acceptance, pointed to a chair then moved to sit behind his desk.

William did not waffle around the purpose of his visit. "I'm very concerned for my daughter." In case Margaret was being followed, he spoke the truth about her visits to the family home. "She has been in our home a few times in the past six weeks. She's unhappy and to be frank, at times frightened of you. What do you say to that?"

"This is indeed a dreadful situation, if in fact Margaret is what you say."

"Are you questioning my word?"

"Absolutely not, I assure you." Thomas clenched his fingers and shrugged.

"Well then, what are you saying? Margaret's lying?"

Thomas placed his hands flat on the desk. "Margaret is spirited and young. I would suggest she is maturing into her role as a wife and hopefully, a mother one day soon. Don't you agree?" He leaned across the desk, challenging William's point of view.

William ignored the physical posturing, remained seated with his back resting against the chair. "I agree that Margaret is spirited, young and new to the role of wife; however, she is unhappy. When she visits, she rarely laughs." He fixed his look on Thomas' dark eyes.

"I must say I don't see that, certainly not lately." Once again he clenched his fingers. "I did have some minor business troubles in the winter. I resolved them quickly. Troublesome workers can quickly ruin a business, don't you agree?" His mouth smiled but his eyes remained cold.

"I'm sure they can. But let's get back to Margaret. She appears frighted at times. Have you seen this?"

"Absolutely not. I cannot imagine what would frighten her. Perhaps the cook has told one too many ghost stories. According to Margaret, she's a great storyteller." He smiled, settled back in his chair.

William remained silent, waiting for Thomas to continue his rebuttal.

"But your story is most distressing, Doctor Bell."

"It is not a story. It seems you do not see any change in Margaret since the wedding. Is that correct?"

"I assure you, I have not."

"And I can assure you, I have." He paused. "I want you to

speak with Margaret about her feelings and concerns. Then you and I will meet here next Monday morning to discuss this further. Agreed?"

"Agreed." Thomas took William's hand in both of his and shook it. "I assure you I want nothing but the best for Margaret."

"On that we agree. We will meet here on the seventeenth at eight o'clock. I want this resolved before your anniversary party on the twenty-second."

Thomas walked William to the door. *Interfering old goat.*

Thomas had no intention of telling Margaret about her father's morning visit nor striking up a conversation with her about their marital relationship. As far as he was concerned, his marriage was his business. He continued his work as if the visit had never taken place.

William paused on the sidewalk. The business of Thomas' look alike would be best handled by Samuel Fraser, the family lawyer. He could use his contacts, make a quiet inquiry.

* * *

"Good evening, Margaret. I trust you had a good day."

"Yes, I met with the church ladies to plan a late fall event in aid of the orphanage."

"Sounds fine. By the way, I'm taking an unexpected business trip to Montreal on Wednesday. My presence is required at a meeting. I will be home on Tuesday, the eighteenth. Expect something from Birks when I return. Now, what has the cook prepared for dinner?"

Margaret didn't care why Thomas was going to Montreal but was delighted when he left. Her diary reflected her pleasure.

Friday, June 14, 1895
With Thomas gone, I am experiencing what I can only describe as new-found freedom. It's akin to an awakening, an inner joy that illuminates my being. My heart is light.

Saturday, June 15, 1895
Today I took the horse-pulled rail car to the end
of the line and walked part-way home.
My life will be so much better when I'm free of
Thomas.

On Sunday William stood to greet Margaret as she entered the family pew. "Where's Thomas?"

"He's in Montreal. He won't be home until Tuesday."

William's lips tightened. "We planned a meeting for tomorrow. Blast that man."

James patted Margaret's hand. "A holiday for you."

"Yes. I had a lovely ride in a horse-pulled railway car yesterday. Several people were talking about the electric trolley cars coming next year."

Grace interrupted. "Let's talk about your adventure over lunch, dear. We must finish the anniversary party details today. I have some ideas about food but the final say is yours. Do you have any additional names for the guest list? We need to mail the invitations tomorrow."

William looked straight ahead. "Shush, everyone. The service is about to begin."

* * *

Margaret hated to spoil lunch but she wanted to know what her father had planned for Thomas. "Can you tell me about the plan for Thomas, Papa?"

"It's already in place. When we have a result, I'll speak to all of you." Then he promptly changed the topic. "You look well today."

"I feel relaxed. It began right after Thomas left for Montreal." She turned to James. "How was your week?"

"The usual lectures, studying and a beer with friends last night. Pretty ordinary."

James hadn't taken to Thomas from the beginning. Perhaps

it was his brazen behaviour at the skating rink or his incessant self-praise. In any case, he disliked the man. His initial inquiries before the marriage turned up nothing. Now months on, he'd resumed his quest to get something serious on Thomas, something that would get him out of Margaret's life. He'd purchased a beard and gone on the hunt, fully expecting it would lead to Thomas' crooked business practices.

William excused himself from Grace and Margaret's party planning discussion to consider Samuel's plan. He was getting impatient. A retired policeman was searching for a Thomas look-like in the dock area, local hotels and men's boarding houses. If that turned up nothing, Samuel would contact a lawyer in Montreal.

* * *

The day before the anniversary party, William could contain his impatience no longer. He went to Samuel's office. "It's been almost two weeks. Do you know anything about that fella?"

"The retired policeman came up empty. If he's working, nobody knows him. My guess is he has his own money and doesn't live here. Based on your sighting, he's a close relative of Thomas' but why he's here is still unknown."

"Thomas gave him something in an envelope. I'm guessing money."

"Then blackmail is a good guess. But why?"

"What about your lawyer friend in Montreal?"

"I've told him to assume the surname is Bishop but without a first name it's almost impossible even when looking at recent convictions. Montreal has a population of over two hundred and fifty thousand people. Do you want me to ask about Thomas?"

"Not right now."

"Okay. See you at the party tomorrow."

* * *

Thomas insisted the anniversary party be held at the Halifax

Club, a private business club where he was a member. Well aware that Thomas would not be interested in ensuring guests were welcomed and have a pleasant evening, William and Grace offered to be the hosts.

Margaret imagined all sorts of possible problems during the party. Her mind was miles away, leaving Cookie to dress her from petticoats to hair pins.

"Is everything all right, my dear?"

"Pardon? Were you saying something, Cookie?"

"Were you this distracted on your wedding day? Are you all right?"

"Just nervous. All those people."

"Be yourself and you'll be fine." Cookie smiled but she knew exactly what was on Margaret's mind. That husband of hers' was a right pain in the bottom. And a brute too.

Thomas called up the stairs. "Are you ready? The carriage is waiting. I'll be in it."

"Take your time on the stairs, dear. Pick up your skirts and take a deep breath. You look beautiful."

Margaret descended the stairs wearing a deep lavender satin gown with short puff sleeves trimmed in cream lace. The full skirt was finished with a wide flounce at the hem and worn as a train. Her reticule of matching lavender silk was decorated with embroidered pansies and pearls.

* * *

Robert was greeted by William and invited to join a small group of guests already deep into a conversation about the upcoming first Natal Day event to be held in August. He remained on the fringe and looked around the room for a glimpse of Margaret. Seeing her, he excused himself and strolled in her direction.

"Hello, Robert." Margaret extended her hand, met his smile with hers.

"And hello to you. You look great in that colour."

"Thank you, my dressmaker seems to have outdone herself,

again." Margaret was discombobulated. She'd run out of words already and fiddled with her reticule.

"What's the matter? Cat got your tongue?" Robert laughed and winked.

"No! Why would you say that? I'm perfectly fine." She pursed her lips.

"I don't think so but..."

Margaret interrupted. "How's the new work? Your mother mentioned something about it at church."

"It's very much the same. The big difference will be the monthly travel."

"That will be tiring."

"Not really. I'll be here every four weeks and see you."

"See me? That's very presumptuous!"

"I consider it a bonus of the work." He laughed.

"Don't be so ridiculous." She took a deep breath. Robert's cologne reminded her of their dance and laughter at the ball.

"Hello, Margaret are you still here?"

"Of course, I am. How are your parents?"

"Fine." He looked around. "I expected to see Thomas rushing to your rescue."

"What do you mean by that?" She could see Thomas cornered by her father near the door. She changed her mood. "Come with me."

Robert only wanted a simple answer but he agreed to follow her.

William was speaking. The conversation looked serious but Margaret interrupted. "Thomas, you remember meeting my friend from school, Robert Fraser."

Thomas looked relieved to end his conversation with William and nodded, keeping his hands in his pockets.

Robert thrust his hand forward. "Good to see you again, Thomas."

"Robert." A hasty handshake followed. Thomas stepped back then put his hands back in his pockets.

"How's business on the wharf? Perhaps we could talk before I return to Montreal?"

"Perhaps." Thomas waved at someone across the room and excused himself.

Robert continued chatting with William while Margaret kept her eye on Thomas. *Bugger, now he's left the room altogether.*

Seeing Thomas go outside, James sauntered out and lit his pipe. "Lovely evening, Thomas."

"Margaret enjoys this sort of thing more than I. If you'll excuse me, I have a brief business meeting." He rushed toward a waiting carriage. As it pulled away a man in a dark suit asked, "Did you get the money from Graham?"

With no way to follow the carriage, James emptied his pipe and joined Margaret, Robert and his father.

"Are you here often?" William asked.

"Once a month now. I have work here and of course it's a chance to enjoy mother's home cooking!"

James was curious. "So not married yet?"

"Haven't found the right one."

"Well, maybe there's still one for you in Halifax." William looked from Robert to Margaret. "Perhaps you two would like to catch-up. James, you and I should speak with our other guests."

Margaret and Robert settled on a sofa near the fireplace. Margaret made frequent glances toward the sitting room double doors.

Robert was quick to notice. "Something wrong?"

"I'm fine."

"Whatever happened to Elaine Gordon? She was a great friend of yours. My mother doesn't seem to know."

"She went off to Ottawa to live with a married cousin." She took another quick glance at the door. "At least that's what her mother told Mama."

"And you. Are you happy being married? I thought you'd wait for me." Then he laughed and slapped his knee. "Just joking, Margaret. You know me. Can't resist shocking people, throwing them off guard." He paused. "How about lunch? Noon on Monday. Meet me at the bandstand."

Margaret was speechless. She would enjoy spending more time with Robert, relive happier times but it would be seen as most inappropriate. Before she could decline, Thomas appeared beside her.

"Just asked your wife to lunch on Monday, old chap. I trust you're fine with us exchanging childhood stories."

Thomas was staring toward Margaret's father, not paying attention. "Sure. Yes. Fine by me. I'll return in a few moments, Margaret. Be ready to go home when I return for you."

"See you Monday at noon, Margaret." Robert kissed her hand. "By the way, you look most charming this evening."

* * *

The day after the anniversary party was business as usual for Thomas. Even though it was Sunday, he was gone by seven-thirty, leaving while Margaret dressed for breakfast and church.

Relieved to eat alone, she considered the many times she'd accepted his appalling behaviour in social situations. Despite the current situation, she very much wanted to challenge Thomas or forever look the fool and miss out on making her wishes clear, winnable. Thomas wanted to be the victor every time. Perhaps it worked in business but it was a distressing way to share a marriage.

After Sunday evening dinner, Margaret settled in to read and avoid a potential altercation. A small glass of sherry was tempting but she didn't want to take the risk.

CHAPTER FIVE

When Monday morning arrived Margaret avoided Thomas until he left for the office, fearing he would remember her lunch with Robert. She dithered over what to wear. After changing day dresses twice and jewelry three times, she settled on the peach taffeta with matching ribbon ties and lace edging on the cuffs. Her small embroidered straw hat matched perfectly.

Going to meet a man who wasn't her husband was both exciting and more than a little unnerving for Margaret. She questioned her own reasoning, then Roberts. Why was he doing this? What on earth would they talk about? Didn't they discuss everything at the party? Her anxiety intensified. Certainly it was out of the question to ever meet him again, even in public. This would be their only lunch. She'd make sure of that.

As her carriage drew close to the bandstand, Margaret admitted she was looking forward to seeing Robert again. Then, a confession. She was frightened to be alone with him, frightened about her feelings for him.

Robert was waiting for her as she stepped off the carriage. He greeted her and together they walked the short distance to the hotel in silence.

Inside the tea room, they were offered a table for two in a window alcove, overlooking the side garden. A tiered tray of small sandwiches and sweets was delivered and their order for a pot of Earl Grey tea taken. They spoke of the weather and recent changes in Halifax until the tea arrived and was poured. Margaret was nervous. She sat stiffly in her chair, eyeing the other patrons, hesitating to start the conversation. She sipped her tea not knowing what she should choose as a topic.

Robert on the other hand, appeared to be perfectly happy in the quietness, his eyes occasionally catching Margaret's as they sipped tea and observed the comings and goings around them.

Finally, he broke their silence. "This is what I've missed, having a lunch and jolly conversation with someone I know well and care about. I'm glad you're here, Margaret." He looked into her eyes.

Margaret flushed. "Very bold words, Mr. Fraser. Don't you have friends in Montreal?" She felt her confidence return.

"A few, all men." Leaning forward, he moved the tiered tray toward Margaret; she selected a chicken salad sandwich and an almond wafer. He turned the tray and picked up ham and cheese and two almond cookies.

"Having fun in the big house?"

"Fun?" Her eyebrows rose.

"Yes, dinner parties, drinks, that sort of thing. It must be great fun." He leaned toward the centre of the table and touched the soft petal of a yellow rose in a glass vase. "Your mother still grow roses?"

"Yes. The old garden ones along the path to the front door are still there, fragrant as ever." She smiled, at ease.

"Back to your parties. Make sure you invite me to one, if I'm here the same weekend. Agreed?"

"Agreed." Margaret couldn't imagine Robert at a party with Thomas in their home. She softened her tone. "We've had one small party with a couple of Thomas' business acquaintances. Thomas doesn't find parties as enjoyable as I do."

Robert nodded, "Bit of a stick-in-the-mud, is he?"

Margaret stiffened her back. "Why would you say that? You don't know him at all."

"Because you aren't yourself, your fun self."

"I beg your pardon. I'll have you know, I'm older and married now."

"What does that have to do with anything? Marriage shouldn't change who you are or does it? I'm not married but I want to be one day. But if that means not being me, I'm not having it." He crossed his arms and settled back in his chair, all the while staring at Margaret.

Margaret arched her back, began to twist her upper body. "Well, don't you sound the set-in-your-ways, know-it-all Mr. Robert Fraser. I'll have you know, I'm still me."

Robert laughed out loud, causing other patrons to stare in their direction.

Margaret lowered her head. "For heaven's sake, now look what you've done."

"I've done exactly what I wanted to do, Margaret Elizabeth Bell Bishop. I got you to be you. I love it." He grinned. "Jelly roll?"

Lunch lasted far beyond the time Margaret expected. In a rush to leave, she hastily agreed to have lunch on July twenty-sixth, clasped her skirts and hurried to catch the horse trolley. Once settled in for the ride, she thought better of her foolish decision. She stared out the window, hoping for inspiration in finding a way out of her reckless behaviour. Lunch once, maybe. Lunch twice, ruinous.

When Margaret saw Thomas racing from a side street towards the horse trolley, she knew she was trapped. She couldn't understand why he would be running away from two policemen and where was his suit jacket? When he hopped on the car, she reached for her fan. Realizing she'd left it at home, she lowered her head hoping he wouldn't recognize her hat.

Three well dressed ladies each carrying several packages squeezed in behind Thomas, forcing him toward the back of the car. Having none of it, he told them to get past as he was getting off at the next stop. Meanwhile, the policemen were yelling and waving their arms from the sidewalk. "Get off, now."

Amid the kerfuffle, Thomas glanced in Margaret's direction,

seemingly with no recognition of her. He crouched down in his seat. At the next stop, he jumped through the barely open door. She watched him run into the hardware store then leave it through a side street exit onto the alley.

At home, Margaret walked straight to the study where she poured a whisky and downed it in one gulp. Her throat burned but it was just what her mind needed, a distraction. She didn't doubt what she saw. Now, what to do about it. She reached the bottom of the stairs when Thomas came through the front door.

"I'm home."

Determined to keep the smell of whisky from spreading, she rushed up the stairs. "I'll be down shortly," Inside the bedroom she took off her hat and applied lavender to her hands, neck and collar of her dress.

When she returned, Thomas offered her a small glass of whisky. "I had such a successful day, I wanted to come home early to celebrate with you. How was your day?"

"Fine." She paused, hoping he wouldn't remember her lunch with Robert. Without thinking, she blurted, "Were you on Barrington Street this afternoon about two-thirty?"

"Good heavens, no. Why do you ask?"

"I saw someone who looked like you on the horse trolley."

"You are mistaken. Maybe you need glasses."

"No, I'm sure it was you." It was the liquor talking and she couldn't stop herself.

"Margaret, were you drinking before I came home?"

She looked at him incredulously, hoping it worked. "Why on earth are you asking?"

"Because that is the one and only reason for this remarkable accusation you are making. When I say I was not on Barrington this afternoon, I was not on Barrington. Now, let's have dinner. You've just ruined a pleasant evening."

Lunch with Robert reminded Margaret how unlike her old self she'd become during the past year. She closed her book and settled back in her reading chair, allowing thoughts of their younger, carefree days drift through her mind. She felt a deep ache for that loss. Robert had annoyed her today, because he could see through her. He could not be allowed back into her life. She could not trust her heart.

* * *

Thomas lived for control but controlling his twin Timothy was proving impossible. It was now more than two weeks since Timothy demanded and been given money. Why hadn't he demanded money again? What was he up to? Joe, Thomas' snoop was costing him money but he couldn't afford not to spend it.

"Mr. Bishop, there's a man here to see you."

Joe stepped into Thomas' office before being asked. "Hello, boss."

"Close that door." Thomas was visibly irritated. "What have I told you about showing up here?"

"Relax boss, that secretary of yours don't look like she gives a sweet damn about this place." He looked around the office. "Nice place 'ya got here, boss."

"Get on with what you have to say."

"Right you are. Spotted a retired copper sniffing around them gambling places and hotels at the wharf."

"What does that have to do with anything I need? I'm no wiser about what Timothy is up to!"

"Hold 'yer horses. Give it time. He wears workin' clothes but don't work. I'm workin' on gettin' into his hotel room. This Sunday's my big chance. The part-timer's on."

"You better be on to something. He's here for a reason."

"Wanna hear somethin' funny? The old policeman wearin' a moth-eatin' army uniform is snoopin' around. Some disguise in a city filled with soldiers. Ain't too bright, that fella."

"You talk to him? Who's he looking for?"

"I dunno, yet."

Thomas shook his head. "Find out. Meet me here Sunday. Make it after five."

* * *

Thomas repeatedly feigned interest in social events and entertainment but he was a phony. Their disastrous winter social season had been Margaret's proof. But she was not going to miss the upcoming summer season filled with regattas, dances, promenades and concerts. She was determined to nudge Thomas into society gatherings to cultivate opportunities for personal pleasure under the guise of business opportunities for him. What harm could come from a little self-indulgence and challenge for her mind?

Her first opportunity presented itself at the annual church picnic on Sunday. Thomas deserted her soon after their arrival on the church grounds. Relieved, she mingled freely among the parishioners, many of whom she'd known since childhood.

While strolling toward a group of ladies, a stranger's voice stopped her in mid-step.

"Hello, please allow me to introduce myself. My name is Anna Hopkins. I recently moved to Halifax. May I ask your name?"

"Of course, I'm Margaret Bishop."

"Hello, Margaret. Have you lived here a long time?"

"All my life."

"Perfect, are you willing to introduce me to your fair city?"

Margaret had never met such a forward woman. Although Anna's natural smile and warm brown eyes were pleasing, Margaret found her off-putting. "Perhaps we should get to know each other first?" Margaret smiled.

"Absolutely. I'm from England. My husband's work brought us here. I have to be prepared to move at a moments' notice and fend for myself every time I'm uprooted. We don't have any children. You?"

As their chat continued Margaret discovered she had much in common with Anna. Both were the same age, avid readers, without children and the wife of a man devoted to his work. George Hopkins was a senior British officer at the Garrison.

Anna had been a society reporter for a women-only publication in Britain. She recognized Margaret would be her way into Halifax society and hopefully her return to a society column in the local paper. She needed to pursue this relationship.

Margaret was fascinated by Anna's work. Being a reporter sounded most exciting. Getting to know Anna would be the ideal person for her to discover some type of pursuit other than church activities and needlepoint.

For better or worse, each had a deeply personal reason for cultivating the other.

"Ready for home, Margaret?" Thomas clasped her arm.

"Thomas, I'd like you to meet Anna Hopkins, recently arrived from England."

"Hello." He nodded toward Anna.

"Nice to meet you, Thomas. Margaret and I have planned a lunch later this week."

Thomas nodded again. "Ready, Margaret?"

"See you Thursday, Anna."

Out of earshot, Thomas was quick to check up on Anna. "Who's that Anna person?"

"She's the wife of an officer at the Garrison. I want to make her feel welcome. She's my age and we have a lot in common." Margaret swallowed hard. It took considerable restraint not to add, why do you care?

"Very well. She's probably sensible, well-connected. I approve." Then he patted Margaret's hand. "By the way, I will be returning to the office for a brief meeting before dinner this evening. I'm meeting a business owner."

Joe's big idea was a big zero. His hotel friend told him Timothy left Sailors Hotel last Thursday.

Thomas didn't believe anyone, Joe included. "Check that hotel every two days for the next week. If Timothy shows up, tell me. Otherwise leave me alone. You'll get your money when you do something."

Margaret waited patiently for Thomas to return for dinner.

She hoped he'd be relieved she'd found an interesting acquaintance in Anna, leaving him more time for himself.

"Dinner is ready, Thomas. Meeting go well?"

No. Let's eat then I have work to do in the study."

Dinner was a silent meal. Margaret went to bed early and read.

* * *

On Thursday Margaret arrived early for lunch, eager to hear more about Anna's life in England.

Anna strolled in and dropped a stack of newspapers on a chair near Margaret. "Hello." Her voice was filled with excitement.

"Hello, Anna. You brought newspapers?"

"Yes, a few examples of my work in England. I thought we could discuss the topics and make a plan to meet with your local papers. You could work with me."

"My, you don't waste time do you."

"Time wasted is time lost. I mean to make a name for myself in the newspaper business. Halifax appears to be a fine place to continue what I've already begun. What shall we have to eat? The fish sounds good. Shall we order?"

"Of course." Margaret was taken aback by Anna's bold behaviour. "If I may ask, how did you begin in the newspaper business?"

"My father's in the publishing business. It pays to have connections. Do you have any connections in the newspaper business here?"

"No, I'm afraid I don't."

"I met your father at the picnic. Would he know someone?"

"I will see them Sunday. I could inquire then." Feeling put-upon, Margaret changed the topic. "Do you have brothers or sisters?"

"An older sister. She likes being at home with three children so we have little in common. You?"

"An older brother, James. He's going to be a surgeon."

Margaret became comfortable as they moved on to more familiar topics; family, weather, social events.

"Back to your brother and medicine. That's a discussion for a big pot of tea. Do you realize how society frowns on women studying medicine." Anna was not really seeking an answer and continued. "If a woman wants to be a doctor, she should be able to do it. Period." She paused then began in a louder voice. "In addition to medicine, I'm equally angry about women not being allowed to vote here. We're considered second-class citizens, you know. I plan to do something about it in my lifetime."

The room went silent. Margaret dropped her head, not wanting to be recognized. Anna didn't. She thanked the few women who offered guarded applause.

Margaret was embarrassed. She knew these discussions took place in small gatherings of women. But being younger than most married women in her social circle, she was not always welcome in their hushed conversations. She remained silent, rearranged the napkin on her lap.

Anna stared at Margaret. "Are you okay?"

"I'm fine, just thinking of something I must do later today." Her words faded away at the end of the sentence.

"I'm quite enjoying this lunch. Shall we meet next Thursday?"

"Of course." *I wanted something exciting in my life and its name is Anna.*

"Good, let's return to the newspaper plans. I'll tell you about how my words get in the paper.

Margaret walked home slowly, appreciating the summer sun and flowers in the front gardens. Time with Anna opened her eyes about work and being a woman in 1895. Anna's work sounded stimulating. She met people, expressed her opinions, produced something others wanted. It sounded exciting. Anna's outburst about society was also revealing. In a moment of awakening, she felt connected with other women in the room. Perhaps she could be part of this movement for women's independence.

"Welcome home, Mrs Bishop. Nice lunch?"

"Thanks, Cookie. I would describe it as different."

"Hmm, sounds interesting. You'll have to tell me about it another time. There's a berry pie almost ready for the oven."

Margaret took a glass of lemonade to the sitting room. Anna was spontaneous, a quality Margaret admired. She considered her own style to be less hasty, not fraught with unexpected outcomes. Then she smiled to herself. If her parents thought she was impetuous, they needed to spend some time with Anna Hopkins! She laughed out loud.

After careful thought, Margaret made a decision. She would decline Anna's suggestion they work together. She'd say Thomas preferred she not work. It wasn't the whole truth but close enough to give herself an excuse. She filled several pages in her diary before Thomas arrived home for dinner.

After dinner Margaret felt serenely apart from Thomas' stream of complaints about his world of work. She reflected a second time on Anna's words, her own fledgling desire to be more independent and reversed her earlier decision. She would tell Thomas later. When the time was right.

CHAPTER SIX

HALIFAX, NOVA SCOTIA
JULY 7, 1895

Following Thomas' usual departure after Sunday lunch, Margaret introduced the topic of newspapers to her parents and James. She intended to keep Anna's name out of the discussion. She could then honestly tell Anna no one knew anyone in the newspaper business.

"Newspapers are nothing but a few peoples' views and are no better than gossip rags." James drew heavily on his pipe.

William smiled. "And how did you come to that conclusion?"

"I read them from front to back. There's too much politics, partisan politics at that!"

"Well, after all they are written by people, people with opinions. And don't forget, we've had a newspaper here since the mid seventeen hundreds. During all this time, I'm sure we've had a variety of opinions."

"But remember the government funded them in the early days. Then editors got money from running advertisements but the editors were usually politicians. Hear what I'm saying?"

"That's true. In recent years though, readers are more interested in what's happening across the country. Immigration, the Stanley Cup last year. I'm pretty sure the reader interest is going to get stronger and not just about politics."

Margaret wanted another viewpoint. "Mama, do you read the newspaper?"

"I do. I read everything but don't always agree with what's

being implied. I especially like the advertisements and drawings, very creative." She leaned toward Margaret. "But I'm curious, why did you bring up newspapers?"

Margaret felt compelled to give an honest answer. "My new acquaintance, Anna Hopkins worked for a newspaper in Britain before coming to Halifax."

James could see where this was going. "And she's working for a newspaper here?"

"Not yet. She meets with a newspaper man next week."

"Ah. She's got lot of opinions, correct?"

"Yes, she does. What are you implying?"

"Nothing directly at the moment."

"That's a partial answer. What is the rest of your answer?"

"What is Anna planning for you?"

"I'll tell you when I know myself." *That's a partial answer, too. Smarty Pants.*

"Okay, you two. Let's move on to something equally interesting but less controversial. I suggest the Natal Day celebrations coming up in August."

* * *

The new week brought new challenges for Thomas with commensurate irritability at home. He swore he'd locked all the papers in the office cabinet before leaving late Sunday afternoon but an empty envelope was on the floor under his desk Monday morning. There was no plausible explanation but that it had fallen while he was gathering up everything on Sunday. When it happened again two days later, he knew someone was out to get him and knew how to do it.

* * *

By the time Thursday morning arrived, James was completely flummoxed. For four straight nights he'd pulled on his beard and wandered around the wharf and taken two carriage rides home from the Halifax Club. As far as he could tell Thomas had stayed at home. As a sleuth he was quickly becoming a failure.

* * *

Margaret dreaded having to tell Anna she hadn't found a newspaper connection. She wanted to be part of the exciting new newspaper adventure but her fear of Thomas made it impossible. She practised her excuse before the looking-glass and set out for lunch.

Right on time, Anna walked proudly into the room, all smiles. "Wonderful news. I met someone with a newspaper connection on Saturday in the Public Garden." She paused and sat down. "Do you know a Mrs. Samuel Fraser? Her name is Regena. She mentioned you were a school friend of her son, Robert."

Margaret remained silent, knowing Anna would continue on with her next thought.

"Seems Mr. Fraser has a connection for us. Isn't this the most extraordinary news? And to think, I found it in the park! I'm sure it's a sign of good fortune."

"It is indeed fortunate for you."

"For us, Margaret, for us! I've made contact with the paper. Mr. Ellis will see us next Wednesday, the seventeenth at two o'clock. We can have lunch and make final preparations just before the meeting. I presume this will work for you."

"I apologize but I will not be able to attend the meeting with Mr. Ellis." She stopped momentarily. "At the present time I believe your marital situation and mine are very different. Currently, Thomas prefers I volunteer my time for good causes."

Anna was quiet for a moment. "You can volunteer with me. It wouldn't be every day and I could use your connections to help your volunteer activities. I'd write about them."

"I'll think about your idea."

"He probably thinks people will assume he doesn't earn enough money."

"Maybe."

"George objected when I wanted to work. My father was on my side and spoke with him. So, I understand your trouble with Thomas."

"Thank you."

Their conversation continued pleasantly about church and city events.

Margaret was quite sure she would not hear from Anna in the near future as no lunch date was planned. Speaking with Thomas about volunteering with Anna was not high on her list but her safety was. Working with Anna would have to wait.

* * *

Papa had not mentioned a weekday lunch for weeks so Margaret suggested one after Thomas left for the office on Sunday afternoon, his usual excuse to get away from the family. Nobody was fooled and they enjoyed the time without him. She would have lunch with her family on Thursday.

* * *

Thomas was irritable all week. Knowing his temper, Margaret dared not ask if there was a problem at the office. It was simply a matter of hours or days. Thursday lunch couldn't come soon enough.

"Goodbye, Cookie. I'm walking to Mama's for lunch."

* * *

By that evening, Thomas was pacing continuously. "What's your father up to these days? He left a message with my secretary today making an appointment for tomorrow morning."

"I have no idea." She moved away from his reach.

"I thought you had lunch every week with your family."

"They've been busy with relatives. Mama's two cousins from Boston have been visiting. You met Minnie and Erma at the wedding." That part was true. Today's family lunch was best left unmentioned.

Thomas wandered toward the study. "I'm having a scotch before dinner." At the door, he turned. "Your father better not be interfering in my personal or business life. If he does, he'll pay the price."

After Thomas fell asleep, Margaret crept into the guest room and slept soundly until a bolt of light jolted her awake. She counted the seconds until thunder rumbled, only reaching two. She sat up in bed and wrapped the wool blanket tightly around her body. A second flash crackled across the sky as heavy rain pelted the window. The booming noise was on top of her head. She was not cold but couldn't stop shivering. She'd always been frightened of lightning storms. Mama told her it was better if it rained when the lightning came. It would put out the fire the lightning might start. She wasn't sure that was the truth but the idea was soothing. Within minutes the storm moved away and the sky began to lighten. Margaret guessed it was nearly six o'clock. Cookie would be up so she went downstairs for tea, dressed in her nightgown and matching dressing gown.

"Well, well. Aren't you up early. I'm guessing you're not a fan of lightning."

"I'm actually frightened of it."

"Me, too. When I was a little girl, I was caught in a terrible rain storm with my parents. Lightning struck a tree on the side of the road and the horse bolted. Papa lost the reins over the side of the buggy. All we could do was hang on and hope for the best. Like many frightened horses, Hansen headed for home. He took us straight to the barn door." She smiled. "Ready for breakfast?"

Thomas had a special talent for side-stepping problems he'd created himself. He greeted Margaret with a 'good morning' then remained silent throughout breakfast, hidden behind the newspaper. This move also delayed his departure to the office, forcing her father to wait outside in the damp morning air. It was a cunning move to signal his control.

As Thomas stood to leave, Margaret looked him in the eye. "I hope you treat Papa with respect this morning. After all, he is my father."

"Of course, my dear. Have a relaxing day." He patted her shoulder. Her body stiffened.

"What time do you meet?"

"At nine-thirty. Why?"

"I thought we might have lunch together."

"Maybe another day."

She was pleased with Thomas' rejection.

* * *

"Good morning, Doctor Bell. My secretary is away this morning. Trust you didn't wait too long."

"Not at all. I enjoyed the fresh air after the overnight storm."

"Come into my office." Leaving the door open, Thomas struck the first blow. "Please accept my apologies for abruptly leaving before our scheduled meeting on the seventeenth. I received word of an urgent matter from Montreal and presumed Margaret would have told you before you learned of it at church on Sunday."

William ignored the apology. "Do you have a twin brother?"

Thomas' shocked expression gave William his answer. "I thought so. I saw him outside your office weeks ago. Sit down and explain yourself. And no lies. My daughter's future with you depends on it."

"I'd like to hear that answer myself." Margaret stood in the frame of the doorway, hands clasped together to prevent them from shaking. Her stance belied her shaky legs and butterflies in her stomach. Then the room went black.

"Margaret, can you hear me?" William knelt beside his daughter, holding her head in his hands. "Margaret, speak to me."

"Papa?"

"Yes, my dear. Do you have pain anywhere?"

"No." She raised her upper body then dropped it immediately. "The room's spinning."

"Rest where you are. This will take a few minutes. Thomas, roll up my jacket. Put it under her head. Is there a blanket?"

"What happened?"

"You fainted. It will take a few minutes to feel better. We're going to see Doctor Lewis."

"But."

"Thomas, hail a carriage."

Thomas was relieved. He'd have time to perfect his Timothy story and Margaret looked fine.

"Thomas, I'll meet you here on Monday morning."

"Very well." Then Thomas looked in Margaret's direction. "I'll come home early, my dear. You've mentioned the military drill at the Grand Parade Square. Let's attend this evening."

Inside the carriage Margaret spoke freely. "Is this true? A twin?"

"I believe so. I saw someone who bore a striking resemblance to Thomas outside his office several weeks ago. My plan wasn't working fast enough so today I made a guess and flushed him out myself. You feeling better?"

"Much. I don't need to see Doctor Lewis."

"I didn't think so." He winked and grinned.

"The twin explains my horse trolley story late last month. It wasn't Thomas after all. But why didn't he tell me about a brother? Why is the brother here?"

"I'll get to the bottom of it." He paused. "Be careful between now and Monday. Just listen."

"Thomas is taking me to the Halifax Club for lunch on Sunday. I'm not happy but I have to keep up appearances."

"That's a stroke of luck. I was about to make up an excuse for you not to be with us after church. Your mother and James don't know about the look-alike and I want to keep it that way until I figure out what's going on."

True to his word, Thomas came home earlier than usual. He reminded Margaret of the military drill then asked about her health. He was almost likeable. She knew what would be expected at bedtime.

Lured by the phony kindness, Margaret was sorely tempted to ask about Timothy. She let the feeling pass and went upstairs with Cookie to select a dress, shawl and hat for the evening's outing.

The following morning Thomas bounded down the stairs early. "Good morning, my dear. I trust you have a plan for your day, perhaps an afternoon in the Public Gardens?"

"Nothing at the moment. I presume you will be working?" She forced a broad smile.

"Yes, but first I'm going to the North Street Station to meet the train from Montreal."

* * *

At the Bell home, James raced down the stairs. "No breakfast for me, Hazel. I'm going to meet the Montreal train."

"But, breakfast…"

"I'll find some little place near the Station."

Every so often James yearned to watch the Montreal train arrive and see all the excitement as passengers and people awaiting their arrival came together. He took a carriage north on Barrington Street.

As a boy, James spent many happy hours with his wooden train set. His first train ride to Truro at twelve confirmed his decision. He decided to be a train engineer. Flying past trees, farm houses and animals was going to be the life for him. Somewhere along the way, medicine side-tracked his dream.

He let out a deep sigh, one with more than a wee bit of regret. A visit to the Station would bring his joy back. Inside a small eatery, he found a window table and took in the view of people in motion and the station.

The impressive North Street Station opened eighteen years earlier. It was decorated pressed brick with a mansard roof and two-storey central clock tower. The first floor contained general ticket offices, a reading room and general waiting room. A separate ladies' waiting room had plush seats, a marble fireplace and a separate ticket office. James was more intrigued by the second floor balcony. There, the railway supervisors oversaw operations in the large glass-covered passenger shed. It contained five enclosed tracks and platforms. Outside was a sixth rail track for private railway cars where the wealthy could disembark in privacy and hook their private cars up to steam heating from the station.

While finishing the last of his tea, James watched people gather for the train's arrival. Children ran to embrace visiting family, lovers kissed, men in military uniforms exchanged crisp salutes. One military man in particular was familiar, a parishioner from Saint George's who saluted then took a suitcase from a gentleman in civilian clothing.

There was no time to ponder the officer's name. Thomas was standing directly in front of his window waving toward a grey-haired man carrying a well-worn leather satchel. He raced out the door, pausing briefly to put on his beard. Thomas and satchel man were walking toward the covered staircase which led from the station up to Barrington Street's sidewalks and streetcars.

The ocean liner and immigration terminal were only a few blocks away. James guessed Thomas was leaving the country with a satchel full of money. But when his targets walked past the terminal and continued south on Barrington Street, he shielded himself by mingling with other pedestrians. Fortunately satchel man had a slight limp preventing them from moving quickly. When Thomas and satchel man stopped at a hotel entrance, James walked past, then returned to loiter nearby, slowly lighting his pipe.

It was impossible to hear all their brief conversation. However, James could see satchel man had a round face and bushy eyebrows. As they turned to leave the hotel entrance, Thomas accepted the satchel. "See you next month, Graham."

"For sure, boss. Twenty-fourth, same place."

James watched Graham disappear into a group of Saturday

morning shoppers, then followed Thomas and the money straight to Bishop Import Export's front door.

CHAPTER SEVEN

Margaret entered the Halifax Club uneasily, expecting to see small klatches of men smoking cigars, reading newspapers and looking at her. She was pleased to see several fashionably dressed women seated on their own or with others, reading newspapers and chatting among themselves.

A man seated alone waved in Thomas' direction. As they approached, he stood and extended his hand to Margaret. His overdose of cologne was pungent. She stepped back after shaking his hand.

"Well, well. You must be Mrs. Bishop."

"Ralph, I'd like you to meet my wife, Margaret. Margaret, Ralph Dickson."

"Mr. Dickson." Margaret delivered a no-nonsense smile and nod.

"Call me Ralph, please. I'm sure we will be seeing much more of each other." Dickson's eyes ran up and down Margaret's body. "A most delightful dress, my dear."

Dickson caught Margaret's furtive glance. "Hilda isn't with me. She rarely comes to my meetings." He winked. "Shall we go to the dining room."

Thomas had set her up. This was a business meeting pure and simple, used as a ploy to keep her from her family.

During a brief lull in the business conversation, Margaret took charge for her own purpose. "Ralph, have you and Hilda enjoyed any of the Citadel concerts?" She deliberately kept her eyes trained on Dickson.

"Why yes, we have. I imagine both of you have as well." He cast a flirtatious smile in her direction.

"I've been thinking Thomas and I should attend."

"You two must go. There is one this coming week, on Thursday." He turned to Thomas. "It's a good opportunity to rub shoulders with some interesting and influential people."

"Sounds like a worthwhile evening. Make the arrangements, Margaret."

Despite Thomas' intent, Margaret enjoyed the food and also managed to add a concert to their social calendar. The only unpleasantness about the outing was Ralph Dickson. She would not be fooled twice.

In the carriage, Thomas complimented her on the business opportunity at the concert she had created. She grimaced knowing what would be expected of her later.

* * *

Given the length of time Thomas had to prepare, William expected to hear a whopper of a story about Timothy on Monday. He settled into his chair in Thomas' office and began with a simple comment. "Tell me about your brother."

Thomas immediately explained away his twin Timothy as a troubled boy who in a fit of rage, killed their parents. "Timothy was placed in an insane asylum soon after the murder. I was adopted. The day you saw him at my office was the first time I'd seen him in thirteen years. He wanted money, said he'd leave town when he got it. That's the whole story." Thomas crossed his arms and smiled.

"And what have you done about this so-called one and only visit?"

"It's in the hands of the local police. I expect they're in touch with the police in Montreal. I haven't heard anything and I'm not really involved." He shrugged, casting off any need for personal concern.

"Not involved! Surely to heavens you must be worried for your own safety and Margaret's too. Aren't you contacting the police every few days?"

"I'll contact them today." Thinking he'd put an end to the conversation he stood, shoved his hands into his pants pockets and took a step toward the door. "I'm a business man. I let the police do their business and I do mine."

William remained seated. "Wait a minute. You had to have seen Timothy prior to the morning of the money exchange. How else would you have known he was coming for money." He paused. "So?"

"He left a letter with my secretary, telling me how much money he wanted and the day and time he'd show up." Thomas returned to his chair.

"You didn't tell the police beforehand? You may be sharp about business but you're damn dull about people." William stared hard. "Let me get this straight. You said this blackmail letter was left with your secretary. So, someone looking exactly like you showed up at your office and left a letter for you with your secretary. I don't believe your answer. Didn't your secretary find this strange, ask you questions?

"No, she did not."

"I don't believe you! Try again and this time, tell me the truth."

"That is the truth. My secretary told me a poorly-dressed man gave her a letter addressed to me. She never said the man looked like me. Never!"

"So, let's continue. You have a letter demanding money. It's from your brother, a brother you haven't seen for years. And the unbelievable part is, you actually gave him the money. That part I saw myself." He paused. "Didn't you try to find him after he got the money? Did you find him? Where was he?" Hearing no replies, William continued. "You better tell me what you're not telling me right now or..."

"Or you'll what?" Thomas' face was scarlet, his eyes riveted on William.

"I'll simply go to the police this minute and tell them what I know." He paused. "Sounds like I may have to anyway."

"You can't do that. He said he'd tell the police."

"Tell them what and why did you hand over money?"

"He said he'd say I was in on the murder."

"So, you haven't been to the police at all, have you? Why would you be afraid to go to the police? Your brother murdered your parents, not you. He was put away, not you."

"Timothy was always unpredictable. I thought he'd take the money and leave town."

"But why are you so reluctant to go to the police? Timothy was tried, convicted and placed in an asylum."

"Not exactly."

"What do you mean, not exactly?"

"Timothy was always a problem, stealing, lying, beating up other children. Lots of people wanted him locked up. There wasn't a trial. He was put into the asylum that very night."

"Okay. We'll leave Timothy for a moment. Let's talk about you. You were adopted. How'd that happen?"

"The police talked to somebody and they took me for a ride into the country and left me with a couple in a small village. That's what happened. That very night." Thomas nodded his head rapidly.

"But you were twelve. Surely you must remember more than a car ride. We'll talk about your details another day. Back to Timothy. How did Timothy kill your parents?"

"Knife from the kitchen, while they were asleep. Then he came to wake me. He made sure I had blood on me too, rubbed it on my hands. Then he sent me to the neighbours to tell them."

"Are you really from Montreal?"

"Yes. At eighteen I went to Montreal to find work."

"And?"

"The port was busy. I found a job loading and unloading ships."

"Where did you live?"

"In a wooden house near the river. With other workers."

"Why are you in Halifax?"

"Someone I worked with was from Halifax. It sounded like a good place to live."

"I have more questions about your move to Halifax but right now finding Timothy is a priority for everyone's safety. I'm going to the police station. I'll give them all the details you have provided."

"I can't go to the police station today. I have several meetings. Your information should be all they need."

William ignored the excuse. "Make time for me at noon tomorrow, here." He left Thomas' office and stood on the sidewalk. He had a puzzle for the police. But first, he had to go home. Returning to the police station he asked to speak with a detective. The desk constable took him into a room with a tall window facing the street and offered him a seat on a well worn wooden chair. A large desk was stacked with several piles of paper, a pen, ink pot and large tea mug. The detective's chair didn't look any more comfortable than the one he was sitting on himself. He stared at the file cabinets and breathed stuffy summer air for what seemed an eternity.

"Good day, Doctor Bell. I'm Detective Sergeant Gilfoy." He extended his hand to William who stood to greet a slim middle-aged policeman well over six feet tall. "Have a seat. What can I do for you?" Gilfoy ran his hand through an unruly mop of curly black hair, then looked at William with intense blue eyes.

"I have a mystery on my hands." William handed over Margaret and Thomas' wedding picture. "Do you recognize this fella?"

"Can't say as I do but let me show it to the officers at the front. The fella looks like an upstanding citizen."

William waited patiently. At least the detective left the door open.

"Seems your picture fella was locked up in Rockhead overnight twice in mid June. Looks are deceiving." Gilfoy returned the picture to William.

William tapped the picture. "What would you say if I told you my fella is not your fella?"

"But, my fella's the spittin' image of your fella."

"Please sit down, Detective Gilfoy. I have a story about my fella and I need your help. First of all, do you know anybody on the Montreal police force? A sharp detective would be ideal."

On the way home from the police station, William spoke with Thomas' secretary and cancelled his next-day meeting. "Tell Mr. Bishop I have no news for him."

William took a carriage to Samuels' office then walked home to sit in the back garden where he was overcome by shortness of breath.

Grace brought sandwiches and a pot of tea. They ate together in silence.

Eventually, Grace put down her cup. "What's troubling you?"

"Thomas is certainly not who we think he is. His past involves a troubled twin who may or may not be in the city. I've involved Samuel and the police but I fear it's too late for a quick and easy outcome."

"Should we bring Margaret home?" She began to cry.

"I'm not..."

"Pardon me, Doctor Bell." Hazel called from the back door. "Your patient is here."

"Thank you. I'll be in directly." He turned toward Grace. "I'm not convinced we need to do that today but it is not out of the question once the detective contacts me."

* * *

"Margaret, Margaret. Wait for me." She turned to see Anna darting across Hollis Street.

"I haven't been in church for a while. How are you? My meeting with Mr. Ellis went well. Are you available for lunch later this week? How about Wednesday noon at the usual place?"

Margaret nodded and Anna hurried off in the opposite direction, her parasol bobbing up and down as her shoes barely touched the sidewalk.

Margaret shook her head. Anna was the only person Margaret knew or had ever known who could have an entire conversation with someone without that person saying a single word.

* * *

John Gilfoy was a believer in personal connections to get a job done right. He decided to forgo a telegram. By late afternoon, Constable Henderson was on his way to the North Station carrying Gilfoy's brown canvas luggage, bound for Montreal. Inside the bag, he carried a detailed and urgent request for the Montreal police along with food and a change of clothing. Gilfoy expected a detailed reply regarding Thomas Irving Bishop by railmail in a few days.

* * *

At home that evening, Thomas was unusually quiet. When asked about his brother, Thomas casually responded the Timothy matter was in the hands of the police, 'thanks to your father'.

"That's wonderful news." Margaret smiled and let the subject drop.

"I'm sure we'll soon see the last of Timothy." He looked at Margaret and smiled.

* * *

Margaret stood in front of her closet, staring blankly at her day dresses. Thomas' callous attitude about his brother was another disheartening blow. She cried during the carriage ride.

"Hello, Margaret. How are you?"

Anna's voice was full of joy, a quality Margaret craved. "I'm well. You?" She hoped the powder concealed her red nose and cheeks.

"Excited. As I said, the meeting with Mr. Ellis went well. He's willing to support my column on the condition I provide him two acceptable samples by the end of this week. George introduced me to a few band members so I've completed one column already about a concert at the Citadel. Now, I'm working on a Sunday promenade column. I should finish later today."

"I'm impressed. Let's order."

"I just know I'm going to get the column." Anna stared at Margaret. "You look flushed. Are you feeling well?"

"I think I have a cold coming. I'll be fine."

Anna tilted her head. "Are you sure?"

Margaret hesitated. "I didn't sleep well either."

Anna picked up her cup. "If you say so." She took a sip of tea. "Can you help me with something?"

Margaret couldn't imagine helping anyone. She could barely keep her own life in order. "How could I possibly help?" She sipped her tea to distract her unhappy thoughts and keep Anna from seeing her teary eyes.

"I'd like you to think about possible ideas and people for the column. You know so many people."

Margaret was on the spot for an answer. "I haven't mentioned volunteering to Thomas so I can't see how I could possibly help."

"All I need is your guidance about the city and its people."

"What do you mean by guidance?"

"Well, you tell me about interesting people and I could speak with them."

"Excuse me ladies, I have your lunch."

"Thank you." Margaret used the interruption to collect her thoughts. "Do you promise not to write gossip about these people? Not that I know any gossip."

"Yes, I do. I'm more about good deeds than misdeeds."

"But doesn't Mr. Ellis expect you to write gossip to sell newspapers?"

"I told him I don't write gossip."

"Are you going to tell people that I sent you to talk to them?"

"Yes, I think I should. It's a way to introduce myself. Otherwise, they might not let me in the door." She laughed, then refilled Margaret's cup and her own.

"I don't know. It feels uncomfortable, awkward."

Anna took a sip of tea, smiled. "I love Earl Grey." She put down her cup. "If we did this, who would you suggest first?"

Margaret thought for a moment. "Mrs. Duncan from the church. She's very involved with the choir, chairs one of the fundraisers and volunteers at the orphanage."

"See, you already know what to do. She's an ideal person. She knows you and your family. Can we start with Mrs. Duncan?"

"I'm sure she would like to talk about her volunteer efforts." Margaret couldn't believe she agreed to do something she'd planned to dismiss. "You are very convincing."

"Thank you for helping. Let's finish lunch and meet next week. I should have Mr. Ellis' decision by then." She reached for Margaret's hand. "I think there's something troubling you. You don't have to talk about it, but take care of yourself."

CHAPTER EIGHT

HALIFAX, NOVA SCOTIA
JULY 26, 1895

Sailors Hotel occupied the last piece of land on a dead end street beside the Halifax wharf. Its faded green paint and grimy windows stood in stark contrast to a front yard filled with cheery yellow dandelions. Acrid fumes from ships belched toward its windows, shut tight even during the heat of summer.

City residents tended to give Sailors a wide berth as they rushed to reach businesses on the bustling wharf. Despite its exterior flaws, Sailors was a safe haven for those down on their luck or in the city with limited funds. Sailors also had a shadier side. It was a location for clandestine business deals and miscreants hiding from their enemies or the police, believed by them to be one and the same.

Bessie Ryan worked at the Sailors Hotel reception desk six days a week. She offered a friendly welcome to one and all. In addition to her pleasant disposition, Bessie possessed two valuable skills. Number one, she could bake. Scones showed up on the front desk daily, except Sunday. For many, this was their only sure meal of the day. Number two, Bessie's sharp memory for people's faces was legend. On more than one occasion the police sought her assistance in locating or identifying a person of interest.

During June, Bessie was baffled by a guest with two very different sets of clothing. Every day, Mr. Timothy dressed in well-worn work clothes, but on three evenings she saw him near the hotel wearing a fancy suit and hat. Her curiosity was piqued. It took great control for her to mind her own business. When Mr. Timothy left on June twenty-seventh, she put his unusual behaviour out of her mind. When he returned on Friday, July twenty-sixth Bessie's curiosity took flight.

* * *

By ten o'clock Friday morning, the Bishop's cast iron stove had pumped out enough waves of heat to send Margaret outside. Cookie was baking bread and making cakes. She bustled around, seemingly unfazed by the muggy heat.

"I like to bake, Mrs. Bishop. It's relaxing."

Margaret shook her head and escaped to the front yard, choosing to sit on the oak bench under the apple tree. Ignoring her book for the moment, she leaned back to catch a glimpse of deep blue sky framed by fluttering green leaves.

The tree on the parcel of land had been saved by the builders working on the Bishop home. It rewarded its owners with apples for pies, cakes, dumplings and puddings. This was the tree's in-between time. No longer adorned in showy flowers of spring, the tree held precious, brightly hued ripening fruit. Margaret breathed deeply, caught a fleeting scent of apple on a light puff of wind.

Days before, Margaret decided not to have a second lunch with Robert. Though unhappy and frightened by Thomas, she could not risk a friendship with Robert. It would be dangerous. Married women did not have close male friends. Robert would understand her position and disappear from her life. Margaret's acquaintance with Anna had become a welcome diversion. Her confidence and ambition offered Margaret a glimpse into another world for women. But Anna, James and her parents must remain all she needed. She picked up her book and began to read.

"Mrs. Bishop? Mrs. Thomas Bishop?"

Margaret looked up. A young boy stood beside a bicycle at the front gate. "Yes. May I help you?"

"May I come in ma'am? I have an envelope for you."

"Of course."

He dropped the bicycle, opened the gate and handed Margaret a blank envelope. As he turned to leave, Margaret looked at the envelope. "Young man, where did this come from? Who gave you this envelope?"

"Can't say ma'am. Have a good day, ma'am."

Margaret snapped the seal on the envelope and removed the note.

> My Dear Margaret,
> I trust you are enjoying this lovely summer morning.
> I expect you have decided not to join me at the hotel for lunch so I have a new plan.
> My parents missed your anniversary party and are most pleased to have us join them for lunch today.
> I will meet you at the bandstand at eleven-thirty and we will walk there together.
> Warmest regards,
> Robert

Margaret jumped up, pulled her watch from the waist of her skirt. The book and its bookmark parted company and tumbled to the ground as she raced for the front door.

"Cookie, can you help me?"

"Yes, Mrs. Bishop. What's wrong, my dear?" She swiped flour off her brow with the back of her hand. "Seen a ghost under that old tree? There's one there, you know. Pa told me years ago. Remind me to tell you the story." Cookie was unflappable and her stories rambling but Margaret knew she was just the sort of woman she needed in her life.

"Come upstairs with me, please. I have lunch with Mr. and Mrs. Fraser. I have to change my dress."

"This isn't like you, Mrs. Bishop. You never forget social engagements. Now myself being older, I have an excuse. Why just last week I forgot to pick up my sister's favourite gooseberry jam from Melva who lives across the street from us." She calmly dressed Margaret in a lavender linen dress with high white collar and cuffs, all the while telling a story about the neighbour's roving dog stealing newspapers.

"Stand still, my dear. You're jittering all over the place. These shoes?"

Margaret nodded while putting on her gloves.

Cookie walked around Margaret, pinning a few errant auburn curls in place. "There, that should do it."

"Where's the small hat with the purple flowers? Oh, dear. Maybe the veiled one? No, no. It's too fussy. Bring the small one, please."

"There, you look lovely. Here's your pearl reticule, goes with the pearl earrings. Off you go. Now take your time. You can be fashionably late. I heard young Agnes Milford talking about it on the trolley the other day. Did you know she's expecting again? In that little house an' all."

Margaret waited impatiently for a carriage, repeatedly asking herself why she didn't pay any heed to the note and put a full stop to this friendship renewal then and there. She told herself this would be the last lunch.

* * *

Robert waved from the bandstand and Margaret returned the greeting with a single flick of her wrist. Neither spoke during the short walk under a shady canopy of ash trees. As the light breeze carried the scent of Robert's cologne past her, Margaret's resolve began to fail. She glanced sideways. He really was terribly handsome. A pleasurable sensation rippled through her body, her cheeks warmed.

At the Fraser front door, Regena patted Margaret's hand.

"Welcome, Margaret. It's so lovely to see you on short notice." She glanced at Robert.

"Sorry, Mother. I had a meeting this morning, right after the train arrived and..."

"Yes, yes. I understand. We're pleased to catch up with Margaret. Come, Hazel has everything ready. We're having one of Robert's favourites, sweetbreads ragout."

Margaret forced a smile. *Oh dear god, organ meat from veal and lamb. The relish better be strong and the bread plentiful. Could have been worse...jellied beef tongue.*

The Fraser dining table was impressive. A snow-white crocheted tablecloth topped with gleaming silver, Limoges china and sparkling Baccarat stemware.

The hour passed pleasantly with discussion of family health, local events and upcoming socials.

* * *

Margaret had barely reached the sidewalk when she rounded on Robert. "What game are you playing here?" Her stare left no room for a glib reply.

"There is no game where you are concerned, Margaret."

"What do you call this then, tricking me to your parent's home for lunch. Your mother had no inkling of this until you forced her into it. She was most gracious and carried it off well. You should be ashamed of yourself, a grown man." She paused for a deep breath. "You are going to make a great deal of trouble for both of us. I should have stayed home." She pinched her mouth, eyes flashing.

"But you didn't." A lop-sided smile appeared on Robert's face.

"Don't you dare adopt that attitude with me. Ladies don't embarrass their hosts, in this case your mother. You played that card too."

"Ever heard of hiding in plain sight?"

"What silly nonsense is that? I'm having none of it, whatever it is. I'm putting an end to this charade before I lose my good reputation, marriage and commitment to it."

"You have a good reputation but you definitely don't have a good marriage."

"And how would you know that, mister know-it-all? My marriage is none of your business."

Robert stopped walking as did Margaret. "I plan to enjoy your company with no intention of hiding our socializing. I repeat, this isn't a game." He resumed walking.

Margaret rushed to catch up. "Well, it most certainly is a game. You're making a fool of me and I won't have it."

They reached the entrance to the Gardens. "Good day, Robert." She turned to walk away.

"Yes, it was a good day. See you next month, the twenty-third. Bandstand at eleven-thirty."

Margaret turned around, ready to put an end to that idea. Instead, she saw Robert walking away, waving his hand in the air. She flounced off down the street.

Anna was crossing Spring Garden Road near the Public Gardens when she saw Margaret and a man. Astonished, she stopped dead causing a carriage driver to yell, "Get off the street, madam."

Anna popped up her parasol and crossed the street to prove herself wrong. It couldn't possibly be Margaret. But it was. She was stomping away from a man about her own age. The man was waving his hand in the air and coming toward her. It wasn't James. It didn't look like a tryst but what else could it be? Her lunch with Margaret next week would be most interesting.

* * *

Sitting in her carriage on the way home, Margaret scolded herself for being caught up in this muddle. *You're to blame for this. He infuriates you. Why do you continue to meet him?* The answer came quickly. She could be herself with Robert. Heaven knows, she needed to be herself. Her world was filled with enough hurt and blame. Besides, what harm could come from lunch once a month?

* * *

On Saturday, Robert returned home after meetings to pick up his suitcase and say farewell to his mother. "I'm back."

"Good. You have a bit of time to spare. We need to discuss this complication you have started." Her no-nonsense words echoed down the long front hall. "Come to the drawing room." Regena entered the room, closed the double-doors, sat straight-backed and stared at him.

In Robert's memory, the drawing room doors were closed only once before. It was a day in eighteen eighty-seven when he was eleven. He was told to stay out of the drawing room, go upstairs and stay in his room.

Robert's curiosity got the better of him. Instead of staying in his own room, he crept into his parents' front bedroom and peeked through the closed curtains. He watched as a horse-drawn cart rumbled down the street. Four hefty men carried a large wooden box into the house then went away. When his mother called him downstairs, he stood ramrod straight beside his mother and father. Grandpa Fraser was inside the big box. The drawing room was never the same for Robert.

"What are your intentions regarding Mrs. Margaret Bishop?" Regena stressed the word, 'Mrs'.

"Margaret and I are getting reacquainted, enjoying each others' company, that's all."

Regena lifted her head toward the ceiling, breathed deeply. "Have you thought about the consequences for Margaret with this 'enjoying each others' company'?" She dropped her head, clasped her hands together tightly. "Her marriage could well be over, probably charged with an 'adultery' divorce, be spurned by society and have her family shunned by friends. Do you want that life for Margaret? By the way, you'll likely get off Scot free, which is absolutely no excuse for you to carry on like this. I'm ashamed of you."

"I won't let anything bad happen to her. I won't."

"While your intentions are admirable, you do not have control over everything and everyone, including Margaret's family but especially, her husband. Frankly, you cannot continue this friendship and presume her husband and parents will see it as acceptable. This is not easy but I'm going to say it. I'm asking you to consider what harm you will undoubtedly cause then make a clearheaded decision about this friendship with Margaret before you return next month. Agreed?"

"Sure."

"Thank you. Let's get your bags ready for the train."

* * *

Robert's life had been without problems for twenty-one years. He came from a wealthy family, had many friends and received a good education. His six foot frame and blue eyes were complemented by a kind nature and warm personality. People liked him immediately and he didn't betray their first impression.

Robert was confident he had plenty of experience to work out a clear-headed plan of action to rescue Margaret from her doomed future. She deserved better, someone to make her laugh again.

* * *

The Montreal-bound passenger cars sat idling on the tracks of North Station, Halifax as its passengers made their way along the wooden platform, most carrying food and drink for the day and a half journey.

Robert joined a long line of passengers walking toward the wooden step stool placed at the rear entrance of the passenger car. Inside the car, he stopped to glance at his ticket for the seat number. Two men behind him were in a deep conversation.

"Mais oui, I bet he's still a crook, Claude. I'm pretty sure I could find proof."

"I don't believe you, Pierre. He's far from Montreal now. That was his past as a young man, a child really. What's this proof you mentioned?"

"I'll tell you when we find our seats."

"D'accord."

Settled in his seat, Robert opened the Halifax newspaper then heard the same voices coming from the seat behind him.

"That was a successful trip. Now, tell me about the problem you think we have."

"I don't think we have one, Claude. There is one."

"Okay, okay. But a problem is not the same as someone being a crook, n'est-ce pas? Where's your proof Thomas Bishop is a crook?"

They had Robert's undivided attention. He stopped reading the Herald.

"Right there." Pierre tapped on piece of paper. "Look at our company copy for the May statement, line twenty-three. The amount our head office was charged by his Halifax office for the company's shipment to Boston. Here's the receipt from his office, verifying the amount we paid to Bishop Import Export for container boxes. It's far different on the June statement."

"What does that mean? So two numbers aren't the same. Besides, how could you possibly remember one number on one page in a ledger from two months ago?" Claude cast a doubtful look toward Pierre.

"How? I'll tell you how. Look at the June Statement. I personally signed the May cheque because you were away. Bishop charged twice the amount in June for the same number and size of containers we shipped from Halifax to Boston in May. What do you say now?"

"We have a problem."

"We do. He's far from Montreal and thought he was free to carry on with his usual crooked ways."

Robert's only task before the train reached Montreal was to get Pierre's full name and his company from the baggage tag. Sitting in front of them was a clear disadvantage. Where were their bags? On the floor? On a hook above their seats? He stood up to look for their baggage while opening and closing his own. *Damn, not on a hook. They're on the floor.*

*   *   *

James was very familiar with the outside of Sailors Hotel by late July. He'd passed by Sailors many times while following Thomas. Smoking a pipe through a fake mask was not easy or enjoyable. He preferred to sit or stand still so he leaned against a bollard near the Sailors in the early evening of Friday, July twenty-sixth. To his surprise, Thomas was standing outside the hotel speaking French to a well-dressed, tall, bearded man. But Thomas was dressed all wrong, wearing work clothes and shabby shoes. As he looked around the immediate area, James spotted a woman dressed in black sitting on a bench close to the hotel entrance. Even with the veil, he could tell her gaze toward Thomas was unwavering. When Thomas entered the hotel alone, James decided to wait for him to come out. Three hours later, he gave up and returned home.

*   *   *

Robert arrived in Montreal empty handed. In spite of two opportunities to read the bag tags, he didn't have what he needed. His very last chance to trace Thomas Bishop was now or never. He put a pencil and his bag tag in his pocket, took a deep breath and bumped against Pierre Armstrong's back on the last step off the car. "Excuse me, monsieur. Sorry."

As Armstrong turned to accept the apology, Robert saw what he needed, then hurriedly wrote Armstrong's name and address on his own tag.

CHAPTER NINE

Margaret fidgeted throughout the church service, anxiously waiting for her father's private talk with Thomas following Sunday lunch. The police were looking for Thomas' brother who could tell the true Bishop family story. Thomas' lies would be laid bare and his pompous behaviour would take a beating. With the meal finished, the main event was about to begin. Margaret began to relax. William excused himself and invited Thomas into the study, a cozy reading room between the main house and his medical office which had a separate outside entrance for patients.

James looked toward Margaret. "Is there something we should know?"

She smiled openly. "We should wait for them to join us. We'll find out together."

James was trying to read her face. "I'm guessing you know more than Mama and I."

Margaret knew too much to wait patiently. Instead of answering she paced the room, her long skirts swishing with each stride.

James stood and went to the liquor cabinet. "If I hear raised voices, I'm going in there. In the meantime, a glass of sherry is in order."

When the study door opened Margaret held her breath, only to see Thomas step into the sitting room looking his usual confident self. She expected him to be at least a bit cowed.

William began. "Thomas and I have discussed the limited information available to us from the local police. Thomas' twin Timothy is being sought by the Halifax police." He turned to Thomas. "Anything you wish to say?"

Timothy is at Sailors! James inhaled abruptly, causing him to cough.

Margaret stared at him. "You alright, James?"

"I'm fine, just swallowed the wrong way. Go ahead, Thomas."

"Timothy has been in an asylum in Montreal since he was twelve. He escaped and somehow found out about me and came to Halifax for money. I have not seen him since he appeared outside my office last month." He looked at William. "That was the morning you saw him." Looking at everyone else, he continued. "I don't expect any of us will see him again." He smiled at Margaret. "Would you like to remain a while longer with your parents and James? I have to return to the office for a few hours."

"Certainly. Will you be home for dinner?"

"Absolutely, but late. Eat without me. Just Montreal business to put to rest before the morning."

William followed Thomas. "I'll see you to the door."

James refilled his pipe. There would be no stopping his father from going to the police station the minute he knew about Timothy. For the time being, he'd keep what he knew to himself.

When William returned, Margaret's tone bordered on outrage. "What happened in the study, Papa? I thought you would set him straight on his whole charade."

"All in due course, my dear. I decided to keep the detailed information from the police and Samuel's private search to myself. No need to tip my hand too soon. Let's leave it with the police and Samuel for the time being." He turned to face Grace and James. "Now, you two need to know everything Margaret and I know. I'll have a glass of sherry, too!"

James listened to his father's efforts to deal with Thomas. He made no comments, asked no questions. He had one damaging Thomas story to tell the family but not today. He wasn't prepared to reveal his own troubles in order to discredit Thomas. His recollection rushed back.

It was the night of June twenty-first when James saw Thomas open the back door of a seedy pub a block off the wharf and walk straight past the bar toward the gambling tables. James dropped his head, knowing full-well the pleasure Thomas would take in exposing his gambling habit to the family. When a man wearing a shabby flat cap beckoned Thomas to his table, James stole a couple of glances and listened.

"You got it?" Flat cap asked.

"Wouldn't be here otherwise."

"Give it over then."

Thomas passed a money packet over the man's glass of ale.

"Careful there. Ale ain't cheap." Flat cap held the packet under the table and counted the money. I'll take care of it this weekend."

"Make it tomorrow not Sunday." Thomas nodded and left.

Since James was winning, the other men wouldn't take lightly to his quick departure to follow Thomas. His pursuit of Thomas came to a dead end.

"James, are you with us?"

James nodded toward his father.

"I thought you'd have something to say about Thomas."

"Just thinking about what Thomas might be up to later today. His comment about having 'Montreal business to put to rest before the morning' was telling."

Margaret looked toward James. "You think he's up to something tonight, don't you?"

James nodded. "I do. He's never spoken so boldly about business before. Anyway, thanks for lunch. I'm off upstairs to study for the rest of the afternoon then out for the evening."

Margaret looked up as he rose from the chair. "Be careful."

* * *

After dark James settled into his vantage point near Sailors Hotel, his pipe unlit to avoid being noticed.

"Hey, mister. Got a light?" A drunk aimed his body toward James' bench. "Nice evenin' for a sit down near the water." He dropped onto the seat and fell against James as he leaned forward to light his cigarette. "Oops. Sorry about that. Thank you, kind sir."

"You're welcome."

The friendly drunk began swaying back and forth, wafting foul-smelling whiffs of body odour. "Come here often, do 'ya?"

James covered his nose. "No."

"Ah, a man of few words." The friendly drunk's hand shook as he aimed the cigarette toward his mouth.

"That's me."

"Lookie, there. It's the mean one in a black veil. Told me to piss off the other night." He fell against James. "Oops. Pardon me."

"What night was that?" James turned his head away and took a deep breath.

"Can't 'member. Thinks she owns this 'ere place. Acts all hoity-toity like." He leaned forward, took a long draw on the cigarette and exhaled.

James breathed in, thankful for the slight breeze swirling the smell of smoke in his direction.

"Fancy dresser and mister beard ain't 'ere though." He straightened up. "You gotta beard. You 'im?"

"Tell me about the fancy dresser."

"All important lookin'. Suit 'n all."

"Beard?"

"Naw."

"Did fancy dresser ever go inside?" James pointed toward the hotel.

"Not tha' I seen. That don't say he didn't." He elbowed James. "There's that flat cap fella. He's 'ere lots."

James grinned. *You are too.*

The drunk stomped out his butt. "Must be leavin'." After a few shuffles his legs held and he wandered off toward the wharf.

Flat cap left at midnight and James half an hour later, passing by the woman in the black veil. He doubled-back in thirty minutes to find she was gone and the area vacant.

On Barrington, James hailed a carriage to the Halifax Club and asked it to wait. Not a member, he could only inquire if Thomas Bishop was inside by quietly offering the doorman money.

The doorman pocketed the money. "He's been here all evening. Have a good night, sir."

* * *

Between patients on Monday, William's mind wandered to the police inquiry. Gilfoy had warned him it might take a couple of weeks. William was quite certain his patience wouldn't last that long. Margaret was at risk and James might be more involved than he let on. He went to bed late but found sleep would not come. He tossed and turned, sensing something big was about to happen. All sorts of terrible possibilities came to mind.

Eventually, Grace poked him in the side. "Get up and read."

As the sun rose, William closed the book with no recollection of anything he'd read. After the last patient left his office early that afternoon, William had enough waiting. Rather than worry Grace, he told her he was going for a walk along the wharf and would be back by dinner time. As planned, his walk took him directly to the police station. Inside, he came upon a kerfuffle near the front desk. A woman was telling her story between great sobs as the desk clerk guided her into an interview room. William moved to the far wall.

Carrying a mug of sweet tea, Gilfoy entered the interview room and closed the door. Before he could ask a question, the woman poured out her story.

"It smelled somethin' fierce what with the heat 'n all. I opened the door. Poor fella. Lord luv 'im. Who would do such a thing?

Ever so quiet he was." She wiped her eyes with a large white hanky. "Bless 'im." She opened her mouth to begin again.

Gilfoy spoke quietly. "Tea?" He motioned for Bessie Ryan to sit.

She perched on the edge of the seat with a heavy sigh, took a big sip of tea and fell back into her chair. "Ta."

"Miss Ryan, do you know the man's name?"

"He wrote down Mr. Timothy. I'm not sure that's right, if 'ya know what I mean. Sometimes they use made-up names, 'ya know. He seemed right nice enough, though." Her eyes flooded.

Gilfoy had no doubt Bessie was in shock. He asked gently. "When did you last see Mr. Timothy?"

She sighed. "This past Friday. Late afternoon it was. Oh my, oh my."

"Okay." He nodded. "Two constables will walk you back to the hotel then search the room. They'll remove Mr. Timothy's personal items and let you know when they're finished. Then you can clean his room." He paused. "I would like to speak with you again tomorrow. A constable will bring you to the station." He bid goodbye to Bessie at his office door, returned to his chair and dropped his head into his hands. His plan to get Timothy's story was reduced to rubble. After a few moments he opened the office door. "Sorry to keep you waiting, Doctor. Come in."

William wanted to be wrong. "The young man in the hotel is the twin you've been looking for isn't he?"

Gilfoy nodded. "I believe so. One of the constables recognized him as the fella he took to Rockhead in mid June."

William ran his hand back and forth over his forehead. "Where do we go from here?"

"Have a seat, Doctor. Well, it's a murder. We'll do an investigation. Perhaps it's settling a gambling debt or payback for some personal matter. I'll send a constable to check-out why he was in Rockhead, then visit the liquor and gambling spots. Maybe Miss Ryan at Sailors Hotel will identify someone who paid him a call." He paused. "Your son-in-law will be interviewed eventually.

When I get the report back from Montreal, it may have something useful pertaining to Timothy. It's a shame I didn't have a chance to talk about your concerns with him."

"Indeed." William nodded gravely. "I look forward to hearing about that report. Will you inform Thomas of the death?"

"Yes. I'll go to his office before I go home for the day."

William began walking home. Feeling short of breath, he hailed a carriage to see Margaret. Timothy was dead. She needed to be prepared for Thomas' response, whatever it might be. He kept their conversation brief.

"Come home if you feel unsafe. Promise you will."

"Yes, Papa."

During dinner, William shared the news of Timothy's murder with Grace and James.

"What about Margaret?"

"I've told her. She'll come here if need be."

"When did this happen, Papa?" James asked casually but his curiosity was in overdrive.

"According to Detective Gilfoy, most probably late Sunday. The body was found earlier today."

"So Sunday the twenty-eighth." *Who's that woman in black?*

* * *

Before leaving the station to see Thomas, Gilfoy looked at the contents of the evidence box from Timothy Bishop's hotel room. It revealed nothing of consequence, work clothes, under-clothing, night shirt, outer jacket, boots, socks, straight razor, shaving mug, soap, razor strap and a small amount of money but no wallet. Robbery didn't appear to be a motive. The description 'ordinary items of an ordinary man' didn't fit what had taken place in that hotel room. The torso was brutally sliced. Gilfoy hoped the autopsy tomorrow would open up a line of inquiry. He headed out for Thomas' office.

* * *

Thomas was leaving his office building when Gilfoy approached him. "Good evening, Mr. Bishop. I'd like to speak with you in your office."

"I'm on my way to a meeting so if you aren't here to badger me or arrest me, you can tell me right here on the sidewalk."

"Very well, Mr. Bishop. I regret to inform you your brother Timothy has been murdered."

"Hmm." Thomas nodded. "I'm not surprised. Hearing of his death is akin to hearing of a stranger's death."

Gilfoy held his tongue. "Can you offer any ideas on who might have wanted to do him harm?"

"Not really. I didn't know the man. He was certainly unpleasant as a child." He quickly added, "If that's all, I'll leave you to the investigation." He turned on his heel and walked away. Out of Gilfoy's sight he hailed a carriage and went home, surprising Margaret with his earlier than usual arrival.

"Has something happened?" She hoped her voice sounded suitably surprised.

"Apparently Timothy has been murdered."

"I am sorry to hear that, Thomas."

"Why? I barely knew the fellow."

"He was murdered. Don't you want to know who did it and have the person brought to justice?"

"Well, of course someone should pay but it doesn't involve me. Let's forget about all this murder business. What's being served for dinner?"

* * *

Late on Tuesday evening, Constable Healy began his rounds of the many drinking and gambling spots, at least the ones he knew about. He was unwelcome and on occasion, threatened. Owners of licensed and unlicensed premises didn't want the cops sniffing around. It was bad for business. If Timothy Bishop frequented any of the likely spots, he'd passed unnoticed.

CHAPTER TEN

HALIFAX, NOVA SCOTIA
JULY 31, 1895

Murder In Sailors Hotel

The headline laid claim to half the front page of the Wednesday morning newspaper. Murder was the topic on the street and gossip at work. The victim's name was not disclosed. It assured big newspaper sales for the following day. The publisher was more than pleased. Murder sold newspapers.

Thomas picked up the morning newspaper from a street vendor and casually tucked it under his arm. He smiled with relief. He had a great deal of business to finish before day's end, including a response to a troublesome letter from Montreal received in Monday's mail. Creating the curt response of denial and rebuttal in his mind, he walked the last block to the office in confidence.

* * *

Margaret fretted about lunch but staying home would be ill-mannered. Anna would have seen the morning newspaper and might want to talk about the murder. Disclosing her family's personal affairs at this point in their relationship would be socially unacceptable.

To Margaret's surprise, Anna was waiting for her. A large pot of tea, two cups and a tiered plate of assorted sandwiches were already in the centre of the round table covered by a blue linen tablecloth.

Margaret smiled. "You're early. You must have good news."

"I have. Mr. Ellis approved my column. I will speak with Mrs. Duncan on Friday, thanks to you. Ready for tea?"

"Yes, please. Congratulations, I knew you would be successful."

"I can't contain my curiosity any longer. Who was the man I saw you with at the Public Gardens Friday afternoon?"

Margaret picked up her cup, steadied her thoughts and breathing. Realizing Anna had not seen them at lunch, she countered the question with a dismissive reply. "That was Robert Fraser, a friend of the family. We were in school together." She reached for a sandwich. "When will Mrs. Duncan's interview be in the newspaper?"

"Mr. Ellis says in two weeks." Anna was not a quitter. "Does Robert live here?" She quickly added justification for her probing question. "He might be a person to interview." She reached for a jellied tongue sandwich.

Anna didn't believe Margaret's explanation and Margaret knew it. She offered a cavalier reply and shrugged dismissively. "He lives in Montreal, a bit out of your interview spot."

Anna plunged on. "But his family is here so he'll be back."

"Most probably. It doesn't concern me. Who's your next interview?"

"I don't know. I was thinking of asking Mrs. Duncan to refer me to someone. It would be a good way to get the column started. What do you think?"

"I think it's a perfect plan."

They moved on to talk about social and church events. Robert was not mentioned again. Margaret was not fooled by Anna's acceptance of her answers. Anna was in the newspaper business. There would be more questions to come.

"Bye, Margaret. See you in church on Sunday."

* * *

Gilfoy received his summons to Timothy Bishop's autopsy shortly after lunch on Wednesday. He wasn't pleased with the timing but nobody kept the coroner waiting. He popped a mint in his mouth and a few in his pocket then headed for the university on foot. Walking was one of Gilfoy's great pleasures. He could think and exercise at the same time.

"Come in, come in, Gilfoy. I presume you can legally identify this man." He pulled the sheet off the face.

"This is Timothy Bishop. He's the identical twin of Thomas Bishop, who lives in the city." Gilfoy lifted his eyes, fixed them on the coroner.

"Fine, that gets us started. Suppose you want the details. I would say Mr. Bishop died late Sunday. He was stabbed. The blade was not overly long, the aim was good, pierced the heart. Lots of blood. As you know, no knife was found at the scene. Have a look at the upper body." Doctor Stillman pulled the sheet to Timothy's waist. "What do you see?"

"I'd rather not but..." Gilfoy covered his nose with his handkerchief and stepped back from the grotesque wound that once was Timothy Bishop's chest. "Oh, my."

"Exactly. You should look for a serrated knife. The murderer gouged the victim at least three times to create the jagged rips. Lots of venom fuelled this killing."

"Thanks, Doctor."

"You don't look too well, John. Fresh air's what you need. Have a good afternoon."

"Thanks, again." Gilfoy stepped outside. *This was personal, vengeful.* He walked quickly. Bessie Ryan might be able to get him closer to the answer.

* * *

When Constable Ferguson entered the Sailors Hotel that afternoon, his job was to escort Bessie Ryan to the station for a more thorough interview with Detective Gilfoy. He didn't expect to be hustled back out onto the street.

Bessie handed Ferguson a scone. "Have a raisin scone, constable. Eat it on the way. I've real serious business with your detective fella." Bessie scooted out the door and up the street. Ferguson rushed to catch up.

"Hello, Miss Ryan. I hope you feel better today. Thank you for coming in again."

"Least I could do, Detective. The poor fella. Killed in 'is own room. Nice fella he were too. Ever so polite. His family's goin' to be some upset. And where are they? I never heard the last name Timothy in Halifax. S'pose it's possible what with the new people workin' in factories and them British soldiers by the dozens."

"Yes, the city's growing fast. Tea?"

"Lovely."

"Ferguson, sweet tea for Miss Ryan."

"Follow me, Miss Ryan." Gilfoy moved toward the interview room.

"Bessie please, Detective. I'd be lookin' around for some fancy-dressed lady if you call me Miss Ryan again." She arranged her long navy cotton skirt and petticoats carefully then crossed her hands on her lap.

Gilfoy opened his note paper. "Okay, Bessie. Do you remember when Mr. Timothy first arrived at Sailors Hotel?"

"Looked all that up before I came, I did. It were a Thursday, the sixth day of June."

"How did he pay? And how long did he stay?"

"Cash for seven nights. Dumped a pile of coins on the desk. Looked like all the money the poor fella had."

"So he left after the week?"

"No, said he took a likin' to the place, found hisself a job, he did and paid for two weeks with cash from a wad 'a paper bills. How'd 'ya suppose he got that so quick like?" Bessie looked Gilfoy straight in the eye, clearly expecting him to answer her question.

"What happened after the two weeks, on the twenty-seventh of June?"

"Never seen 'im again til he showed up last Friday morning. Poor fella paid for a week, he did. Little did he know he'd be dead right soon."

"Anyone ever visit Mr. Timothy?"

"Not inside the hotel, I ever seen. One time I heard 'im talkin' to another fella in French. Between the hotel and the wharf they were. I was standin' outside for a little break."

"When was that, do you remember?"

"Right easy that question is. It were last Friday. Real late in the day it were."

"Can you describe that man?"

"Wearin' a bowler, 'bout Mr. Timothy's age. Taller though. Dark hair. Beard."

"Did they sound angry?"

"More serious like, business like. Shook hands when the French fella left."

"Think hard. Any words you heard."

"I don't understand a word of French, except 'bonjour'."

"Anything else about the conversation?"

"Your goin' to think it funny. There was this woman alone on a bench starin' hard at 'em the whole time. What do 'ya think she'd be doin' that for?"

"Can you describe her?"

"Couldn't see her face. Must've been in mournin', wearin' a black dress, hat and veil. All that black on a hot day. Poor thing."

"Back to Mr. Timothy. Anything else or unusual about his stay come to mind?"

Bessie took a deep breath. "His clothes."

Gilfoy had seen Timothy's clothing. They were ordinary. "Clothes? What about them?"

"Why would Mr. Timothy wear a fancy suit and hat sometimes?"

"When did you see Mr. Timothy in this fancy suit and hat?"

"June. Late in the day it were. I remember that part. Never saw him inside in a fancy suit though."

"Did you see him wear a suit and hat last Saturday or Sunday?"

"No. That don't say he didn't 'cause I don't work Sundays."

"If you do recall the June dates, let me know. Who works Sunday?"

"My cousin, Freddy."

"Can you arrange for your cousin to come to the station today or tomorrow?"

"Fraid not. Took time for a sick family member in New Brunswick. Back in a couple of weeks, maybe more, maybe less."

"Let me know when the visit's over. This has been most helpful, Bessie."

CHAPTER ELEVEN

HALIFAX, NOVA SCOTIA
AUGUST 01, 1895

Thomas was not surprised to discover a large envelope under a thick slab of grey slate at the front door of his office building. It bore no return address. He grinned and shrugged. People in shady businesses operated in the shadows. He too, often received and delivered goods and money after the sun went down. He threw the rock to the side of the building and unlocked the door.

Thomas' public operation of Bishop Import Export was always open for business. He eagerly courted members of his private well-to-do circle to visit him any time during business hours Monday to Friday. The private side was a different story, a continuation of the one he brought with him from Montreal. Separated by considerable distance and head office, Thomas' risky creativity blossomed. Import and export branched out to include lucrative offshoots, including fraud, bribery and coercion.

Ready for a full day of work, Thomas put the blue envelope aside and unlocked his cabinet drawer removing two ledgers and the locked money box. He knew the money box was full as his secretary had given him several sealed envelopes during the week. He looked forward to making entries and notes, especially in the red ledger, the one his secretary Miss Elgin never saw. He set to work.

Maude Elgin, a middle-aged woman who always wore black revealed precious little of her personal circumstances. It didn't matter to Thomas. He wasn't in the least bit interested in Miss Elgin or her tedious little life. Maude took this as a blessing. She had her own motives for going unnoticed. She never questioned why she was not to open any envelopes personally addressed to Mr. Bishop nor did she express interest in his business. Thomas found these qualities reassuring. Miss Elgin was an excellent gatekeeper. Thomas paid her well for just that reason. The perfect secretary for an imperfect business owner.

By the end of May, Miss Elgin had concluded Thomas was involved in serious wrongdoing. Skilled at deceit herself, she could and did open all Thomas' locked doors and drawers. And why not? She had her own set of keys to everything in Bishop Import and Export thanks to a clever locksmith who could be bribed. The local theatre was first-rate for her costume needs. Dressed as a man, she walked the streets a few evenings each week to root out Thomas' business dealings with assorted law-breakers. In early June her plan expanded, thanks to a newcomer in Halifax. Her plan was coming together nicely.

* * *

"Have a pleasant evening, Mr. Bishop." Maude smiled to herself and left the office.

Thomas ignored her. Well pleased by the growing amount in the red ledger, he put aside everything except the blue envelope. He poured himself a large scotch, finished it, then slid a knife through the seal and removed the contents.

THE GAME IS UP. BANDSTAND. THURSDAY, EIGHTH. 9:00PM.

After throwing the knife and letter across the room, he tipped the bottle to his lips. The long walk home failed to dampen his anger nor lessen his intoxication.

Margaret took the brunt of Thomas' cursing while he swayed down the front hall, calling out names of people she'd never heard before. He swung in her direction twice and missed but connected with her right arm on the third try. She reached the stairs and bolted up the steps, locking herself in the guest room. Her legs turned to jelly, dropping her unceremoniously into her skirts. She leaned her head against the door. A whiff of alcohol wafted through the keyhole. Margaret shifted her body. For her efforts, she received a painful jab from her shoulder to wrist. Despite the throbbing arm, she crawled to the bed and pulled herself onto it. She would keep quiet for as long as it took, silently praying the door would hold until Thomas' pounding ended.

Thomas' slurred threats continued. "Margaret, 'member what I told you, I win. Trying to ruin me. Won't work. I know things about them, got my own people. You lose." He hammered on the door. "Talk to me, damn you. You can hear me. Get out here." Groans. "Get. Out. Here. Now. Help me up. Do as you're told or else. You, your bloody family. Trying to ruin me. I'm smarter. You'd be nobody without me."

Margaret stopped paying attention, turning her thoughts to escape. She'd be safe if Thomas couldn't force the door open or if Cookie arrived from her sister's home before he woke up. Eventually, Thomas' silence allowed her to fall into a fitful sleep.

When the first light of day peeked through the bedroom window, Margaret woke to the sound of Thomas' heavy snore. She crept to the door, unlocked it and stepped over him before he knew what happened.

"Morning, Cookie."

"Morning, Mrs. Bishop. You're up early. Did you read about the murder at Sailors in Wednesday's paper? That place has all sorts of trouble and has for years." Cookie turned from the stove. Seeing Margaret's dishevelled hair and rumpled day dress, she averted her eyes to the pots on the stove.

"Yes, I did. Tea ready?" Margaret sat at the table, her eyes down.

An unspoken agreement of silence continued as Cookie served tea, toast with an egg and Margaret ate her breakfast.

Some questions are best left unasked. Cookie knew perfectly well what the answers were.

When Thomas came down stairs, he avoided the kitchen all together, talking as he made his way to the front door. "I'm off to the office. Don't expect me until very late tonight. I might go to the club."

Cookie broke the silence. "You look unsettled, not yourself. Would you like me to prepare a hot bath?"

Margaret winced while moving her arm to reach for the tea pot.

"Good heavens, what's the matter with your arm?"

"I hit it against the newel post last night. I can be so clumsy, at times. And yes to the bath, if you wouldn't mind helping me. I'll finish my breakfast and be up shortly."

As Margaret entered the bathroom, the soothing scent of lavender reached her nose. "Lavender in the bath. Thank you."

"If it relaxes Her Majesty Queen Victoria, it'll work for you. Now you call me when you're ready and I'll help you dress." She paused a moment. "You may not like me interfering but I'm going to. You must go to your parent's home immediately. Tell them what's happened. They'll help."

* * *

"What's happened, Margaret? You look distraught."

"Thomas." She burst into tears.

"Go to the drawing room. I'll get your father. Hopefully, he doesn't have a patient with him."

Margaret poured out the details of Thomas' drunken episode. Grace was quick to suggest she move home, forthwith. Margaret had never seen her mother's face so fierce.

"Something happened yesterday. He was drunk and out of control. I intend to sleep in the guest room with the door locked until this is settled." As an afterthought, "Cookie is with me. I know she understands my circumstances."

"Is she trustworthy?"

"Yes, Mama. I'd trust her with my life."

William nodded. "That's good. I'm hopeful the Montreal information will reveal Thomas' entanglement in financial crime."

Margaret added, "And Timothy's murder?"

"I'm far less hopeful about the murder." William pursed his lips.

"I remain terribly worried about your safety, dear. You must take a key to this house. Hazel's usually here but you might need to get indoors quickly. I will accept no argument from you."

Margaret took a breath, looked at her mother, "There's another matter you've not mentioned, perhaps by choice. If I stay here, we will have to endure gossip. It will be swift, sharp and unforgiving. In short order, we will be cast out of our social circle. I doubt you want to be shunned, Mama."

William commented on the exchange. "That issue will take a long time for a fair resolution, my dear. In the meantime, let's focus on your safety. As you wish, try a few days at home with Cookie."

Margaret continued. "Thomas mentioned three names during his tirade. I know it's not likely, but do either of you know someone with the first names Andrew, Claude or Pierre who might know Thomas?"

Her father was the first to speak. "I know one. Andrew. He's a dentist." He paused. "These names you mention are more likely from Thomas' past, maybe even his childhood." He looked toward Grace. "Anyone you can think of?"

"Well, there's Andrew Nesbitt but he's always been called Andy. Pierre works at the shoe repair shop off Barrington Street. He's much older than Thomas. Neither one seems likely to be involved with Thomas. Claude is not a name familiar to me."

Margaret looked directly at her father. "Why isn't the detective interviewing Thomas? I'm sure he knows something or is hiding something." Her tone became more strident. "He might leave town. Then what could be done? He's not above anything now.

Look at me." She undid the buttons and rolled up her sleeve, immediately regretting it.

Grace gasped. "I'm fine, Mama. Just really, really angry."

"It's too soon for an interview with Thomas. Detective Gilfoy's gathering local information before he talks to anyone who might have a reason to murder Timothy. He'll also wait for the report from Montreal. It's unlikely Thomas would leave town while this is going on. He'd look suspicious." He added, "Two things are happening here, Thomas' abusive behaviour toward you and a murder. The two may not be linked at all."

Margaret sighed. "I just want all of it to be over."

Her father patted her hand. "It may take longer than any of us hope."

During lunch, Margaret promised to lock herself in the guest room every night and stay close to Cookie when Thomas was in the house.

* * *

Sunday morning Margaret leaned over the second floor banister. "Thomas, are you going to church this morning?"

A sharp response drifted up from the study. "No. I'm far too busy for any social events today."

"Fine."

"And cancel going to that Natal Day celebration tomorrow."

Thomas locked the study door behind him and took a bottle of scotch to his desk. He stared at the crumpled blue envelope. *Time to call in my Montreal favours.*

* * *

Margaret considered the Wednesday lunch more failure than success. She'd upended her budding friendship with offhand answers about Robert. But how could she possibly describe him to Anna. To try would be embarrassing at best but more likely ruinous and end their friendship altogether. Today, she had to face Anna after church and try to mend the relationship.

Following the service, Margaret spotted Anna walking toward the sidewalk. Armed with faltering courage, she hurried toward her. "Hello, Anna. Pardon my intrusion. Do you have a moment?"

"Of course. So good to see you. I'm in a rush to see George before he leaves the house. He's off to some sort of meeting for the rest of the day. On a Sunday. Can you believe it? Can we have lunch Thursday at our usual place?"

"Of course." Margaret turned to see the carriage was waiting and her mother waving. She promised herself not to become upset over Thomas or talk about Anna over lunch.

* * *

Despite Thomas' refusal to attend the Dartmouth Natal Day events the following day, he was there. Avoiding the area where Margaret and her family were seated, he crept around the edge of the crowd looking for one of his Montreal regulars to do a job Thursday evening. Distracted by his own needs, he failed to spot the bearded man walking several paces behind him, seemingly engrossed in an event flyer.

When James left the family to do a walk-about, he never imagined he would see Thomas. But there he was, waving toward a man wearing a dirty blue cap and shabby coat. As the two met, James spotted a well-dressed bearded man with his binoculars trained on Thomas. *Well-dressed bearded man. The drunk at Sailors mentioned him.* James moved toward him for a closer look.

Binocular man was not happy. "Merde." He'd been jostled, his binoculars were on the ground.

When James looked in Thomas' direction, he was gone. By then, the French-speaking, bearded man was also lost in the crowd.

CHAPTER TWELVE

On Thursday morning the envelope from Montreal arrived at Halifax Police Headquarters. Constable Henderson lifted it up and down in his hand then went into the detective's office. "Feels like a long read, sir."

Gilfoy leaned across the desk. "Thanks, Henderson. You did a fine job. Looks like the personal delivery paid off. Once I've finished reading, I'll want to discuss it with you."

"Thank you, sir."

"Close the door and no interruptions 'til I say so."

Absolutely, sir." Henderson left with a smile on his face.

John Gilfoy studied the large envelope in his hands. Since the discovery of Timothy Bishop's body, he'd experienced a deepening sense the Montreal report would enlighten him 'way more than his initial inquiry had intended. He looked forward to the information casting a light on Thomas' past and in turn, creating dark shadows on his present. Other persons of interest might also emerge. He placed the envelope on his desk then picked up his tea, strong, laced with sugar and a splash of milk.

A man had been murdered in Gilfoy's city and it was his job to determine the motive and find the murderer. Despite the few murders in Halifax, Gilfoy was well aware of the possible motives... love, greed, fear, jealousy, revenge and occasionally, sheer habit. After considering the factors relevant to Timothy Bishop's death, he selected jealousy and revenge as likely motives. They would drive the initial inquiries. He'd begin with a focus and be open to broadening the possibilities as evidence was gathered, examined and discussed. The other motives might come into play later. He drained his cup, stood and opened the door.

"Henderson, you there?"

"Yes, sir. Tea sir?"

"Yes. Bring a full pot, sugar bowl, milk and the evidence box from the Bishop murder scene."

"Right you are, sir."

Gilfoy opened the envelope then emptied its contents on the desk. He quickly grasped the level of detail from the Montreal police was a message for him to pay attention to every word on every page. He skimmed the salutation and first paragraph. His eyes locked on the itemized list of included reports. "Holy smokes," escaped his lips. He read the list aloud.

* * *

Reports regarding the death of Mr. and Mrs. Matthew Bishop

1. September 08, 1882 summarized report – the murder investigation of Mr. Alan & Mrs. Cecile Bishop, parents of minor twins Thomas and Timothy

2. September 09, 1882 police interview report – Thomas Bishop

3. September 09, 1882 police interview report – Timothy Bishop

4. September 09, 1882 mental health reports –Thomas and Timothy Bishop

5. September 11, 1882 murder charge report – Timothy Bishop

6. September 11, 1882 report committing
   Timothy Bishop into the care of Dr. Alfred
   and Mrs. Ethel Jarvis, (supervision by
   psychiatrist Dr. Hector Ormond)

7. September 12, 1882 report placing
   Thomas Bishop in the care of Mr. Edgar
   a Mrs. Alice Dumont in Montreal until
   Thomas reaches the age of eighteen
   years in 1888 (supervision by Dr. Hector
   Ormond)

Three witness statements (dated September
08, 1882) regarding the murder of Mr. and
Mrs. Bishop are included.

Reports regarding Mr. Thomas Bishop and police matters:

1. March 11, 1891 embezzlement charge
   laid against Thomas Bishop

2. October 09, 1891 embezzlement charge
   laid against Thomas Bishop

3. May 12, 1892 embezzlement charge laid
   against Thomas Bishop

4. August 03, 1892 embezzlement charge
   laid against Thomas Bishop
   The charges laid against Mr. Bishop were
   dismissed – witnesses refused to testify.

Interviews regarding Thomas Bishop in 1888 and 1892

– provided by Mr. and Mrs. Dumont on July 18, 1888 and September 12, 1892
We believe Mr. Thomas Bishop left the city of Montreal in February of 1893.

Regards,
Alexandre Dupuis
Chief Superintendent
Montreal Police Department
Ville de Montréal, Quebec

"Your tea and the evidence box, sir."

"Thanks, Henderson."

While exhaling long and loud, Gilfoy eyed the sizable stack of documents before his eyes. His task was to unearth facts, seek-out motives and hunt for evidence in the creation of proof. Proof which would point to the person who carried out a crime. This was a giant puzzle. John Gilfoy loved puzzles.

From the cover letter, Thomas was not implicated in the death of his parents in 1882 nor found guilty of theft of funds from his employer in 1891 and again, in 1892. Gilfoy pondered over these findings and how Thomas successfully avoided responsibility. He intended to examine all details and names in this paperwork. Bishop's treatment of Bell's daughter would have to wait.

After a few moments of quiet thought, he prepared a mug of sweet tea, opened his notebook and began with the Bishop murders, September 08, 1882.

* * *

Margaret arrived for lunch with Anna a few minutes before noon. She sat on the edge of her seat, braced for Anna's usual exuberant entrance and launch into an excited barrage of news about her life during the past few days. She anticipated Anna's first question about Robert would be casual then she would dig in with more queries to unnerve her. Margaret intended to have none of it. She decided to give a quick response and change the subject, more than once if necessary.

When ten minutes passed, Margaret wondered if she'd misunderstood the arrangement or if Anna was ill with no way to contact her. She remained seated five more minutes, looked at her watch, then returned it to her reticule and stood up. *How embarrassing.*

"Oh, Margaret, I'm ever so sorry. Please forgive me. Please sit. We need tea, lots of tea. Where is the waitress? I'm so embarrassed."

"It's fine. You're a bit late, that's all." She looked into Anna's eyes. Something was very wrong. Her eyes were bloodshot and swollen.

The waitress glanced at Anna then turned to Margaret. "Ladies, may I take your order?"

"Go ahead, Margaret. Whatever you choose will be fine."

As soon as the waitress left, Margaret reached for Anna's hand. "Can I help?"

Anna took a deep breath. "I need someone to talk to, someone I can trust." She began to cry openly.

Margaret was embarrassed for both of them. This sort of display was just not done in polite society.

She leaned forward. "I'll listen if you want me to."

"Thank you. But why are you whispering?" Anna looked around the room, expecting to see someone they knew.

"Mama warned me about people who tittle-tattle. Didn't your mother tell you about them?"

"You're right, I should have remembered. Let's eat quickly then go to the Public Gardens. I feel better already, knowing I can talk with you especially as I have to return to the office later this afternoon."

Inside the Gardens, Margaret waited for Anna to begin her story. When she didn't, Margaret spoke. "I'm glad you feel better." and continued walking.

After a few moments, Anna opened up. "George tells me I get 'overheated' sometimes. I had one of those times. There was a big argument at the newspaper office early this morning. I'm excitable, always have an opinion, which gets me into immediate trouble. I got involved, went home annoyed then became angry with George about some trivial thing. He stood his ground and reminded me to not lose my temper because that's when people make mistakes, say things they'll regret and can't take it back."

"George sounds like a very calm person."

"He's a good person. He has to be to put up with me." She laughed to make light of her statement. Then she fell silent. Margaret waited. "It comes from his background, self-restraint and of course his military training. Lots of men, lots of orders and routine. We met at a weekend house party, hosted by his older sister, Celeste who I met at a gallery opening in London. I was the reporter and she was the gallery's benefactor. His family has money."

"But he supports your work?"

"Yes." She hesitated. "To be honest, he'd like me to be a bit more like Celeste and a bit less like me." She smiled. "I'm from a working family. I want to work not host tea parties. We have our moments. Some of them are fiery. It's all with words though. He never calls me names, belittles or hits me."

Envy crept into Margaret's thoughts. "You're very fortunate. Not everyone is." She winced. She'd unwittingly given Anna an opening to question her comment. She wasn't ready to talk about Thomas' behaviour.

Anna continued, seemingly oblivious. "It feels good to talk openly. Thank you. I needed someone to listen. Someone I can trust." She smiled and squeezed Margaret's hand. "Anything new with you?"

"My life has been somewhat unsettled recently."

"So the newspaper was correct about the murder at Sailors?"

Margaret was relieved about Anna's presumption. "Yes. He was Thomas' twin brother but they hadn't seen each other for many years. Thomas has been quite agitated about it all."

"I'm sorry to hear that but I understand he could be troubled even though so much time has passed. If you need to talk just tell me. Promise?"

"Yes. Thank you. Maybe next time."

"See you at church Sunday?"

"Yes. Bye, bye, Anna."

Margaret lingered in the Gardens before taking a carriage home. The stunning colours and delightful scents could not draw her away from jumbled thoughts of Robert. She had no intention of seeing him again but counted the days to their next lunch. He aggravated her to no end but she was happy being with him. He spoke of a bright future yet her present was a calamity.

* * *

Thomas taught James one valuable lesson, how to be patient. Drawing attention to himself was the last thing he needed while tracking Thomas. He leaned against the red spruce across the street from the Halifax Club on Hollis Street while casually eating his cheese sandwich. Thomas was inside the Club no doubt enjoying a first-rate dinner. Two trolley cars slowed but James waved them on, then filled his pipe and took the first puff as the sun dropped behind the horizon and the electric street lights came on.

When Thomas eventually stepped out of the Club, James tapped his pipe on the tree trunk then tucked it into its leather pouch. He expected Thomas to walk toward the wharf where he frequented his preferred bars and pubs, several unsavoury. Not tonight. Thomas glanced at his pocket watch and began a brisk walk south toward Sackville Street then west. They were going to the Public Gardens.

When Thomas stepped onto the bandstand, James pressed

his body firmly against the back of an elegant female statue. He wrapped his arms around her considerable bust and peered over her shoulder, experiencing a strong urge to whisper an apology for his brazen behaviour.

Thomas had already begun slinging angry questions. "Who are you?" He grabbed the woman's arm.

James squinted to get a better look at the woman. Black dress, black veil.

* * *

Gilfoy called it quits for the day. "Good night, Constable Healy. See you tomorrow." He stepped onto the sidewalk just after the sun set. He'd made good progress in the review. Tomorrow, he'd finish up his notes. Despite being dog-tired, he couldn't resist taking a detour into the Public Gardens. No matter the time or season, it always brightened his spirits. As he approached the entrance, he heard people yelling.

"You're just like your father and you're gonna pay. You're a crook and I've got proof."

"How dare you threaten me. Who the hell are you? Put that knife away."

Gilfoy inched closer to the bandstand, hunkered down behind a flowering rose bush.

"I'm your aunt Jessie. Your bloody family ruined my life. Now I'm going to ruin yours."

"You're the one who sent the threatening letter! I've got people who'll shut you up."

Gilfoy didn't recognize the woman's voice but knew the man. He leaned forward, trying to see the woman's clothing. She was dressed in black, complete with hat and veil.

"Good evening, Detective. Having a close look at the rose bushes, sir?"

The booming voice startled Gilfoy. He jumped up. "Stop. It's the police. Craigswell, a man and woman. Run left, I'll go right. "

It was a lost cause. Too many paths and multiple places to hide but Gilfoy was pleased. He had a new lead into Thomas Bishop's world. The woman in black was a new piece of the puzzle. *Was she really Thomas' aunt? If she had proof, why didn't she come to the station?*

* * *

James loved the thrill of gambling and kept it from his family. While he occasionally admonished himself about gambling, he had no such notion about his passion, tracking Thomas. He wanted proof of the man's fraud. In the throes of the chase, he felt justified in his action to rid Margaret of a flawed man. Tonight was the biggest thrill so far. He'd heard someone had proof of Thomas' guilt. He wanted to identify the woman in black but that proved impossible once the police arrived. Thomas and the woman ran off in different directions. Having to avoid the police himself, he soon lost track of the elusive woman in black in the wharf area.

When the policeman gave up his search, James resumed his own hunt, weaving back and forth through side streets and between buildings. Convinced he'd find the woman in black near Sailors in the coming days, he began the walk home. Thomas' guilt was within his grasp.

Minutes later, he met a man wearing a shabby coat and dirty blue cap rushing away from a nearby street light. He was reminded of the man speaking with Thomas on Natal Day. Then he spotted a bundle of dark clothing under the light. Approaching slowly, he realized it was not discarded clothing but a person. He quickly dropped to his knees to check for a pulse but found none. It was a woman, her torn black veil revealed gruesome rope marks on her neck. Hearing voices, he yelled for help, then ducked behind a storage shed.

"Jesus Murphy, what's happened here?"

"She's dead." The second man crossed himself.

"Nothin' we can do. We better go for the coppers."

"We is right. I ain't stayin' here by myself."

CHAPTER THIRTEEN

MONTREAL, QUEBEC
AUGUST 9, 1895

Robert woke to an overcast Montreal morning. The grey clouds hanging low over the city were the perfect match for his frame of mind. His mother's words were direct. 'Make a clear decision about this friendship with Margaret before you return next month'. She'd made it sound like he had a choice but her intent was end it.

Robert left for work without an umbrella and was soon forced to huddle under the overhang of a nearby office doorway, hands stuffed in his coat pockets. His fingers touched the bag tag. It was his only option to find out about Thomas. It also meant he could lose his job. He clutched the tag for the remainder of his walk to the office then picked up the phone and made the call.

"Bonjour, good morning. Montreal Shipping. How may I help you? Comment puis-je vous aider?"

"Good morning. May I speak with Pierre Armstrong?" Robert folded and unfolded the tag several times before a male voice answered.

"Pierre Armstrong speaking. How can I help you?"

"Good morning, Mr. Armstrong. We haven't met." *Damn. Why did I say that?* " My name is Robert Fraser. I am an employee of a large bank in the city. I have reason to believe you can assist me with information about a man by the name of Thomas Bishop, current resident of the city of Halifax.

Silence. Robert expected to hear a click, severing the connection. "Are you there, sir?"

"Yes, Mr. Fraser. Are you available to meet after work today?"

"Absolutely. I'd prefer we not meet in either of our places of work. Would the Red Maple Pub be suitable?"

"Good choice. Five-thirty?"

"See you then." Robert breathed deeply. *As Grandpa used to say, in for a penny, in for a pound.*

* * *

Thomas didn't trust anyone, least of all that deranged woman at the bandstand who claimed to be his aunt and accused him of fraud. She'd been his secretary for months as Maude Elgin and sure as hell didn't look anything like his father or mother. Rumours about him being a crook would ruin him in Halifax, lead to a police investigation. He needed to clean-up any evidence she might have. Pleased to have Margaret out of the way in the guest room, Thomas rose before daybreak to start looking for his so-called aunt's lodgings.

There was a women's boarding house near Thomas' office. He'd start there and broaden his search if needed. He approached the three-story sandstone building in full stride, stepped up to the wooden storm porch and knocked on the door.

A stern-faced woman wearing a shabby green print cotton dress opened the door a few inches. "Stay right there. What 'ya want?"

"Morning, madam. I apologize for the early hour. I'm looking for one of your boarders on an urgent family matter. She is an older woman with grey hair, sharp features and always wears black day dresses. Her name is Maude Elgin. Does she reside here?"

"Nobody here looks like that. Name ain't right either. Try the boardin' place two streets north." She slammed the door in Thomas' face.

Thomas made three more boarding house stops but the search

came up empty. He checked his pocket watch. It was eight o'clock. Time to be in the office. He sat at his desk, scattered papers over it then placed the black ledger in plain view and pretended to work. When Miss Elgin failed to come to work by noon, he enjoyed a drink of scotch.

* * *

Margaret breathed a sigh of relief when she discovered Thomas was gone for the day. She wanted to speak with Cookie about friendships. Margaret had no doubt Cookie had heard a few stories and could offer sage advice.

* * *

Overnight Gilfoy replayed his bandstand encounter, hoping to piece together a connection between Bishop's fraud and Timothy's murder case. Before sunrise he washed and dressed in the bathroom, crept downstairs to the kitchen, ate a scone then walked to the bandstand. Standing behind the same rose bush, he willed the place to give up details his mind had not. Maybe a missed word or intuitive understanding would come to mind. Nothing. He resumed his brisk walk to the station.

Gilfoy spoke with Henderson about the bandstand episode and added, "Perhaps Thomas' mystery aunt in mourning will deliver the much-needed evidence in the fraud charges this morning." Then he settled at his desk to review what he'd written yesterday and write short summaries from the Dumont's 1888 and 1892 interviews.

Psychologist's findings:

Thomas had a remarkable ability to remain detached from trouble he was directly responsible for creating. Displayed controlling behaviour. Treated brother Timothy as prey, parents as targets of ridicule. "bossy pigs who are going to hell". Prescribed laudanum.

Timothy remained traumatized by his brother's accusations

and parent's death. Recommendation Timothy be placed in an approved family home with ongoing supervision by the family doctor. Needs counselling.

After parent's murder:

Thomas talkative — gave detailed story, said Timothy murdered their parents, Timothy came to their shared room and "rubbed blood on me." Timothy was inconsolable. Denied the murder accusation.

Neighbours:

Thomas came to them after the murder. Calm. Blood on hands.

Timothy distraught, crying, incoherent. Blood on his hands.

Thomas and Timothy inside police station:

Thomas said Timothy was often angry with parents. They locked him in a little room under the stairs when he was bad.

Timothy was barely able to speak. Said he didn't ever hit his parents or hurt them. Said Thomas lied about rubbing blood on him. Couldn't describe the little room under the stairs.

Boys' night clothing taken as evidence. Thomas' nightshirt bloody blotches and missing a button. Timothy's nightshirt bloody smears.

Dumonts July 18, 1888

Thomas was fostered with them. Nothing was ever his fault. Refused to accept family rules, argued. Took laudanum

Dumonts September 12, 1892 (Contacted by police re fraud investigations)

Thomas returned to Dumonts for Christmas 1890 and 1891, big gifts, money, boastful about important job in Montreal, stayed a few days, they sensed he was hiding something or from someone both times (fraud?)

Gilfoy rubbed his forehead. The Dumont details were at odds with his recollection of Doctor Bell's details on Thomas. He reached for Bell's report and proved himself correct. Thomas lied to Bell. Timothy was not placed in an asylum. Thomas wasn't adopted. He was fostered by Edgar and Alice Dumont. No big job. Where did his money come from?

* * *

"What's the matter with you, William? That face would terrify a small child! You better tell me before anyone outside this room sees you." Grace put her cup back on its saucer.

"I'm tired of waiting for news from Gilfoy, that's what. He must have some news from Montreal and the constables out and about in the city. At lunch time I'm going to the police station. I plan to sit there until I get some answers. Margaret's future is at stake. She's a prisoner in her own home. I've had enough!"

Grace smiled. "Be considerate, dear."

He rolled his eyes with a smirk on his face. "I will. You know I will." His face became serious. "I'm worried."

"So am I. I know an admission of a marital problem is not done, but it's time for Margaret to come home and stay."

* * *

Glancing at his watch, Gilfoy realized it was almost ten o'clock and still no sign of the woman from the bandstand. He jumped up and grabbed the door knob just as Henderson was about to knock. "Something happening?"

"Yes, sir. A woman's body was found at the pier last night. The constable says she was wearing a black dress and veil. Think it's our lady?"

"Maybe. Let's see what the coroner finds. If it's her, things just got a lot more complicated." Gilfoy returned to his desk. "Bring in the Timothy Bishop evidence box. I also have to update you on the Montreal report."

Gilfoy emptied the box of clothing and picked up the envelope containing a dark blue button. "Why would Timothy keep this button with him? What kind of button is it? Any ideas?" He handed the button to Henderson who rolled it around between his thumb and index finger.

"I think it's a child's button, sir. My nephew's nightshirts have buttons like this one." He shrugged and returned the button.

"You may be on to something there, Henderson. My grand-daughters' nightgowns have pink buttons. Let me read the notes from the night of the murder. There it is." Gilfoy's words took on an optimistic tone. "Thomas' nightshirt was missing a button!"

"But what does that mean? I hate to say it sir, but you'd never get Thomas Bishop on the stand with a button as evidence." He shook his head. "Is it really from Thomas' nightshirt? How did Timothy get it the night of the murder and where did he hide it that night? Imagine the jury's doubt."

"You're right but it might come in handy later, some how." He hesitated then began again. "I'm acting on a hunch here. Telegraph the Montreal Police. Ask them to search the names Jessie Bishop and Maude Elgin, possibly connected to the Thomas Bishop fraud cases or their own criminal activity.

"Will do. Jessie Bishop, sir?"

"It's a guess. Jessie might be a sister of Thomas' mother but let's try Bishop first. I'd rather not be forced to ask Thomas for his mother's maiden name."

Henderson glanced toward the evidence box.

"Leave the box with me. I'd like to have another look at Timothy's clothing before the end of the day."

* * *

"Mrs. Gilmore, do you have some friends who are better than others?"

"Better? What do you mean?"

"Well, women you can really talk with. And not worry."

"I always enjoy our little talks but this morning's chat is most confusing. What do you want to talk about, my dear."

"Friendship and trustworthy women. I'm sure you have women friends. How much do you really tell them?"

"First of all, not all friendly women are the same."

"Whatever do you mean?"

"Well, the best way I can say it is, friendly women and real friends. Real friends know you and love you no matter what. The other kind are not that. My mother used to call them fair weather friends. They're interested in what you do, ask lots of questions then you find out they've told everybody." She paused. "Make no mistake, men can talk too. My mother told me about a couple she knew. She made the spit balls and he threw them."

Margaret laughed out loud. "That's funny."

"And true. Your biggest problem will be finding out which ones are which."

"How do I do that?"

"Don't be sharin' too much at the beginnin', for sure. Don't gossip yourself. Listen. If someone gossips to you, they'll gossip about you just as fast."

"Thank you, Cookie. That was most helpful."

"If you don't mind me askin', don't 'ya have close women friends? You know, from school."

"No. Most are married, moved to Boston, other parts of Nova Scotia. Only two are here. I asked them to be my bridesmaids but we aren't really close friends."

"Ready for lunch? I have leftover baked ham. A brown bread sandwich and pot of tea? Sweet pickles?"

"Sounds delicious."

"Bet 'ya didn't know what the definition of eternity is."

"I don't."

"A baked ham and two people. My sister told me that one."

After lunch, Margaret was comfortably settled in the sitting room with a pot of tea and the Walter Scott novel, *Kenilworth*. Rays from the afternoon sun fell across the hardwood floor and warmed her feet resting on the velvet footstool. Margaret was captivated by the story, seeing in its pages her own private agony amid the public perception of her privileged life.

* * *

The usually quiet front office of the police station was buzzing with constables. Their earnest tones told William Bell something unusual had happened. When fellow physician and coroner Jacob Stillman walked directly into Gilfoy's office without knocking, he resisted the impulse to leave right then and there. He had a mid afternoon patient appointment. Recalling Grace's advice, he looked at his watch then sat back in the chair.

When Stillman and Gilfoy exited the office together, Stillman nodded to William as he went toward the exit door.

Gilfoy beckoned William into the office. "I'll be quick, Doctor. We've another murder on our hands."

"Related?"

"Maybe." Gilfoy opened his arms, shrugged his shoulders. "I know this is a long shot but it's a woman who might be Thomas' secretary. Know her?"

"Only to see her."

"Good enough for me. The coroner just told me her reticule held a room key, a much smaller key and an embroidered hand-kerchief." He hesitated. "As a doctor, would you mind looking at the body?"

"Not too keen mind you, but I will. How soon would you need me?"

"Now."

By mutual consent without a word being spoken, William and Gilfoy walked in silence to the morgue, housed in the university's pathology laboratory. Both men had previous visits to the morgue, both with identical outcomes. The foul odours had lingered long and strong for both of them causing nausea followed by brief loss of appetite. When cheery Doctor Stillman welcomed them into his operating theatre, each placed a mint in his mouth, then held a handkerchief over his nose.

"I'll be quick, fellas. This lady died by strangulation. There are no wounds or bruising on the body, except on the neck. Pretty straight forward for me but likely not for you, John." He then turned to Doctor Bell. "William, I'm puzzled as to why you're here."

"Not by choice I assure you, Jacob." He smiled. "I may be able to identify the victim."

"Okay, let's get on with it." Doctor Stillman lifted the white sheet to reveal the pallid face.

"It's her all right. Maude Elgin, Thomas' secretary."

"Hmm, I'm not convinced that's her real name. May I see her handkerchief, Jacob?"

"Of course. It smells of lavender and the embroidery's a lavender design. I doubt either one will help with the name."

"Maybe not but I'd like to have a longer look. It's evidence so I'll sign it in at the station. Oh, and the keys, too. Just put everything in her reticule."

"It's all yours. See 'ya fellas."

Outside the morgue, William took a deep breath. "I have to get back to the house for a patient. Best of luck with whatever you're thinking about the handkerchief."

"Thanks."

* * *

Gilfoy made himself a mug of sweet tea with milk then breathed deeply, clearing his nose of any lingering morgue odours. He removed Timothy's work jacket from the evidence box and spread it over his desk, slowly patting it down while smoothing it out. He placed his hand inside the right pocket, fingers tight together, feeling for any odd shape or loose thread. Nothing felt out of place, until his forefinger sensed a slight unevenness in the lining at the bottom of the pocket. A few scissor snips later, Gilfoy was reading a letter.

June 03, 1895

To Whom It May Concern,

My name is Timothy Bishop. I am a bank investigator seeking information on Thomas Bishop, former resident of Montreal.

Should you come into possession of this letter contact Mr. Benoit Allard with the Montreal Police.

Timothy Bishop   Benoit J. Allard
Timothy Bishop   *Benoit Allard*

"Henderson."

"Sir."

Gilfoy handed the letter to Henderson. "A bank wouldn't authorize Timothy to investigate a family member! Contact the Montreal police about Benoit J. Allard then come back to see me. We need to find Jessie Bishop's room."

Gilfoy walked out to the front desk. "Ever see a key like this before, Constable Healy?" He put the key on the front desk.

"A bedroom door? Got an interesting fob though." Healy squinted and slowly turned the fob over. "Looks like a small crown on it. No letters. A house key, sir?"

"Too small for a front door."

"Name of a building then?"

"Maybe." Gilfoy went back to his office, continued looking at the key.

"All done, sir." Henderson looked at the key on the desk.

"I left my magnifying glass at home. How's your eyesight, Henderson?"

"Fine, sir. No spectacles for me yet. Something I can read for you?"

"This small key fob has something on the back. Healy says it's a crown. Have a look."

"Healy's right, it's a crown. You suppose it's for a room in the Crown?"

"A boarding house?"

"It's on my way home."

"Off you go then. Take an evidence box. When you finish bring the items back here tomorrow. We'll talk then. Boy, oh boy. If you're right, we got lucky. It could have taken days."

* * *

"Good evening, Monsieur Armstrong." Robert stood to greet and shake hands with the middle-aged man scanning the room. "I'm Robert Fraser."

"You look familiar. Have we met?"

"Not formally. Come to my table." Robert had chosen a small table in the corner, far from the bar. "A few weeks ago I intentionally bumped into you getting off the train from Halifax."

"Yes, yes, that's it. What's this all about?"

"To be direct, Thomas Bishop. I met the man in Halifax and came away with a bad impression. Then when I overheard some of your conversation with another gentleman on the train, I wanted to speak with you. I admit I bumped into you on purpose in order to obtain your name from the luggage tag."

"That was inventive. Is your agenda business or personal?"

"Both. A school friend is married to him and there may be reason to believe he is less than honest in business dealings."

Armstrong was staring over his wire-rim glasses. "You work here in Montreal, Mr. Fraser. How are you connected with Halifax, aside from your friend?"

"My family lives in Halifax and my bank business requires I visit Halifax monthly."

"Bank? Is your bank involved in this matter?"

"No." He hesitated then continued. "It's personal. Frankly, I'm more than a little concerned about my employment as it relates to my involvement in this matter."

"Understandably. How do you want to proceed? Or maybe I should ask, do you want to proceed?"

"If you're interested, I am."

"Then Robert, I'm Pierre. We should have a bottle of Mr. Molson's beer together. My purchase."

CHAPTER
FOURTEEN

HALIFAX, NOVA SCOTIA
AUGUST 9, 1895

Control ruled every aspect of Thomas' life. He lived for it, thrived in its presence. On Friday afternoon he paced in his office, afraid of losing his personal toughness and finding himself at the centre of a police investigation. His thoughts raced, repeating themselves over and over. What evidence of fraud did Maude Elgin have? Had she already given it to the police? By four o'clock he could no longer face the uncertainty alone. He locked the door and went home. At least he'd be safe there, have a drink and try to have a conversation with Margaret. It was time for her to return to the marital bed and provide comfort to her husband.

Margaret was in disbelief hearing Thomas enter the house much earlier than usual. "What's happened?"

"Nothing. Let's have a drink before dinner." He wandered toward the study.

Margaret followed, alert to an unknown problem and sat in the chair closest to the door.

Thomas poured two drinks and walked toward her. "I must apologize for my behaviour these past few weeks. I'm sure you think me a terrible husband. To tell you the truth, I do have a great deal of worry right now, none caused by me I might add." He gave Margaret her glass and returned to the liquor cabinet. "To be honest Timothy's death has caused me considerable sorrow, even though I haven't seen him for all these years." He gulped the scotch. "After all he was my brother. I'm sure you can understand, having a brother yourself." He studied Margaret's face.

"Of course."

"Where was I? Oh, yes, my worries." He refilled his glass and began drinking before sitting down. "To make matters worse my secretary, Miss Elgin did not come to work today. I did inquire about her at a local boarding house. Apparently, she does not live there. I do hope she's not unwell. I would miss her efficient work." He shifted his gaze from the window to stare at Margaret. "Spoken with your parents lately?"

"No, not in the past few days." Her heart raced, breathing quickened.

Then the mood changed. "I have an idea. We could have a dinner here again. Do you think our cook could manage a larger gathering here, say a dozen people for dinner in a few weeks?"

Margaret made a great effort to offer a pleasant reply. "Mrs. Gilmore will need help with preparation and serving but she is quite capable of planning and preparing for such an event."

"Wonderful. You decide on a date, my dear." He rose to refill his glass as a loud knock on the front door stopped him mid stride. "Are you expecting someone?"

Margaret shook her head. "You?"

Thomas ignored her question and filled his glass, placing it on a side table. He moved behind his chair and gripped the back with both hands.

Cookie entered the study, hands folded over her apron. "It's for you Mr. Bishop. A Detective Gilfoy from the city police. Shall I ask him to come to the study, sir?"

"Certainly. He probably wants to inform me of an arrest in my brother's death."

After a quick glance at Margaret, Cookie backed out of the room.

"Right this way, Detective." Cookie was tempted to eavesdrop behind the closed French doors.

"Good evening Mrs. Bishop, Mr. Bishop. Sorry to trouble you

at home but I have urgent news to deliver." Gilfoy spun his hat in his hands.

Thomas was quick to get the man on his way. "You've found Timothy's killer. I'm pleased. Thank you for coming to inform us." He took a step toward the study door.

"Before you go any further Mr. Bishop, this is not about your brother. Your secretary, Miss Elgin has died. Her body was found late last night."

"That is distressing news. She did not show up for work today. That is not like her. Died at home, did she?" Thomas returned to stand behind his chair.

Gilfoy ignored the question, asked one of his own. "I have information that you were seen at the bandstand with her last evening. Is that correct?"

"No, I most certainly was not." Margaret noticed Thomas' hands grip the fabric of his chair. She guessed the detective did as well.

"This person is quite certain it was you. Then it must have been someone who closely resembles you if, as you say, you weren't there."

Thomas swallowed hard. "What would I have to do with Miss Elgin's death?" He lifted his head and pressed his lips together, determined to regain his composure.

"Tell me about Miss Elgin. When did she start to work for you?"

"Around the beginning of April."

"References?"

"She said she needed a job but hadn't worked for a few years. She offered to work for nothing for two weeks. I took her up on the offer." He took a deep breath.

"She have family in the city?

"I wouldn't know. She didn't talk much."

"Anyone ever visit her at work?"

"Not that I'm aware off. In any event I wouldn't encourage that sort of thing." He crossed his arms.

"Think she ever met your brother, Timothy?"

"Why would she?" Thomas shrugged.

"Is that a no?"

"I don't know."

"So you don't know if they met, correct?"

"Maybe they met, I don't know."

"So, it is possible they knew each other." Ignoring Thomas completely, Gilfoy turned toward Margaret. His tone softened. "Mrs. Bishop, did you know Miss Elgin?"

"No, detective. I've never met her."

Gilfoy shifted his eyes to Thomas. "By the way Mr. Bishop, where were you around nine o'clock last evening?"

"At home." It was a careless answer and he knew it immediately. Margaret was fascinated by the detective's ability to unbalance Thomas. A grin passed across her face.

"Well, thank you both for your help. Mr. Bishop, I'll undoubtedly need to speak with you again as we close in on the murderer. Make yourself available this coming week. And with regard to your brother's murder, I will have more details within the week. Good evening, I'll see myself out."

As soon as the front door closed, Thomas stood over Margaret. "Don't look at me like that. I couldn't tell him I was gambling, could I? I have a reputation to keep. And besides, I'll have someone vouch for me."

James did not see Thomas in his usual late afternoon Friday haunts. He decided to check on Margaret. As a man exited the Bishop home, he took a few backward steps to stand behind a maple tree. It was one of the policemen from the Public Gardens bandstand. When he began whistling, James knew Thomas' evening had been ruined. He took no pleasure in knowing Margaret would pay the price for the policeman's visit.

Margaret furrowed her brow. "Whatever happened to that poor woman? You saw her every day. You must have noticed something."

"Why would I? She wasn't anyone I knew. I don't encourage

idle talk in the workplace. She came, did her job and left. Let's get back to those dinner party plans."

Cookie came to the study door. "Dinner is ready."

Thomas glanced at Margaret as he picked up a bottle of red wine from the liquor cabinet. "Wine with dinner?"

Margaret shook her head. A woman Thomas knew had died. Excessive drinking seemed most inappropriate.

Fuelled by several glasses of wine, Thomas flirtatious chatter during the meal meant only one outcome. Margaret steeled herself and played the game to ensure her safety.

Satiated, Thomas fell into a deep sleep. Alone in the locked guest room, Margaret cried herself to sleep.

* * *

Gilfoy was intrigued by the possibility of a handkerchief solving a murder. He placed the hanky on the kitchen table. Magnifying glass in hand, he peered at the intricate spray of embroidered lavender flowers bound together by a delicate lavender-coloured ribbon tied into a bow.

Nettie Gilfoy was overcome with laughter when she spied her husband staring at the handkerchief. "You brought home a hanky? And what happened to a jig-saw puzzle for evening entertainment?"

"Hush now, Nettie. I need to concentrate."

"What in heaven's name are you looking for?"

"A murdered woman's name."

"And the hanky is going to speak to you!" She shook her head. "I'll pretend you didn't say that." She tousled his hair and picked up her knitting.

A quiet half hour passed before Nettie stood and put the kettle on for tea. "Did the hanky speak?"

"I'm close. There it is, you sneaky little devil. Come here, Nettie. Look at the ribbon. What do you see?"

"A very pretty lady's hanky that smells of lavender. How lovely."

"There are two distinct shades of lavender thread in the knot. Follow each colour, slowly."

"The 'J' is easy." Nettie squinted, her nose almost on the glass.

"Take your time."

"Hmm. Yes, the J then a B." She lifted her head. "JB. Somebody you know?"

Gilfoy nodded. "Told 'ya. Hankies can talk. How about that tea? Put a drop of whisky in it. Yours too."

CHAPTER FIFTEEN

MONTREAL, QUEBEC
AUGUST 10, 1895

In early April 1894 Eloise Chartrand's great loss would become Robert's good fortune. Eloise's husband, Alphonse died fighting a house fire in the Le Plateau-Mont-Royal borough district of Montreal. Left with a small cozy house but no income, Eloise decided to sell her cherished home and find a room in a boarding house where she would perform menial tasks to offset the rent.

In mid April of the same year, The Bank of Montreal offered Robert a permanent position in their head office. He'd spent a year and a half with his aunt and uncle. Now he was financially able to live on his own but struggled to find a suitable place within walking distance of the bank. His search ended when his supervisor introduced him to Eloise.

More than a year later both couldn't be happier with the arrangement. Robert was handy at repairing things, a good conversationalist and Eloise loved to cook.

Eloise was also good at reading people. By the end of July she knew all about Margaret and was worried. Well aware she had only her own marriage experience to draw on, she offered no advice to Robert with no plan to do so. What she could and did do was listen and pose the occasional thoughtful question.

The tempting aromas of bacon and coffee wafted up the stairwell just as the sunshine broke through the clouds and streamed across Robert's quilt. It was Saturday, normally a restful day but not today.

After hearing Robert's explanation of the situation in Halifax, Pierre Armstrong offered written proof of Thomas Bishop's employee fraud. When asked for details, Pierre admitted the company retained the proof but had not pressed charges. The company president believed exposing an internal scandal would erode public confidence in their business. He demanded a written apology from Thomas and his immediate resignation from the position. Thomas was nineteen at the time.

Lying in bed, Robert acknowledged Pierre Armstrong's information was helpful as proof of Thomas' fraudulent behaviour but worth little in convincing Margaret to walk away from her marriage. He had fourteen days before his next Halifax visit.

* * *

Henderson rushed through an early Saturday breakfast and found Gilfoy waiting for him.

"Morning, Henderson." Gilfoy patted the evidence box on his desk. "I saw this box in the evidence room with J Bishop on it. How was the meeting at the boarding house?"

"Good. It was the right place and the owner agreed to me looking around Jessie's room."

"I take it you found something."

"Somethings, sir." Henderson reached into the box and pulled out a rolled up blanket.

"A blanket?" Gilfoy's eyes rolled.

"It was at the bottom of the bed. Neat as a pin, it was. Unroll it, sir." Henderson looked very pleased with himself while this was happening.

"Men's pants!" Gilfoy held them up. "And a beard." He shook his head. "How'd she get those things, especially the beard?"

"My guess is the theatre company at the Citadel. Why'd she need the beard and pants, sir?"

"We'll have to do more work to answer that. Good work, Constable."

"There's more, sir. She had a small wooden jewellery case. The little key in her reticule opened it."

Gilfoy lifted the key out of the box. "How'd you find the case?"

"My little sister has a treasure box so I was thinking this lady would have some keepsakes. She hid it well. I guess knowing the lady who runs the boarding house had a key to her room."

"Where was it?"

"The room has an armoir, real plain it is. It's got three small shelves inside. You can move them up and down. They're near the top on one side. She moved the top shelf up to squeeze the case between it and the top of the armoir. The jewellery case is wood, you'd miss it real easy. She had three office kind of keys and a knife inside. The blade is like a saw, would make a jagged wound, just like you said about Timothy Bishop's injury."

"Well done, Henderson."

"Another thing, sir. The room smells like lavender. Timothy's shirt had a whiff of lavender. There a connection, ya think?"

"Could be but a hard one to make. Lavender is very popular."

Henderson hesitated, looked out the window. "There was one other thing in the case, sir. A lock of hair tied with a pink ribbon. The paper attached read 'Elizabeth Marie'." He paused. "I got tears in my eyes, sir. She have a child?"

"I don't know. Maybe the report from Montreal will tell us." He paused. "You're human, Henderson. There's no shame in crying."

* * *

Saturday morning in the Bishop home was precisely what Margaret expected. Thomas joined her for breakfast, feigning concern by pouring her tea then quickly turning to his own needs by complaining of a headache. Then his strategy changed again.

"On my way home yesterday, I spotted a new jewellery shop. I'm going to buy you the opal broach in their window. Let's look at it immediately after breakfast tomorrow, on our way to church. I'll go first thing Monday and buy it."

"You're attending church tomorrow?"

"I'm looking forward to having the family lunch with your parents and James of course. He's a dark horse. I wonder what he's been up to these days?"

"Why would you ask that? James is studying to be a doctor. How on earth would he have time or the interest in being 'up to something'?"

"He's very fond of you. I'm sure he wouldn't want anything to happen to you."

"Of course he's fond of me. I'm his sister." She stopped talking and looked warily at Thomas. "What are you saying? Someone's going to hurt me?" Her eyes widened.

"Calm down. You're not in danger."

"But why would you say James wouldn't want anything to happen to me?" Her eyebrows went up.

"Stop ranting. You always jump to conclusions, get emotional about everything."

"I most certainly do not. When did I do that? Name one time." Her brows came together.

"Listen to yourself. You've just done it...raising your voice, waving your arms about. I rest my case. Have more tea and settle down. And put powder on your red face. I'm off to the office."

* * *

As Margaret expected, after the church service Thomas strutted around shaking hands, greeting people, playing the part of a fine upstanding citizen. She was able to avoid most of it while speaking with Anna and planning their lunch for Tuesday.

The family lunch began with the usual pleasantries. Margaret remained on edge. It was only a matter of time before Thomas triggered a clash with James.

Through the main course, Thomas held court with his

incessant chatter at the table. Then during dessert, he looked directly at James. "What do you do for fun, James?"

"Fun? I don't have much time for fun but I occasionally enjoy a beer with friends. Why do you ask?"

"Ahhh, that's why I saw you outside the Anchor Pub near the pier last Thursday night."

"And were you inside or walking on the pier yourself?"

Thomas dropped his eyes briefly, "I'd been inside meeting with a couple of business people, had food and drink and saw you as I was leaving."

"If you say so." *You were nowhere near the pier but I saw you at the bandstand.*

Thomas refused to give up. "Detective Gilfoy told me someone reported seeing me at the bandstand last Thursday evening. Would you know anything about that?" He stared across the table at James.

"Fraid not. Wasn't me. Margaret, could you pass the tea, please."

Thomas then turned toward William and Grace. "And what about you, Doctor and Mrs. Bell? Same question. Same night."

William jumped to his feet, followed by James. "How dare you ask such an atrocious question. We will not be maligned in our own home. Apologize immediately or leave." William's face was scarlet, his breaths in short gasps.

"I'm off to the office for the remainder of the day anyway. The death of my secretary has caused considerably more work for me. I'll see you at home, Margaret. Good day."

Following Thomas' departure the stillness was palpable. He had all but declared them complicit in or hiding knowledge of a murder.

William breathed deeply. "Grace, could you ask Hazel to prepare a fresh pot of tea and bring it to the sitting room, please."

Margaret guided her father to a chair. "You must sit down, Papa."

"Give me a minute to catch my breath."

When Grace and Hazel returned with the tea, William was ready with a plan.

"All of us need to remain calm. Not one of us is guilty or connected in any way to the death of Timothy or Thomas' secretary. Margaret, I want you to stay here for a few days. James and I will speak with Mrs. Gilmore this afternoon and ask her to prepare meals and do the usual chores during the day. I will have her pack clothing for you. She will not stay overnight in your home, beginning tonight. We will leave a note for Thomas. He needs to understand there are real and immediate consequences to his outlandish accusations."

Margaret interrupted. "Cookie will be safe with her sister."

William continued. "Excellent. At this point I want to tell you what I know about the death of Thomas' secretary as he may be involved. I met Miss Elgin in Thomas' office many weeks ago. On Friday, Detective Gilfoy asked me to accompany him to the morgue to help identify the body found at the pier. It was Miss Elgin but Gilfoy is of the opinion that may not be her name." He looked at Margaret. "Do you know something about Miss Elgin?"

"No, but Detective Gilfoy visited us last evening. He told us Thomas was seen at the bandstand and Thomas denied it. He told the Detective he was at home that evening. He wasn't. That's why he confronted the three of you." She looked from her brother to her parents. "Do you think Thomas is capable of murder?"

James was not ready to tip his hand. "I expect Gilfoy's visit really unnerved him. Today, he wanted to intimidate us, keep the spotlight off himself. He's got lots of enemies. Sooner or later somebody is going to fight back. Things will get worse for him, very soon."

Margaret leaned forward in her chair, stared at James. "Do you know something or are you just being dramatic, making up things like lots of enemies. Who are these enemies you're talking about and how do you know them?"

"I know many people in Halifax from school and social

gatherings. I listen and ask questions. As a woman, you do not have the same easy way into society."

Margaret opened her mouth to object but James continued quickly.

"I didn't mean you shouldn't have the same way in but society sets the rules. Men have more freedom than women. That's just the way it is."

"That's now." Margaret's voice took on a commanding tone. "I have a friend who thinks society needs to change now. So do I and I'm going to do something about it." She froze, barely believing the words herself. Her wide eyes darted from James to her mother, settled on her father. The ticking clock sounded like bomb blasts in the still air.

James began clapping. "Well done, Margaret. The young woman you were is back."

"It's good to know you have spunk again, my dear. "

William nodded. "Your mother is correct. I'm very pleased, too."

Margaret realized her Tuesday lunch with Anna was going to be a corker.

* * *

Thomas arrived home late Sunday evening. Instead of finding Margaret, he found a warm meat pie under a tea towel and a letter addressed to him. He ripped it open, read it, then threw it into the stove. "Damn them all to hell and the sooner the better."

CHAPTER SIXTEEN

HALIFAX, NOVA SCOTIA
AUGUST 12, 1985

Cookie quietly closed the front door of the Bishop home and hurried into the kitchen where she stood behind a kitchen chair, fully prepared to swing it at Thomas.

Thomas burst into the kitchen, avoiding eye contact with Cookie. "Finally, you're here. Clean the kitchen and take the rest of the day off. On second thought, take the rest of the week off. I seem to be the only one living here these days." He stormed out, cursing to himself down the hallway and out the front door.

"Yes, Mr. Bishop." Cookie called out after he closed the door. She was overjoyed to be 'dismissed'. She knew Margaret was safe. The rest of the trouble would sort itself out. She did her work and went off to her sister's for a little holiday at home.

Thomas seethed about the damn detective playing games and insulting him in his own home, tricking him into lying. By noon, with little work accomplished and no desire to talk business at the club, he began drinking and pacing. Soon he was shouting. "If that damn Gilfoy knew something, he should have interviewed me already. That bloody Bell family will pay. Nobody gets to keep my wife from me." At five o'clock he walked to the closest hotel with a decent dining room.

* * *

"There's no such person as Benoit J. Allard in the Montreal police department, Henderson."

"What do you mean, there's no such person as that Allard fella, sir? Timothy Bishop said so in his letter."

Gilfoy nodded slowly. "Have a seat, Henderson. You're right about that letter. Timothy did say so in his letter."

"Why'd he do that? It didn't help."

"Not us but himself. He bought time by hoping to send the finder on a wild goose chase."

"Wait a minute. He musta known he could be killed! How else would we've found the letter?"

"Well, he might have known he could be killed but I believe it was more for insurance to protect himself. He was in Rockhead for drinking and fighting but he didn't need the letter at that time."

"But, if Timothy didn't come to Halifax to catch his brother, why was he here?"

"Murder." Gilfoy spoke confidently. "Here's my theory. Timothy came to Halifax not to investigate fraud but to commit murder, Thomas' murder."

"But he got killed, sir. His victim got to him first?"

"Not necessarily. Thomas could have been the intended victim and not kill Timothy."

"So, someone killed Timothy for Thomas?"

"Maybe. Who killed Timothy and who Timothy wanted to kill are likely different people."

"Besides being in a pickle, where does that leave us, sir?"

"With the evidence. We've missed something." Gilfoy ran his hand through his hair, leaving it untidy. A curly lock fell over his forehead. "Maybe I missed something in those Montreal reports about Timothy."

"But Thomas was the one with problems."

"The obvious one, yes. Maybe Timothy had problems too. Different problems."

Henderson nodded. "So there's more to Timothy than we thought."

"I'll have to prove Timothy harboured his resentment of

Thomas' mistreatment for years and finally was able to act on it. When he found proof of Thomas' fraud he came to Halifax to blackmail him, then plan his murder. I need documented proof and witnesses."

"But he's dead, sir. Is there any need to prove his guilt?"

"In my mind, yes. It will close the file. It's a Timothy, Thomas and Jessie Bishop puzzle."

Henderson nodded. "Only one person is alive and he doesn't have all the answers. Or does he?"

"We may never know if Timothy knew Jessie Bishop was in Halifax on her own blackmail mission aimed at Thomas. As far as we know, he never knew her. But when he showed up at Thomas' office to hand over his blackmail envelope, Jessie knew who he was and she had a new opportunity. Both Thomas and Timothy could be blackmailed. I believe she looked for Timothy or saw him on the street and followed him to Sailors, found out where he was staying. Eventually, she saw Thomas visit Timothy there."

"That explains Bessie Ryan's story about Timothy's different clothes, sir. Maybe Jessie killed Timothy, thinking Thomas'd be blamed. She'd get rid of both of them."

"Hmm, I don't think so. If she wanted money she couldn't risk Thomas being arrested for murder. That's why she confronted him at the bandstand, the night she died."

"Then why'd she kill Timothy if she'd get money from him too?"

"There could be something else about Jessie and the Bishop family. Something personal, not just money. The report from Montreal should be here in the next day or two. Let's hope a strong motive shows up there."

"Ya think Thomas killed Jessie, sir?"

Gilfoy counted the evidence on his fingers. "One, he has a motive. Two, I overheard the bandstand argument. Three, he was quick with an alibi for that evening in front of his wife who by the way, raised her eyebrows. For my money he better have a reliable alibi if he plans to claim innocence."

"What if Thomas didn't do it, sir?"

"Talk to Bessie Ryan again. She saw Timothy talk with a bearded fella speaking French. Has she seen him since?"

* * *

Margaret had no intention of being accosted on the street by an angry husband. She took a carriage to lunch with Anna. Lunch would focus on her own future regardless of what the rest of the week held. She pushed her current situation with Thomas to the back of her mind and stepped onto the sidewalk.

Anna waved toward Margaret, her pleasure clearly revealed in a broad smile. Margaret felt a brief moment of unease about Robert but regained her composure and returned the wave. Today, she'd strengthen her friendship with Anna and declare intent to make a difference in her own life, follow through on her bold statement of Sunday afternoon.

Anna was full of energy and ideas, talking about George's work. Margaret waited patiently for her to slow down before speaking.

"The last time we spoke you mentioned how George is so calm when you get overheated. You don't always agree, I understand that. How do you make your relationship better?"

Anna paused before answering. "You've never seemed interested in personal topics before but I like it." She smiled. "We're quite different personalities and our backgrounds are different too. Early in our relationship, we had an honest conversation about our life together. We still have those conversations. My marriage has been a big change for me, getting used to George's orderliness and rigid routines. His life hasn't really changed in Halifax. The camaraderie and regimental traditions remain solid in his life. He came here with a purpose and a plan in place. I came with him and gave up everything. I lost my newspaper life, I'm often lonely. He can't make my life for me but understands my frustration. That about sums it up." She looked at Margaret with a lopsided smile. "How are things with Thomas lately?"

"It's probably best I not speak here. Let's go to the Public Gardens after lunch, be away from eavesdroppers. We can chat under our parasols without being overheard."

As Margaret and Anna entered the gardens, a well-dressed bearded man smiled and tipped his hat. "Afternoon, ladies."

They nodded then popped up their parasols to avoid further interruptions and provide shade from the afternoon sun.

"My marriage is very different. I'm married to a man I know very little about."

"How can that be?"

"Thomas moved here a few years ago. His parents are dead and he refuses to talk about his past. His business success is impressive but as a person, he's unfeeling. I should have seen through him."

"Don't blame yourself. Some people are very good at fooling others."

"What I do know is that he is focused on making money. Nothing else matters." Margaret stopped, unsure she should tell Anna more about her own life.

"Your life sounds lonely but not that same loneliness as mine."

"He takes his business problems out on me. We've never had the kind of conversations you spoke of and I truly believe we never will. I've tried but he tells me I'm too emotional. He doesn't care."

"But you must be wrong on that. He married you."

"And I know why. I was his entry into Halifax society and business contacts. What a fool I am!"

"What are you going to do? Divorce is a social spectacle with statements in the paper, awful accusations and admissions just to get out of a marriage. You don't want that, do you?" She paused. "Can you live together but separately, if you know what I mean?"

Margaret was in a quandary. Should she expose her vulnerability? "No. He's mean when he's drinking, forces me to do things then buys gifts."

"How awful for you. I'm so sorry. Can your family help?"

Margaret hesitated. "Yes. Thomas is not what any of us thought." She began to cry. "This is harder to say out loud than I imagined." A heavy sigh. "I'm currently staying with my family." She pressed on. "Thomas' secretary was found dead on the pier late last week. He's drinking, angry with the police. It's dreadful."

"The death was in the paper a few days ago. Not much seems to be known about her. Did you know her?"

"No." Margaret stopped walking. A long pause followed.

Anna reached for Margaret's hand.

Margaret whispered. "I believe the police suspect Thomas is involved with her death."

As Margaret dabbed the tears from her cheeks, Anna spoke quietly. "This is unbelievable. Are you in danger?"

"I don't believe so, except from Thomas' anger, of course."

"No wonder you're with your family. You must stay with them until this is over one way or another. You are most welcome to call on me for anything, including staying with us."

"I have something else to tell you. A family discussion brought it on. James mentioned how unequal social freedom is for men and women. His comment rankled me. I blurted out I was going to do something about it. So I am. Maybe my quick retaliation got me into trouble but I'm a woman of my word. I also need to regain my old self. I hardly recognize me!"

"In the midst of all this personal trouble, you're looking to the future. Good for you. I have an idea. Since you brought up inequality for women, how would you like to get acquainted with the suffragette women in the city?"

"You know them?"

"Getting to. First, I'd like you to meet them. We could work together on reporting to the paper. What do you think?"

"It sounds wonderful."

"Good. I'll see you here on Wednesday next week." She leaned forward and kissed Margaret's cheek. "Be careful and take care of yourself, my dear friend."

"You too, Anna."

CHAPTER
SEVENTEEN

While getting dressed on Wednesday morning Margaret noticed her favourite pair of black shoes needed mending. Her first thought was to walk to Barrington Street and enjoy all the front gardens on the way but her better sense won out and she decided to take a carriage.

"Good morning, Mama. Thank you for waiting for me."

"It's lovely having you here even though the circumstances are dreadful."

"I'm going to the shoemaker after breakfast. Is there anything you need?"

"No. Please be careful. Thomas might see you and make a scene."

* * *

Thomas did see Margaret leave the shoemaker's shop and shouted at his driver to halt. He leaned out of the carriage and waved his hand, beckoning her to come closer. Thinking herself safe in public, Margaret slowly approached the carriage and stood a step away from the window. Thomas immediately reached out and pulled her arm inside the window. "Keep your mouth shut and get in or I'll yell you're a tart selling your wares."

Margaret stepped into the carriage. "Where are you taking me?"

"To our home and our bed. Now shut up, sit down and do what you're told."

Margaret grabbed her skirts and sat down opposite Thomas on the sidewalk side of the carriage. Minutes later when the carriage stopped to allow a pedestrian to cross the street, she opened the door and jumped.

"Oh, my goodness, madam. Are you alright?"

Margaret opened her eyes and saw a shopkeeper standing over her. She was lying on the wooden sidewalk with no recollection of how she managed to avoid hitting the carriage step on her way to safety.

The shopkeeper repeated his question. "Are you alright, madam?"

Margaret sat up. "Yes, thank you. Can you hail a carriage for me?"

"Of course, madam." He helped Margaret stand, then shook his head in amazement. "I've never seen a woman fly before."

Margaret tilted her head.

"Your feet never touched the ground, madam."

Margaret knew she would have bruises, a small price to pay for what she might have endured.

* * *

The Montreal papers arrived just as Gilfoy returned from a meeting at city hall. He picked up the Jarvis report and went to his office. Doctor and Mrs. Jarvis were interviewed in 1888 when Timothy was released from supervised care and again in 1892. Both now deceased. He then proceeded to review the report on Timothy. He was a quiet child who came to the Jarvis home immediately following the murder of his parents in 1882. Continued with his medication. Didn't care about his brother. A loner with no interest in friends or activities. Obsessed with murder stories. Sought out a job in local bank at age eighteen. Keen interest in bank fraud. Rented a room in town in 1888. Visited the Jarvis home in 1892. Moved to the bank's Montreal office in 1892 to investigate fraud and embezzlement cases.

Gilfoy stared out his window. "And that's where he ran across Thomas' name and a likely place to look for him."

Gilfoy picked up the other requested information. The name Maud Elgin was not known to the police but Jessie Bishop was. He read on. Jessie Bishop, born in 1854, the younger sister of Matthew Bishop. She fell on hard times after being written out of her parent's will. The will described her as a fallen woman. She was disowned by the family. At twenty, unmarried and with a baby, Jessie appealed for help from her brother Matthew. He turned her away, citing how her disgraceful behaviour would ruin his young boys, Timothy and Thomas.

Jessie sought refuge in a Montreal homeless shelter where the infant subsequently died of smallpox. Bitter and in deep mourning, she started a proclivity for wearing black, often with a veil. Shelter workers found her work cleaning homes. The pay was meagre but kept her alive. Eventually, she was employed to clean a large business building. Reportedly, she liked the work.

A second police report explained why. Cleaning the building after work hours was a lucrative source of information for Jessie. She rifled through documents, searching for family contacts. After 1877, telephones enabled her to directly contact businesses, inquiring about Matthew, Thomas and Timothy Bishop. If challenged, she described herself as a family member visiting the city, looking for her brother and nephews. When an employee working late caught her in the act, she was dismissed. Charges were laid but later withdrawn after her miserable life story was revealed. Jessie had no compunction in revealing her tragic existence and who was to blame. She was hell bent on getting retribution.

In late 1893, Jessie reluctantly returned to cleaning homes. At that time she demanded the police help her find her family. They discovered Thomas Bishop's name in their own files and quietly contacted the homeless shelter. She cobbled together enough money to ride the train to Halifax intent on confronting Thomas.

Gilfoy dropped the sheets of paper on his desk and lowered his head into his hands. *Revenge. But who among us would have suffered so greatly and not considered redress. Obsessed to catch her own prey, she was blind to being prey herself.* Troubled by what he read, Gilfoy grabbed his lunch. "Murphy, if anyone needs me I'll be at the bandstand. I need a walk to clear my head. Some days I quite dislike this work."

* * *

When Henderson returned to the station, he found Gilfoy sitting at his desk, a concerned look on his face. He placed a plate wrapped in a tea towel on the desk. "Something from my mother. You don't look so good, sir. Something troubling you?"

"You're right." Gilfoy took a deep breath. He looked at the tea towel. "I'd never say 'no' to your mother's baking. She knows I have a sweet tooth. What did she send today?"

"It's a sour cream pound cake but the best part is, she sent a jar of strawberry jam too."

Gilfoy poured two mugs of tea, added sugar and milk. They relished a few minutes of calm before he told Henderson about Jessie and her wretched life.

"So there was a baby, sir."

"Yes, you found her pink ribbon. Elizabeth Marie's pink ribbon."

* * *

Living alone, Thomas had quickly fallen into his bachelor routine of working in the office until hunger drove him to a local hotel for drinks and a meal. Long after dark on Wednesday evening, he left the hotel intending to walk home. In his inebriated condition, he failed to hear the footsteps approaching from a dark alley.

CHAPTER EIGHTEEN

Constable Henderson found and recognized the body shortly after midnight. It was a savage thrashing. He blew his whistle for help then heaved his last meal toward the nearest tree. Splatters and clumps of food slithered down the trunk, its fetid smell mixing with the metallic odour of blood.

The body was warm, its pulse weak. As the wagon carrying the body moved off toward the hospital, Henderson turned his thoughts to his next task, the victim's family. Leaving other officers at the scene of the crime, he took a police carriage to the home of Margaret Bishop. In spite of his efforts, there was no response. Well after two o'clock, he firmly knocked three times at the Bell home. Henderson knew Thomas Bishop's reputation. There would be no need to ask the family awkward questions.

Hearing the insistent knocking, Doctor Bell grabbed his dressing gown. Grace stirred and opened her eyes. "Another middle of the night baby, dear?"

William swung the front door open expecting to see a wide-eyed father-to-be asking for help.

"Hello, Doctor Bell. I'm Constable Henderson. I must speak with your daughter, Margaret. Is she here?"

"She is. What's this about?" William's brain filled with all manner of possibilities.

"Her husband Thomas is in the hospital. I've come for her."

"Come in, Constable. Have a seat in the sitting room. I'll be back as soon as possible."

Henderson waited impatiently, spinning his cap in his hands. Bishop's face was barely recognizable. He feared the man would not be alive by the time they reached the hospital.

Margaret rushed into the room, followed by her parents. "Is he dead?" Her voice was barely above a whisper.

"No, Mrs. Bishop but we must leave now."

James heard the sounds of the commotion drifting into his room not long after he crept into bed. He put on his dressing gown and inched toward the second floor railing. From the floor below the voices of Margaret, his parents and a unknown fourth person were speaking in hushed tones.

"We'll accompany you, dear." Grace reached for Margaret's hand.

"No, Mama. I must learn to cope with my own life, such as it is."

"But Margaret." Grace's voice took on a strident tone.

"Please, don't insist on accompanying me. I need to be strong. Please allow me that."

"Now, Margaret." William's voice was firm.

"No, Papa." Her voice matched his but with a steely edge. She sounded stronger than she felt.

James moved down the stairs and into the sitting room. He could not afford to be absent.

"James, don't tell me you want to accompany me!"

"Accompany you where? What's all this about?"

"To the hospital. Thomas is there. He's been injured. Badly."

After Margaret left, James excused himself and returned to bed. He wanted Thomas to pay for his criminal behaviour and brutish treatment of his sister. Thomas' death was an outcome he saw coming. He stared at the ceiling, recalling all the suspects he'd seen while tracking the man.

* * *

Henderson was prepared for his gruesome news to bring on Margaret's uncontrollable shivering. He placed the rug over her knees and sat on the opposite bench. "The ride won't be too long, Mrs. Bishop. I'll take you inside. A nurse will meet us at the desk just inside the front door."

Outwardly, Margaret appeared in control. Inwardly, she was jelly. "Constable, did you see my husband?"

"No, Mrs. Bishop." His answer was a straight-up lie to save the gentle-looking, brown-eyed woman seated opposite him. The destruction to Bishop's body was best kept unsaid. He lowered his head, placed his hands on his knees, signalling he had little desire for conversation.

Margaret was undeterred. She pulled her wool shawl tighter around her shoulders, her rocking motion more vigorous. "Can you tell me anything?"

Henderson did not want to answer but he couldn't bring himself to let her walk into the hospital without a warning. "It's serious, ma'am. Mostly on his head."

"Thank you, constable." She paused, smiled weakly. "Henderson, isn't it?"

"Yes, ma'am." Henderson looked kindly at his fellow passenger. She looked fearful. It would become worse.

With nothing more to say, Margaret turned toward the window. The crisp rhythmic 'clip clop' of horses' hooves were a welcome diversion. Lamp posts diffused an amber glow, laying bare the human creatures of the night. Her stare was frozen on snippets of scenes outside her carriage window. Women stood alone or in pairs looking for a customer to pay for their favours. Food for tomorrow depended on their 'takings'. Men, young and old loitered in front of shabby pubs and run down gambling dens, their cigarette smoke swirling away from their lips, melting into the warm night air. All this lay in sharp contrast to her day visits to businesses and shops now shuttered for the night. She tried to look away but her eyes were perpetually drawn to the other world outside her carriage. She drank it all in.

What Henderson saw was not new to him but he held his tongue. He had an opinion on everything and a fierce sense of duty to uphold the law. He guessed this carriage ride in the early hours of the day was Margaret's first close-up view of a different world, the underbelly of her polite society.

"We're here, Mrs. Bishop." Henderson escorted Margaret from the carriage and introduced her to a nurse immediately inside the hospital door.

The stiff white apron, white cap, long skirt and sturdy shoes portrayed no-nonsense. "Hello, Mrs. Bishop. I'm nurse Pender. Thank you, Constable."

Margaret was overcome by the pervasive unpleasant smell of cleaning fluids. She looked toward Nurse Pender expecting an explanation but received none. She concluded the nurse no longer noticed the eye-watering fumes. The walls began a slow roll past her eyes. Nurse Pender eased her into a chair as the floor came up to meet her.

Nurse Pender leaned forward. "Feeling better, Mrs. Bishop?"

Margaret nodded then looked up. "What is that dreadful smell?" Hearing no reply, she turned to Henderson. "Thank you, Constable Henderson."

"You're welcome, ma'am. Take care of yourself."

Nurse Pender carried on. "I was about to warn you of your husband's condition just as you crumpled toward the floor. Take my arm and we'll walk toward his room."

Margaret looked puzzled. "To warn me?"

"Yes. Your husband's head is fully bandaged. He is restrained and…"

"Restrained! He's tied down?" Margaret gripped her reticule with both gloved hands.

"The bed sheets are tightly bound around him. It will prevent him from moving, speed the healing."

"What's wrong with him?"

"I'm not permitted to speak about your husband's condition.

The doctor has complete authority in disclosing and discussing a patient's condition."

At Thomas' door, Nurse Pender touched Margaret's arm. "Are you ready to see your husband?"

"Yes." She stepped into the room, without any thought as to what she might see. She gasped then grabbed the nurses' arm. "I need to sit."

"Of course."

Margaret stared at the body encased in white sheets, covered by a blanket. The head was completely wrapped in bandages with streaks of dried and fresh blood obvious. She looked at the face. Most of it was misshapen. The puffed-up, distorted nose melded with the red eye sockets. She wasn't certain if it was really Thomas. It could be anyone off the street. She felt queasy. "Can I speak to him?"

"Yes, but you won't get a response. He hasn't spoken since his arrival but his eyes opened briefly, once. I'll bring Doctor Adams to see you now. He's Lieutenant Doctor Adams, attached to the British Military at the Citadel." Nurse Pender took Margaret's hand. "Please stay seated while I'm gone."

Margaret stared at her husband's still form, not wanting to touch him. He looked dead. She breathed into her handkerchief, treasuring the calming effect of lavender. She was eight again, standing beside her mother at grand-papa's casket inside Saint George's Church. The memory of overly sweet lilies had turned her stomach.

A wiry, middle-aged man with his white coat flying behind him rushed into the room. He stretched his hand toward Margaret. "Mrs. Bishop, I'm Doctor Adams."

Margaret attempted to stand up but thought better of it.

"Are you not well, Mrs. Bishop?"

"No, just a moment of dizziness." Her second attempt to stand was successful. "This is quite overwhelming. Injured husband, middle of the night..." Her words faded away.

"Yes, yes, of course. Well, your husband is in serious condition.

He's in a coma, sometimes called a deep sleep and has not made a sound since arrival. You may notice his breathing is irregular. That is common at this stage." He abruptly stopped speaking. "Perhaps you would like to sit down?"

Margaret nodded then eased onto the chair. "The nurse told me he opened his eyes. Is that a good sign?"

"I hope so. I imagine you have more questions but I'm afraid I don't have many answers."

"He looks like he's asleep. When will he wake up?"

"I don't know. My military experience would indicate days, possibly weeks."

"What's in his arm?"

"We are putting liquid into the body. It was developed about ten years ago in Britain. I brought some equipment with me when I was transferred to Halifax, earlier this year."

"Can he hear?"

"I don't know that either. He's certainly not responding to anything going on around him." He paused. "Anything else, Mrs. Bishop?"

"No. May I stay a bit longer?"

"By all means. I'll tell Nurse Pender to come for you in a half hour. Would that be suitable?"

Margaret nodded. "Thank you, Doctor." She looked at her watch. Her head was buzzing. *Who wants you dead?* She thought about a future without Thomas. A widow's life was lonely but she was living it already. *Perhaps my freedom will come soon but for the time being, that decision is out of my hands.*

When Nurse Pender returned, Margaret picked up Thomas' wallet, watch and keys from the small table near his bed. She moved past the motionless body of her husband and out of the room without looking back. Dawn was breaking when she stepped through the hospital's front doors. The sunrise was a fire of reds and yellows, lighting up clouds in colours beyond the talent of an earthly artist. Within minutes the splendid image was gone, replaced by the full sun. A new day lay before her. She waved toward a carriage driver and instructed him to take her home and wait for her.

Inside the house, Margaret gathered up all the ledgers and papers from Thomas' study and spirited them out the front door.

"Get everything you need, Mrs. Bishop?"

"Yes. Thank you. Now we'll go to the home of Doctor William Bell. Do you know it?"

"Yes, ma'am. Been there many 'a time."

Margaret stared at Thomas' travel bag sitting beside her in the carriage. The secrets Thomas worked so diligently to protect were now in her possession. She intended to find someone who would make sense of it all, whether Thomas was alive or not. This was her opportunity to take charge of her life and she was not going to let it slip away.

* * *

"Good morning, dear." William rose from the breakfast table and reached for the large leather bag. "What's in this? Rocks?"

"Evidence from Thomas' study. I plan to do something with it, preferably before he wakes up, if he does."

For the time being, William was not prepared to discuss her plan. "Very well. I have patients to see." As a post script he added, "I gather from your comment Thomas is alive?"

"Yes, but in a coma. I don't think his future is looking bright." Saying the words out loud gave her a sudden gush of relief. A fleeting thought of Robert crossed her mind. Her heart fluttered.

"We'll talk later today. Have breakfast then a rest. I suggest we take the contents of the bag to Samuel. He'll have an opinion of how to legally handle this situation."

Margaret ate breakfast with her mother and went to her room for a rest. Sleep came swiftly and so did a dream filled with images and pleasurable sensations of loving Robert. She woke feeling warm and satisfied.

* * *

Henderson completed the Bishop assault report as Gilfoy walked into the station to start his day.

"Morning, Henderson. Quiet night?"

"Not at all, sir. I'll explain in your office."

Gilfoy posed no questions as the facts flowed from his most skilled constable. The only word he could formulate was 'why' and he asked it.

"Well sir, I've been working on that question myself. Aside from a Montreal thug after him, everyone else with a motive is dead." He broke off his response. "I know, I know. That was not the right thing to say but who else is there?" He shrugged.

"Well, there might be someone else. Got men on the scene looking for evidence, asking questions in the area?"

"Been there since early this morning. By the way, Bishop's watch and wallet weren't taken."

"Okay. Keep on it." He stood up. "Change of plan. I want you go home for a sleep and come back late afternoon. We'll talk more then."

"Thank you, sir."

* * *

Margaret went to the hospital in the late afternoon, more out of curiosity than care. Seeing no change in Thomas, she left after less than fifteen minutes and received a disapproving look from the nurse as she exited the front door.

Quite naturally, Thomas was the main topic over dinner in the Bell home. At the end of the back and forth questions and comments about Thomas, William offered his plan as a first step.

"I'll speak with Samuel tomorrow about Thomas' papers and make an appointment. He'll know how to handle the situation. Margaret you should come to the appointment with me. I understand your strong desire to use Thomas' possessions against him but perhaps it's too early to begin any legal proceedings against a man unable to defend himself. Let's have Samuel offer his advice. Agreed?"

"Absolutely."

James decided it was time to make his knowledge known. He asked them to join him in the sitting room.

"Before we continue speculating about Thomas and his beating, I'll tell you what I know about him and the recent murders." Quiet enveloped the room. "For months, I've been following Thomas." No one uttered a word. "He's not an honest business man." He wanted to say he's a bloody crook but that would be unnecessary. Instead, he looked at Margaret. "He meets with people and money exchanges hands, lots of money."

"For heaven's sake James, out with it. Did my husband kill someone?" Margaret shifted her body toward him, her eyes fixed on his. She felt her heart thrum.

"Thomas did not kill his secretary. I was following him that evening. I discovered her body."

William all but shouted, "You what?" His mouth dropped open.

"I did. She was on the pier. Fortunately, two men came along and went off to report to the police. I've kept this information to myself. If Detective Gilfoy lays a murder charge, then and only then will I provide Thomas an alibi. I dislike the man immensely, to say nothing of the fact he's not good enough to be married to my sister."

If William had any concerns about his son playing detective, they didn't last long. He wanted facts. "His brother's murder, know anything about that?"

"That answer isn't so easy. Thomas was in the Halifax Club from early evening on. Two others were in the area of Sailors but I don't know if they were involved in Timothy's murder. I'll speak about everything with Detective Gilfoy tomorrow. I expect you want to be there, Papa."

CHAPTER NINETEEN

HALIFAX, NOVA SCOTIA
AUGUST 16, 1895

Clarence Snell waylaid Gilfoy the moment he stepped through the front door of the police station. He rushed to block the detective from entering his office, all the while stabbing the newspaper's headline: Prominent Businessman Brutally Assaulted.

Snell's eyes darted back and forth between Gilfoy and the newspaper, a smirk on his thin lips.

"Detective Gilfoy, this city's going to the dogs. Two murders and now a well-known businessman is lying in a hospital on his deathbed. The city's being overrun by thugs. It's a..."

Gilfoy cut through the barrage of words. "Do you have a question, Mr. Snell?"

"What's Mr. Bishop's condition?"

"You'll have to speak with the hospital about that. Anything else?"

"What are you going to do about putting a stop to this criminal activity?"

"As you are well aware Mr. Snell, investigations take time. We are making good progress on the murders you mentioned. Regarding Mr. Bishop, this is our first full day of investigation. I'm sure you grasp the impossibility of an answer at this time. Have a good day, Mr. Snell." Gilfoy stepped around Snell and entered his office.

Gilfoy was annoyed with himself. He'd planned to interview

Bishop this week and now the man was lying unconscious inside the Victoria General. *Damn and blast.* He opened his door a crack to find out if Snell was gone and discovered Henderson standing on the other side, hand poised to knock.

"Snell's gone, sir. Bessie Ryan's here. Her cousin's home from New Brunswick. Can you do that interview tomorrow?"

Gilfoy replied in a clipped tone. "Yes. Anytime tomorrow is fine."

"Will do, sir. And sir, Miss Ryan hasn't seen that French-speaking man since the Friday before the murder. The flat cap fella's gone too."

"Come in when you've spoken with Miss Ryan about her cousin."

"Be right back, sir."

Gilfoy ran his hand through his hair as Henderson returned and closed the door. "We're in a real pickle now, thanks to me. Thomas Bishop can't be interviewed. He lied to my face in front of his wife about the bandstand last week. I should've acted sooner." He sat back in his chair. "It doesn't seem fitting to speak with Mrs. Bishop today, nor even tomorrow."

Henderson leaned in toward Gilfoy's desk. "If you'll pardon me saying so sir, I don't think there's much love lost between those two. My guess is, Mrs. Bishop might want to speak with you." He settled back into his chair.

Gilfoy looked hard at Henderson. "Is this gossip? I don't put trust in that tittle tattle business. And I won't have you doing it either."

"I don't, sir. Mrs. Bishop was staying with her parents when Mr. Bishop was assaulted." He opened his palms and shrugged, hoping to get the exchange on a more amiable footing.

"Fair enough." Gilfoy nodded. "I'll leave it for a few days though. Bishop may improve or not by then. Let's move on."

"Perhaps Bessie's cousin might be the one with new particulars on the Jessie Bishop murder, sir."

"I appreciate your positiveness. She works one day a week. Any leads on the Bishop assault?"

Henderson shook his head.

* * *

Cookie Gilmore dropped the newspaper like it was on fire. "Oh my heavens, Maisie. Come here."

"Who died now? Another of our old friends? That damn tuberculosis again."

"Thomas Bishop."

"He's dead?"

"Let me finish. Somebody has beaten him up. Look." Cookie passed the paper to her sister.

"What will 'ya do?"

"Look after Margaret, of course. Bloody man got what he deserved."

"No, I mean right today. What 'ya going to do today?"

Cookie didn't have a fast answer.

* * *

"Good morning, Doctor Bell. I'm afraid you'll have to wait. Detective Gilfoy's in a meeting, sir."

"Thank you, Constable Boudreau. Let him know Doctor Bell and his son have information regarding Thomas Bishop's secretary."

"Yes, sir."

Within seconds, Constable Boudreau was back. "Go in, Doctor Bell."

"Come in, Doctor Bell. Boudreau, bring in another chair, please."

William waited until the office door closed. "Detective, this is my son, James. He's here to offer evidence in the murder of Thomas Bishop's secretary."

"Gentlemen, this is Constable Henderson. He's on the case with me. Please go ahead, James."

"Let me begin by saying, I feel no concern for Thomas Bishop. My sister is married to the man and my intent was to right a wrong I created before they married."

Henderson's eyes opened wide. He glanced at Gilfoy who was quick to ask, "And what wrong was that?"

"Bishop is deft at fooling people for his own benefit. I failed to see it and I failed to scrutinize him thoroughly before he married my sister. As a result, Margaret is married to an unsuitable man, to put it mildly."

Gilfoy nodded. "Very well. Now tell us what you know about Bishop that relates to the murder."

"Thomas did not kill her."

Gilfoy was intrigued by James' matter-of-fact statement and could hardly wait to hear the details. "Go on."

James began his detailed story with his presence in the secret gambling room, seeing Thomas accept money from a man called Graham on July twentieth and ended with the evening of August eighth when he found the woman's body on the wharf. He concluded by saying, "You should also know I wore a beard while tracking Thomas."

William winced at James' gambling revelation but was pleased he'd openly admitted his presence in such a place.

Gilfoy leaned across his desk, chin resting in his hands. Now that his prime suspect was cleared of the murder, he had a new challenge. *Who was responsible for Jessie's death? And Timothy's murder was still on the books.* "Thank you, James."

Gilfoy's interest in the man called Graham prompted a spur of the moment decision. "Would you help identify this Graham fella at North Station on the twenty-fourth?"

"Certainly."

"On one condition. You only identify the man then step away from the scene, immediately. Agreed?"

James nodded. "Yes, absolutely. My pleasure."

Gilfoy rose. "Thank you, gentlemen. I look forward to getting information on the twenty-fourth. Be here by six-thirty am. We'll make a brief plan and leave together."

James knew what was coming as soon as he and his father reached the sidewalk.

"Thank you for including everything in your statement to the police."

"You don't have to skirt the issue, Papa. I gamble and enjoy it."

"We'll talk about that another time. In the meantime, I need to see Samuel, bring him up to date. See you at dinner."

* * *

Samuel was seeing a client out as William rushed up the stairs. "What's the matter with you? Did you run here?"

"I seem to be overly tired these days, can't get my breath. It'll pass."

"I'd suggest a good doctor if I didn't already know one. Now what can I help you with?"

* * *

Margaret left for the hospital before William returned to his office. Her visit was a repeat of the day before except for a well-dressed bearded man sitting on the bench in front of the hospital. She walked toward him and sat on the same bench.

Recalling the Public Gardens episode with a bearded man on Tuesday, she ignored social norms and spoke to him so as to take a closer look at his face. "Waiting for a carriage?" Dark eyes, scar above left eye.

"Non, madame. Resting."

"Hmm. Lovely day."

"Oui. Au revoir."

He speaks French. Margaret watched him cross the lawn toward South Park Street. She sensed she'd discovered something of importance.

* * *

At dinner, William was about to tell everyone the details of his visit with Samuel. Margaret put down her fork and knife then interrupted him. "Why did you do that? This is about me. I do not want to be treated like some helpless woman. How do you expect me to become more worldly when you dismiss my request to be involved, not to mention you told me I was going with you!"

"I did not intentionally exclude you. I was near Samuel's office this morning and went in. I saved us time. It's as simple as that." He took a breath. "Now, let me tell all of you what Samuel said about the ledgers and papers from the house. Margaret, as you believe Thomas' ledgers and documents are incriminating and you want to provide this information to the police, you can. Essentially you believe you have in your possession evidence of a crime." He covered his mouth and coughed. "You can also tell the police they may want to search his office. In that case, they'll need a warrant from Judge Bailey. I suggest you see Gilfoy on Monday." Hearing no comments, he inquired about Thomas.

"No change but I noticed a bearded man on the bench outside the hospital. He had a scar above his left eye. I've seen him before."

James wanted to hear more. "Where?"

"The Public Gardens. Why?"

James wasn't interested in answering her question.

"Well-dressed? Real beard?"

"Yes and his beard didn't come from the theatre's costume room. Why?"

"I've seen someone who looks like him around Sailors."

"And for the third time, why?" Margaret intended to get an answer.

"He may be following you because I believe he was following Thomas. You didn't speak with him did you?"

"Yes. He speaks French."

* * *

Margaret rushed through Saturday breakfast and took a

carriage to the hospital. She planned to stay in the hospital until lunch. If bearded scar-man appeared, she'd know it. She was seated inside the main doors when he arrived. The urge to flee surged through her body but she casually lowered her book to make sure he had a scar. Bearded man nodded at the nurse then walked with purpose down the main hall. Margaret had no choice but to follow. Clearly he'd been inside the hospital before as he went straight to Thomas' room. She dared not go in. Without a doubt, he knew Thomas.

Trusting he would not try anything harmful in the hospital, Margaret retreated to the chair inside the front doors. Within minutes, he was in a carriage and out of sight. She looked in on Thomas, finding him as death-like as ever and left the hospital herself.

* * *

Freddy Ryan was none too pleased to be seen entering the police station. Folks who worked at the docks prided themselves on keeping themselves to themselves. The police station might not be a place where folks smoked so best not take a chance. There was plenty of criticism at home from Bessie who called smoking a 'filthy habit'. The butt was crushed under a heavy work boot.

For the first time in his life, Gilfoy met a woman close to his own height. He hoped Freddy couldn't read the surprised look on his face. "Good morning, Miss Ryan. Thank you for coming in to help us with our inquiry,"

"Happy to help, Detective. My name is Frederica. People call me Freddy." She gripped Gilfoy's outstretched hand.

"Tea?"

"No, thanks."

"Come into the office. Bessie tells me you were at the Sailors Hotel Sunday evening, the twenty-eighth of July. Is that correct?"

"Yep. Bessie takes Sundays off."

"Tell me about that evening at the Sailors."

"It was a strange one, alright. Real odd."

"Go on." Gilfoy wasn't about to guess what she might say next. She was one of the more interesting witnesses he'd interviewed in years.

"I smoke." Freddy paused, expecting the detective to have something to say about that. Most people did. "I went out for a smoke and they were outside. Never seen the like. Dark it was. I'd say around eleven, maybe eleven thirty. I don't have a watch. Too fancy for me, 'specially where I work on the dock. Where was I?"

"They were outside."

"Right you are. They were outside in the dark. It's hard to tell about the dark after it's dark." Freddy paused. "I saw three of them. I'm pretty sure they couldn't see each other though. Spaced out they were on different benches, all of 'em in black. Or maybe just dark colours. Sittin' still. The lady for sure was in black. She was closest to me. Well, not real close but close enough to make out the black hat and veil, black dress, black gloves and one of them reticule things. Never owned one meself. I put my things in my pants pocket. What would she be doing out at that hour?" Freddy looked at Gilfoy.

He shrugged. "Carry on."

"It were funny to watch 'em. I was smokin' so had somethin' to do. They were jus sittin'. All of 'em were facin' toward the hotel. Strange bunch, if 'ya ask me."

"And the other two people?"

"Right you are. Two men with beards. Clothes looked good, far as I could tell. Now mind you, I weren't real close to 'em."

"Anything happen?"

"I went back inside, got a rag, pail 'a water and dust cloth from the cupboard, cleaned the room for holding folks travel bags. After that, I stepped outside the front door to get some fresh air, like. They were gone. Well, the men were gone and the lady slipped out past me with her head down. Rushed around the corner of the hotel, she did."

"So she was inside the hotel?"

"Oh, yes. Bold that one, don't 'ya think?"

"She was inside while you were cleaning the little room?"

"Yep. She was leavin' fer sure."

"How long did it take you to clean the room?" Gildoy waited patiently for a rambling reply. He had the time and needed the answer.

"Well, I don't have a watch, like I said before. The room has several shelves. Some were pretty dirty and dust everywhere, 'a course. Even if you do it everyday. I'd say close to fifteen minutes. Just guessin' 'a course."

"The victim's room was on the main floor. Did you hear any noise, voices?"

Freddy shook her head. "But I sing to myself sometimes. I like hymns."

"Anything else you remember?"

"Lavender. When she scooted past me, goin' out. I smelled lavender. Would that mean anything?"

"Perhaps. Thank you, Freddy. You've been very helpful."

* * *

Anna sent a note to Margaret following Thomas's incident, expressing her concern and suggesting they talk after church about their planned lunch for next week. She had no intention of visiting Margaret on Saturday afternoon until she saw a bearded man follow her from the newspaper office to her home. She was frightened and immediately took a carriage to the Bell's home.

"Good afternoon, Mrs. Bell. I do apologize for coming unannounced. May I speak with Margaret?"

"Of course, Anna. It's lovely to see you again. I'm sure she will appreciate your visit. These are difficult times."

"Thank you."

"Make yourself comfortable in the sitting room. Tea?"

"Yes, that would be lovely."

Anna could barely wait for the pleasantries to be over, tea served and she was alone with Margaret.

Margaret spoke first. "There's something wrong, isn't there?"

"Yes, terribly wrong."

When Anna finished, Margaret asked if he had a scar.

"I don't know. He wasn't close enough for that but I'm pretty sure he's the man who nodded to us at the Public Gardens."

When Margaret asked about clothing, Anna described what the bearded man was wearing at the hospital.

"I think we better tell James what we know."

CHAPTER TWENTY

George Hopkins was adamant about his position on the matter. After hearing Anna's plan to accompany Margaret on her visit to Thomas Sunday afternoon, he left no room for discussion. "Absolutely not."

"But George, it's the only way we can confirm this man is following us. James will be there but out of sight."

"Anna, I've carried out sufficient military operations to know the both of you are placing yourselves in imminent danger. This man may be doing more than simply following you and Margaret. He patted the bed. "Come sit beside me. You and Margaret are at great risk. I forbid you to do this."

"Forbid! I beg your pardon. I am not one of your foot soldiers who salute and obey." Anna picked up her skirts and stormed out of the bedroom.

George followed. "Okay, I see you are bound and determined to do this."

"Are you're saying you'll help?"

"On condition I speak with James about this after church. Put on your hat. We have to hurry."

* * *

After the service, George asked James to speak with him alone. "I understand you're planning to help Anna and Margaret identify this bearded fellow at the hospital later today. I'll tell you right now, it's not safe. This sort of thing is police work. What precisely are you planning to achieve?"

"I don't know what Anna has told you but I believe this fellow is involved in criminal behaviour. He's been seen in locations where a crime has been committed, including murder."

"Dear heavens. Are you undercover police? Anna told me you're planning to be a doctor."

"No. I'm studying medicine at Dalhousie University."

"Then why are you playing detective?"

"The simple answer is because my sister's husband is a crook."

"Connected to this bearded man?"

"I believe so, yes."

"So about this man. What are you doing today?"

"I want to see him to confirm what he looks like and is a match for the man I've seen at Sailors Hotel. Margaret and Anna have seen him in the Gardens. He's likely followed Anna. Margaret saw him in the hospital yesterday."

"And you think he'll be at the hospital today?"

"We don't know for sure."

Margaret waved in their direction. "James, George. Join us. We're all going for lunch with Mama and Papa."

"Do your parents know about this plan?"

"No. Are you in?"

George nodded. "Anna's bound and determined she's going so I better keep an eye on her. Think he could have a gun?"

James shrugged. "Don't know. I want to see him, that's it."

By mid afternoon, lunch and a lengthy conversation ended. William called for a toast to new relationships and George responded, "I can't recall a better time since arriving in the city. Thank you for such rousing conversation and a delicious meal. To a long and happy friendship, right Anna?"

"Certainly."

"It's time for me to go to the hospital. James, would you accompany me today?"

Grace and William bid farewell to everyone and returned to

the sitting room. Grace picked up her embroidery and William a book.

"Lovely young couple." Grace sighed.

William knew she was comparing Margaret's situation with Anna's. "Yes, they are. They have a bright future ahead."

* * *

As planned, Margaret and Anna arrived at the hospital together and made their way to the front doors. George was already in position a good twenty feet away, leaning against the brick wall. James sat on the bench closest to the front doors, wearing his beard and smoking a pipe. His hand signal would alert George to take action and follow the man into the hospital.

Margaret and Anna walked through the main corridor toward Thomas' private room. Upon entering the room, Anna gripped Margaret's arm but remained silent as they approached the bed. She'd never seen someone who looked that pale who wasn't dead. She whispered, "Are you sure he's alive?"

"Oui, 'e is." A pair of strong hands shoved them to the floor. "Stay down. I 'ave a gun."

When the footfalls faded away, Margaret and Anna rushed through the front exit. Outside, they waved frantically for James and George.

George ran to them. "What happened?"

"He was already inside. He had a gun." Margaret took a deep breath.

Anna finished the sentence. "We didn't see him but he has a French accent."

"What should we do?" Margaret looked at James but it was George who answered.

"James, it's time for the police to take charge. Don't mention my name. The rest of us are going home.

* * *

"Good afternoon, Detective Gilfoy. Do you ever go home?"

"After church I decided to get an early start on the week. How can I help you, James?"

"It seems a French-speaking, bearded man is trying to kill Thomas."

Gilfoy jumped up. "What! Come in."

At the end of the story, Gilfoy stared hard at James. "Stay right there." Then he opened the door and walked to the desk. "Healy, send a constable to the hospital to stand guard over Thomas Bishop until midnight and someone from midnight until eight tomorrow morning. I'm going to the hospital to speak with the doctor in charge and wait for the constable. We're looking for a bearded man with a scar over his left eye who speaks with a French accent. He may have a gun."

Gilfoy turned to James. "Why on earth did you take that on?" He shook his head in disbelief.

"I wanted to see him, find out if he was the same man I'd seen before, at Sailors."

"And if he was, would you've tried to stop him?"

"No, no. But I didn't expect he'd take a gun into a hospital."

Gilfoy shook his head again. "James, the man's a criminal. He pays no attention to the law, rules or society's expectations. Someone could have been killed." He paused. "Have you seen other suspicious characters around Sailors?"

"Yes."

"Come back tomorrow when you have time. We need to talk. For now, go home and stop playing detective. This man means business. Let us deal with it."

"Thank you, Detective."

* * *

Margaret returned home shaken but determined not to alarm her mother.

"How was the hospital visit?"

"Thomas is the same." Unable to keep up the pretense, she

broke into tears. "A man with a gun came into his room. He pushed Anna and I to the floor."

"Come, sit beside me. What was Anna doing there?"

"She was with me."

"But James went with you. Where is he?" Her hands flew to her mouth.

"He's fine, Mama. He went to the police station. He'll explain everything when he comes home. George was with us too."

"George! The four of you planned this and didn't tell us at lunch. I can't believe four clever people did something so foolish. That man could have shot any of you." She rose from the chesterfield and turned to Margaret, her concern turned to anger. "This senseless activity has gone on long enough. You and James need to stop this dangerous behaviour now." Her grip tightened on her skirt.

"I just wanted to see the bearded man, get this problem over."

Grace paced the room. "The over part I understand but all four of you trying to do police work is foolish and dangerous. As your mother, I am very annoyed." She returned to sit beside Margaret. "George should have known better. You two better keep his name out of this. His military superiors wouldn't take his part lightly." Her storm of emotions was over. "I'm sure Papa will have plenty to say later today. The detective will likely have a word or two with you tomorrow when you deliver the ledgers."

"I'll be fine, Mama. I'm only going there to give him Thomas' papers.

* * *

"Good Morning, Mrs. Bishop." Gilfoy was struck by Margaret's fragile form. She looked about to collapse. "Come with me. Have a seat."

"Thank you."

"I understand you are offering physical evidence against your husband Thomas, as related to theft and fraud. Is that correct?"

"Yes."

Gilfoy looked into Margaret's eyes and saw the suffering she'd endured in the past year. His own daughter was only a few years older. His heart ached. "I understand you have some papers for me."

"Yes."

Gilfoy took the papers and put them on his desk. "Would you like a cup of sweet tea?"

"Yes. Sounds lovely."

When he returned, Margaret was sitting ram-rod straight, hands clenched on her lap. Two streams of tears rolled down her cheeks. "I hope you can make my problem go away."

Gilfoy felt his own eyes fill up. He went to his desk for a handkerchief. "I'll do my very best, Mrs. Bishop."

"Thank you."

"Is there anything else you would like to say about your claim and paper evidence?"

An awkward silence filled the small room. Gilfoy searched Margaret's face. She was holding something back.

"Secrets make you weak, Detective. They can destroy you." She was barely speaking above a whisper.

"Do you have a secret, Mrs Bishop?" He asked in a low voice.

She twisted the handkerchief. "Thomas' love of money is the least of his sins. My husband is a brutal man. I want his life to end so I may have one of my own."

Gilfoy felt a chill. "Do you have suspicions about your husband's attack, Mrs. Bishop?"

Margaret felt the heat spread from her neck to face. "This has been a most trying time. My apologies for taking your time." She stood, "Good day, Detective."

Unsettled by her careless personal comment, Margaret decided a walk might help her to think more clearly. She decided against another hospital visit, had lunch with her mother, then took a carriage to her own home to collect day dresses for the coming week. She lingered in the kitchen, thinking about Cookie before walking through all the main floor rooms and closing the doors behind her. Upstairs she saw the apricot dress Robert liked. Her body warmed at the thought of him and her flushed face was reflected in the looking glass. Having selected all the dresses she would need, her eyes fell upon the apricot day dress again. She hesitated then added it to her arm.

* * *

James was tempted to postpone his planned meeting with Gilfoy so soon after yesterdays' hospital fiasco. With no way to send a quick message, he swallowed his embarrassment and went to the station.

"Come in, James. I'm eager to hear what you have to say about the bearded fellow and others you've seen." Then he abruptly broke off and stared at James intently.

James leaned forward in his chair and dropped his eyes to the floor.

"Young fella, you're up to your neck in police business. You must stop now. If you're not already, you will become a target. It will end badly."

"I'm finished with the exception of spotting that Graham fella on Saturday."

"The police will be with you on Saturday. There's a difference. Now, tell me everything you know about those people you've seen at Sailors and around town."

* * *

In five days Thomas had shown no sign of recovery. Detective Gilfoy would take care of Thomas, the criminal. Margaret intended to take care of Thomas, the husband. She crept downstairs to the study and sat at the desk where she composed a poem. Free from the ties that bound her to cruelty, Margaret placed the letter inside the drawer of the night stand, thought about Robert and went to sleep.

CHAPTER TWENTY-ONE

Grace stood at the bottom of the stairs. "Margaret, are you having breakfast today? It's nine o'clock. "

"Yes, Mama. I'll be down soon."

"I'll wait for you."

When Margaret arrived in the dining room, her mother was smiling. "You look rested, my dear."

"I slept well for the first time in days. My mind is less troubled."

"No doubt giving Detective Gilfoy the ledgers gave you great relief." She passed Margaret the toast rack. "This afternoon I'm going to the church to work on the orphanage fundraising ball. Come with me. It will give you a nice change and you'll meet some of the other women."

"No, thank you. I'm going to the hospital this morning then having lunch with Anna. She's going to give me particulars on the suffragette ladies in the city."

"Oh?" Grace's eyebrows went up.

"Yes. They have a group here. I thought I would find out what they are all about."

"Oh!"

"Anna wants me to write about them for the newspaper. I've volunteered to do the research. Sounds ever so interesting."

"Oh."

* * *

"Good morning, Mrs. Bishop. Doctor Adams is on morning visitations. Do you wish to speak with him?"

"Has there been any change in my husband?" She held her breath.

"No, I'm so sorry. He remains the same."

"In that case, I doubt Doctor Adams and I have anything to speak of."

"Very well, Mrs. Bishop."

Margaret moved her chair close to Thomas' bed and studied him. His head bandages were fresh. His position was unchanged, right down to the placement of his arms and hands. She opened her reticule and removed the sheet of paper then began, barely above a whisper.

"Thomas, your control over me is ended. I will not be intimidated or abused by you. Today I am giving myself permission to live my life as I see fit. I will seek permanent separation from you through the courts. My decision is steadfast. If you wake and object, I will fight you with any and all means. This poem expresses the hope I have for my future."

> ### sleeping garden
> our marriage is the cruelest season
> a cold and empty bed
> frigid landscape full of fear
> beneath a frosty blanket
> asleep in a garden plot
> my heart is a tangled root
> unruly and rebellious
> waiting, wild with ecstasy
> for freedom, hope and growing strength
> to blossom into spring

Margaret walked out of the hospital into the sunny afternoon head held high, looking forward to lunch with Anna.

* * *

Margaret stepped out of the carriage just as Anna arrived. Anna was the first to speak.

"You look calm and refreshed. Have you not had trouble sleeping since Sunday? I certainly have. It was a dreadful experience. George regrets his involvement but realizes his presence was a comfort to me. Did James' conversation with the detective go well?"

"I'm very well. Let's go inside and continue our conversation."

"Sorry, I do go on when I'm worked up about things."

"That's certainly understandable. James spoke with the detective again yesterday. He was sternly reminded to leave everything to the police, which I dearly hope he will."

"Have you seen Thomas recently?"

"This morning. Nothing has changed with him. I see no point in going every day. In fact, I don't know when I will go again, maybe Sunday. Daily visits are pointless."

"After seeing him myself, I understand why you feel that way." She unfolded her napkin. "But he is your husband."

"I said my goodbye this morning. He's breathing but frankly, he's dead to me."

"And what do you mean you said goodbye?"

"I said farewell to him this morning, told him I was getting a divorce." She picked up the menu. "Let's order."

Anna had no response that seemed fitting. She studied the menu.

With the waitress far from hearing distance, Margaret continued. "I gave Thomas' office papers to Detective Gilfoy yesterday." She stopped herself from opening up about their conversation. It felt too embarrassing, even for a friend.

"What's going to happen now?"

"First, a police investigation. But with Thomas in a coma, I can't imagine he'll be charged. He'll die and so will the case."

"You sound so confident, free."

"I'm not sure it's freedom I feel. Set apart is a better way to describe it, on my own, seeing my life from a distance."

They continued with lunch, each with their own thoughts.

The silence was broken by Anna. "Do you want to discuss the suffragettes?" She hastily added, "We can do it another time, if you'd rather not."

"I need something worthwhile to do with my time. Let's talk about it today."

"What will your family think of this?"

Margaret chuckled. "Mama was speechless this morning. Papa will support me. James will applaud. Well actually, James is a question mark. No doubt he'll have an earful from Mama before I return home!"

Anna passed her papers across the table. "Look over the names and notes. We can make a plan during lunch next Tuesday, if that's all right with you."

Before lunch, Anna had checked the calendar. Robert should be coming to Halifax soon. When it appeared their lunch was coming to an end, she asked casually, "Will you be having lunch with Robert again?"

"He'll be here Friday morning."

"Is that a 'yes'?"

"Of course."

Anna tried to keep the surprise out of her voice. "You're going?"

"We are old friends. It's perfectly harmless. He makes me feel uplifted, despite our differences."

"Differences?"

"You know, when people don't see things the same way."

Anna nodded but remained quiet. Thomas was already dead to Margaret but not to society. Seeing Robert at this time would be most improper. Were they really just friends? She wanted to say something.

"Why are you looking at me so strangely?"

"I..."

"It's about Robert, isn't it?"

"Yes. I..."

"You're never at a loss for words. Why now?"

"Because, I don't know what to say about the lunches."

"What about them?"

"You're married."

Margaret laughed. "Anna, you of all people!" Her hands flew up in the air. "You're the one who gets worked up about women not being treated equally. You're the one working on suffragette stories for the newspaper." She stared at Anna. "Why can't I have lunch with Robert without you being concerned over society's rules?"

Anna reached across the table for Margaret's hand. "Because I'm not concerned about the rules but about you, my dear friend. Right now, you could be easily hurt."

"By Robert? That's absurd. He's a good friend. He means me no harm."

"He probably doesn't but ask yourself, what does he want from this relationship?" She glanced at her watch. "Good heavens, I have to go. There's a meeting at the newspaper in ten minutes."

"Off you go then. I'll finish the tea." Anna's question about Robert lingered. She sat back in her chair. Why does he want to see me? Nothing improper, of course. Her body warmed. She leaned forward and filled her tea cup. *What if he desires something I'm not prepared to give?* Failing to answer her own question, her conviction slipped, ever so slightly.

* * *

At dinner, Margaret finished explaining her new work with Anna.

Grace's face was stern.

James was the first to offer support. "I think it's a great idea. After all, she has a good deal of free time now with no household to manage. What's your concern, Mama?"

"Time isn't the only standard to judge one's participation in an activity, James. Society has expectations of women."

Unable to hold her tongue any longer, Margaret spoke up. "Would you two please stop talking about me as though I'm not here. Remember, I'm not joining the group, I'm contacting them. Anyway, it's clear Mama objects to and James supports my interest in suffragette activity. Papa, you must have an opinion. I would like to hear it."

"You certainly sound like your determined younger self." He chuckled. "From what I understand, these women are working hard to secure the vote for women and I agree with them. But how you see yourself within this group and live your views will be the challenge. By the way, is Anna involved?"

"Not directly. She's asked me to contact the suffragettes for the purpose of newspaper articles."

"I know you're not joining the group at this time but I suggest you consider what impact you expect it might have on you in the future. Looking forward is always a good idea, at least in my humble opinion. Now, let's move on to dessert. I hear it's lemon meringue pie."

* * *

Robert stepped off the Friday morning train from Montreal with two intentions. Number one, get the fraud evidence to the police station and two, get a reminder message to Margaret about lunch. But first, he'd rush home and drop off his luggage.

"Morning, Mother. I'm dropping off my luggage and going to meetings. See you later."

"Don't run off. There's news about Margaret."

Robert sat motionless as his mother relayed the story of Thomas' assault. "Margaret is staying with her parents until

Thomas is well enough to return home." She stared at Robert, hoping he would not visit Margaret at the Bell home. "I have few facts but the newspapers are referring to his condition as a coma."

"Thanks for letting me know. From what I've seen of him, he's not the friendly sort. I'll see you at dinner."

Robert's plan to remind Margaret about lunch ended on the spot. With no time left after the police station visit, all he would have left was hope. He clutched the envelope containing evidence against Thomas close to his chest and stepped into a carriage. With Thomas convicted or dead he had a clear path to Margaret's affection. With a coma, his life with Margret was a pipe dream.

* * *

"Good morning, Mr. Fraser. Come into my office. What brings you to the police station this morning?"

"To be blunt, I have evidence of fraudulent activity regarding Thomas Bishop. It's from a reliable source in Montreal." He handed over the envelope. "I understand Mr. Bishop is unwell."

"Thank you. You're correct about Mr. Bishop. Have a seat. Tell me about this evidence you speak of." With Jessie Bishop's death and no paper evidence of Thomas' fraud found in her belongings, Gilfoys' case against Thomas rested with the man's ledgers. Robert Fraser had just given him a gift.

* * *

"You seem distracted this morning, Margaret. If it's the suffragette meetings, delay them until you're ready."

"I'm ready, Mama. Other things on my mind." She waved her hand dismissively.

"I noticed you haven't visited Thomas since Tuesday." The tilt of her head and raised eyebrows were meant to ensure Margaret understood her statement was really a question.

"I'll go on Sunday afternoon."

"Good. "I know you're feeling some freedom but you are his

wife and people notice these things. By the way, you look lovely in apricot, dear. You should wear that colour more often."

"Thank you, Mama."

*　*　*

As Margaret approached the bandstand Robert came into view. He walked toward her. "Hello." then reached for her hand. "I'm sorry your life is in such turmoil."

"Thank you." Seeing Robert again flooded her heart with relief then joy. She truly wanted to spend time with him. He would bring care and kindness to her day. The tears began. She took a deep breath to settle herself. "Let's speak of other things, at least for a while."

"The apricot dress suits you. You've worn it before."

She smiled. His presence was something she'd been missing for too long.

"Let's walk to the hotel for lunch. How is your family?"

"As they say, no time like the present, you might as well hear about James' detective work. He started following Thomas months ago and proved Thomas was not guilty of his secretary's murder." She hesitated. "And I gave the police Thomas' ledgers after his assault. His past is not free of criminal activity."

"Since we are confessing, I brought evidence from Montreal that will help the police with their fraud case against him."

"Why would you do that? That's the job of the police."

"Just like James, I want you free of that man. You deserve better."

She laughed. "You sound exactly like James. How did the evidence come about?"

"I overheard a conversation on the train and contacted the person in Montreal. He offered me information about Thomas."

"Here we are. Window table, please."

"Right this way sir, madam. It's lovely to see you both again. Earl Grey and a multi-tier plate?"

It's lovely to see you both again. Margaret looked around the room. *Who else remembers us?* She kept her eye on the window.

"What are you doing?"

"Sorry?" She glanced at Robert then returned her gaze on the window.

"Margaret look at me, please. Lunch should take your mind off your situation. Why are you looking out the window?"

"I hope nobody sees me at lunch with a man who isn't part of my family."

"If they do, you have a perfect excuse. I'm a friend from out of town. End of story."

"I hope so." She recalled Anna's comments.

"Excuse me madam, sir. Your lunch."

"So, what's the news from Montreal?"

"Nothing new there but Mother gave me an ultimatum last month."

Margaret laughed, "Okay. What did you do this time?"

"It's not about me. It's about you."

"Me? I..."

"Don't speak, please. Let me finish."

"Mother insists I stop seeing you. I do not agree with her."

"Well, she is correct. It's not proper for a married woman to be seen socializing with an unattached man." She heard Anna in her head. "It's another society rule that must change. Why can't women have men as friends? It's absurd." She smiled. "Anyway, back to your mother. Why would she say such a thing? We're old friends."

"She's convinced my intentions are not simply friendly." He looked into her eyes.

"After seeing us together at one lunch in her home? That's ridiculous."

"My mother is very observant."

"Observant about what?"

"Me."

"You? What is there to explain about yourself to her? We are friends."

"I don't disagree with her observation and I care about you." He held her eyes with his.

"Of course you do." She faltered. "Oh, I see now. This can't be."

"Why not?" He took Margaret's hand. "Your circumstances are changing."

Margaret quickly turned the topic back. "What's your mother going to do if we continue to have lunch together?" She reluctantly pulled her hand away.

"I have no idea but if it comes to that, I'll choose you over my family."

"Now Robert, it's your family. You can't possibly do that."

He changed the topic. "Do your parents know you are having lunches with me?"

Margaret shook her head.

"Anyone else?"

"My friend, Anna."

"I guessed this would happen."

"What would happen?"

"This conversation cannot take place here. We need to talk about Thomas, family, all of it." He paused. "I've found a private place to talk after lunch. It's just around the corner, a lovely sitting room on the first floor. The house is empty all day."

"That's not at all proper. I couldn't possibly go there." She sat back in her chair. "Not at all proper."

"That's an easy reply to dismiss the idea of a meaningful conversation. It doesn't solve anything for either of us. I want us to talk about our circumstances, our feelings. That is unless you never want to have lunch together again. Is that what you want?" He waited for Margaret's reply. None came. "Can you truthfully tell me you are prepared to live part or all of your life with Thomas in a coma or in jail? To be blunt, you aren't happy now so how can you be happy with that sort of future? Can we talk?"

"I'm afraid."

"Of what?"

"Surely you know gossip travels quickly."

"That's an easy answer and it's not a good one either."

Margaret became agitated. "You're wrong on that, Robert. Men do not face the same censorship as women. Your mother knows what a misstep, even a small one on my part will change my place in society forever. Your life will be untouched. It's not fair."

"I know it's not fair. I also know you have the spunk to help change exactly what you're talking about." He leaned forward. "But all that doesn't make my question and your answer any less important today. We deserve time to talk about your future and mine. That's all I'm asking. If we don't have this conversation today when will we ever have it?"

CHAPTER TWENTY-TWO

HALIFAX, NOVA SCOTIA
AUGUST 23, 1895

Margaret was terrified of being seen on the side street with Robert. Her mind was in a struggle with her heart. She kept her head down until they were inside the safe haven.

When Robert closed the front door, she gazed around the sizable two-story oak foyer then up the central staircase. "This is a beautiful home. It's very calming."

"It was a family home but has a new life. Wait until you see our room."

"Our room!"

Robert turned the key in the lock and stepped inside. "This room is one of four private rooms on this floor. They are generally used by business leaders who don't want their conversations overheard. Unlike clubs, there are no staff to disturb people and no meals served."

Margaret remained in the foyer clutching her reticule, her eyes darting about. "I smell sweet peas." She moved past Robert. "You can't miss that jasmine and orange blossom scent." She walked past the red velvet ottoman. "There they are." She leaned toward the flowers on the mantle. "Lovely." Her back remained to the room.

When Robert closed the door, she turned around, kept her eyes on the floor.

"Where would you like to sit, a flowered chair or chaise lounge?"

"The chair is fine." Margaret sat straight-backed, her gloved hands on her lap.

"Footstool?"

"No, thank you." She'd only ever been alone in a room with Papa or James until she married Thomas. It felt most inappropriate. She twisted the drawstring of her reticule.

Robert moved his chair opposite Margaret's and sat down. "Comfortable?"

She tapped the upholstered arms of her chair. "The honest answer is no."

"Neither am I. It feels a bit like our dance classes, holding another person so close and hoping not to step on their feet!" He grinned. "Remember?"

Margaret laughed. "Or skating in public the first time. I remember falling so many times, James continued shouting, 'need a pillow', which of course made more people look at me."

Robert chuckled. "I recall my games of Checkers with James. He was a bit of a pain sometimes."

"Was? He still is!" Then the smile faded from her lips.

"Your world is changing quickly. How are you feeling these days?"

"Uncertain. Everything has changed. I'm living with my parents. I have a husband in a coma and my friend Anna has offered me a chance to work with her." She sighed. "But you brought me here so you better start."

"First, I want you to know I don't want anything bad to happen to you."

Margaret's chin went up. "I certainly hope not. But I'm absolutely certain you did not bring me here to tell me that. Remember, I have a marriage. I can't possibly keep seeing you, even for lunch. It's not done."

"Do you think our lunches are as simple as that?" He paused.

"They aren't for me." Hearing no response, he changed topics. "What do you think will happen to Thomas?"

She shrugged. "He could die, wake up or live in a coma forever. It's early days."

"And have you given any thought to what you might do?"

"Of course, I have. Don't be so daft as to think I don't have a brain and don't use it. Really!" She crossed her arms and lifted her chin, ever so slightly.

Robert tilted his head toward her and raised his brows. "And?"

Robert's intent was becoming clearer. She must become more cautious with her words. "Well, the detective has plenty of evidence to make a case for a fraud or embezzlement charge. If he wakes up, he should go to jail." She spoke the words without emotion.

"If he goes to jail, what does that mean for you?"

She flashed back to her last hospital visit. She wasn't about to mention the farewell to Thomas. "In that case, I suppose a person would have a couple of choices."

"And if he doesn't wake up?"

"I suppose divorce is one choice. But how long does one wait?"

Robert ignored the question, "I did not expect such frankness."

"You asked. I spoke in generalities."

"What do your parents and James think?"

"About my thoughts? I haven't spoken of my thoughts to them."

"No, their thoughts about Thomas."

Margaret fidgeted with the closure of her reticule. Robert was becoming too personal. She cautioned herself to be careful, again. "James dislikes him. Mama and Papa don't particularly care for him."

"And why is that?"

"How he treats me." She lowered her head. *Watch yourself.*

"How does he treat you?"

She kept her head lowered. "Well, you've met him. He's not exactly affable."

He could see Margaret struggling. "And what does that mean?" He needed her to acknowledge her situation for the sake of her own future, not just his.

She shrugged, "He's not exactly caring nor easy to talk with."

"It sounds as if your marriage is not happy."

She clenched her reticule, looked Robert straight in the eye.

"You have no idea what my marriage is like. And don't presume to do so!"

Robert could tell his words were hurtful. "I'm sorry. I should not have forced you to defend yourself. You're right. I don't know what a marriage is like. But I can see you are suffering from the marriage you are in. It hurts me to know you are unhappy. He's not a gentle man, is he?"

Margaret jumped to her feet. "This is not about me and my marriage." She glared at Robert, stormed past the sweet peas to a window draped with heavy brocade curtains. She parted the white sheers then let then them fall back in place. "You come to Halifax once a month and presume to know all about my life then have the unmitigated gall to suggest I pour out my life story to you? I think not, Robert Fraser."

"But I think it is about you and your marriage. You mentioned divorce."

"It happens in marriages and what bloody business is it of yours?" She remained stiff-backed, staring at the curtains.

Robert could see her back heaving as she fought to control her breathing. "Because a person who mentions divorce one minute does not angrily defend her marriage minutes later." He stayed seated, afraid for both of them.

Margaret's thoughts swirled and her heart thudded. She reached for the window ledge, missed and dropped to her knees.

"Margaret!" Robert rushed toward the window and knelt beside her. "Are you hurt?"

Margaret shook her head. "Just embarrassed." She straightened her back.

He took her gloved hands. "Are you ready to stand?"

Margaret looked into Robert's kind eyes and felt safe. She nodded.

He guided her to the lounge and sat beside her, still holding her hand. They bodies were touching. Neither made an effort to move away.

"Why are we really here, Robert? You know Thomas is alive, your mother is opposed to our friendship, society is unbending."

"What about the two of us?"

"'There is no 'us'." She pulled her hand away. "There can't be."

"Why not?"

"You must be joking. How could we be together when even a friendship is wrong?"

"I'm not joking. How you replied is an easy answer to throw away everything we've just talked about. We are friends. Society has no right to deny us that friendship. I want us to keep talking about our circumstances, our feelings." He took her hand again. "Are you prepared to live part or all of your life with Thomas in a coma or in jail?"

Margaret kept her head lowered. "I'm afraid."

"Of what?"

"Surely you know gossip travels quickly."

"I agree, it does. I also know it is mostly about jealousy."

"And you believe if tittle tattle is simply all about jealousy, that is justification for us to be more than friends? What a ridiculous notion."

He asked another question. "In addition to society, anything else frighten you?"

"I don't need you to rescue me." Her strong words belied the pale face.

Robert leaned forward, afraid she might shatter at the slightest touch. "Do you really think I believe you're helpless?"

She didn't want to jump into a secret relationship with Robert but she didn't want to chance losing him either. "No, but I've already misjudged one man."

"He's a fraud, Margaret. I'm not him."

She fell against Robert and began crying. "He destroyed so much of my life, how do I begin again?"

Robert wrapped her in his arms and whispered. "You can have a future with me." He removed her gloves and cradled her face in his hands, kissed her lovingly.

Margaret returned his kiss with her own.

Robert reached for Margaret's hat pin, removed it and the hat then moved the lounge pillow to cradle her head and laid down beside her.

"This will never work." Margaret pushed Robert away.

"It won't work if we give up. Do you want to give up?" He put his arm around her shoulder, kissed her cheek.

"No."

* * *

Margaret rushed toward Barrington Street. Once there, she paused to collect her thoughts. Her intimate time with Robert felt surreal until an unmistakable wave of heat surged through her body betraying her outwardly calm composure. Her body had a mind of its own, revelling in the recent delight. She'd never felt such pleasure with Thomas. She opened her parasol to hide her flushed face.

"Carriage, madame?"

Margaret used the ride to create a story about her afternoon. She stepped out of the carriage with confidence.

"My goodness Margaret, you do look flushed. Are you feeling unwell?"

"I'm fine Mama, just a bit warm in this dress. I should have worn one with a shorter sleeve."

"It looks dreadfully rumpled."

"My fault. I was not careful while seated in the carriage." She patted the wrinkled front of her dress, releasing the scent of Robert's cologne. "I'll take it off immediately." She rushed toward the stairs.

"You might find it helpful to have Mrs. Gilmore come here to take care of your needs during these trying times." Then quickly added, "Did you see Thomas today?"

"No, Mama. I'll go Sunday, I promise."

Margaret dreaded the family dinner conversation. Explaining away her afternoon would not be easy. It was too soon to declare her intent to be free of Thomas and speak of her fledgling freedom without sounding like a woman lacking a moral compass. She would need an alibi. She changed her clothing and sat down in her room to read. It was pure folly to think a story would replace the memory of her time with Robert. She laid the book aside and picked up a far better choice, a boring embroidery sampler. That too was a silly notion. Instead she closed her eyes and enjoyed pleasant thoughts.

* * *

Robert walked home after the late day meetings, his head swirling with questions about Margaret and their future. The question that laid heaviest on his heart was how long could their deep affection for each other last with so many obstacles in their path. Perhaps their September lunch would hold a brighter future.

"Hello, I'm home."

"You look tired, dear."

"Meetings."

"I presume you saw Margaret today. How is she?"

"Her life is upside down. Thomas is still in a coma. As you probably know, she's living at home again."

Regena breathed deeply. "It's a wretched situation for the whole family. She needs all the friends she can get."

Robert waited for her motherly advice about Margaret but it didn't come.

"Have a rest before dinner."

Robert took his mother's suggestion, knowing tomorrow would be another day filled with meetings then the evening train to Montreal. He fell asleep quickly and dreamt of Margaret.

* * *

Margaret's dread was born out immediately upon entering the dining room. Three solemn faces looked in her direction. Her father was standing in a corner by himself. "Is something the matter? Why are you in the corner?" She held her breath.

William began. "A former patient of mine died this afternoon. The illness was tuberculosis and I may have been exposed. That does not mean I will contract the illness." He stopped to catch his breath. "I must isolate myself from the three of you and my patients. The hospital physician believes if I don't develop any symptoms within the next two weeks, I should be okay. Let's assume the best."

"My basic medical training is finished next week. Could I be of some help?"

"Thank you, son. That's kind of you. I've contacted a couple of friends who can cover for me starting tomorrow. I've been a little tired lately so a rest will be good. Hard to believe you'll be an MD in two years."

"I start my two-year supervised practice late next month. Doctor Ellis is my first supervisor. Know him?"

"One of the best family physicians in the city. You will learn a great deal from him. Be prepared to work long hours. He believes in home visits." William looked across the room. "I will isolate myself from all of you beginning now. Hazel will serve all three of you in here. She will leave my food on the table in the foyer." He coughed. "I will sleep in the guest room, beginning tonight and stay outdoors as much as possible. I've had a cough and been tired off and on in recent weeks but that may have nothing to do with tuberculosis. Nevertheless, I will not starve; I'll have a lovely bed and a great chance to catch up on all the reading I haven't been able to do. And Grace dear, don't ask me if I'd like to try embroidery or that other thing you do so well, cross-stitch. When I'm outside, come and join me at a distance. I won't say 'don't worry' because you all will anyway."

The unspoken topic of tuberculosis hung over them like the merciless killer it was. All three were frightened William's absence at the dining room table was a foreshadowing of what their lives might soon become.

CHAPTER TWENTY-THREE

James ate breakfast quickly and arrived at the police station in good time to join Gilfoy, Henderson and Healy for a quick review of their plan before taking a carriage to North Station.

Gilfoy looked at James. "This Graham fella doesn't know he's getting a welcome party so I doubt he'll wear a disguise. Tell us what he looks like and what he might wear."

"Right. Shorter than I am. I'd say five feet eight inches with a limp. Wore a shabby dark suit last month. That about covers it. Oh, satchel was well-worn. But he gave that one to Thomas."

James was looking forward to a ringside seat for the police chase. Instead, Graham stepped off the train and in full view slowly looked around, presumably for Thomas. His shabby suit and the limp were dead giveaways.

Gilfoy casually approached the man. "Good morning, Graham. Are you looking for Thomas Bishop?"

"I am. Are you his representative?"

"No, Graham. I'm a representative of the Halifax Police Department. Hand over the satchel and put your hands behind your back." Henderson and Healy emerged from the crowded platform. "Henderson, cuff this gentleman. Healy, join Henderson and march this fella to the paddy wagon and on to Rockhead Prison. Thanks, gentlemen. Good work." He turned to James. "Sorry to spoil your fun. Would a pot of tea and cornbread muffins with honey make up for your disappointment? After I log in this bag of money, of course."

"Sounds fine to me."

* * *

James returned home to discover his mother sitting beside Margaret, his father on the opposite side of the room.

William was first with a question. "You get him?"

"He's in Rockhead. At the train station, Gilfoy asked if he was looking for Thomas Bishop so he can't weasel out of knowing Thomas. How are you feeling?"

"Bored." He muffled a cough into his handkerchief.

"Already? It's been one day!" James leaned forward in his chair. "I've reconsidered a surgery specialty. It'll take a few years after my MD. Would you consider accepting me as a fellow physician in your general practice?"

"Of course. Best news of the day. Young Doctor Bell sounds first rate." He paused. "But old Doctor Bell doesn't sound so good!"

They all laughed, the first good laugh they'd had in weeks.

* * *

William's absence at church prompted several questions. All were answered with reasonable excuses without a mention of the word tuberculosis.

Anna approached Margaret after the service. "Hello, Margaret. Are you feeling well?"

"I didn't sleep well last night. I've so much on my mind. But I'm looking forward to lunch Tuesday."

"Dare I ask about Thomas? Any change?"

"There's been no word from the hospital. I'm going after lunch."

"Would you like me to go with you?"

"I'll be perfectly fine. There's a guard on duty."

Anna hugged Margaret and waved good-bye.

Anna was her dear friend but standing in front of a church

hardly seemed the proper place to mention Robert. Then there was Papa's possible illness. No wonder Anna was concerned about how she looked. Lunch on Tuesday would be awkward at best.

* * *

"John Gilfoy, why on earth are you going to the office this afternoon? Sunday is a day of rest."

"Now Nettie, don't fret so. I'll be back in a couple of hours and we can go for a walk in the Gardens. By the way, that was a tasty roast."

"Never mind trying to butter me up, Detective Gilfoy. I'm holding you to that promise of a walk." They kissed good-bye.

Gilfoy was ready to charge Thomas Bishop with embezzlement. Saturday night, Bishop Import Export had been searched, documents and money seized and the locks changed. An hour on paperwork today would allow him to begin the legal proceedings discussion early tomorrow morning. Tomorrow, the company's and Thomas Bishop's personal bank assets would also be seized. Gilfoy rushed down the street, past the Gardens and into his office in jig time.

"Sir?"

"Afternoon, Murphy. A large mug of tea with the usual fixins'."

Gilfoy looked at the several pages of testimony from Graham Acton's interview in Rockhead prison. Acton had been willing to tell everything for a lesser sentence, including playing both sides of the brother's illegal activities.

Thomas was the boss of a crime syndicate in Montreal which included thieves, con artists and enforcers. Thanks to Acton, Henderson had a long list of felons to share with the Montreal police. When pressed about a bearded, French-speaking partner in crime, Acton denied any knowledge of the man.

Even with proof of Thomas' guilt, Jessie Bishop's missing proof of Thomas' fraud continued to trouble Gilfoy. Was Jessie bluffing at the Bandstand? Did her landlady burn the papers then deny ever seeing them? Perhaps he would never know.

* * *

Back home in Montreal, Robert poured himself a cup of coffee and cut a slice of lemon pie. Eloise poured herself a coffee and sat at the kitchen table with him. "You have a serious look on your face this evening. There must be an explanation."

"Lots of things happening in Halifax. There's too much work at the bank for a two-day, monthly visit. Margaret's husband is in a coma."

Eloise's hands flew to her mouth. "Mon dieu. Que s'est-il passé?"

"He was attacked."

"And Margaret?"

Robert looked out the kitchen window, exhaled heavily. "Her life is upended."

"Je suis désolé. You do not need to tell me your private business." She started to rise from her chair.

"Please stay seated. Margaret and I care deeply for each other." He smiled. "I think we both knew we cared for each other years ago but I left. Then an awful man came into her life and hurt her."

Eloise nodded. "Despite losing Alphonse in the fire, I still believe things happen for a reason. Maybe that coma is for a reason too."

"You're a wise woman, Eloise. I hope you're right."

* * *

On Sunday afternoon Constable Henderson was guarding Thomas room. He stood up as Margaret approached. "Hello, Mrs. Bishop. How are you, ma'am?"

Margaret offered him her best imitation of a smile. "Quite well, Constable Henderson. And you?"

"Fine, ma'am. Thank you. Please go in." Margaret hesitated in the doorway. The scene before her was a photograph, not real life: same chair, same bedside table, same wrapped body. She had much to tell Thomas but with no reason to speak aloud, she didn't bother. Then Thomas twitched his left hand. Margaret gasped so loudly Henderson stepped into the room.

"Ma'am?"

"Get a doctor."

Henderson stepped out of the room and waved at the closest person in a white coat. "We need a doctor."

"What does it mean, Doctor?"

"According to your husband's chart, there have been no other signs of movement. For example, he's never been observed opening his eyes. I suspect it's a seizure caused by your husband's brain injury. On the bright side, it will be positive if the movement continues to occur and eventually involves the arm. I'll speak with Doctor Adams in the morning and of course the nursing staff will continue to monitor him. Anything else, Mrs. Bishop?"

Margaret glanced at his name tag "No. Thank you, Doctor Griffin." After his departure, she walked into the hallway and bid 'good day' to Henderson.

On the carriage ride home, Margaret held back her tears, kept her hands motionless on her lap while her thoughts were moving fast, thinking the worst.

"Madam, we're here."

Margaret sauntered toward the roses alongside the path to the front door. She closed her eyes, breathed the sweet scent and lingered, delaying the inevitable first question.

"I'm home."

"How's Thomas, dear?"

Margaret removed her hat and perched on the edge of a chair. "I don't know. He moved his hand." She burst into uncontrollable tears. They flooded her cheeks, mixed with mucus and ran from her nose. "I can't have him back in my life. I won't."

"Now, now dear. Stiff upper lip. It can't be all that bad."

"You think he should be back in my life! I won't have it."

James slipped out of the room to get her a fresh handkerchief and find his father.

"You're overly excited. You misunderstood what I said, Margaret I meant..."

William stood in the doorway. He flashed his palm towards Grace, adding a quick smile then turned to Margaret. "What's happened at the hospital?"

"Thomas moved his hand while I was there."

"And what did the doctor say?"

"It's probably a seizure because his brain is injured. It doesn't mean anything unless his arm moves."

"Well then, we just have to wait and see what happens." He turned to the hall where James was standing. "Can you ask Hazel to bring a pot of tea?" William stepped into the drawing room, isolating himself on a chair in the far corner.

"Thank you, Papa. I was beginning to enjoy a bit of freedom and it's being ripped away. It's so unfair."

"You know nothing about Thomas' injury is certain, Margaret. I think it is too early to be talking about freedom. It's not appropriate."

Margaret stared at her mother. "What am I supposed to do? Stay in my room?" She clenched her fists. "He's not dead but neither am I."

"Society expects you to use your sense of right and wrong. You can't do as you please. You must see this ordeal through to the end."

"And what is this end you talk about?"

"I believe it's dependent upon Thomas."

"Well, he's either going to die or go to jail. Are you saying I cannot have a life until one or the other occurs?"

William stepped into the stalemate. "When you speak of freedom, what exactly are you talking about, my dear?"

"I want to work with Anna, have lunch with her, be able to meet other people for lunch." She stopped short of mentioning Robert's name knowing her mother would be rendered speechless, probably fall out of her chair.

James put on his best smile. "Tea is served."

* * *

Henderson thrived on the action and unexpected experiences of a police constable. Today was his fifth shift at the hospital. Guarding Thomas Bishop's room was the most tedious police work he'd ever encountered. By the end of his first shift, he was familiar with all the hospital entrances and exits as well as possible hide-outs near Bishop's room. On the second shift, he introduced himself to every nurse and doctor who walked by. Nurses wore uniforms and name tags, doctors wore white coats with name tags so it made life simpler. Today was Thomas Bishop's eleventh day in the hospital. Henderson was inclined to think the bearded, French-speaking man was long gone from Halifax.

Sunday was a day of rest. Businesses closed and many people attended morning church services. Sunday afternoon was an ideal time for family and friends to visit hospital patients. The hospital was filled with visitors. Henderson was quick to notice the potential danger. It would be the perfect time for someone to blend in and wait for a chance to slip past the guard and into Bishop's room. He began scanning the hallway for any suspicious movement. After Mrs. Bishop left and the afternoon wore on, Henderson become less certain today was the day for mister beard to visit.

"Have a good evening, officer."

"You too, Doctor Griffin." As he was speaking, Henderson noticed a doctor leaning against the opposite wall. He was holding a piece of paper. It blocked Henderson's view of the name tag. The doctor was beardless so Henderson dismissed his presence.

Moments later, Henderson's vision of the doctor was blocked by a large family group passing in front of him. He caught a glimpse of a white coat entering Thomas' room. He charged in to find a doctor with his hands over Thomas' mouth and nose.

"Stop. Halifax police." Henderson blew his whistle then smashed a chair over the doctor's head.

A passing nurse ran into the room and found Henderson

snapping handcuffs on a man wearing a white coat, lying face-down beside Thomas' bed.

"Officer Henderson, what are you doing? That's a doctor." She took a towel from the night table and held it on the man's bleeding head.

"Call for a doctor then see if you can find this fella's name tag. It could be under the bed."

The man on the floor opened his eyes. Realizing he was cuffed, he looked at Henderson and swore in French. When Henderson helped him up, he spat in his face.

When questioned, the French-speaking man confessed he was an associate of Timothy Bishop sent to Halifax to kill Thomas. Following Timothy's murder, he stayed on to finish the job.

* * *

Gilfoy glanced at his watch. "Nettie's not going to easily forgive me for this one."

Henderson was busy writing his report on the arrest and lock-up of the hospital suspect. "Pardon me, sir. I couldn't quite understand what you said."

"I should have been home over an hour ago and right about now strolling in the Gardens with Nettie."

"I've met your Nettie, sir. I'm sure you'll be forgiven. Blame it all on me."

Gilfoy laughed. "Thanks for the idea. I'll try it out. Great work today, Constable."

"Thank you, sir. That job in the hospital isn't my kind of work though. Too much sitting down."

"Are you telling me you don't want to move up the ranks, take on more paperwork, have a desk?"

Henderson thought for a minute. "No, sir. I'm saying I like my job to have excitement, some paperwork but not a lot of sitting down."

"Fair enough. I think a sergeant's job would fit your description. Are you in agreement if I put your name forward for a promotion?"

Henderson was so surprised he simply nodded then managed a 'Thank you, sir.'

"Then let's finish up here and go home. On second thought, you go home. I need to speak with Margaret Bishop."

"I'm not responsible for that decision and don't you be tellin' Nettie I was. Good evening, sir."

CHAPTER TWENTY-FOUR

HALIFAX, NOVA SCOTIA
AUGUST 26, 1895

In one hour Detective Gilfoy was scheduled to meet with the Crown Attorney Albert Logan. In order to lay an embezzlement charge against Thomas Bishop, Logan would need to declare Gilfoy's evidence to be admissible, reliable and complete. Gilfoy had full confidence in his paperwork and witness statements but Thomas Bishop was unavailable and would be for the foreseeable future. He stepped out of the station with an uneasy mind.

Albert Logan rose from his leather chair and stretched his lanky body across the desk, reaching for Gilfoy's outstretched hand.

"Good morning, John. I believe you have an embezzlement charge for review." Albert's usual easy smile was absent. The dark circles under his eyes were noticeable.

Gilfoy nodded. "I do."

"Assets seized?"

"Yes. Company office Saturday evening. The company and personal ones at the bank this morning."

"Excellent." Logan sat down and removed his spectacles. "Have a seat and tell me the story."

Gilfoy placed the documents on the desk and sat. He proceeded to outline his case and identified his problem. "The intended accused is in a coma." As an afterthought, "Who should receive Mr. Bishop's copy of the charge?"

"Well, the coma complicates the case. And with regard to Mr. Bishops' copy of your paperwork. Does he have a lawyer?"

"I don't believe so. If he did, I'd think the lawyer would have spoken with the police by now."

"Perhaps. In any case, I recommend you speak with his next of kin to determine the status of legal counsel and if none, present the copy to that person."

"That would be his wife."

"Is she involved in this charge?"

"As a witness, when it goes to trial."

"Then I recommend she find a lawyer to hold the documents as Mr. Bishop is in no position to seek legal advice. This lawyer should have no connection to Mrs. Bishop or her family. Now to the charge itself. I cannot immediately see my way clear to lay your charge for the very reason you gave me. The man's unable to understand the claim against him let alone defend himself. How long has he been in this coma?"

"Almost two weeks."

"The fella on the front page of the paper?"

"The very one. So, can the charge be delayed and for how long?"

"As we're dealing with a serious medical condition, I can't specify a time for a deferment. I could consider a pending recovery deferment but that could mean days or years."

"To be straightforward, I want some sort of delay because I don't want this man to get away without a visit to the court room."

"You do realize this man might wake up and be mentally incapacitated?"

"I do but his victims need a sign the law is taking some course of action, is working on their behalf."

Logan stared at his desk top and drummed his fingers. Looking up he said, "I understand your point. I'll review all your documentation and advise you on my final decision by the weeks' end."

"Thank you."

Logan slid Gilfoy's documents to the side of his desk and moved to join him on the other side of the desk. "How's Nettie, children and grandchildren?"

"Doing well. The little ones are growing like weeds." Gilfoy asked uneasily. "And Elizabeth?"

"Recovering slowly. Thanks for asking. Losing a grandchild is a dreadful thing. Have time for tea?"

Gilfoy obliged, sensing Albert's need to spend time with a longtime friend and speak of matters other than the law.

On his return walk to the police station, Gilfoy stepped inside the city's Court House. Some thirty odd years after a series of fires destroyed its predecessor, the stone building with elaborate interior, arched doorways, wood panelling and pressed metal ceilings never failed to impress him. Seeing the courtrooms, robing rooms, jury rooms and law library affirmed his dedication to the law. He looked forward to Thomas Bishop's presence in the building, however long it took.

* * *

"You look lovely, Mrs. Bishop. Enjoy your lunch with Mrs. Hopkins."

"Thank you, Hazel."

Despite Hazel's agreeable manner and care of her clothing, Margaret missed Cookie's stories and sensible advice. Living with her family was a reminder of Thomas' control. She chafed at her mothers inferences regarding her social status. It was time to return to her own home. Her life's path needed to be of her own making, complete with blunders and successes. She would tell everyone her decision this evening.

"Good bye, Mama. I'm going to lunch with Anna."

"Are you seeing Thomas this week?"

"Yes." She hurried down the hallway, preferring to wait outside for the carriage. Her thoughts jumped from one thing to another and back again...returning to her own home, Thomas,

Robert, Papa's illness, Mama's interference, James' gambling, suffragette work.

* * *

Anna had no doubt Margaret was headed into imminent trouble. A husband suspended in time and an admirer very much in the present spelled disaster. She intended to nudge Margaret into understanding exactly that today, hoping she still had a friend after lunch.

Anna was barely in her chair when she asked a question. "How was Thomas yesterday?"

"His hand twitched while I was there."

"He's waking up?" She covered her mouth and muttered through her fingers, "Oh, my!"

"Hello, ladies. Tea and assorted sandwiches with sweet pickles?"

"Sounds lovely." Margaret waited until they were alone. "The twitch would have to continue and the arm move before it would be considered a real improvement. He will wake or die. Right now neither one seems about to happen."

"You look calm."

Margaret closed her eyes. "I'm pretending." She opened her eyes. "To do otherwise would be foolish, just the sort of behaviour my mother would use to keep me at home. She's already implied I'm a woman without a moral compass because I'm not doing what society expects."

"Are you saying you're returning to your own home?"

"Excuse me ladies. Your lunch."

"Thank you." Anna acknowledged the waitress without taking her eyes off Margaret.

"Yes. I'm telling everyone this evening. To stay is to admit I'm incapable of taking care of myself."

Anna nodded. "You'll be alone."

"Cookie and I will be just fine."

"I sound nosy but what about money? Thomas owns

everything, even what you brought to the marriage. It's legal but unfair. How will you manage?"

"Thomas asked what was in my cedar chest and I told him fancy linens. That was the truth but not all of it. Grandfather Bell left me money in his will. It was certainly a surprise to my parents. Not enough for a lifetime but fine for now."

Anna chuckled. "You know me. I always have a plan for our lunches so here is my next matter. The suffragettes. Do you remain interested?"

"Yes. It's one thing I can manage. No surprise, Mama's not enthused."

"I understand you need to do more than visit the hospital. Here's the address for the Halifax Suffrage Association. I'm sure you'll find its first president very keen to speak with you. I've enclosed a few questions to get you started. Take good notes. Anna Leonowens is her name."

"It's really going to happen? Now I'm nervous!"

"You wanted something to do."

A companionable silence followed.

"I'm pleased you sound so positive today but I worry about you."

Margaret frowned. "Why?"

"You're unhappy living at home, your husband's in a coma, your future is uncertain. That's why. By the way, how was lunch with Robert?"

"It was pleasant to see him again." She flushed from her neck to cheeks as her body responded to raw thoughts of desire, her craving for Robert's lips on hers, his hands on her body, their intimate coupling. "He's very concerned for my happiness."

Margaret's flush answered all Anna's unasked questions. She leisurely finished her tea and refilled the cup, waiting for Margaret to add more to her reply.

"Do you have any advice on moving away from parents?"

Anna recognized the ruse and gave a straight forward answer.

"The army tells us where and when we're moving. There isn't any discussion, with anybody."

"Oh, of course. How silly of me."

Anna abandoned her earlier plan. She'd already confirmed Margaret was in a relationship with Robert and moved on to social events.

* * *

Grace Bell returned from her church meeting to find William wandering in the back garden, arms behind his back, head down. Usually he admired the apple trees along the back fence or pulled weeds from among the roses, daisies and hollyhocks. She walked through the herb garden, barely noticing the heady scent of sage and mint. "Are you alright?"

William lifted his head and suggested they talk about a few things. "You can sit on one bench and I the other."

Separated by a double row of onions, they sauntered toward the back of the house.

Grace looked worried. "Are you feeling worse?"

"No, but we need to settle the future before I might be. With the potential of tuberculosis, it's time for a talk about Margaret, James, the house and money. I'll go first. We need to update our wills with Samuel. I cannot envision Margaret being allowed to live in Thomas' house for the long term. If he comes out of this coma and lives, he'll be in jail. If he dies, the house will be sold. According to the law, she owns no part of it."

"So we need to speak with her."

"I believe she already knows these things, dear."

"She's certainly not acting as if she knows. It's terribly worrisome."

"I'm concerned too and that is why Samuel should meet with us. That brings me to James. He seems keen to join my practice so living in this house for the long term is logical."

"Yes, of course."

"I'm not convinced Margaret would be agreeable to living with you and her brother again."

"Why wouldn't she be?"

"I think that's hope on your part. I cannot imagine her happy to be overseen by a mother and older brother."

"But that's how it will have to be if Thomas dies or is incapacitated anyway. What else could she do?"

"Live with another young widow? I don't have a good answer but traditions are changing, dear. The suffragettes are working towards the vote and fairness for women in other parts of their lives. More women will work outside the home. Anna Hopkins is an example. Margaret could too." He paused. "What do you think of James having ownership of the home and Margaret receiving the family money after your death? That would provide for her independence in the future."

"This conversation is very upsetting. Are you telling me you're going to die soon?"

"I'm not saying anything of the sort. I simply want our children to have a fair plan in place. Traditional wills give everything to the boys and girls get nothing, supposing they will marry and be looked after by a husband. Do you think my idea is fair?"

Grace nodded. "It's very fair for the future but what about the present? Margaret could decide to leave any day. We can't stop her. She's so wilful."

"If she leaves, I don't know how she'll survive. I'm worried. She has a bit of money from my father but that won't last long."

"She needs to stay here. Food, dresses, lunch with friends and Mrs. Gilmore all require money."

"As you say, we can't stop her." He paused. "I'd like Samuel to come here. We can keep him a safe distance from me, in case I am carrying tuberculosis. Shall I send a message to him for Friday afternoon?"

"Yes, of course. When will we discuss this with the children?"

"Whenever you are ready, my dear."

* * *

James' suspicion about his father's illness all started with the discussion about tuberculosis. He'd taken particular note of his recent fatigue and shortness of breath and recalled a few coughing episodes earlier in the year. Did he really have a brush with tuberculosis or was he hiding something? Margaret's troubles were enough worries for the time being. He decided to mention his concern after the two-week tuberculosis period ended.

* * *

"You're quiet this evening, Margaret. A penny for your thoughts."

James was quick to step in. "I imagine she has many thoughts, Mama." He smiled toward Margaret. "You might need lots of pennies."

"I don't know about the thoughts but I do have a decision. When we've finished dessert, I'll find Papa and tell everyone together."

James wanted an excuse to watch his father from the kitchen window. "I'm finished. He's likely in the garden. It's his favourite haunt these days." James was astonished. His father was shuffling along the rows, pulling only those weeds he could reach without too much effort. His first instinct was to rush out the door and be a doctor. Instead he opened the door and stepped outside. "Papa, Margaret wants to speak with us. Come in when you're ready."

"I'm ready."

James noticed how quickly his father walked to the kitchen door then how laboured his breathing became inside the kitchen. "How are you feeling, Papa?"

"A bit tired this evening. It's amazing how a little gardening can wear you out."

"Let's go hear what Margaret has to say. I'll bring you a glass of water."

Inside the sitting room, Margaret began confidently despite

her jittery stomach. "I imagine all of you know what I'm going to say so I'll say it. It's time for me to return to my own home. The longer I remain here, the more dependent I'm becoming. Leaving was bound to happen anyway so it's best I do it now. I'll be here for Sunday lunch and other times. Anna asked me to help with her newspaper work and I agreed. I will be doing my first interview soon. Tomorrow I will see Cookie and leave Thursday."

James had no idea what to say so he kept quiet.

William nodded without comment.

Grace began to cry and ran out of the room toward the garden. She was followed by William who consoled her with words as he sat on the bench and she stood a distance away, among the rose bushes.

"I know you don't agree, dear, but perhaps it will be for the best, even if it only lasts for a short time. The experience will serve her well."

CHAPTER TWENTY-FIVE

Breakfast was a silent meal in the Bell home. William was eating in his room. James was gone before Margaret came downstairs and Grace offered her daughter a polite 'good morning' without a smile. Margaret nodded in return.

Hazel pretended she didn't notice the frosty mood in the room. "Good morning, Mrs. Bishop. Would you like an egg and toast?"

"No thank you, Hazel. Toast with jam and tea is fine."

"Very well."

Margaret ate quickly and stood up. "Have a good day, Mama. I have shopping to do before seeing Mrs. Gilmore and going to the hospital."

"Have a pleasant day, dear."

* * *

Cookie Gilmore lived with her older sister Maisie, also a widow. Margaret was quite taken with their small two-story wooden home, a few blocks from the wharf. She was greeted by a festival of multicoloured hollyhocks leaning against the front of the house. Calico curtains hung in both of the front windows. The single-ring brass door knocker shone brightly in the morning sun. She tapped the knocker and waited.

Cookie appeared, wiping her hands on her apron. "Come in,

Mrs. Bishop. Pardon my appearance. Maisie and I are baking up a storm."

Cookie's welcome did not sound at all surprised. Margaret guessed she'd been waiting for this day since Thomas' attack, almost two weeks ago.

"Thank you." Margaret stepped into the front hall and was straight away cocooned in the rich scents of cinnamon and vanilla.

"Maisie, Mrs. Bishop and I will be in the sitting room. Keep an eye on those pies."

"Now don't you be goin' worryin' about those pies. I'll be in ever so shortly with tea."

Maisie's sing-song manner of speaking caught Margaret's attention as it was so different from Cookie's straight forward manner. Unlike her taller, dark-haired sister, Maisie was a short woman with brown hair, round face and rosy cheeks.

A wave of scented air overpowered Margaret the very second Cookie opened the door to the sitting room. Vases of sweet peas were on the window ledge, small tables and the bookcase.

"Oh, my!" Margaret felt her cheeks heat up. The scent summoned her memory of the secret room with Robert.

"Sit down, Mrs. Bishop. Are you feeling weak? I can understand. Your husband's..."

"I'm fine, Cookie." Margaret rummaged in her reticule for the small fan, waved it in front of her face. "There, that's much better."

"It's so kind of you to come for a visit." Cookie hesitated. "I thought about visiting you at your family home but it didn't seem appropriate what with everyone there and Mr. Bishop's accident and all." She straightened her skirts and sat down. "And how are you, Mrs. Bishop?"

"I'm quite well, Cookie. That is why I'm here."

"Oh?"

"I will be returning to my home tomorrow and want to know if you are ready to return with me?"

"I would be delighted to."

"Excuse me ladies. I made lemonade, not tea. It's so warm, isn't it though. The shortbread cookies are fresh from this morning. They turned out lovely, they did." Maisie placed the glasses, pitcher of lemonade and a plate of cookies on the table, smiled then left.

Cookie poured the lemonade and offered Margaret the cookies and an embroidered napkin.

"I imagine you are curious about how all this will work without Thomas' money."

"It's really none of my business, Mrs. Bishop."

"Perhaps I better tell you the details."

Cookie listened to the story of Thomas' attack, his coma, her new adventure with Anna and her desire to return to her own home, despite her parents' concern. "It's really my mother who is not in favour of my independence. I don't expect she will visit us soon, but I plan to attend church and Sunday lunch as usual. Papa tells us times are changing and I intend to be part of the change."

When Margaret bid farewell, Cookie kept her thoughts to herself, only telling Maisie she was returning to work tomorrow. Margaret spoke as though Thomas was already dead but how was she planning to live without his money? In spite of all her concerns, Cookie was looking forward to being with Margaret again. She planned to keep the dear girl safe and well.

The visit with Cookie lifted Margaret's spirits immensely. Cookie told several amusing tales about the neighbours and she laughed often. She was tempted to mention Robert. Perhaps she would invite him for lunch one day. He'd enjoy Cookie's stories.

* * *

Margaret intended to make a quiet entrance into Thomas' room. Instead, a loud gasp escaped her lips as she moved behind the temporary screen at the foot of his bed. Thomas was naked from the waist down. She was repulsed by unpleasant memories and turned her head away.

"Hello, Mrs. Bishop." Nurse Pender pulled the sheet over Thomas' lower body. "I'm bathing your husband and re-positioning him in order to prevent pressure sores. Would you like me to come back later?"

Seeing Thomas' naked body was a disturbing reminder of his cruelty. She clenched her fists and fought to keep her voice neutral. "No, finish what you have to do. I'll sit in the front waiting room. Any additional movements?"

"Not that anyone has seen. I'm sorry." She paused. "I'll let you know when I'm finished."

"Thank you." Margaret's inclination was to keep walking past the waiting room. Instead, she reasoned an hour's observation of Thomas' still body would help ease her concerns about his recovery. She made a mental note to bring a book for the next visit.

* * *

In Montreal, Robert was surrounded by stacks of balance sheets, income and cash flow statements stacked neatly over much of his desk. A construction company recently applied for a bank loan to undertake an enormous expansion on the Montreal waterfront. The company's performance report and his recommendation on the loan were due the next morning. He rubbed his eyes and walked to the window. His thoughts drifted to Margaret and their time together. What happened seemed like a dream but his arousal did not come from a dream. It was real. Margaret had sacrificed her present life believing in a better one with him. He could not let her down.

* * *

Margaret arrived home to hear James excitedly describing something new in his life. "The sessions begin next week, on Monday evenings."

Grace beckoned to Margaret. "Come in. James has news."

"I'm proud of you, son. This is excellent news."

"Thank you, Papa."

Margaret was confused. "A new class?"

"Sort of. I'm joining a small group of fellow students who gamble and want to stop. A terrible thing happened to one chap and his friends decided they better do something to help themselves. A professor is leading the group."

"Good for you. I'm proud of you too. Can I help?"

"Yes, you can. Here's the information for family and friends."

"Thank you." Margaret looked at her father, sitting alone in the corner. She wanted to embrace him, tell him how much he meant to her, feel the reassurance of his love in these disordered times. Her heart was breaking for him, for herself. She could not imagine her life without him. Surely he would not die of tuberculosis. "Papa, when I'm settled in the house, I want you to come and visit me. We'll sit in the garden. But first, Cookie and I have to get rid of the weeds! We'll find out how bad it is tomorrow." She laughed to make herself feel better. It didn't help much.

* * *

Late Thursday morning, Margaret slipped the key into the front door lock but didn't turn it. It was a big moment in her changed life. No Thomas and no fear. Robert. Work and freedom. A new beginning.

"Morning, Mrs. Bishop. Something the matter?"

"No, Cookie. Everything's perfectly fine."

Cookie was carrying a basket covered by a tea towel. "I brought some flowers to cheer up the kitchen table."

"Lovely. Let's go inside." The hall smelled of dust and stale air. Margaret sneezed. "Goodness, it's so stuffy here. Let's open the windows. You take care of the kitchen and I'll go to the dining room, sitting room and study."

The study door was open. Margaret recalled leaving it open when she left with all the money, papers and ledgers immediately after Thomas' attack but not the last day she came for day dresses. The door should be closed. Nothing appeared to be disturbed.

As Margaret returned to the kitchen, her body responded to the scent of Cookie's sweet peas. Her hands remembered the brocade sofa and Robert's warm body, the short curls of hair on his neck.

"I need to step outside for a few minutes." She opened the kitchen door and breathed in cool air on the shady side of the house then looked across the side yard. The entire garden needed attention. Cookie's herbs were in a losing battle with weeds. She leaned forward and removed the tallest ones then continued toward the back of the house. She stepped toward the study window. Paint on the ledge and window frame was deeply gouged. She rushed back to the kitchen.

"Cookie, I'm going to the police station. I believe someone has been in the house since I was here a few days ago."

"Never! Another reason for us to be here. Nobody would try that when we're in it. Lay-abouts!"

"I think we better check upstairs before I leave."

* * *

"Is Detective Gilfoy available? I'm Margaret Bishop."

Gilfoy's door was partially open. "Come in, Mrs. Bishop. What has happened?" What he heard was not expected. Everyone he knew connected with Thomas was either in jail or being closely watched since the Graham Acton interview. "When do you believe this occurred?"

"Sometime since Tuesday afternoon."

"Anything missing?"

"Nothing noticeable. My housekeeper and I have been through all the rooms. As you know, I took the paperwork and money from the study long ago."

"Yes, I recall that. A smart move on your part. I'll have a constable take a look around later today."

"Thank you." Margaret rose to leave.

"Do you have a few minutes?"

Margaret nodded.

"Do you know if your husband has a lawyer?"

"He never mentioned one. Maybe a lawyer in the Halifax Club?"

"Thank you. Can I assume you've returned to your own home, Mrs. Bishop?"

"I have. Thank you, Detective."

Gilfoy remained standing, his mind on Margaret's safety, now alone in her own home.

"Healy, Mrs. Bishop has discovered evidence of a likely break-in at her home. Can you ask Ramsay to examine the grounds, study room window and the room itself sometime later today?"

"Yes, sir."

Gilfoy picked up his notebook and headed for Rockhead.

* * *

"Good afternoon, Mr. Acton. I trust Rockhead is treating you well." Gilfoy received a cold stare for his effort.

Acton glared, his lips pinched together. "Why you here? I told you everything I know."

"Maybe. Let's review those names and descriptions you told me several days ago." He pulled out the notebook.

"Why?"

"Humour me."

Gilfoy came away empty-handed. In the office, he found the names and descriptions James had given him. The smelly drunk was not on Graham's list.

* * *

On Friday morning, Albert Logan decided to take a walk to the relatively new police station to meet Gilfoy. The old station had been replaced five years before in 1890. At the time, its condition inside was so bad Logan avoided it at all costs, as did the policemen who worked there. In fact, they preferred to sit outside rather than inside.

"Detective Gilfoy, please."

"Yes, sir."

Gilfoy rose from his chair. "Never mind, Boudreau. Come in, Albert. Have a seat."

"I won't keep you in suspense, John. I've approved the charge with a pending recovery clause and added a review of Mr. Bishop's condition every three months. The police department will be required to contact Mr. Bishop's physician for his current condition in a written form. If, between the review periods, Mr. Bishop's condition changes his physician will be required to notify your department. I trust you will be able to negotiate this with the physician. If you meet with resistance, call me and the Attorney General's office will resolve the problem."

"I'm relieved. Thank you. Now I can move on to the charges for others in the scheme. Have you time for tea and apple cake?"

"I always have time for apple cake!"

* * *

Grace Bell paced in the garden. William was in bed and her children were not in the house. She pretended to tend the flowers but truthfully, she could not see them through the flood of tears rolling down her cheeks. Margaret was unaware or wilfully ignoring her uncertain future and in her heart she knew William was not well. She looked forward to Samuel's visit, expecting William to open up about the true need for the will to be reviewed. She needed the reassurance his truth would bring.

Hazel called from the kitchen door. "Mrs. Bell, Mr. Fraser is in the sitting room."

Thank you, Hazel. Will you wake William and bring in the lemonade tray."

Grace patted her tears away, practised a smile then walked down the hall.

Samuel rose from his chair and took Grace's hand. "Good afternoon, Grace." He didn't fail to notice the redness of her eyes and flushed cheeks.

"Hello, Samuel. It's so good of you to come. I've been in the garden so I'm a bit warm. Please, have a seat."

When William entered the room he waved at Samuel. "Don't get up. I sit in the corner these days. Before you think I've been a very bad boy, I have to say I may have been in contact with tuberculosis. I'm half way through the two-week waiting period."

Samuel's eyes widened. He was speechless for a long moment. "So you're changing your will?" He hoped his tone of voice lacked the alarm he felt.

Grace forced herself to remain silent. She reasoned her tactic would illicit the most information from William.

"Change may not be the best word. We want to ensure the children are taken care of. Margaret's circumstance has changed dramatically."

"Because of her husband's condition, I presume?"

William nodded. "He remains in a coma. You should know, his business dealings are under police review."

Samuel's face revealed his surprise. "Oh!"

"If what I suspect happens, Margaret will be left with nothing. She will have no right to the home nor any of his money. It will likely be taken as proceeds of his criminal activity."

"So what we are dealing with today is protecting Margaret's future and ensuring James is not left disadvantaged."

"Well said."

"For my understanding, are Margaret and James aware of your wishes?"

"No." Grace and William responded at the same moment.

"Then let's begin."

"May I add something first?"

"Of course, Grace."

"Margaret has been living with us for weeks but returned to her marital home today. She appears to believe she's somehow entitled to the house in spite of the law. I'm very worried, Samuel."

Grace thought William was listening to her, waiting to add his opinion. He remained silent. She looked toward him and realized his mind was elsewhere.

"William, anything to add?" Samuel inquired.

"No, let's begin."

While Grace and Samuel focused on words and paper, William reflected on his daughter. The will itself would not secure Margaret's future happiness. She was becoming increasingly distanced from her mother. Reconciliation appeared impossible.

* * *

When Gilfoy knocked on the door of the Bishop home he received no reply. He lifted his hand to knock a second time when he heard voices from the side of the house. He followed the laughter.

Margaret and Cookie were on their knees, each with a bucket by their side. Limp weeds hung over the sides of the buckets. A few had missed the mark and were lying on the ground, clumps of dried soil hanging off the ends. Both women had streaks of dirt on their brows, from swiping them with the backs of their dirty hands.

"Good afternoon, ladies."

"Detective!" Margaret jumped up while also trying to push her errant auburn curls under a sun bonnet. "I look a sight." She looked at the envelope in his hand. "Did I know you were coming and forget?"

"No, but I do have papers for you."

"You better come in the house."

Cookie rushed past Gilfoy. "Good afternoon, Detective. Mrs. Bishop, I'll get the lemonade ready."

"Considering the dirt on my clothing, we should stay in the kitchen. Follow me through the side-door into Cookie's domain."

Cookie bustled around for a few minutes, placed the lemonade, glasses and ginger cookies on the table and returned to the garden.

Margaret poured the lemonade. "So, what are these new papers?"

"In short, they are the legal papers charging Thomas I. Bishop of Halifax with embezzlement. As I do not believe your husband has a lawyer, I must give them to you, as next of kin."

"But he can't go to court. He's in a coma!" She passed the cookies to Gilfoy then helped herself.

"This charge addresses that by adding a review of his condition every three months."

"He might never go to court!"

"That's correct."

"Or he might die."

"Correct."

"Does he need a lawyer?"

"I can't advise you on that. If your family has one, I suggest you speak with him. But your family lawyer cannot represent your husband."

"I assure you, that would be the last thing Samuel Fraser would do. More lemonade?"

"Please, half a glass."

"Thank you for being so direct with me."

"Just my job, Mrs. Bishop." He sipped his drink. "If you don't mind me asking, how is your husband?"

"He's the same as he was on August fifteenth, completely cared for by nurses and checked daily by the doctors."

"I'm sorry this is such a difficult time for you. I'm sure you feel there seems to be no end in sight."

"Thank you. I have to think about my own future no matter what happens."

"Thanks for the refreshment. It's time I return to the station."

Margaret saw Gilfoy to the door and returned to the kitchen door. "Cookie, you can come in. Detective Gilfoy's gone. I must tell you some things. Sit with me. The detective just gave me the police papers charging Thomas with embezzlement. Nobody knows what will happen. He may die or stay in a coma, forever."

Cookie knew first hand, what kind of horrid person Thomas was. She did not express any sorrow for his situation. "And you. How are you holding up?"

Margaret hesitated. "I'm more worried about Papa than myself." She didn't want to mention tuberculosis so spoke of his shortness of breath and tiredness.

* * *

Constable Ramsay sighed with relief when the sun went down. Afternoon foot patrol wearing a police uniform in the summer heat was wretched. He tried to stay on the streets with shady trees but that didn't always work. Thankfully the Bishop home was on his route and it was shady. He timed his next walk past to be in the dark. The late day had been quiet and Ramsay looked forward to a bit of evening excitement. An attempted break-in at the Bishop house would be perfect. He patrolled the back fence carefully and often.

Joe McCuaig was mad as hell at Thomas Bishop for not paying him what he was owed. He knew the bugger was in the hospital but that didn't help him any. Joe wanted the money and intended to get it somehow. He figured he'd pay himself by taking a few things from Bishop's house, sell them off at the wharf. His first try went wrong when he didn't see anything of real value in Bishop's study. During the second try, he opened the study door to search the rest of the house. Thinking he heard a knock on the front door, he scurried back inside the study and crawled out the window, earning several scratches along the way.

Tonight he planned to go for the good stuff rich folks kept in the dining room, silver and such. But hapless Joe failed again. Constable McCuaig whacked him on the rear end with his club and cuffed him before his feet left the ground under the study window.

* * *

After lunch on Saturday, Margaret and Cookie stood in the

middle of the flower and herb garden admiring the beauty of their hard work.

"Remember yesterday? It was so overgrown, it was nearly impassable in places. It needs a proper vegetable garden though." Margaret pointed beyond the perennials. "Over there."

Cookie wished that could be true but she wasn't thinking about vegetables. Margaret's welfare needed to be protected, in spite of her occasional headstrong behaviour. One day soon she needed to find out if Margaret was ignoring the truth of her situation or simply defying her mother.

On Saturday afternoon, Constable Ramsay rang the Bishop doorbell. "Good afternoon, may I speak to Mrs. Bishop?"

"Come in Constable." Cookie rushed into the study.

"Who's there, Cookie?"

"The police. What's happening now?"

"Good news, I hope."

"Good afternoon, Mrs. Bishop. I'm Constable Ramsay. That fella who took it into his head to break into your house is in Rockhead for a while."

"And are you the policeman who caught him?"

"I am, ma'am."

"When did this happen?"

Last night, ma'am. 'Bout midnight."

"Well, come in Constable. Your hard work deserves a thank you. Have lemonade and cookies with us."

"Ma'am, I don't think I should."

"I'm sure Detective Gilfoy would approve."

CHAPTER TWENTY-SIX

HALIFAX, NOVA SCOTIA
SEPTEMBER 1, 1895

With the hymn book close to her face, Anna leaned toward George and murmured into his ear. "There's something wrong with the Bell family."

"What?"

"Shh. William is absent again."

"Probably an emergency, a baby or some medical problem. You have a vivid imagination."

Anna ignored George's quick dismissal. She knew a story when she saw one. She'd ask Margaret after the service.

"Good morning, Anna. What a lovely day."

"It is. I noticed your father was absent again today. I trust he's well."

"He has a cough and decided to stay home, in case it's a cold." She smiled. "I have good news though. I moved home Thursday and I'd like to have you come for lunch one day this week."

"That sounds lovely. I have work and volunteer obligations every day, except Friday. Is Friday fine?"

"Yes. It works perfectly. I promised myself to complete the suffragette interview this week so we can discuss it then."

"And Thomas. Anything new?"

"No change." She'd keep the story about the break-in until Friday. "Everyone's in jail and Gilfoy's legal charge for Thomas is prepared."

* * *

William was more restless with each day of his confinement and Margaret's absence was an added worry. When Monday morning arrived, he told Grace he was going out for a walk then hailed a carriage to see Margaret.

"Doctor Bell, how good to see you." Cookie hesitated. "I don't believe Mrs. Bishop is expecting you but do come in."

Margaret rushed down the stairs, "Papa, how wonderful to see you. Come to the garden."

"Tea will be out shortly." Cookie returned to the kitchen.

"How are you feeling?"

"Tired of being tired. Only four days until we can all sit together and I can hug my daughter." He looked across the flower beds. "My, oh my. You two have been busy girls."

"Sit on the bench, Papa. I'll get a kitchen chair for myself."

Cookie placed the tea, biscuits and jam on a second kitchen chair. "Mrs. Bishop, you need a small table for the garden. I'll have a look around the house for one." She nodded at William. "Have a nice visit."

"You have a first-rate housekeeper, my dear and she's right you need a table. I'll bring one from our garden later in the week."

"That's a good idea. I don't think Cookie will find a suitable one here." Margaret laughed then looked closely at her father. "I'm guessing you're here for more than tea and idle conversation."

He grinned. "You're always clever to catch onto things."

"You think I've made a big mistake in returning home?"

"I'm concerned. We should talk about the future and what might happen." He paused. "I'm assuming Thomas hasn't got a will. Am I correct?"

"I didn't see one in his papers."

"Shall I begin with what I know?"

"I do know this house is not mine, Papa."

"That's right and everything in it. You know that too?"

Margaret straightened in her chair. "That's not right." Her

voice grew louder. "The cedar chest is mine. You and Mama gave it to me. My silver service and ornaments are from Grand-mama and Grand-papa Bell. My wicker rocking chair was given to me by Mama's dear friend, Mary. My dolls are here too. The tiny tea set is in my china cabinet." She crossed her arms. "I won't let any of my things be taken." She lowered her voice. "What other things should I know?"

"If Thomas dies, I expect his property will be sold and the money will go to repay the money he has stolen. If he doesn't die but needs to be cared for, any remaining money could go toward his care."

Margaret stared fiercely at her father. "I won't look after him. I absolutely refuse. Period."

"I doubt you could do it alone any..."

Margaret cut through her father's words. "I won't do it at all. I mean it, Papa."

William slowly finished his tea, letting her anger settle. "Have you thought about where you will live when the house is gone?"

Margaret didn't respond. She closed her eyes and remained silent. Her silence gave William the answer.

"I've tried not to."

William glanced at his watch. "My carriage should be here soon. Time for me to return home, have lunch and a nap. Give some thought to my last question, my dear. I'll come Thursday afternoon with the table, if that's fine with you."

"Of course." She kissed his hand. "Before you go, I must tell you something. Thomas hired a man to spy on people but never paid him. Last week, the police arrested him for attempted robbery. Here."

"He broke in while you were with us?"

She nodded. "This should be the end of my Thomas problems, aside from dealing with him."

"You have so many worries, my dear girl." He kissed her hand. "You know you can always talk to me about anything."

"I know, Papa. And I love you for that."

In the front yard Margaret waved and called out, "Bye, bye, Papa." then watched until the carriage disappeared from her view. Finding a place to live was a far distant second compared with her fear of losing her much-loved father.

When Cookie left the house that evening for a visit with her sister, Margaret went into the study, picked up a pen and paper then walked into the dining room. Silver service set, three crystal vases, two petit point chairs, china cabinet. The list was two pages before she went up the stairs. Cedar chest, framed cross-stitch family crest, three quilted bedspreads. She returned to the study with a three-page list and sat at her desk. How on earth could she remove these articles and where on earth would she put them?

*　*　*

Margaret expected her monthly menstrual flow to begin during the next few days. As she was often irregular, she collected her flannel cloths and pinned one to her underpants.

After breakfast, she went to the garden and cut a few asters for the study and prepared for her meeting the next day. Anna's notes and questions were very helpful. Within the hour she was ready to meet the famous Anna Leonowens. She glanced at the flowers on her desk then spun her chair around. The room with its windows overlooking the side and back gardens was perfect.

During the following afternoon, Margaret spent a fascinating hour with the first president of the Halifax Suffrage Association. Anna was born in 1831 as Anna Edwards in India to British colonist parents. She arrived in Halifax in 1878 with her husband, general manager of the Bank of Nova Scotia. Anna was already a celebrity thanks to her travel, writing, lectures and as governess in the Court of Siam. She infused Margaret with her zeal for bettering the lot of women, especially in education and women's suffrage. Margaret left her first work assignment ignited about the possibilities for her new life.

The following day when William arrived with the garden table, Margaret was still gushing over Anna Leonowens and her efforts on behalf of women. William was delighted to see Margaret so happy and thankful for the possibilities in her future. He intended to tell Grace what he saw and heard, hoping she would feel reassured for Margaret and other women with the changes coming in the lives of women.

William chewed his sandwich with a grin on his face. "Cookie makes a tasty egg salad sandwich. What's in it?"

"Her secret ingredient, chopped apple, not onion."

"I'll have to tell Hazel." He lifted his cup. "Here's to tomorrow, the fourteenth day of my isolation. I'll be free. Can you come for dinner tomorrow?"

"I most certainly can but I might not be hungry. I'm having lunch here with Anna."

"No matter. I want you to come anyway." He reached for his pocket watch. "How long have I been here?"

"Two hours, perhaps."

"I better look for the carriage." He rushed to the gate. "It's here."

When Margaret caught up with him, William was catching his breath. "Darn old age."

He's forty-nine. "Bye, Papa. See you tomorrow for dinner."

* * *

Friday morning started with good news, Margaret started to spot overnight. Not much but it was a beginning. A companionable lunch and afternoon with Anna was just what she needed. The dining room table was set with a lace tablecloth, flowers, her best luncheon dishes and the silver tea service. Cookie had outdone herself with dainty sandwiches in assorted shapes and roly-poly jam pudding for dessert. When Anna arrived Cookie left the house, using a shopping trip as her reason to leave the young women alone.

After the garden tour and comfortably settled in the dining room, Anna was eager to hear all about the suffragette interview. "What's she like?"

"Well, she's older that I thought she would be. Aside from that, I rarely had to say a word. I had a difficult time keeping up with her comments! Did you know she helped create the School of Art and Design here? She had much to say about how women deserve a fairer chance in education, in everything really. Here are my notes. I'm sure you'll put together a good article."

"Did you enjoy the interview enough to do another?"

"I did. It was wonderful. I've been experiencing so many troubling days, it was a relief and pleasure to do something new." She sighed deeply and smiled.

"Very well. I'll arrange another for mid month. This one might take more work if the person isn't as fond of talking!" Anna helped herself to another sandwich and more tea. "I presume Thomas is the same."

Margaret nodded. "But I have a new complication. Apparently he owns everything, including my possessions so I have to take all my belongings out of here."

"Don't you think that's a little hasty?"

Margaret shrugged. "He could die tomorrow or wake up next week. Either way, he's not having my things." She paused. "Actually, I believe everything will be sold to pay off his crooked business debts. But nobody is selling my property. That's all there is to it." She smiled. "Now, about you. How is work at the paper?"

"I'm happy to say the bickering has subsided, at least for now." She laughed. "This dessert is delicious."

"Cookie is a treasure. I don't know what I would do without her."

"Let's hope you don't have to."

"Do you have to rush off somewhere else?"

"No. My afternoon is free."

"Come to the study. We'll have a glass of sherry in the middle of the day."

Anna stopped at the open study door. "What a beautiful room. Military quarters, even for officers isn't nearly as pleasant." She moved toward the desk. "Looks like you've made it your own, flowers, a book, writing paper. I understand why you don't want to leave."

Margaret poured the sherry. "Come to the window facing the back garden. What do you see?"

"Big trees."

"Yes, well there is that but look at the window ledge."

"Someone's damaged it."

"A burglar, while the house was empty. He was caught last week."

"Good heavens. Your life is filled with stories, not all are good of course. You should start writing a journal of your adventures."

"Nobody would be interested in my life."

"You might be surprised. People are naturally curious."

"And just plain nosy too. Let's sit and catch up on recent social events."

"George and I are attending a full-dress military dinner tomorrow evening."

"Sounds very fancy."

Anna nodded. "Gowns, medals, food, drinks and speeches."

"I missed the most recent orphanage fundraising committee meeting. What happened?"

While Anna explained the orphanage's needs, Margaret quickly finished her sherry and poured another. She turned to Anna. "Sherry?"

"No, thank you. I'm already warm and relaxed."

"Me too." Margaret took a big sip of sherry before asking, "Have you been to the orphanage?"

"Just inside the matron's office." Anna paused. "I'm not sure I could visit the children."

"Me neither." She sipped again. "Poor things" She began crying.

"What's the matter?"

"I don't know. I feel terribly sad, yet I feel silly." She hesitated a moment. "Isn't that silly too." She began laughing then hiccuped. "Pardon me. Good job Mama can't see me." She smoothed her dress, straightened in her chair. "I really like you, Anna. You're fun, have lots a ideas." She stared off into the distance trying to focus, blinked several times.

"I like you too, Margaret."

"I like Mama even though she is so darn straight-laced." She finished her second sherry. "And Robert, of course. He makes me feel special, very special. Loved." Margaret's mind caught up with her mouth. She stopped talking and looked in Anna's direction.

Anna filled the void. "Can I get you a glass of water?"

"That sounds delightful. Water would be delightful." She laughed. Her eyes wandered about the room.

Despite Margaret's squinting, Anna knew Margaret was not seeing straight. She had seen this before, many times. Some soldiers enjoyed the drinks at parties too much. George wasn't immune either. Margaret was more than a bit tiddly. "Here you are. Just sip."

"Thank you. Did I say something I shouldn't have about Robert?"

"You said you liked him."

Margaret opened her mouth to disagree but quickly shut it.

They sat in silence letting the warmth of their friendship banish the awkwardness of the earlier conversation, Margaret sipping her water and Anna, the remainder of her sherry.

Margaret looked at her watch. "I feel better, not so silly and sad."

"What time are you expecting Cookie to return?"

"Soon."

"I'll wait with you."

* * *

Margaret needed more than a little help to dress for dinner with her family. Cookie added extra lavender perfume to Margaret's undergarments plus a few dabs on her reticule. She would not have Margaret smelling of sherry, lovely though it might be.

During the carriage ride Margaret vowed never again to have two glasses of sherry during lunch.

William was visibly tired during dinner. Grace insisted on asking him how he felt every few minutes, completely negating any real conversation. James was unusually quiet, giving most of his attention to his food. Margaret struggled to bring up social topics but they died a quick death. Her niggling sherry headache didn't help. She looked forward to a good nights' sleep until she went to the bathroom. The spotting had stopped hours ago.

CHAPTER TWENTY-SEVEN

Early Saturday morning Cookie began gathering household linens and clothing to be washed first thing on Monday. She would have a head start on the usual Monday chores. With Margaret in the bath, she gathered Margaret's undergarments and several menstrual cloths. Downstairs she separated several cloths from the household items and dropped them into a small bucket of soapy water. Only three were lightly spotted.

Margaret put on a cheerful face and started her day. "Good morning, Cookie."

"Good morning. It's a lovely day. Do you have plans?"

Margaret took a deep breath. "I should go to the hospital but I'm tired. Maybe it's the hot days. I'll go after church tomorrow." She filled her tea cup. "Anna loved the roly-poly so much I told her to take the remainder home for George. I'll have to ask her if she actually gave him any!"

"How was the meeting with the suffragette woman?"

"Fascinating. She's travelled the world, done so many things. She's inspiring."

Margaret finished her tea and went for a walk in the neighbourhood. Children playing and mothers pushing prams were exactly what she was trying not to think about. Returning home, she picked up a book to read. When her book couldn't keep her attention, she opened the knitting basket and finished a scarf she'd begun in February.

Margaret's restless activities did not escape Cookie's notice. "Mrs. Bishop, would you like to visit Maisie with me this evening?"

"That sounds delightful. What shall we take?"

"Just ourselves. Maisie will have food and the board games ready."

* * *

William was warmly welcomed back to church. He offered his thanks along with a version of the truth. "As a family doctor, you never know what's going to happen on Sunday." Then he quickly entered the sanctuary.

William the man, husband, father and physician wasn't the least bit comfortable with lying. Seeing the troubled looks on the faces of his family, he asked himself if he truly was a truthful man. Didn't his family deserve to know the truth? But would his honesty be for them or a selfish act to assure himself of his family's love?

William looked at Margaret. She was staring toward the stained glass window, lost in thought.

James reached across his sister to pat his father's knee. "Feeling all right, Papa?"

William nodded. During the past week, he'd noticed James looking at him more carefully than usual. *Perhaps he's made his own diagnosis.*

After the service, Anna rushed toward Margaret. "Sorry for the last minute invitation. Can you come for tea after your hospital visit today?"

"Yes. But..."

"I'll tell you all about my idea then." And off she went, hurrying to catch up with George who was walking slowly with his hand out, ready to take hers.

Margaret felt a pang of jealousy. Anna's life was so perfect.

* * *

The family lunch surprised Margaret. The usual topics of Papa's health, James' keen interest in autopsies, Mama's volunteer efforts and her own newspaper work never came up. Weather, changes in the city and social events were boring but welcome. She was grateful for the mindlessness of it all. James' change of mood was gratifying. Maybe she was concerned for him over nothing. Overall, she listened more than spoke while bracing herself for the hospital, a necessary evil before the stimulation of another idea from Anna.

* * *

The hospital corridor left little room for walking. Visitors looked around, people asked directions, others offered help by pointing fingers. Children were full of questions.

Margaret lingered in the waiting area, not ready for the deathly quiet of Thomas' room. Then, taking a deep breath, she launched herself into the busy corridor only to bump into a young woman who was in the family way. She hesitated then stumbled over her words. "I'm, I'm sorry. Are you hurt?"

"Goodness, no. Are you feeling unwell yourself?" The young woman rested her hand on Margaret's arm.

Margaret shook her head and moved away unsteadily. Seeing the pregnant woman left her shaken. After a few moments, she moved quickly to the refuge of Thomas' silent room.

Finding Thomas unchanged, she carried the chair to the window and sat with her back to it. Her book failed to capture her attention. She gave up and closed her eyes. The afternoon sunlight warmed her body but offered no respite from her tangled thoughts. Until now, her well-ordered mind had given direction to her future plans. Today, it was failing her miserably. Was her body about to let her down too? She left the room without even a sideways glance toward the man in the bed.

* * *

"Come in, Margaret. Welcome to my army life. Please sit down."

Cramped was the first word that came to Margaret's mind. Anna's front room obviously served as the only room for visitors. Evidence of Anna's work was strewn over a low table set in front of a comfortable looking sofa, covered in multi-colour cotton chintz. The two side chairs were covered in matching solid colours. The front windows were covered with chintz curtains.

"This is so cozy." Margaret looked across the front hall into the dining room. A round table and four chairs with upholstered seats were in the centre of the room "You have a Boston fern in the dining room. I can see a few fronds."

"My father gave me money so I could buy one when I came to Canada."

"I like them too. I should buy one."

Anna jumped up. "Come upstairs before I explain my idea."

Margaret agreed but was totally baffled by what idea Anna might have in mind.

"This is a spare bedroom. It would have been the children's room, if we had any." A fleeting look of sadness passed across her face. "And it's empty."

"It's actually quite large." Margaret opened the curtains. "The window looks over the back garden."

"Let's go downstairs. I'll tell you my idea."

"Does George know about this idea?" Margaret waited to hear the answer. She suspected George might be in the dark as much as she was. "By the way, did he get any roly-poly?"

"The answer is 'yes' to both your questions. Come to the kitchen. I'll make a pot of tea and we can eat cookies and work on the details."

"Details of what?"

"Moving your things here." Anna poured the tea then outlined her plan, including who would help.

"You're offering to keep my possessions in your home? George has helpers?"

"If you have a better idea, speak up."

"What happens if you need the room for visitors, your parents, a relative?"

"I can't imagine anyone coming to visit. England is so far away and it's expensive to travel. We are posted as part of the British military. Our home is England and one day we will return there."

Margaret never thought about Anna leaving. "When will you leave?"

"It isn't our decision. But I don't think it'll be soon. Now, back to the spare room. I can't think of a better use than helping you, my dear friend."

Anna's words washed over Margaret. It was the breaking point in a string of days filled with doubt, worry, panic and every other nasty feeling she'd had in her life. All of the nasties were bottled up inside her. She buried her head in her hands and wept.

Anna sat in silence, allowing the stillness to enfold them. She knew all about life's overwhelming pain. She held Margaret through the tears, soggy handkerchiefs and unfinished sentences until there was nothing else to hear but deep sighs and stuttered breathing.

Margaret looked at Anna through bloodshot eyes. "Why did you keep quiet just now?"

"Words don't always help in the darkness. When you return to the light, words become powerful. When you're ready, we'll talk." She released Margaret from her embrace.

Margaret held a fresh cup of steaming tea, took a drink and began. "I'm angry Thomas might wake up. I don't want him to. I don't want to live with my parents forever." She dropped her eyes. "I'm frightened." She sipped the tea. "I might be pregnant." She forced herself to keep quiet about Robert. There would be a time for that, just not now. "How do you know about dark places?"

"After losing two babies, I put up a good front. I carried on as if nothing happened, that I could manage grief. Deep down, I was angry with myself for disappointing George, my family. I carried an impossible burden alone because I believed it was my problem and mine alone." She took Margaret's hand. "Lately, I've seen myself in you. Angry, distracted, pretending to be happy, in charge, too much sherry."

They both gave a short, suppressed laugh.

"How did you get out of your dark place?"

"My anger took control. I became someone even I didn't like. George distanced himself and my family reminded me of how I wasn't fun anymore. One day I lost all control, couldn't get out of bed, couldn't stop crying."

"What happened?"

"George asked questions. I told him how angry I was and why." Anna sighed deeply. "He rescued me. I can't imagine living without him."

"But my anger is different. It involves other people. I..."

Anna talked over her. "But you have no control over other people. If Thomas lives or dies is not up to you. If you're going to have a child, you're going to have a child."

Margaret interrupted. "It's not that easy, Anna. I understand what you are saying about Thomas. But if I'm with child, it won't go away. What will happen to me?"

"I'll help you. If Thomas dies, you're a widow with a child. If he lives and cannot help, you're still a mother who will need help."

Margaret made no effort to respond.

"Margaret."

"I wish it was that simple. I'm in love with Robert. If I am expecting a child, it's his."

CHAPTER
TWENTY-EIGHT

Margaret made the mistake of standing too close to Thomas' bed. He grabbed her arm and yelled, "Whore. It's not mine, is it?"

Margaret slapped him across the face with her free hand as Robert stepped inside the room and inched toward the bed.

Robert stretched out his arm. "Take my hand."

Enraged, Thomas grabbed her throat and screamed, "You'll rot in hell."

Margaret swung again. "Stop. Stop."

Cookie kept her distance from the bed. "Wake up, Mrs. Bishop. Wake up."

Margaret swung and hit the pillow again. "I hate you."

Cookie clapped her hands. "Mrs. Bishop, it's Cookie. Wake up, Mrs. Bishop. Wake up."

Margaret opened her eyes and stared toward the sound.

"You're at home, Mrs. Bishop. Take your time." Hearing no response, she continued. "You've had a bad dream."

Margaret sat up then began to shiver. She pulled the blanket to her face. "It was so real. Sit with me for a minute."

"Of course."

"Did I say anything out loud, mention any names?"

"You yelled a few angry words."

"I've never been frightened by a dream before." She fell back against the pillow.

"Would you like to take breakfast in bed before dressing?"

"No. Today's a new day. I have things to do and Papa's coming for a visit."

Cookie knew little about bad dreams. Perhaps Maisie could help. She seemed to get people to tell her the darndest things. She'd make time today to get smarter.

* * *

William Bell was skilled at getting people to talk about themselves but not so forthcoming about himself. Little wonder Margaret was uneasy about his visit. There were deeply personal things she needed to keep to herself for the time being.

"Hello, Papa."

"Hello, my dear." He held Margaret's hands in his while looking into her eyes. "You look tired, dear. You appeared distracted in church and at lunch yesterday. Is there something more than Thomas on your mind?"

"I have good news. I'm moving my possessions to Anna's spare room. I need to decide on a day."

"Are you moving as well?" He managed to keep the alarm from his voice.

"Good heavens, no." She frowned. "Why on earth would I do that?"

"Are you sure there isn't something else troubling you?"

Margaret admitted to a bit of recent tiredness then quickly added. "I don't always sleep well. Let's talk about something new. I'm going to see Mr. Fraser after you leave."

"Whatever for?"

"Detective Gilfoy suggested I speak with him regarding Thomas, to ask if Thomas needs a lawyer now that the embezzlement charge has been prepared. This is good news." She smiled.

"Samuel is a family friend but don't be concerned about meeting him as a lawyer. He's easy to speak with. You'll be fine."

"I'm sure I will. After all, it's the first step toward putting Thomas in jail. Let's have refreshments and speak of other pleasant things. Are you taking patients again?"

"Mornings only. I decided to spend more time in the garden with your mother this week. The flowers are in full bloom, apples are smelling so good. It's such a peaceful place filled with colour and aroma." He swirled the lemonade and smiled.

* * *

Samuel Fraser was standing beside his secretary's desk when Margaret entered his law office.

"Good afternoon, Margaret." He stepped toward her. "Would you like a tea before we begin? Perhaps lemonade?"

"No, thank you. Papa and I had refreshments earlier."

Samuel pointed toward his open office door. "Well then, let's go into my office." He followed Margaret into the sun-filled room, closing the door behind him.

The wall directly in front of Margaret had a large velvet-draped window overlooking the harbour. An office desk sat in front of the window, a gas light and telephone to one side. An arrangement of red roses in an etched crystal vase sat on the other. The calming scent of the flowers wafted through the room.

"Please have a seat." He pointed toward two large armchairs directly in front of the desk.

Margaret sat, her back straight, gloves in her hand. As Samuel moved behind his desk, she took the opportunity to look around the remainder of the room. On her right, a pendulum clock was centered on the wall. Two walnut work tables holding several stacks of papers sat underneath it. The opposite wall to her left was filled with books, most with embossed spines. She took a deep breath to settle herself and prepare for questions.

Samuel leaned forward and rested his hands on the desk. "After church yesterday you asked to speak with me about Thomas. How can I help you?"

"I presume you know Detective Gilfoy?" Margaret took another deep breath.

"Most certainly but how does he fit into this?"

"He suggested I ask if Thomas needed a lawyer. You see, I asked him that question when I was given legal papers called..." She hesitated, felt dim-witted. "Darn, I can't remember."

"The criminal charge against Thomas?"

"Yes. I apologize. I have a few worries." *Why did I say that!* She fussed with her gloves.

"I know this is a difficult time. Events in your life are uncertain and you have no control over them. The unknown can be quite frightening. I'm here to help but first, two questions. Do you want a lawyer for Thomas?"

Margaret felt Samuel's steady eyes on her own. "Me? Heavens, no!" She sounded callous, reminded herself to refrain from such churlish talk.

"That brings me to the second question. Do you think he needs a lawyer?"

She sat back in the chair. "He's in a coma. He'll be charged if he wakes up. What would a lawyer do for him now? He could go on like this for years." She began to cry.

Samuel left his chair to sit in an armchair beside her and took her hand. "Thank you for answering my questions. At the present time, your husband does not know if he needs a lawyer. I'll find a lawyer to take possession of the charge documents. You can let me know when Thomas' condition changes and then I'll pass the information on to his lawyer. Does that sound fine with you?"

Margaret nodded, prepared to stand up but Samuel did not release her hand.

"Regena and I know Robert has a deep affection for you. The coming months will be difficult. As you mentioned, Thomas' coma could continue for a considerable length of time. We want you to know you can come to us for help or advice, at any time. Promise me you will."

"I will, Mr. Fraser. You're very kind."

Samuel watched as Margaret held the hand rail and slowly descended the stairs to the first floor. He stood in the same spot for several minutes after her departure. He had not made the Fraser family's offer of support lightly.

* * *

"Well, that was a relief." Margaret removed her hat and sat on a kitchen chair.

"I gather the meeting with Mr. Fraser went well."

"He said he would find a lawyer for Thomas."

"That's good news. Perhaps you should have a rest before dinner."

An hour later, Cookie found her asleep in the study, feet on the footstool and a book on the floor. She hated to wake her but needs, must. "Mrs. Bishop, dinner is ready."

Margaret stood and immediately sat down. "Oh, my." She covered her mouth. "I feel a wee bit sick."

"Did you eat something while you were out this afternoon?"

Margaret shook her head.

"Sit quietly for a few minutes, it'll pass. I'll get a bowl, just in case."

When Cookie returned, Margaret was standing "It went away quickly. I'm fine now. Too many worries, I guess."

After clearing the dinner dishes and preparing for the next day's breakfast, Cookie found Margaret in the study. It was the ideal time to talk about bad dreams.

"Mrs. Bishop, it's past my bedtime. I'm surprised you're still up. You've had a full day."

"I had a nap this afternoon." She patted the sofa. "I need a funny story."

Cookie sat down, unsure how to begin.

"Is there something wrong?"

"No, it's just that I went to see Maisie while you were with Mr. Fraser."

"There's nothing wrong with that. You're not a prisoner here."

"I wanted to ask her about bad dreams. I hope you don't mind."

"And did Maisie know anything?"

"Well, Maisie told me a story about our sister-in-law, Addie. Last month, Addie's parents and a younger brother came to visit for two days. They kept makin' excuses about leaving. Nothin' but a pile of trouble, they were. Ate them out of house and home, tried to bamboozle them out of money. After a few days, Addie began to have bad dreams, waking up in a lather of sweat, cryin', frightened. Her husband Fishy went to the doctor."

Margaret laughed. "Fishy?"

"He's a fisherman. His name's Orville. The doctor told Fishy to get Addie talkin' to him about the dreams, who was in them and what she might be afraid of in them. Then he asked Fishy to do somethin' to cheer her up, get her mind off things. Fishy went home, listened to Addie's bad dreams about the relatives tryin' to steal their home. That very day, he sent the bad apple relatives packin'." She patted Margaret's hand. "I'm thinkin' you're dreamin' about somethin' scary too." She looked into Margaret's eyes. "And I'm guessin' you'd feel better if you talk to someone about your bad dream."

Margaret was not ready to tell anyone about the bad dream. "Thank you, Cookie. Let's see if it happens again."

* * *

After lunch on Friday Margaret took a carriage to Anna's newspaper office, hoping she was free to talk. Sitting on a bench at the harbour, she took Anna's hand. "I'm going to have a baby."

"I'll come to see you tomorrow, after breakfast. In the meantime, I think Cookie needs to know." She embraced Margaret. "We'll get through this together."

CHAPTER TWENTY-NINE

Getting out of bed would change the course of Margaret's life. It meant telling Cookie she was expecting a child. If Cookie decided to leave, she would be forced to return to her parent's home. She glanced at the clock. Anna would arrive soon.

"Good morning, Mrs. Bishop. I'm glad to see you stayed in bed to rest. Any bad dreams?"

"No. I thought about something happy before I fell asleep. It worked this time."

"What would you like for breakfast?"

"Tea and toast with jam is lovely. Mrs. Hopkins will be here soon. I will invite her to stay for lunch but don't make anything fancy. Your egg salad sandwiches would be perfect."

After Cookie poured the tea, Margaret asked her to sit at the table. "I have to ask you a question. When you answer, I want you to do what is best for you not me, agreed?"

"I never agree to anything before I hear what things are all about, Mrs. Bishop."

Margaret shifted in her chair, took another sip of tea. "I'm expecting a child."

"This is happy news, Mrs. Bishop. And pardon me for being so forward but I thought as much."

"Thank you." She faltered. "Will you be able to stay and help me?"

"And why wouldn't I, my dear?"

"Well, my circumstances are uncertain."

"Now you never mind about that. Your health is the most important thing. Don't be worrying over Mr. Bishop. What will happen with him will happen anyway, child or no child. Finish your breakfast and I'll boil the eggs for sandwiches." She turned to the stove. "I bet your parents are pleased."

"I haven't told them. Only you and Anna know."

Cookie almost dropped the eggs. She'd never heard of a cook being one of the first to be told when a society lady was expecting a child.

* * *

Anna's arrival was the usual sparkle and bounce of someone embracing life. Margaret could hear her from the front door. "Good morning, Mrs. Gilmore."

"Come in, Mrs. Hopkins. Mrs. Bishop is in the study. A cup of tea?"

"Sounds brilliant."

"I'll bring a fresh pot."

As Cookie approached the study with the tea, Anna was finishing a sentence. "...so you have to tell him." Cookie placed the teapot and two cups on the small round table Margaret had moved from the sitting room. She took a few steps down the hall, away from the study then muttered, "The bloody man's in a coma. Why on earth would Margaret tell him about the baby? That young Anna is silly."

With Cookie gone, Anna spoke. "I gather Cookie's staying?"

"She is. She assumes Thomas is the father."

"And so she should. Speaking again of Robert, you do have to tell him. When is he coming to the city?"

"Next Friday."

"So you should tell him next week or next month. After that, you'll be putting on weight."

Margaret rubbed her forehead. "What a muddle I've made."

"There are two people in this muddle, my friend."

"Yes, but men always get the easy way out."

"From what you've told me, Robert is not one of those men." She pressed on. "So between now and Friday you need to make a decision about telling Robert. But for now, let's work on the what we can do. Is Monday a good day to move your personal items?"

"Yes. What can I do?"

"Put the small items on the dining room table, dishes, silver that sort of thing. Leave your hope chest and other large items where they are. George will bring a few of his men and the boxes from the army storeroom along with a wagon and blankets to cover the furniture. By the way, they'll come about three o'clock. Next is your interview. Can you meet with someone Tuesday, early afternoon?"

Margaret was swept along with Anna's words. "Yes. Who am I interviewing?"

"I have two people in mind and will have an answer by Monday morning."

"Sounds like a mystery. I'm curious."

Anna grinned. "Now back to your pregnancy. I imagine you've been thinking about telling your family."

Margaret sighed deeply. "It's barely left my mind."

"You could wait a while but I don't know what advantage there is in doing so."

"Should I tell them without mentioning Robert, treat them like Cookie?"

Anna's eyes flew open. "Are you really expecting me to answer that question?"

"No. But I don't know the answer myself." There was a heavy silence while Margaret argued with herself.

"Ladies, lunch is ready."

* * *

A growing discomfort got the better of Margaret during the

Sunday church service. The pew felt tight but of course it wasn't. It was her own unease about what was to come when she followed through with her overnight decision. When the final hymn was finished, she could hardly wait to get out of the sanctuary.

As usual, a large carriage waited on the street for the Bell family to emerge from St. George's. Except for another morgue story from James, the ride was quiet.

At the lunch table, all eyes were on Margaret after her announcement. She made no mention of Thomas. "I know it is startling news. I understand if you're not pleased."

William frowned. "It's not that we are unhappy for you. I for one, am surprised."

"Congratulations, Margaret. I have no idea what a brother does in this situation but I'm ready to help. Tell me what to do."

"Your circumstances are greatly changed, dear. It's best you come home. Hazel and I can look after you."

"The baby's not due for months. It's too soon to even consider moving anywhere. Speaking of moving, my personal belongings will be moved to Anna's spare room tomorrow."

Grace straightened in her chair. "Your things are going to Anna's?"

"Yes, I intend to keep my personal items away from Thomas, in case he wakes up."

"But you're going to have a child, dear. You cannot be taking your things from the house."

"Are you saying you want me to raise a child with that man, Mama?" She silenced the room. "Speaking of that man, I should make an appearance at the hospital. Thank you for lunch."

As she stood, Margaret looked at her mother. "Papa has been to visit, perhaps you and James could come one day later this week. We could sit in the garden, have tea." She moved around the table kissed everyone goodbye and left.

William rose and followed Margaret out the front door. "I love you, my dear girl." He kissed her on the cheek and held her hand until a carriage was in sight. "I'll come for another visit in the morning."

* * *

"Who could that be so early in the morning?" Cookie rushed to the front door.

"Good morning, Mrs. Gilmore. I'm here to see Margaret."

"Come in, Doctor Bell. She's having breakfast." *She's told them.* "Pardon me, I have a few things to do upstairs."

"Papa!" Margaret stood to embrace her father. "Sit with me."

"I'm here to apologize." He kissed Margaret then took a cup from the cupboard and poured himself tea before sitting. "You gave us quite the surprise yesterday and James was the only one who acted appropriately. Congratulations, my dear girl."

"Thank you, Papa."

"Anything else besides that little bit of nausea you mentioned?"

"Tiredness." She twirled her fork in the poached egg.

He frowned. "You may have to raise this child without a father. That's not going to be easy."

"I know." She pushed the breakfast plate away, pulled her cup closer.

"Well, it's one thing to know something and another to live it. Keep that in mind, dear."

"I will. I don't want him near this child, ever."

"I understand."

* * *

Not long after lunch, the doorbell rang. "Good gracious, another visitor. It feels like a railway station." Cookie hurried toward the door. "Mrs. Hopkins!"

"I know, it's me again. Two days in a row. Maybe I should move in!"

Move in? I think not. "Mrs. Bishop is resting. I'll go upstairs for her."

Through the open door, Anna could see the dining room

table. It was covered with Margaret's personal treasures. She was tempted to go in and admire the beautiful things but this was part of Margaret's life on display, ready to be taken away. Tears came to her eyes.

Margaret came down the stairs slowly, her hand sliding along the oak railing. "Anna! Did I misunderstand something?"

"Sorry to interrupt your rest. I have news of the interview."

As they entered the study Margaret spoke. "I am more tired than I imagined. It's best you do the interview tomorrow." She closed the door.

"That's part of why I'm here but first, what happened with the pregnancy news on Sunday?"

"Everyone was surprised. They presumed it's Thomas' child and I didn't tell them otherwise."

"I think that's best for a while. Now, about the interview. You can interview me tomorrow! I'm going to tell the story of a military family moving to Halifax. I think readers will find it interesting. Now, I must go and let you rest."

Margaret began to cry.

Anna hugged her tightly. "What's happened?"

"James was the only one who seemed happy for me. Papa came yesterday to apologize for his response. I feel such a fraud."

CHAPTER THIRTY

Margaret descended the stairs and walked through the main floor of her home. Her footfalls on the wood floor echoed down the hallway. The rooms were hollow, stripped of her personal touch. Furniture from her grandparents, special dishes, silverware, crystal, photos and wall hangings, all gone to Anna's. She'd left the study untouched. Her books, writing paper, pen and flowers a proud display of Thomas' banishment from her life. She took deep pleasure in looking at the room and sitting in it.

"Breakfast is ready, Mrs. Bishop."

"The downstairs sounds so unfriendly, as if it's annoyed with us."

"But the kitchen is still homey." She placed Margaret's plate on the table. "Will you be leaving the upstairs as is?"

"Yes. The upstairs furniture was put in the house by Thomas. What he purchased means nothing to me."

Cookie busied herself at the stove, an excuse to avoid further conversation on the subject of Thomas.

"Mrs. Hopkins will be here for an interview after lunch. Also, it's been weeks since my mother and James visited me. I expect they will this week. Can you make sure we have some sweets for the next few days?"

"I enjoy making sweets so I'll start the planning right after breakfast. Did you sleep well?"

"I did. Thomas can't get my personal things now."

* * *

For more than a year Robert returned to Halifax once a month, arriving early Friday and leaving late Sunday. His telegram baffled his parents.

Will arrive Saturday am STOP Too much news for a telegram STOP Robert

* * *

After lunch Anna breezed through the door, smiling broadly toward Cookie. "Good afternoon, Mrs. Gilmore."

Cookie nodded. "Mrs. Hopkins."

Margaret called out. "Come down the hall, Anna. I'm in the study."

"Feeling well today?"

"So far. I slept well." She waited until Anna removed her hat and was seated. "This isn't just about my move to Halifax. It will also be a suffragette story, about the disenfranchisement of women. Do you know that women here lost the right to vote forty-four years ago? They'd already had it until the word 'male' was added to the voting rules in eighteen fifty-one. Can you believe it? It's plain wrong!"

"Drink some lemonade. You're far too excited for me at the moment."

They were both silent for a few minutes then Margaret asked, "Why all the excitement about suffragettes today?"

"I met someone from the Suffragette Association who is keen on getting women's voting rights back and women holding political office."

"So if you have the information you need, why are you here?"

"Because I want you to listen to the plans the Association gave me and help me make it a story both men and women would want to read. And I'll add your name to mine. I want it on the front page of the newspaper!"

"A picture would help. Readers like them."

"Now you understand why I want you to work with me."

"Let's begin."

* * *

Cookie needed her worry about Anna answered. Over dinner, she went straight to her concern. "Mrs. Hopkins seems to be a busy young woman."

"Far too busy for me, especially now."

"Does she have a lot of friends who are also busy?"

"No. I believe I'm the only one. Her husband is with the British army and she works for the newspaper."

"Children?"

"Sadly, no." Margaret sat back in her chair. "Cookie, I believe I know what you're trying to ask. You're concerned about me and I'm grateful. Your good advice about friends so many months ago helped me be a friend to Anna and she in turn, is a friend to me. She is naturally more spontaneous than I but her heart is kind and her feelings genuine. Her life has not always been easy. I'm going to need her in my life in the coming months. I hope you can see her in the same way I do."

"I trust your judgment, my dear. Mrs. Hopkins has passed the test." Cookie reached out and squeezed Margaret's hand.

* * *

Cookie was surprised when she met James at the door early the following morning. She glanced at the waiting carriage. "Your mother isn't with you?"

"Oh, Mrs. Gilmore, I have the most dreadful news. Papa has passed away." His eyes overflowed with tears. "I've come to take Margaret home with me."

"She's in the study. I'll go with you."

Margaret stood as James entered the room. "Mama didn't

come?" She looked toward the doorway, saw Cookie and dropped into her chair. "Something's wrong isn't it?"

James moved to her chair and fell to his knees. "Papa's gone, Margaret." As the sobs began, he held her close in his arms.

Cookie quietly left the room, her own eyes overflowing. Upstairs she packed undergarments, nightgowns, hairpins, handkerchiefs and black gloves in a small bag. She searched for a black mourning dress among Margaret's day dresses and gowns but found none. Then she realized Margaret would have been much younger when her grandparents died. She did not pack any day dresses as Margaret would be wearing black for weeks, if not months. She did find a veiled black hat along with a beaded, black lace shawl which she carried over her arm down the stairs. *These two things will have to do for the carriage ride.* On the way through the kitchen, she pulled several handkerchiefs from the clean laundry basket. Folding them would give her something to do as James comforted his sister in preparation to leave the house and endure an unspeakably sorrowful ride to her family home.

* * *

The grandfather clock played a short melody then chimed ten times as James took Margaret into the sitting room. She recalled its first chime on a Christmas Eve afternoon years before. Two burly men patiently held the clock while her father struggled with its best placement in the front hall. When the clock was hung and it played a tune and chimed, everyone clapped. The memory of Papa and the men toasting the clock and Christmas would be forever etched in her mind. Margaret rushed to her mother. "Oh, Mama, how will we live without him?"

Gracie kissed Margaret cheeks. "Shush now, my darling. We must buck up. Hazel has a black dress on your bed. She'll help you get ready." She patted Margaret's hand and sent her on her way.

Margaret turned around. "Where's Papa?"

"He'll be home soon. It's best you change now. People will be arriving soon."

James paced the garden paths with a glass of scotch in his hand while Margaret was upstairs and his mother sat stoically in the drawing room. Deep in his heart he'd sensed Papa's tuberculosis was a ruse to keep his family in the dark. His own medical training pointed to a heart condition, yet he kept silent. He asked himself what kind of doctor would he be to do such a thing. He wasn't worthy to be a physician.

As Margaret descended the stairs, four men carried a black cloth-covered coffin through the front door. Her stomach dropped at the thought of her father in a box. Her eyes watered then she dropped onto the step. She was still sitting there when James came in from the garden. He took her hand and together they walked toward their father's coffin. After a few minutes they stepped away and sat on either side of their mother.

Hazel came into the room. "Mrs. Bell, the vicar from St George's is here."

"Good afternoon, Grace, James, Margaret. Please accept my deepest personal condolences to you all. William was an upstanding husband, father and physician. Our church community will sorely miss him.

"Thank you." Grace's voice was barely audible.

The vicar made the sign of the cross in front of the casket, uttered a short prayer over the body then turned to the family. "Shall we pray." When he finished, he spoke again. "I will return tomorrow evening to spend more time with you and complete the funeral service details. If you have scripture readings and hymns you would like for the service, let me know then." As he grasped each hand he whispered, "God bless."

Seeing the vicar leave, those waiting outside began a slow, steady walk to view the body then express their condolences to the family, beginning with Grace.

Margaret stood stoically. She thanked those who passed in front of her without truly seeing them until Anna and George stood before her. They were her undoing. She lost her composure and tears flowed. Unable to stand any longer, she stepped backward and sat in the armchair. Anna moved behind her chair as George moved along to speak with Grace and James, before leaving the room.

Anna leaned toward Margaret's ear. "Close your eyes, take a few deep breaths and stand when you're ready. You don't want to faint. I'm leaving the room now."

Before Margaret was ready to stand, Samuel and Regena Fraser stepped into the room causing Margaret's thoughts to race wildly from her father to her baby and Robert. When they moved on, she couldn't recall what they or she said.

Margaret did not expect to see Detective Gilfoy and Constable Henderson in the seemingly endless line of people. At first she assumed they were present simply because it was a duty call. Her opinion changed completely when both of them spoke comforting words of sympathy and Gilfoy recounted a fainting episode in the station when her father helped revive a robbery suspect. Gilfoy was able to contain his composure. Henderson tried but was utterly unsuccessful.

As the late afternoon wore on into early evening, the neighbours and close family friends who arrived to pay their respects lingered to reminisce, filling the main floor. Hazel had prepared several plates of small sandwiches and sweets which were on the dining room table. She made repeated trips with pots of tea but was becoming worried about what would happen in the evening. It would be an embarrassment to the family if she failed to take care of their guests. She was so anxious she jumped when someone knocked on the kitchen door.

"Hello, Hazel. Would you like some help?" Cookie and Maisie stood on the step holding several baskets of food.

"You two are a godsend. I was getting worried."

Cookie took charge. "You and Maisie can refill the empty plates. There are more baskets in the carriage. I'll get them."

* * *

James bid the last visitor farewell after nine o'clock then

returned to the sitting room and asked his mother and sister if they wanted something to eat. "Hazel set aside a few sandwiches and sweets for us. I, for one, am hungry."

"Make up a plate for me and a cup of tea, James. I'm staying with your father until he's gone from us forever."

"I'll sit with you in the kitchen, James."

Cookie was anxious to see Margaret but it was not proper for her to be seen in the sitting room, especially without a black dress. Hazel wore one so she could move in and out of all the rooms as needed.

When Margaret and James came into the kitchen, Cookie almost fell to her knees in thanks.

Margaret ran to her and took hold of her hands. "What are you doing here?"

"Your father was a fine man, cared for by so many people. We wanted to help Hazel and your family. How are the both of you?"

James spoke up. "It's difficult. Thank you both for coming." He was overcome with the reality that his father would never speak on behalf of the family again. That weight had come to rest on him. He took a handkerchief from his pocket and wiped his eyes.

Cookie did not dare stay inside a moment longer. She picked up a few baskets and walked to the kitchen door. "Rest well and we'll be here to help tomorrow." Her hanky was in her hand before the door closed behind her.

James and Margaret ate in silence each lost in their own thoughts until James spoke. "His death was a pleasant one."

"What do you mean?"

"I spoke with him shortly after breakfast. He was taking a cup of tea to the garden. I said I'd get a book and join him. He talked about the flowers and how the garden was his favourite place, even in the winter. A few minutes later he spoke of a tightness in his chest then he took a deep breath and drifted away, leaning against me on the bench. I felt his pulse and he was gone."

Margaret spent the dark hours of the night staring out her

bedroom window. From the downstairs, she heard sobs and her mother calling her father's name. In the quiet moments, she considered why her mother was such a firm woman, not often showing her gentler nature. Near dawn she came to understand more completely the immense pressure society placed on women to conform to its rigid expectations. That pressure had taken away her mother's freedom to fully share herself with others, especially her family. What a loss, one she was not going to repeat herself. She felt a great sadness for her mother.

* * *

Many people came to the Bell home the following day, most arriving late afternoon. Throughout the day, James and Margaret sat with Grace. Few words were spoken as Grace was in another world, one she refused to leave. When she left the room to refresh herself, she asked James or Margaret to take her place saying, I don't want him to be left alone. Hazel brought her meals on a small tray. And for a second night, she stayed with William.

The next morning, a horse-drawn carriage would carry William's body to St. George's Round Church for a service then interment in the church cemetery.

CHAPTER THIRTY-ONE

Following an early Saturday morning meeting at the bank, Robert walked into his parent's home and found it empty. Ruby, the housekeeper would be shopping but his mother was always home to greet him. Thinking she was in the garden, he dropped his suitcase at the bottom of the stairs and walked into the kitchen. A note addressed to him leaned against a bowl of apples.

Dear Robert,
William Bell passed away suddenly on Wednesday. The funeral is this morning. Ten o'clock at St. Georges.
Mother

St. George's Church was over flowing with mourners. Robert was prepared to stand outside but never expected to be standing in the cemetery alongside a few dozen others, steps away from the open grave. It unnerved him. His parents were Doctor Bells age. He averted his eyes then moved back several paces to stand under the dappled shade of a towering oak where the open grave was no longer visible. His new spot also afforded a clearer view of the path from the church steps toward the grave-site. His thoughts returned to Doctor Bell's life, how his death would change the family. James would become head of the family, his responsibilities multiplied, including the care of his mother. Margaret would be adrift without her father's steady advice and unwavering support. The man was always unruffled, firm in his beliefs yet open to acknowledge and consider the views of others.

Deep in thought, Robert was slow to realize all quiet conversation around him had ceased. A cough from an older gentleman standing some ten feet away brought him back to the present. William Bell's final journey had begun.

Church officiants lead the procession. The casket, carried by six sturdy men was followed by Grace, James and Margaret. An untold number of mourners accompanied the Bell family to William's final resting place.

Margaret and her mother were shielded from both the curious and caring by their heavy black veils. As they passed in front of Robert, he reached into his pocket for his handkerchief. A dried sweet pea blossom dropped to the ground. It was a memory from the August afternoon his relationship with Margaret changed forever. He rescued it and returned it to his pocket.

* * *

Regena took off her hat and gloves leaving them on the hall table before she noticed Robert in the sitting room. "Hello, dear. I thought you'd be back at the bank by now. Something happen?"

"No, I'm taking time away from work."

"So, you're staying for a few days?"

"For a week."

She sat in an armchair beside Robert and leaned toward him. "Is something wrong?"

"No, not with the bank. I haven't had much time away from work since February and summer is a good time to be in Halifax, spend time with family and friends."

"Be honest with me. Is this about Margaret?"

"In part." He changed the topic. "The bank is talking about

sending me back here to open a new department." He lowered his head, stared at his clasped hands. "I knew Doctor Bell all my life. I liked him." He shook his head. "I can't imagine what James feels like. He hasn't even finished his schooling. Now he has responsibility for the family. Perhaps we can get together later this week." He looked at his mother. "Is Papa in the office?"

"Yes. Are you going to see him?"

Robert nodded.

"Lunch first?"

"I ate an apple." He wandered off toward the front door.

* * *

After three days of being buoyed up and carried along by conversations with mourners followed by sleepless nights, the Bell family came home to a silent house. William's absence was painfully real. The hall clock ticked, his garden hat hung on a peg at the back door, his favourite garden bench sat empty, the blossoms he enjoyed spread fragrance through the air. The loss was crushing.

While the family was at the service, Hazel cleaned and rearranged the sitting room and set out lunch, doing her best to help them return to normal.

"Hello, everyone. Sandwiches, desserts and tea are in the dining room. I expect everyone needs to rest. Dinner will be ready at the usual hour. If you need anything, I'll be in my room." She rushed to her room, laid down on the bed and sobbed until she had no tears left.

The family lunch was silent, each of them remembering the morning filled with emotion and wondering what was to come. Margaret needed to see Robert. Their child's future was at stake. Grace wanted Margaret to remain in her family home. James pondered a new future. None of them were able to openly share their private thoughts and needs. The grief was too raw.

After lunch, Margaret removed the heavy black dress and

crawled under the covers. Her tears had dried up but a crushing ache pressed on her heart.

* * *

"Mr. Fraser, your son is here to see you."

"What a great surprise, son. I didn't expect to see you until dinner."

"That would be the usual, Papa but I'm home for a week."

"A week? That's lovely. Maybe we can get on the water, do a bit of sailing?"

"Sounds like a fine idea." Robert hesitated, struggling with how to begin.

"Well, have a seat." Samuel searched Robert's face. "What's on your mind that couldn't wait a few hours?"

"Ah, a direct opening question from the lawyer." Then he laughed. "But before you ask a question about your question, the answer is yes. I have a couple of things on my mind." He settled into the arm chair. "How are you feeling?"

Samuel smiled then leaned over the desk. "This is because of William, isn't it?"

"Well, it certainly got me to thinking. I'm in Montreal, see you for a few hours once a month."

"To answer your question, I'm well and plan to stay that way." He paused a moment. "I'm going to miss William very much. We were dear friends for years. It's not easy to lose someone close to you." He hesitated then carried on. "Now, what's the other thing on your mind?"

"Margaret."

"You have a question about Margaret?"

"What's going to happen to her?"

"I'm afraid you'll need to see someone who reads tea leaves about that!"

"Seriously, can she leave Thomas? What about the house?"

"Here's my best answer. Margaret could abandon Thomas and start divorce proceedings. The law would consider her action acceptable. However, society's response to what people do is entirely different. If she commences divorce proceedings, she will be the talk of Halifax. She and her mother will be shunned socially. The house is a different matter. It's considered Thomas' property."

"So, she'll have to return home?"

"That's debatable while Thomas is still in a coma. But I imagine her mother expects her to return home now."

"I'm sure Margaret won't have any part of that."

"You sound pretty familiar with Margaret's opinion. How did you come about this information and more importantly, why are you so involved?"

"We've spoken on several occasions." Robert's eyes belied his confident posture.

Samuel nodded but was not prepared to field additional questions. "I think we better leave this for dinner. Agreed?"

Robert nodded, knowing he was about to take a path with no return. He felt relieved and in a way, happy. He and Margaret could begin thinking about their future.

Samuel continued. "I'm sure your mother and I will be happy to gain an understanding of your relationship with Margaret. In the meantime, I'm preparing to read William's will to the family on Monday. If you can entertain yourself with a law book or a conversation with my secretary for about fifteen minutes, we can walk home together."

"I'll talk to Miss Compton."

During the walk home, Samuel and Robert walked in easygoing silence until Samuel brought up the subject of Margaret. "I spoke with Margaret in the office about ten days ago."

"How did she seem?"

"Tentative, distracted. I told her we would be supportive of her during this troubling time with Thomas. I included you." He stopped and looked at Robert. "With William's death, everything is changed for her."

"I feel a strong connection to Margaret, Papa. I'll help take care of her."

Robert's answer fed Samuel's already deep concern. "Be careful. All manner of difficulties can arise from those types of feelings." He reached for a possible reprieve from his worry. "Perhaps your work in Montreal will help this connection pass."

Robert shook his head. "There's serious discussion about moving me back to Halifax to open a new bank department."

"Sounds like congratulations might be in order." He patted Robert on the back and asked when this might happen.

"Soon."

Samuel continued walking.

* * *

Regena Fraser didn't question the unusually quiet start to the family dinner. It never crossed her mind to consider her husband and Robert would be thinking of something other than the Bell family's grief.

Samuel broke her reverie. "Robert and I had a brief discussion about Margaret on our walk home. He's agreed to talk with us about what he describes as a strong connection with Margaret."

Without damaging Margaret's reputation Robert told his parents about the lunches and conversations he and Margaret shared since the anniversary party. "We realize our friendship is more than that. We love each other and want to be together."

Samuel sighed heavily and looked down at his hands. He ran his thumbs around each other. Regena collapsed onto the back of her chair and closed her eyes.

As Robert expected, the room was charged with emotion but no words came from either of his parents. He waited.

Regena began. "Has Margaret told her family? Who else knows?"

Then Samuel. "Margaret's married. How can this possibly work?"

When silence returned, Robert spoke. "Margaret's family does not know. She has spoken to me about divorcing Thomas." He glanced at his father. "We know this is going to be difficult but nothing will happen right away." He took a deep breath. "I'm pretty sure the bank is going to move me back here so that will make things easier."

Regena dropped her head into her hands. "This will be such a scandal for Margaret."

"Margaret and I know there will be gossip, especially as Thomas is still alive but we want to be together. We are not going to hide."

"Okay, son. Sounds like there is no turning back now. You two have made a decision."

"Thank you, Papa. Mother."

CHAPTER THIRTY-TWO

Grace Bell was expected to wear black every day for at least two years, regardless of the season. She came to the breakfast table on Sunday morning wearing a plain black dress, hair unadorned. Her only jewellery was a mourning ring with a jet stone in memory of William.

James was momentarily distracted by his mother's pale complexion. "Good morning, Mama. Would you like to attend church today?"

Grace shook her head and ate a mouthful of egg then moved the remainder to the side of the plate.

When Margaret appeared James frowned, shook his head in her direction.

Margaret kept her greeting brief. "Morning, Mama."

"Morning." In a voice slightly above a whisper, Grace continued. "Hazel is going to the dressmaker tomorrow. I've asked her to order three black dresses for each of us. Two of yours will be a simple pattern, adjustable for your condition. Do you want another veil?"

"Yes. The weather is much too warm for the one I wore at the funeral. Thank you, Mama."

James and Margaret ate in silence until Grace left and closed the door to the garden.

Margaret put her cup down and looked at James. "She ate like a mouse, same as yesterday! She's not sleeping either. I've heard her walking through the house late into the night."

"Give her a few days." James reached for the toast rack. "Pass the jam, please. By the way, you must be awake if you can hear Mama walking around during the night. How are you?"

"Fine. The nausea has truly begun, only mornings so far. I've told Hazel so she understands what is happening." She finished her egg. "What will we do if Mama doesn't improve?"

"She will, be patient. And you, dear sister, don't add another worry to your own list."

"Is that the doctor or brother talking?" Hearing no reply, she asked another question. "How's the gambling group?"

"Grand, actually. Our meetings and occasional planned activities together are working for me. I can't speak for the others." He took a big drink of tea. "So I imagine you'll be staying here now."

"Why would you assume that, my dear brother? You're here for Mama and I have a home." She finished her toast.

"I thought you would stay with Mama, especially in your condition."

"No, no. I'll be fine. In fact, I intend to return home in a few days." She finished her tea. "I can visit Mama any day." She stood up. "That reminds me, I should go to the hospital this afternoon." She meant to slip the idea past James and leave the room but he was too quick for her.

"Wait a moment. Is that something you should do?"

Margaret shrugged. "Maybe. In the meantime, I'm going to lie down."

"Don't forget, Samuel is here to read the will tomorrow at eleven."

* * *

Margaret needed to talk to Robert about the baby. She'd tell Mama she was going to the hospital but take a carriage to the Fraser's home. Socializing while in mourning was absolutely unheard off but she'd made up a question for Samuel about Thomas. It would sound far-fetched and she'd look the fool but what choice did she have? When Hazel knocked on the bedroom door, she quickly lay down.

"Come in."

"I have a message for you."

"Is someone waiting for a response?" Margaret opened the envelope.

"No." Hazel left the room without another word. *Who would have such unmitigated gall to disturb a home in mourning?*

My Dearest Margaret,
I must speak with you this morning. Please meet me at your home at eleven o'clock. I'll be in the garden.
        Love, Robert

She put on her black veiled hat then looked for her mother, to say she was going to see Thomas. When she found Grace sound asleep, she waved down a carriage before anyone could miss her.

* * *

At the house, Margaret waited until her carriage was out of sight then opened the side gate to the garden. Robert was pacing back and forth in front of the kitchen door. When she saw him, she was overcome and rushed toward him.

He held her close until she stopped crying then stepped back a half step. "I'm so sorry about your father." He moved the chairs so they sat opposite each other, holding hands. He noticed dark circles under her eyes.

They were both silent for a few moments then Margaret spoke. "I shouldn't have come but I need to see you. Why did you ask me to come here?"

"Your life has been uprooted. I should be here with you. I promised."

Margaret stood up and took the house key from her reticule. "I think we should go inside. Your note said you must see me. I expect it's not something anyone should overhear. "As she turned the key in the lock, she turned to Robert. "I have something to tell you, too."

Robert looked at her more closely, trying to read her face. She turned away before he could come to an opinion.

"We'll go to the study. It's the most comfortable. Before you ask, I've moved my personal possessions out."

"To your mother's home?" He hoped not. If so, she had already accepted her fate.

"Now you're being silly. I won't be staying with Mama. Anna and George Hopkins have my things." Robert looked puzzled. "Anna is my dear friend."

"I know it's only a few days but how are you faring with your mother and James?"

"Mama hasn't said so in so many words, but I know she expects me to remain with her. I'll stay for a few more days." She squeezed Robert's hand. "I know I sound unfeeling but I need to find my own way through all of this. I can't fall into the old ways." She pointed to an armchair for Robert and sat in one herself.

"And James?"

"Not himself, pensive, more quiet than usual. I imagine he's feeling the new burden."

Silence settled over them again. Margaret was on edge, not knowing what she was about to hear.

Robert broke the silence. "You're not finding your way alone. I will help."

Margaret nodded. "I know." She'd let him speak first. Her words would change his world. "What's the something you need to tell me?"

"My parents know about us."

Margaret jumped up, began pacing. "How?"

"I told them."

"You told them! Whatever for? You told them then leave for Montreal?"

"You'll understand when I tell you why I made the decision."

"I certainly hope so." Margaret returned to her chair, began rocking back and forth. As a child she found rocking eased her worries. Lately, it had become a habit.

"First of all, I'm here for the week. I want to see you, at least once before I leave next Monday evening."

Margaret stared at him. "And how on earth do you expect that to happen? I'm supposed to be in mourning." Then an afterthought. "And by the way, while I'll love Papa forever, I don't plan to wear black dresses for two years."

"Sounds reasonable to me. And there's more news. The bank will likely move me back to Halifax. Not immediately but soon. This is great news, don't you think?"

When Margaret didn't reply immediately, his face dropped. "What's wrong? You don't want me here? I know your life is unsettled but in a few months, things will change. I'm sure of it."

It was time. Margaret took a deep breath. "They certainly will change. I'm going to have a baby." She kept her eyes on Robert, looking for his first reaction. It would tell her a great deal about her future.

Robert felt woozy, unable to speak.

Margaret waited patiently.

Then he smiled. "I hope I'm the father."

Margaret nodded but kept silent as Robert stood and pulled her up from the chair and held her in a close embrace. "This is happy news. He gave her a light kiss on the cheek then held her at arms' length. A slow smile worked its way across his face and into his eyes. "Who else knows?"

"Mama, James, Anna, Cookie, my housekeeper and Hazel, Mama's housekeeper."

"All those people know I'm the father!"

"Don't be daft. Anna knows. Everyone else presumes Thomas is the father. And before you ask, he couldn't be." Margaret embraced Robert's face in her hands and kissed his mouth. His response ignited her body. For a few moments, the world had righted itself. As Margaret pulled away, she began to weep.

"I know you're worried but I..."

"Worried? I'm beside myself." She sat on the edge of her chair, counting on her fingers. "I've shamed my family, ruined my reputation, destroyed my future and heaven knows what else." She fell back into her chair. "And Thomas is still alive. How do we get through this?" She drew a deep breath to speak again.

Robert knelt in front of her. "I love you. As long as we're together we can do this."

"But we're not together. I'm here alone to face all of it with a mother who is already ashamed of me. When will the time be right to tell people?"

"How would you feel if we start with the truth right now? We tell the truth, don't hide anything. We are expecting a child and you are divorcing Thomas."

"People will talk."

"That's true. There will always be people who gossip. We can't stop them."

"I believe what you're saying but I want to think about how we will do this."

"I don't have a plan this moment. We can think about it tonight and tomorrow we meet and talk again. Yes?"

"Not in the morning. Your father is reading Papa's will. But I'll be here by two-thirty."

* * *

Samuel lingered at the front door of the Bell home, his eyes resting on the black mourning wreath. As he did so often, he brought a document that would change lives. He lifted his hand and tapped on the door.

"Good morning, Mr. Fraser. The family is waiting for you in the sitting room. May I take your hat?"

"Thank you, Hazel."

Samuel was always unsettled at the outset of reading a will. People sat in front of him clothed in black, silent, stone-faced preparing to come to terms with the finality of their loved ones' life. This reading was particularly poignant.

James stood to greet Samuel. "Good morning. Please join us."

"Good morning." Samuel looked at Grace then Margaret and finally, James. "Unless anyone has a question, I'll proceed with reading the will and answer any questions when I'm finished." He looked at each of them in turn, knowing full-well Grace was aware of the contents of the document. "Anyone?" He paused. "Then let's begin."

Margaret's hand flew to cover her mouth when she heard James would assume full ownership of the Bell home and she would receive the financial portion of the estate after their mother's death. Males in the family received everything. She glanced sideways to see James' reaction but couldn't read his expression.

James was now in a tight spot. He had already decided to leave school and was counting on his father's will to provide some funds for his immediate future. His exit from Halifax was in jeopardy.

When Samuel completed the reading, he added, "As Executor, I will ensure William's requests are fulfilled according to his wishes. For example, I will ensure all bills and bequests are paid before any funds are paid to beneficiaries." He looked at Grace. "As you heard, there is a bequest to St. George's."

Grace nodded.

"Any questions?" Hearing none, Samuel told a lie then said his farewells. It was kinder to fake a pending client meeting than accept an offer of tea and an awkward conversation.

* * *

Margaret crept out of the house after lunch to meet Robert. He was waiting at the kitchen door and began to walk towards her. Before he could utter a word, she collapsed into his arms. "I can't do this."

"Where's the key?"

Margaret pulled the key out of her reticule then leaned on the door frame as Robert unlocked the door, allowing them to escape into the privacy of the house.

"The world I know will be gone forever. Mama's already stricken with grief, not eating, not sleeping. I think she wants to die." When her first tear broke free, the rest followed. She bent forward. Her breathing became heavier, denying any chance of words being spoken.

Robert eased her onto a kitchen chair and pulled another close for himself.

As the tears subsided and her breathing became more even, Margaret lifted her head. "The gossip will be unbearable." She breathed heavily.

"If we tell the truth first, I think they won't have as much to say." Hearing nothing from Margaret, he sighed and asked the difficult question. "How do you feel about speaking to our families today?"

"Mama is broken already." She wrapped her arms around Robert. "What we have to do is right but it's so frightening."

"I love you and I'm willing to see all of it through as long as you're by my side. "

"I love you, Robert Fraser."

"Tonight we tell our families about our baby."

"And tomorrow I'll visit Cookie."

* * *

When Margaret returned home, her mother was in a dither just inside the front door. "Where have you been?"

"I went to check on the house. It was broken into once before."

James piped up. "I knew it was something Margaret could explain, Mama."

"The hospital sent a message."

"When did the message come? What does it say?"

James answered. "About half an hour ago. It's addressed to you so I didn't think we should read it."

"Thank you." She ripped the envelope open.

Grace and James stared at Margaret's face.

"It says Thomas is awake. I should come as soon as possible."

James steadied Margaret before she could collapse on the floor. "You're alright. Lean on me."

As soon as Margaret was comfortably seated and sipping a glass of water, James spoke. "When you're ready, I'm going to the hospital with you. Don't argue with me."

* * *

The ride to the hospital was awkward. Margaret stared out the carriage window. Her imagination worked overtime, seeing Thomas dressed, sitting on the bed and demanding to leave the hospital immediately. James' medical training gave him far too many options that could apply to Thomas' awake description. He couldn't think of anything to say that would provide reassurance to his sister so he held her hand.

The nurse at the front desk welcomed Margaret and looked at James suspiciously.

"I'm Mrs. Bishop's brother."

"Very well. Please have a seat. I'll arrange for Doctor Adams to meet you in Mr. Bishop's room."

Within minutes, the nurse returned. "The doctor is ready for you now."

James held Margaret's arm tightly and whispered, "Slow down. You'll faint again. Besides, I doubt he's going anywhere today."

James was correct. Thomas was still in bed, his head wrapped in bandages. His eyes opened briefly when their footfalls crossed the threshold into the room.

"Good afternoon, Mrs. Bishop. Considering your family circumstances, I'm sorry you had to come here today. Please accept my deepest sympathy."

"Thank you. This my brother, James."

The men shook hands and exchanged a brief greeting. James remained near the door and studied Thomas. Margaret moved into the room to stand near Doctor Adams, well beyond Thomas' reach.

"I'll be brief. The nurse on duty earlier today noticed your husband blinking. He appears to be in discomfort, moaning but has not spoken."

James spoke up to stop any comment Margaret might have planned. "I think my sister should be seated for this conversation, Doctor Adams. May I suggest we continue our discussion in your office?"

"By all means. Follow me."

As all three left the room, Thomas opened his eyes and stared at their receding backs.

In the office, the doctor continued. "As I mentioned, Mr. Bishop appears to be in some pain. No major bones were broken but he will be stiff, sore and feeling discomfort."

Margaret asked for confirmation. "So has he spoken?"

"No, but as his recovery has begun, I expect he will soon."

James posed a question. "Could the discomfort be bed sores?"

While nodding, the doctor responded. "Yes. Despite the best care, they can easily become infected. For that reason, I'd like to get him out of bed as soon as is possible." He shook his head. "Bed sores are worrisome. It is a battle we can't afford to lose. Any other questions?"

James answered. "Thank you, doctor. I believe that is all for today."

* * *

At home, James offered to explain Thomas' condition to his mother.

"Thank you. I was going to ask you to do that. When you're finished, we need to talk."

James returned almost immediately from Grace's bedroom.

"Is Mama worse?"

"I can't say she's worse but she's not herself. She barely made eye contact and expressed no interest in Thomas' condition. I know she doesn't care one bit about him but she usually has some biting remark. If she hasn't improved at dinner, I'm going to contact Doctor Lewis. You wanted to talk?"

"Sit down. This will not be quick."

James was stunned into silence, his eyes never leaving Margaret's face. When she finished, he placed one hand over his face, pulling it down over his eyes, nose and mouth, staring in disbelief. "You and Robert. A baby. Is that why Mama..."

"No. I haven't told her."

"And don't until she's improved." He leaned forward. "My congratulations still stand and besides, who am I to judge you? You and Robert have decided to tell the family and face society's gossip. I think that's the right thing to do." He sat back. "Since we are talking about the future, I will tell you my plan. I'm leaving school and Halifax."

"You're what?"

"I shouldn't be a doctor. Someday I'll be able to explain myself better. I hope."

"When are you leaving? Where are you going?"

"Following Thomas was exciting. Finding out who was doing what and why was a big puzzle to solve. I learned things about myself, some I liked, some I didn't. Helping the police catch that fella at the train station was exciting."

"So you're joining the police?"

"No. I want be a private investigator. I've talked to Detective Gilfoy a few times. He told me some railways hire their own detectives. You remember how I wanted to be a train engineer. Well, I'd like to put the two together."

"But you can't decide to be something and immediately make it happen!"

"Gilfoy has the name of a man in Toronto I can contact. Don't worry, I won't leave until we get Mama settled."

* * *

In the Fraser home, the conversation was brief.

"A baby!"

"Yes, Mother."

"And when will there be a wedding?"

"As soon as possible."

CHAPTER
THIRTY-THREE

HALIFAX, NOVA SCOTIA
SEPTEMBER 24, 1895

Hazel received two messages at the front door of the Bell home before she was able to clear the breakfast table. She was none too pleased about it. Messages, comings and goings within a home in mourning was unsuitable, bordering on improper.

From the sitting room, James overheard Hazel muttering to herself in the hallway. "People are getting out of hand."

James snickered to himself, "Wait 'til she hears about Margaret and Robert. She'll pass out."

Robert's message for Margaret was the first to arrive, suggesting they meet Wednesday afternoon at two-thirty and to reply only if she could not come. A post script read,

Parents in shock but have not thrown me out of the house.
Love, Robert

The second message was also for Margaret. Doctor Adams' advised her Thomas' condition had deteriorated overnight.

*We are battling an infection. Come only if you
wish. I will keep you appraised later today.*

Margaret passed the message to James. "What should I do?"

"I'll go. You spend some time with Mama. I think she's in the garden. We can go together tomorrow."

*   *   *

Thomas' face was flushed, his eyelids flickered when James entered the room.

"Good morning, Mr. Bell."

"It's just James, Doctor Adams."

"Very well, James. Your brother-in-law has developed an infection. His temperature is up."

James put his forefinger to his lips. "Can we step outside the room for a few minutes?"

"Certainly."

"I'd rather we talk without the possibility of Thomas hearing."

"I understand. He has an infection. Also, he occasionally mutters a few words. If you intend to be in his room, don't be surprised by what he says. The words are not very complimentary about you and your sister."

"I'm not surprised. What are the chances of recovery from this infection?"

"The chances will be better if we can keep the infection out of the blood. I want him moving but walking will be a challenge."

The doctor's indirect answer did not go unnoticed by James. "Thank you. I'll spend a few minutes in the room then go home to speak with Margaret. I'll accompany her for a visit tomorrow, likely in the morning."

"I'll be here."

James had no sooner crept into the room when Thomas called out, "You whore."

James carried the chair to the wall opposite the bed and sat down quietly. *Let's see if you're playing to an audience or might accidentally tell me something I don't know.*

* * *

"Hello, Mama. The yellow roses look lovely. Want to help me cut some blooms for the sitting room?"

"You go ahead, dear. I'll watch."

A black dress and the summer sun was not a desirable combination. Margaret moved quickly to snip several blooms then retreated to the shaded bench and sat with her mother.

"Where is James? I haven't seen him all morning."

"He went to the hospital to see Thomas."

"And why did you not go?" Her tone was less accusatory than usual but still had a critical edge.

"Thomas' situation has worsened. James wanted to see the doctor. He plans to take me tomorrow."

"I never liked Thomas. Is he going to die? You'd be better off without him."

Margaret remained silent.

"Never mind telling Thomas about the baby." Then she stared off into the distance. "Maybe you should take flowers to your father's grave on Sunday."

"We could do that together, Mama. Will you come to church with me on Sunday?"

"I don't know, dear. Nothing is the same without your father. Not church, mealtime, sitting in the garden, visiting friends. It's all gone. I might as well be gone too." She lifted her head toward the fluffy clouds drifting slowly across the late morning sky.

Margaret put her arms around her mother. Her body felt frail. "Don't say that, Mama. Don't you want to be here to see the baby?"

Grace continued to stare toward the sky. "I'll try, dear."

It was clear their conversation was over. Margaret turned her head away. There was no way she could stop the angry tears. She'd lost her father and was frightened her mother was going to leave too, just when she wanted them to share in her new happiness.

She was thankful her dress had big pockets with lots of room for handkerchiefs.

* * *

"Here you are, ladies. I have lemonade for everyone." James glanced at the flowers. "But first, I'll take the roses in for Hazel. What's she supposed to do with them?"

Margaret responded. "Sitting room."

James returned with a message. "Hazel has lunch ready. Would you like to eat outside Mama?"

"No. Bring the lemonade indoors, James. I'll eat and have a rest."

When Grace left the dining room after lunch, Margaret asked James about Thomas.

"He has an infection. The doctor wants him out of bed but I can't see how they will be able to do it. I'll take you in the morning. Be prepared for colourful language."

"So he's talking about me?"

James shrugged. "Maybe his aunt?"

"I don't think so." She finished her lemonade. "I'm going to see Cookie while Mama's in bed."

"When are you moving?"

"Tomorrow. I'll meet Cookie there just after lunch." She paused. "I plan to be here for lunch every day, beginning Thursday."

"How did Mama seem in the garden?"

"It's time to see Doctor Lewis. I'll explain when I return from Cookie's."

* * *

At breakfast Grace sternly refused food. "I'm not hungry. Now stop being so terribly annoying. Both of you. I'll eat when I'm hungry and not before." She stared at each of them in turn.

Margaret and James reluctantly left the house to visit the hospital. James was the first to air his feelings. "I don't know about you but I felt like a ten year-old at breakfast. That was around the time Robert and I took Papa's fishing rods without asking and went to the wharf. Both of us spent the following two days in our rooms."

"How did you get caught?"

"Robert's father saw us out his office window, came to the wharf and took us home."

"Mama doled out the punishment?"

"Oh, yes. I could see Papa in the hallway trying not to laugh." He leaned forward. "I don't remember you getting into trouble. You must have been miss goody two-shoes."

"Do you remember my friend Eleanor?"

"Vaguely."

"We were about seven at the time. Hazel gave us a few old spoons and baking tins to play house in the garden. We decided to make mud pies and came into the house for water. I knew Hazel put eggs in pies so I thought we should too. Apparently, Hazel was missing a few eggs for her baking so Mama came out to ask what we were baking. Eleanor went home and after apologizing to Hazel, I went to my room for the rest of the day. I had to eat dinner in my room too."

"By the way, what happened to Eleanor?"

"The family moved away a few years later." Margaret stared out the window. "We loved to laugh, dance. I miss being a child." She turned her gaze to James. "I bet you think I'm silly."

"Not at all. It was a time to enjoy life, without worries. Speaking of worries, should we see Doctor Lewis on the way home?"

"Absolutely."

* * *

Margaret and James were stopped just inside the hospital's front door. "Mrs. Bishop, Mr. Bell, could you wait here, please. Doctor Adams wishes to speak with you before you see Mr. Bishop."

The minutes ticked on. James gave up leaning against the door frame and sat down. "Something's happening."

Nurse Pender appeared. "We are so sorry to keep you waiting. We've had to sedate your husband, Mrs. Bishop. Come with me. Doctor Adams will see you in Mr. Bishop's room."

Margaret gasped. "What's happened?" Thomas' face was flushed, his body motionless. A nurse was wiping his brow with a cloth, her own brow damp with perspiration. An empty syringe lay in a basin on the nearby table.

James led her to the chair in the corner. "What's changed, Doctor?"

"The infection is not abating. Mr. Bishop became unmanageable, trying to get out of bed, yelling. I had no choice but to sedate him. We will continue the treatment but his lack of cooperation will slow the rate of healing."

"Dare I ask how long you have to beat this thing?"

"Not long, unless he cooperates."

James turned to Margaret. "Unless you want to remain, I think it best we leave. What do you say?"

"Leave." She stood. "Thank you, Doctor Adams."

James took her arm. Part way down the hall Margaret stopped. "I'm feeling nauseous."

"We'll sit in the waiting room for a few minutes. Do you want to go home or see Doctor Lewis with me?"

"Doctor Lewis."

* * *

The visit with Doctor Lewis was brief. James came to the point without many pleasantries. "Mama will be mad as a wet hen if you come to the house but I'm sure she won't come here. What do you suggest?"

"Keep trying to get her to eat. Food is the best answer. I have a tonic which a few patients have taken for a poor appetite. Let's try it for a few days. It's not something that can be disguised in food or drink. I will see her Monday, invited or not." He stared at James. "And you can tell her that."

James expressed his thanks then stood to leave.

"Margaret, you look a little peaked. Are you unwell? "

"I am expecting a child, Doctor Lewis."

"Congratulations, my dear. A bit of nausea then?"

"Yes. When should I come to see you?"

"If you are feeling well then one day next week would be fine. We will talk about what you can expect in the next few months."

* * *

That afternoon Margaret and Cookie set about the work of opening up the house shortly after one o'clock. The temperature was a comfortable sixty-six with rain expected late in the day.

Cookie brought a batch of cookies from home and set the kitchen table for their afternoon lemonade break.

Seeing two place settings gave Margaret the opening she needed. "I am expecting a visitor this afternoon so we'll need a third glass and plate."

"You want me to have lemonade with you and Mrs. Hopkins?"

"It's not Mrs. Hopkins and yes, I want you with me. Let's finish the work before our visitor arrives."

Not long after, Cookie answered a knock on the front door.

"Good afternoon, I'm here to see Mrs. Bishop."

"And who shall I say is calling, sir?"

"Robert."

"Robert. And the last name, sir."

"Fraser."

"One moment, Mr. Fraser."

As Cookie turned toward the kitchen, Margaret was coming down the hall, her face beaming. "Hello, Robert. Come into the kitchen. We're putting the last of the clean dishes away."

"Perhaps you would like to speak with Mr. Fraser in the study, Mrs. Bishop."

"Yes I will then we'll be back to speak with you."

Inside the study Margaret and Robert embraced each other and lingered over a long kiss.

"I'm surprised you're wearing a dark blue dress."

"I changed my dress when Cookie and I came to open up the house. My day dresses fit and the dark colour is to honour Papa. This dress suits my point of view on my new life." She paused. "If Thomas dies while I'm still married to him, I will not honour his memory by wearing black. I'm sure not all widows wear black."

"That's spunky."

"Papa often used that word." She smiled.

"Were you able to speak with your mother about us?"

"No." Her face became sad. "James and I spoke with Doctor Lewis about her earlier today. She's really determined not to eat. But I did tell James and he's happy for us. I wasn't the only one with news. He's leaving medicine behind and going to leave Halifax."

"That's a surprise. He's so close to an MD. Back to your mother. Do you think she would accept a visit from my mother?"

"Mama has flawless manners. If your mother came uninvited, Mama wouldn't refuse to see her."

"I'll suggest it."

"Make sure your mother doesn't utter a word about us."

"Certainly. Any news about Thomas?"

"James and I saw him this morning. The doctor is concerned about an infection."

Robert nodded but made no attempt to discuss the man. "Ready to tell Cookie?"

Cookie's eyes darted back and forth between Margaret and Robert as she listened to Margaret tell their story. She ended with, "We're going to tell the truth to everyone."

Cookie had never been privy to such detail from society people. "People are not used to so much truth. The two of you could have a pack of trouble."

Robert wanted a more personal answer. "And what do you think, Cookie?"

She was quick to answer. "I'm here to take care of Mrs. Bishop and support her decisions until she asks me not to. I won't gossip but I will tell the truth if I'm asked a question." She looked at each of them individually. "Don't be making a big display of yourselves. People don't like that. Let them see you doing what you believe is right and goin' about your daily business."

"Sound advice. Thank you, Cookie." Robert squeezed her hand.

* * *

In spite of James' very best efforts, Grace would have nothing to do with 'that awful smelling drink.' "And don't you ask Doctor Lewis to come here. Leave me alone until I decide I can live without your father. It could be some time."

* * *

After dark that evening Regena Fraser crept into the garden of the Bell home. The vanilla scent of evening primrose lingered near the kitchen door. She raised her left hand to tap loud enough to rouse Hazel and kept the fingers of her right hand firmly crossed.

As Hazel opened the door a crack, Regena whispered, "shh."

Hazel's dark eyes were round with alarm. "What's happened, Mrs. Fraser?"

Regena beckoned her to step outside.

There was nothing Hazel could do to hide her strands of hair wrapped around the curling rags but she managed to pull her shawl over her shoulders.

"I understand Mrs. Bell is not eating."

Hazel glared. "Who told you that gossip?"

Regena held Hazel's glare with her own. "As you are well aware, this is not gossip." Then with a softened tone she added, "Society be dammed, I will be here tomorrow for lunch with Mrs. Bell. What is her favourite dessert?"

Hazel was clearly offended but knew better than to refuse a

society lady's request. With her hands clenched, she muttered, "Sticky Toffee Pudding".

"Thank you. I will bring dessert. Keep this to yourself."

Hazel nodded and closed the door in Regena's face.

Regena smiled and returned to the waiting carriage.

"What happened?"

"I'll be taking pudding to the Bell home for lunch tomorrow."

"Well done, Mother."

CHAPTER
THIRTY-FOUR

HALIFAX, NOVA SCOTIA
SEPTEMBER 26, 1895

The following morning Hazel remained miffed about her altercation with Regena. She intended to warn Mrs. Bell about that woman at her earliest convenience.

"Hazel's stomping around in the kitchen. What's the matter with her?" James carried on cracking his boiled egg.

Margaret laughed. "Who knows. Lots of things get up her nose. She has her own definition of what's right and wrong."

James leaned across the table and whispered. "Wait 'til she hears about Robert. It'll be quite the performance. Pass the salt cellar, please." He dipped the salt spoon into the cellar then seasoned his egg. "Did Mama have breakfast with you?"

"She ate a few bites of her egg and left. She's not interested in talking."

Hazel appeared at the dining room door, her arms folded over her ample bosom and cleared her throat. "Excuse me. I have something I must tell both of you before I speak with your mother. Last night I had a visit from Mrs. Regena Fraser, at the kitchen door no less." She shot a penetrating stare toward James and Margaret then waited. Hearing no response, she continued. "That woman needs to be told she cannot have a say in what goes on in your mother's house. It's shocking to say nothing of the social impertinence of telling me she's coming here today for lunch with your mother." She cleared her throat and put on her best indignant expression. "And she's bringing sticky toffee pudding."

Margaret smiled. "Mama's favourite. How kind."

James had a puzzled look. "I'm confused, Hazel. Why did she come at night to see you?"

Hazel straightened her upper body, ready to launch her condemnation. "Who knows why she would do such an outrageous thing."

James sat back in his chair. "Well then tell me what she said."

"She said she heard your mother was not eating, no doubt some gossip in a shop. And she wanted to have lunch with your mother. Then she asked me about your mother's favourite dessert."

Margaret spoke up. "What a lovely idea. And she went to all the trouble of coming here to make sure it would be a surprise."

James spoke the thoughts he surmised Margaret left unsaid. "Hazel, our mother is very upset about Papa's death. She is not sleeping well and not eating well either. We need her to get well. I don't give a damn about society's expectations. I am delighted Mrs. Fraser came to see you and she wants to help my mother. Thank you for telling us but we want you to prepare Mama's favourite food for lunch and set the table for four with our best china and silver. And you will not speak of Mrs. Fraser's evening or lunch visit with Mama. Thank you."

"Very well." Hazel waited until she was well down the hall before she emitted a big snort and a condemnation of James. "Cheeky little bugger."

* * *

Margaret was fascinated by Regena Fraser at lunch. Samuel was a lawyer with plenty of courtroom experience, but Regena was a master at the art of conversation. Within minutes of arriving she had Grace relaxed and interested in the latest goings on at church and upcoming arts activities in the city. She never once hinted or suggested that Grace participate, she simply connected her friend with the world outside. By dessert Grace began to smile, ever so briefly. Margaret almost wept. With lunch finished, James and Margaret excused themselves and left their mother and Regena at the table. In the hallway, they embraced each other. Margaret cried with joy.

"What are you doing this afternoon?" Before Margaret could answer James added, "A rest would be my advice."

"A rest and a good book at home sounds perfect." She paused. "Does the hospital know I have moved?"

"Yes. I mentioned it the last time I was there."

"And you this afternoon?"

"Part of my afternoon will be a meeting with my professor about my absences from class and my decision to leave the program. It might not be a pleasant meeting." He grimaced.

"Mama hasn't noticed you've been at home most of the time for the past two weeks?"

"No and I'm dreading the day I have to tell her. I'll leave it until she is feeling better."

"You know I don't want you to go."

"I know but it's something I have to do."

Margaret could tell by the set of his jaw, he would not be swayed but she still didn't understand why he gave up medicine. Some day she wanted the real answer.

* * *

"Excuse me, Mrs. Bishop. It's a note from Anna to me asking if you were able to meet her for lunch tomorrow. Pardon me for being bold but I think it would be more restful for you at home. May I reply and ask her to come here?"

"Yes, please."

Cookie returned to the door and Margaret to her book but not long after, Cookie was going to the door again. Margaret overheard her sigh heavily. "Who is it this time?"

"Mrs. Bishop, this message is for you. Stay seated, I'll bring it to you."

Dear Margaret,
Samuel and I would like you to join us for lunch
this Saturday. I hope you are able to join us.
   Sincerely,
   Regena

"Is someone waiting for a reply?"

"Yes, the young man is in the hallway."

Margaret quickly responded, *Yes, I look forward to our*
time together. then immediately she began to think the un-
thinkable. Robert's name was not included.

* * *

There was always something compelling about Anna that
Margaret found irresistible. Lunch would be no different, filled
with stories and new ideas, diversions she greatly needed.

"Come in, Mrs. Hopkins."

"Anna, please."

"Mrs. Bishop is in the study, Anna. Lunch will be ready
shortly."

"Don't get up." Anna gave Margaret a long hug. "It's only
me. How are you managing and your mother, any better? I'm
presuming James is doing well. What's the news on Thomas and
when did you last see Robert?"

Margaret satisfied Anna's questions and posed her own. "I
need to think about something new. What is the latest news at
the paper?"

Anna hesitated, not sure how to begin. She took the plunge
and began. "I must tell you something I was just told this
morning." She held back a moment. "George is scheduled to
return to England."

Margaret's was frozen in place, her question barely audible.
"When?"

"These things happen quickly, within weeks but sometimes
days." She couldn't stop rambling because to do so would result

in the awful truth for both of them. "Apparently, someone in England requested his return. I don't know why and probably will never know. That's the military, do as you're told. Don't question why." Then at the end, "I don't want to leave."

They both cried.

"I can't take any more hurt, Anna. Inside me is a big empty hole."

They sat, both silent until Cookie came for them.

"Good heavens. What's happened?"

"I'm leaving, Cookie."

"You're not staying for lunch?"

She looked at Cookie, her eyes filled with tears. "No, I'm leaving Halifax."

Margaret spoke. "If there ever was a time for stories, this is it. Cookie, can you sit with us for lunch."

"I most certainly can. Nothing would please me more than telling you two about the old days and old stories." *My dear girl. How much more can you take?*

* * *

Margaret sleepwalked through Friday evening and Saturday morning as Cookie continued a quiet telling of light-hearted tales from her childhood.

"Are you sure you want to have lunch with Mr. and Mrs. Fraser?"

"I have to, Cookie. To do otherwise would be rude."

"Very well."

* * *

Margaret had second thoughts about her decision when Robert did not appear with his parents at the front door.

Samuel spoke first. "Robert will not be joining us, Margaret. I asked him to give the three of us time alone."

Margaret's face reddened. She nodded but could think of no appropriate words.

Then it was Regena's turn. "May I take your hat and gloves?" followed by, "Come into the dining room. Lunch is almost ready." Margaret was wearing a navy blue dress. Regena smiled to herself.

The table setting caught Margaret's eye. At one end of a table for ten, Royal Doulton china and silverware was set for three. Samuel motioned for Margaret to sit on his left and Regena on his right. He took the end seat himself. The scent of sweet-peas lingered in the room. Margaret turned slightly to see a vase of sweet-peas on the sideboard. Her heart fluttered.

"Robert suggested the sweet-peas since he was not going to be here."

Margaret blushed. "I do like them. Thank you. And thank you for inviting me to lunch."

"It is our pleasure. Before we go any further, you are here so we can get to know you better and assure you we will do everything we can to support you and Robert. Regena and I know all about Thomas."

"You are very kind."

Regena nodded her agreement then added, "One thing we cannot stop is gossip. I expect you are going to have a very difficult time during the next...when is the baby due?"

"May."

Regena continued. "During the next eight months."

Samuel rang the bell for Ruby to bring the first course.

* * *

Margaret arrived home to find Cookie holding a message from the hospital.

Margaret read out loud. "Mr. Bishop's condition has improved slightly. Could you come to the hospital and speak with Doctor Adams?"

Cookie was quick to respond. "There's no need to bother your brother. I'll go with you. Take time to freshen up and we'll go when you're ready. How was the lunch?"

"It was lovely. They are so kind."

"Good. They've met my required standards." She chuckled.

* * *

Cookie was not impressed with the brief hospital visit. "Why on earth did that doctor waste your time?"

"I'm sure he wants to make sure I know what is happening with my husband, probably has no idea our marriage is a charade. Thomas didn't look much better and still isn't talking."

"Maybe this is a short rally before the end."

"What do you mean?"

"He'll make a brief recovery then pass away."

* * *

Over breakfast on Sunday, Margaret decided to cut flowers from her garden and visit her father's grave. Stepping inside the church was not a commitment she was prepared to make. As she passed through the cemetery's ornate wrought-iron archway, red and gold leaves were already gathered on the ground. The musky odours of fall had begun. Next to the gently blowing branches of a maple, she stood beside her father's grave. His name, date of birth and death had already been engraved into the headstone. Her mother's name and date of birth awaited its final inscription, her date of death. Margaret's days of uncontrolled weeping were over. Today she cried for what was lost, knowing her father would live forever in her heart.

"Hello, Papa. I've brought you flowers, knowing how you admired my first garden. I miss you terribly. Mama is sad but James and I are determined to help her feel better." She faltered. "I also want to tell you about my baby and hope you understand." She pondered what to say then spoke the truth. "Robert is the baby's father." A red leaf dropped onto her hand then fell away. Papa often patted her hand when he assured her of his love. "Thank you. Papa. I knew you would understand."

* * *

Monday morning's darkness and the sound of water pounding on the window promised a full day of rain. September had a few wet days but this one sounded particularly foul. Margaret lingered in bed, not wanting to face the day nor the reality of Anna leaving and Thomas' recovery. She fell back against the pillow. Why couldn't Thomas leave and Anna stay? She admitted her wish was selfish but deeply needed. She took a deep breath, sat up and thought about Robert and the baby. They were her future. She would keep them in her thoughts, even in the dark times.

Cookie called up the stair well. "Mrs. Bishop. Breakfast?"

"In a few minutes."

* * *

The carriage ride for lunch with Mama was dreadful from start to finish. Her shoes became soaked trying to escape the puddles on her own front walk. As she opened the carriage door to get out, a gust of wind blew rain in her face and pulled at her hat.

"Well dear sister, you look bedraggled. A drowned rat comes to mind."

Margaret stuck her tongue out at James. "You're not very kind, sir."

"But you're in luck. Your new black dresses arrived late Saturday afternoon. Take your shoes off. I found an old pair upstairs. Everything is in your room. You can change before we eat."

"You sound cheerful. Is Mama better?"

James smiled. "No but I must maintain good humour. Now go get out of those soggy clothes."

Lunch was a quiet affair, aside from the pleasantries and talk of local news and events. When Grace left the table, Margaret opened up about Anna and George. "I was counting on Anna to be here with me." Followed by, "Thomas improved yesterday." She couldn't hold back the tears.

"You went to the hospital alone?"

"With Cookie. It was a brief update with Doctor Adams."

James shook his head in bewilderment. "Improved! Let's sit in the sitting room. Bring your tea. The fireplace will feel good on this miserable day."

They were barely settled when a short, sharp knock brought Hazel to the front door. "Come in, Doctor Lewis. May I take your coat?"

"Thank you." Doctor Lewis removed his coat and hat, which was dripping water on the hall floor. "May I speak with Mrs. Bell?"

"She is resting, Doctor. I will ask her."

As Hazel turned toward the stairs, James stepped into the hall. "Thank you for coming, Doctor. Margaret is in the sitting room. Please join her. I'll speak with Mama." Then turning his head, "Hazel, you may continue with your kitchen duties."

"Still feeling well, Margaret?"

"Yes, thank you, Doctor Lewis."

A few minutes later, James reappeared. "Mama will see you in her room. I'll take you up."

When Doctor Lewis reappeared, his face was easy to read but James put up a good front. "Will this be over in a few weeks?"

"As a student of medicine, I'm sure you understand when I say, I don't know."

James pointed to a chair. "Have a seat, Doctor."

Doctor Lewis sat down and removed his glasses. "Your mother has no desire to live. Eating will sustain her body but not her soul. I have to say, this practice of isolation while in mourning is depriving her of her friends. Your mother needs her friends even though society expects she do otherwise." He shook his head. "I've seen too much of this in my time and I don't like it. It's a custom long overdue for change." He pulled his handkerchief from his pocket, cleaned his glasses and put them back on. "You two will have a battle to move her off her point of view but it's my view it will be the only thing to save her." He smiled weakly "Let her wear the black dresses. They don't matter a jot."

Immediately after Doctor Lewis left, James looked toward Margaret. "I can see by your face, you have an idea. Out with it."

"We are going to have a lunch for two or three of Mama's closest friends right here."

James rolled his eyes. "And how do we convince her?"

"We don't. Regena Fraser will. Hail a carriage while I put on my coat and hat."

"Now?"

"Is there a better time?"

"Well no, but."

"Robert leaves this evening and I'll also be able to say goodbye."

CHAPTER THIRTY-FIVE

On the Friday morning of Grace's surprise lunch, Margaret dealt with a bout of nausea, ate a small breakfast and arrived at her family home just before ten o'clock. Her first task was to tell her mother about lunch. That was the easy part. Regena Fraser was expected at eleven o'clock, four friends at twelve. The hard part would be explaining to Regena why her mother had no idea Robert was the father of her child. She moved her hand back and forth over her stomach.

"Regena's coming here and invited other people? The neighbours will take a dim view of such frivolity. It can't possibly happen."

"But it will, Mama. Not because your dear friends want to break the rules but because they want to be with you. There will be no music, no card games." Risking a swift rebuke, she added, "Papa would want you to feel better."

Margaret's firm but sincere words brought a deep sigh of resignation from her mother. And then, "I suppose I should have Hazel arrange my hair."

"I'll do it, Mama." Margaret picked up the hair brush. "Come sit on the dressing table stool."

"Remember, no ornaments, just pins." Grace sat patiently, watching Margaret in the looking glass. "Are you staying for lunch?"

"No. Cookie is trying a new recipe today. It's Spanish Chicken Stew. We will be having it for lunch. If it's tasty, I'll give Hazel the recipe."

Grace studied Margaret's reflection in the mirror. "How are you feeling? I mean about the baby."

Margaret was thrilled. This was the first mention of the baby in days. "I'm well." She paused, hoping her mother would offer advice or perhaps ask another question. When she did not, Margaret continued, "You look lovely, Mama. Mrs. Fraser is coming early. I must go downstairs to meet her."

Margaret reached the bottom of the stairs as Regena tapped on the front door. "Hazel, I'll answer the door."

"Good Morning, Mrs. Fraser."

"Hello, Margaret." She placed a large wicker basket on the hall table. "This is a worrisome gathering for you. How are you feeling? Nausea today?"

"Nausea this morning but I'm feeling very well, thank you." Margaret could smell the toffee pudding.

"Good. What can I do?"

"Nothing really but I do have something to tell you before Mama comes downstairs. Let's step into the sitting room."

Regena frowned. "Is your mother unwell?"

"No. It's about Robert."

"Then let's sit together on the sofa." Seated, she continued. "Your mother doesn't know about the baby?"

"Oh no, it's not that. She knows there's a baby but she thinks it's Thomas'." She rushed to finish on a happier note. "I want her to feel better before I tell her."

"Don't worry. Your mother will be better in a few weeks and then you can tell her." She paused. "Does James know?"

"Yes and he's pretty stern about me resting, eating well."

"Good. Are you staying for lunch?"

"No, but I'll wait for Mama to come down before leaving."

"That sounds fine, dear. I'll look after the rest, including Hazel. I'm sure she's still a bit snappish about me."

Margaret kept silent. A lady doesn't gossip.

Regena patted her hand. "Here comes your mother. I'll send a message later this afternoon. Don't worry. I'm sure everything will be fine."

And it was. Regena's note to Margaret mentioned her mother's "spirits were high', that she ate well and suggested she would consider attending church.

Margaret wasn't confident in her mother's suggestion about attending church but would bring it up during lunch the next day.

* * *

"Church tomorrow? No, my dear."

"Are you tired from yesterday's lunch?"

"No. I certainly don't want to appear a gadabout so soon. It would not be proper. But you should go. I don't know why but James seems to think he needs to stay with me."

* * *

Margaret entered the church after a visit to her father's grave, replacing the withered flowers with fresh blooms. The full pews forced her to a complete halt. She'd never been to church alone and was uneasy sitting by herself in the family pew. Anna's words about braving strong headwinds flashed though her mind. *People will define you. Don't let them.* She put one foot in front of the other, reached the pew and sat down. Her father's absence, mother's illness and James' imminent departure closed in. Her breathing became laboured. Desperate to get away, she inched toward the side aisle. Then a hand rested on her shoulder.

"Good morning, Margaret." Regena leaned toward her. "May we join you?"

"Of course."

Regena turned her head to Margaret and whispered. "We'll be the talk of Sunday lunch in a few homes today. Don't let it bother you."

* * *

In the carriage for lunch with James and Mama, Margaret wondered why Anna was not in church. Tired and preferring her own company, she sat in the solitude of the back garden thinking about visiting Anna later in the afternoon. In the finish, she folded her arms over her abdomen, closed her eyes and thought about Robert's next visit.

An hour later, James found her sound asleep. He touched her shoulder. "Margaret. Wake up."

Margaret looked up, both eyes partially closed. She breathed deeply. "Give me your hands. I'll help you stand up."

"What time is it?"

"It's almost one o'clock. You and Mama were both asleep so I postponed lunch for a while. You look like you're in another world. What's the matter?"

"It's Anna. She hasn't been to the house since telling me they're going back to England. She wasn't in church today either."

"Perhaps you should visit. I could take you."

Margaret gave him a side-eye then moved toward the kitchen door.

"Or you could go on your own." He smiled to himself.

"I've decided to let Anna do things in her own time. Besides, I have to become accustomed to life without her. I have to tell you, I don't like the idea one bit."

"Changing the subject, what made you decide to go to church?"

"I wasn't planning to but after taking flowers to Papa's grave, it seemed the proper thing to do. The Fraser's sat with me."

"That's going to set off the fireworks!"

"Why do people take great pleasure in gossiping about other people's lives instead of minding their own business?"

"You answered your own question. They enjoy it. It makes them feel important."

"Shh. Here comes Mama."

Grace fell back into her old ways at lunch. Although no words were spoken, Margaret was already planning another friend's lunch. She would speak with Regena tomorrow.

* * *

More than a week had passed since Margaret had been summoned to Princess Elizabeth Hospital. The expression 'no news is good news' meant bad news for Margaret. Her ongoing struggle to be free of Thomas forever continued on.

Bolstered by the Fraser's public support in church, she felt a surge of courage. Today, she would defy society and take the first step toward divorce which would surely lead to a blackening of her name. The decision itself was a tremendous relief until a wave of nausea rolled over her stomach and she found herself gagging over the bowl Cookie had placed on her bedside table.

After dinner that evening, Margaret presented herself at the Fraser front door.

"Good evening, Mrs. Bishop. Come in."

"Thank you, Ruby. I'm here to speak with Mr. Fraser."

Samuel rushed down the hall, without a jacket, his shirt sleeves rolled up. "What's happened?"

In her haste to see Samuel, she had totally forgotten what a surprise evening visit might mean to the Fraser household or for that matter, any household. "I apologize. Everyone is fine but I need to speak with you about a legal matter."

Settled in Samuel's study with the door closed, Margaret came to the point quickly. "I need a lawyer who will divorce me from Thomas."

Samuel delayed his response. "On what grounds?"

Margaret immediately realized Robert had kept her confidences about the violence in her marriage. Now she must talk about the violence again. She blanched as all the fear and pain rushed back.

"Are you all right?"

Margaret kept her head down. "I..."

Samuel decided to take a risk. "Is Thomas a violent man?"

Margaret nodded.

"There is no need for you to relive your distress with me. But you will have to with your lawyer." He gave Margaret a minute to regain her composure. "I know just the lawyer you need. His name is Angus Stewart. I'll write down the address. Tell him I sent you."

As Samuel moved to his desk, Margaret asked a question. "Does Mr. Stewart have experience?"

Samuel nodded. "His sister is his most recent case. To be blunt, her husband almost killed her." Then he took a breath. "Do you have a witness to the violence?"

"Yes." *Cookie.*

"Excellent. Now how about a cup of tea with us?"

"Please. I do want to speak with Mrs. Fraser about another lunch for Mama."

"Wonderful. I think there might be a carrot cake in the pantry. Say yes so I can have another piece myself."

* * *

When Margaret came downstairs on Tuesday morning, Cookie was placing raisin scones and fresh strawberry jam on the table for breakfast. "You look pleased about something this morning."

"I am. Mr. Fraser recommended a lawyer who can help with my divorce."

"Oh my. A divorce will bring on terrible gossip. Are you sure you want to do this now?" *That terrible creature should die soon anyway.*

As if reading Cookie's thoughts, she responded. "I can't wait for him to die. I'm going to see Mr. Stewart this very afternoon."

Cookie was not convinced. "But if he lives on or gets better? What then?"

"I'm not counting on his death or him getting better. I'm going to tell Mr. Stewart about his cruelty."

Cookie carefully placed her cup on its saucer. "My word. And how are you going to do that?"

"My journal and you. You'll be my witness, won't you, Cookie?"

"Of course, I will. And happy to do it."

* * *

When Margaret stepped out of the carriage on a side street off Barrington, she literally walked into the middle of a suffragette march. More than a dozen women chanted and waved signs carrying their message. The Vote For Women. Seeing their passion re-ignited her interest in their cause. She took note of a sign that announced a suffragette meeting that very evening. She felt sure there would be others. Several women offered warm smiles as they moved past her.

Standing alone in front of the law office, Margaret experienced her first social censure. A few men and two women stopped to stare at her, read the law office sign then shook their heads as they moved on. She looked up to the sign. Angus Stewart Lawyer. We Represent Women and Men.

Inside the office, a young woman with dark brown hair in a tight bun and high-neck white blouse sat behind a desk. She greeted Margaret with a soft smile. "Good afternoon, madam. I'm Mrs. Stewart. How may I help you?"

"My name is Margaret Bishop. I'm here to see Mr. Stewart."

"Please have a seat. I'll tell him you're here."

"Good afternoon, Mrs. Bishop. A tall, slim man with a big smile and round glasses crossed the room, his hand out to greet Margaret. His shirt sleeves were rolled up and a pencil stuck behind his ear. His unruly black curls were in need of a haircut. "Come in, come in. Samuel told me you wanted to talk to me. Have a seat and tell me why you want a divorce."

Margaret divulged a few details of the abuse and handed over her journal. "I also have a witness."

Stewart leaned over his desk. "Men hold all the cards in a divorce case, Mrs. Bishop. It also becomes a public spectacle when the newspapers get a hold of the proceedings. Your life will be on display. You will be talked about, shunned and shamed by people you don't know and unfortunately, people you do. Does this sound like something you want to undertake?"

"Mr. Stewart, I have been threatened and mistreated far too long. I am not afraid of society. I have family and friends and I want to be free of this terrible man."

"Very well, let's begin."

Reliving her torment was exhausting. Hearing the very public steps to secure a divorce was intimidating but she left in a cheerful mood, thanks in part to Angus Stewart himself.

* * *

Wednesday morning Margaret turned her mind to the suffragettes. She was most curious about what they discussed at meetings and wondered how she could attend one. Anna would know but that relationship was ending. A visit to the suffragette office seemed in order, perhaps Thursday.

As Cookie placed the ham and mustard sandwiches on the table for lunch, James knocked on the front door then wandered into the kitchen. "Good afternoon, ladies."

"Mr. Bell, how good to see you. Would you like to have lunch with us?"

"Absolutely." He looked toward Margaret. "And how is my dear sister?"

"You look very pleased with yourself. What's happened?"

"As you have not been at the hospital lately, I decided to speak with Dr. Adams this morning. Thomas' condition is changing. His temperature is rising and Doctor Adams is unable to bring it down. My guess is the medication is no longer working. You need to know the hospital will be contacting you soon, maybe even later today."

Margaret was silent. The knowledge that Thomas might actually die within hours settled in her mind. After a few moments, she looked directly into James' eyes. "Is this the first time you've recently visited Thomas?"

"Of course. Please pass the pickles, Cookie."

The lunch conversation was humdrum. The weather and the city's news stories took place between James and Cookie. Margaret ate quietly, her thoughts stayed with James' offhanded answer to her query until a question formed in her mind. She stopped eating and fixed her eyes on James. "You're almost a doctor. Tell me how Thomas' slow recovery could suddenly reverse itself?"

Although curious about the answer, Cookie made an excuse to leave the room. "My goodness, I forgot to open the upstairs windows this morning. Please excuse me for a few minutes."

Thankful for the interruption, James waited for Cookie's departure then began. "He has an infected bedsore. The infection is spreading throughout his body."

Margaret was not satisfied. "But he was recovering. What happened?"

"Even with medication, he couldn't fight off the infection. Maybe the medicine was not started soon enough, any number of causes."

"Maybe the medicine was stopped."

"If you mean an error by a nurse or the doctor, I highly doubt that."

"I don't mean that. Perhaps someone intentionally meddled with his medicine. Someone who wanted him dead, got tired of waiting."

James shrugged. "All his fellow crooks and enemies are in jail or dead. Who else would want him dead?"

Margaret studied James' eyes.

CHAPTER THIRTY-SIX

The Thursday morning sky was a perfect match for Margaret's frame of mind. The grey clouds grew darker, a whispering wind became a howl and misty rain turned into a pelting torrent. After breakfast she settled into a comfortable chair in the study to read poetry but dark undertones of danger bedevilled her thoughts. She shivered, closed the book and pulled the blanket close.

Moments later, Cookie came into the room. "Mrs. Bishop."

"It's the hospital, isn't it?"

Cookie sent Margaret out the door toward the carriage wearing a winter coat and carrying a blanket. The city was cloaked in a sky dark as pitch. Only those forced by circumstance were on the muddy sidewalks or huddled in doorways. Horses were anxious to return to the sheds for warmth and hay, their humans for a smoke, tea and conversation.

Margaret found a nurse keeping watch over Thomas. She left immediately to find Doctor Adams. Thomas' face matched the white sheet, his breathing so shallow the chest movement was barely discernible.

Margaret draped her blanket over the chair and placed her book of poetry underneath a fold. It would come in handy as she began the death watch.

"Mrs. Bishop, you've come alone! I expected your brother to accompany you."

"It seemed appropriate I do this myself."

"He's been here several times recently."

"James is very protective of me but this is something I must do myself."

"Of course. As you wish. May I speak with you outside the room?" He shoved his glasses in the breast pocket of his white coat.

In the hallway, Doctor Adams came to the point quickly. "Your husband's condition is worsening rapidly. As your husband breathes, you may hear a rattle from his throat. This is normal as he breathes through his saliva. Your vigil could be lengthy but I expect it will end by nightfall. I understand if you wish to leave earlier. In the meantime, the nurse will bring you a pot of tea now and a sandwich a little later."

"Thank you." Then she settled on the chair and began reading. As the late afternoon hours moved on to early evening, Margaret was surprised James had not made an appearance.

At the end, Doctor Adams was in the room as Thomas took his last breath. He looked at his watch. "Nine twenty-three. His struggle is over." He covered Thomas with the top sheet and turned to Margaret. "Please accept my condolences, Mrs. Bishop. When you are ready, a nurse will take you to the front door. There will be a carriage to take you home."

"I'm prepared to leave now."

* * *

When Margaret arrived home, Cookie was waiting to make a strong pot of tea. After a sandwich and tea with milk and sugar, she helped Margaret get settled in bed.

Thomas' final arrangements would be taken care of quickly, thanks to James and Samuel. A private service in the viewing room at the undertaker's building would occur on Saturday morning then a burial in a remote corner of St. George's cemetery, attended only by the undertaker and the officiating priest. Samuel arranged for a small plaque to be placed at the head of the grave indicating a name and dates of birth and death.

Grace's second friend's lunch on Friday was more subdued than Regena hoped. Immediately following the departure of Grace's last friend, Regena hailed a carriage to see Margaret.

"Hello, my name is Regena Fraser, a friend of Margaret's mother. Is Margaret accepting visitors?"

"Come in Mrs. Fraser. I'm sure Margaret will appreciate your visit. Follow me."

"Mrs. Bishop, Mrs Fraser is here to see you. I'll bring tea."

Margaret started to stand up. "Please stay seated Margaret. Samuel told me of Thomas' death. Yesterday was surely a dreadfully long day for you. How are you today?"

"More tired than I expected. How was lunch?"

"That is why I'm here. Your mother was quite subdued. She ate well but her heart wasn't in it. She agreed to another lunch next week so that is good news. Perhaps Thomas' death was playing on her mind. You are a widow expecting a child."

"I suppose that's possible."

"Excuse me ladies. Tea and scones. I'll be in the kitchen making an apple pie. If you need anything, ring the bell."

"Thank you, Cookie."

Regena poured the tea and passed the scones. "Cookie seems to be quite the treasure. Robert speaks of her in glowing terms. By the way, Samuel sent him a telegram about Thomas this morning. I hope you don't mind."

Margaret let out a heavy sigh, "No, of course not."

"Are you sure you're fine? Perhaps you should see Doctor Lewis again?"

"I don't know." She hesitated. "I mean I don't know how I feel. I've been frightened for so long, it feels odd to be truly free." She drew in her breath. "I'm sure you noticed the empty rooms. Anna Hopkins has my furniture and personal things. But she and her husband are returning to England." She let out a long sigh. "I haven't seen her lately. I imagine they are getting ready to leave."

"Take each day as it comes. I've learned each problem will be solved in its own time no matter how I try to rush it across the finish line. Tomorrow will be the very end of your worries about Thomas. Robert will be here next Friday and that should cheer you up. In the meantime, you and the baby need rest. I know you are in good hands with Cookie." She squeezed Margaret's hands and stood. "No need to see me to the door, my dear."

* * *

Margaret and James slipped through the back alley door of the undertaker's premises shortly before ten o'clock Saturday morning. Dressed in a well-used black suit and carrying his top hat, Jeremiah Wheatley greeted them with a solemn nod, putting his bald pate on full display. The remaining fringe of hair suggested he had been a fair-haired man in his younger days.

The back entrance area was small with one closed door on the left marked 'private'. Margaret presumed this led to Mr. Wheatley's living quarters.

Wheatley turned and walked toward the front of the building. "Follow me please."

Part way along the hallway a closed door on the right gave no indication of its use. It was Wheatley's work room where bodies were prepared for viewing. The other door on the opposite wall opened directly onto the side alley, a quiet place to do the business of death.

Further along the hallway, Wheatley stopped at an open door and stepped inside the room. "Mr. Bishop is resting in here. A priest from St. George's will be here shortly. When you're ready to leave turn right, then right again to find my office."

Margaret stepped inside the small viewing room. Seating was a collection of mismatched wooden chairs, placed in two rows close to the coffin. Most were from old dining room sets, the others were kitchen chairs. A gas lamp hanging from the centre of the ceiling provided dull light for the room. All four walls were covered in dark floral wallpaper. She shivered.

Thomas' coffin was set against the back wall where another gas lamp cast a yellowish tinge to his face and hands.

James leaned against the door frame. He clearly had no intention of entering the room. "Do you want to sit?"

"No." Margaret approached the fabric-covered box, stared at Thomas for a few moments then turned away.

"Good morning, Mrs. Bishop. I'm here to offer a prayer for your husband. Shall we bow our heads."

The prayer was short, Margaret offered a thank you, bid the priest goodbye and followed him out of the room.

Inside the carriage, James let out a sigh. "Well, that's over and good riddance. Do you want to see Mama before going home?"

"Yes, for a few minutes. Does she know Thomas is dead?"

"Yes."

"And?"

"She didn't appear to care. Not even a 'thank heaven he's gone'. I asked Doctor Lewis to come later today."

"I'll come for lunch tomorrow."

* * *

Margaret was sound asleep in the late afternoon when Cookie entered her room with Anna in tow.

"Mrs. Bishop. You have a visitor."

Margaret took a deep breath and opened her eyes.

Anna was pacing at the foot of the bed, her face blotchy, eyes red from crying. "I'm so very sorry to wake you. You're the only family I have here. A soldier brought me. George was shot."

Margaret sat upright. "Shot? Is he..."

Anna nodded. "In the hospital. I can hardly breath." She took a gulp of air. "I held his hand until he let mine slip away." Tears flowed down her cheeks. "What am I going to do? I can't go back to England."

Cookie quietly left the bedroom, put water on to boil and took the largest tea pot in the cupboard down from the shelf. Anna was in shock. A drop of brandy might help. She went to the liquor cabinet.

Upstairs, Margaret was trying to make sense of Anna's scrambled rendition of what happened. So far, it sounded like George was shot while inside the Citadel. A weapon went off while being cleaned.

Anna kept pacing between the bed and the window. "Why was ammunition in the gun?" She wiped her runny nose. "Why?"

Margaret tossed her blanket toward the end of the bed and stood up. "We should go downstairs. You can rest and stay here as long as you like."

Margaret sat quietly letting Anna organize her thoughts.

Anna looked pleadingly at Margaret then Cookie. "What do I do now?" She took a deep breath and dropped her face into a fresh handkerchief. "Why?"

"Have a sip of tea, Mrs. Hopkins. There's a little brandy in it."

"Thank you, Cookie." She looked toward Margaret. "Without George, I'll be lost."

"Yes. Absolutely."

Time and people who care would be the answer. But in the meantime, life would dish out a serving of hell. Margaret knew only too well what hell was like.

CHAPTER THIRTY-SEVEN

In the wee hours of Sunday morning Margaret was too alert to sleep. The day before her should be one of great relief except for the new reality facing her dear friend Anna. She maintained her own morning routine and came downstairs to find Anna already in the kitchen with Cookie, her hair unkempt and wearing the night clothes and gown Margaret had given her.

"I'm an early riser." The weak smile quickly left Anna's face. "George always counted on me to have his tea ready when he came down for breakfast." Her eyes flooded.

Margaret sat down beside Anna and grasped her hands.

"Cookie told me Thomas died a few days ago. You must be relieved."

"I am." After a pause, she continued, "I expect there will be some arrangements for George's military funeral. Is there anything you need to do today?"

"The military funeral is on Tuesday. The Major will visit me tomorrow."

"At your home?"

"I don't remember what he said."

"Do the families in England know?"

"Yes. The Major helped me contact them."

"I'm seeing Mama for lunch today. Would you like to come with me?"

"I won't be very good company." She leaned forward, her shoulders shook as tears ran down her face.

"That's fine. I'll be with you. Let's have something to eat."

Anna left her poached egg untouched but ate toast and jam in between blank stares toward the window and heavy sighs.

Margaret broke the silence. "James will be at lunch tomorrow. Would you like him to go to the Citadel with you?"

"I don't know." She stood up and went out the kitchen door without saying a word.

"Stay seated, Mrs. Bishop. I'll keep my eye on her. She's tramping between the rows of flowers like a woman off her head."

When Anna finally returned to the kitchen, she stood cross-armed in front of the closed garden door and looked straight at Margaret. "I'm going to the Citadel by myself tomorrow."

Margaret glanced at Cookie then back to Anna. "Very well. Have a bath and we'll get ready for lunch with Mama and James. Would you like me to take you home for your clothing after lunch?"

She nodded. "It's Sunday. Where will I find a black dress and hat for tomorrow?"

"I'll have Hazel shorten one of mine for you today. After you see the Major tomorrow, I'll take you to Mama's dressmaker and have you fitted for your own. Is that suitable?"

Another nod.

* * *

Anna's lunch behaviour at the Bell home was expected. She greeted Grace and James in subdued tones and engaged in very little table conversation. When Margaret excused herself to speak with James in the garden about their mother, Anna eagerly went to the sitting room.

By two-thirty, Anna was wearing Margaret's altered black dress, had refused James' support at the Citadel and was eager to pick up her clothing at home. During the carriage ride and then in the house, Margaret noticed a visible change in how Anna carried herself and how forceful her language had become.

By Monday morning, Anna's demeanour was strikingly different. She ate well, spoke like the old Anna about the newspaper and her intent to clear up George's shooting. By mid morning, she was dressed in black for her meeting with the Major.

"Are you sure you want to go to the Citadel alone? We could go together and I could wait in the carriage."

"It's not necessary. I always have plans and ideas. Today will be no different."

Margaret could not keep her concern to herself. She found Cookie in the garden. "I need to talk to you before Anna returns. Please come into the study with me."

"Is there a problem?"

"It certainly feels like one."

"Women's intuition is usually reliable. What are you thinking?"

"Anna has overcome her despair in one day. I think she's planning to do something."

Cookie shook her head. "Probably putting on a good face to make herself feel better."

"It's more than that. She insisted on going to the Citadel alone, says she has plans. I think we have to watch her carefully."

Over the evening meal, Margaret asked about the funeral meeting with the Major, hoping it would be an opening to a bigger discussion.

Anna was quick to reply. "It seems the funeral will be Wednesday not tomorrow. I have other topics to discuss with him. I will be gone all tomorrow morning. Can we go to the dressmaker in the afternoon?"

"I could meet you there at two o'clock."

"That sounds fine. I'm reading a most interesting book so I hope you'll excuse me if I go to bed early."

On Tuesday evening, Anna again offered her book as an excuse to retire early. This time Margaret was not about to play her game.

"We need to talk, Anna. I'd like you to join me in the study."

Margaret closed the study door and sat down. "Please sit."

"What is this about?"

"It's about you or more to the point, the person you're pretending to be. You helped me with my problems. Please let me help you with yours. George has died. Allow yourself to grieve. I'm worried because I believe you're planning something related to George's death."

Anna squirmed in her chair. "I have to try, don't I?"

"Try what?"

"Try to find out why the bullet was in the weapon."

"Thank you for telling me. Let's discuss that another day. Tomorrow is George's funeral. I want you to be you. Come with me."

When Margaret opened Anna's bedroom door, Anna burst into tears. On the bed was the black mourning dress, shawl and veiled hat Margaret wore to her father's funeral.

"Hazel shortened it."

"How can I thank you?"

"Be yourself tomorrow. The man you loved died. I will be there with you. Cookie and James are also attending."

"I love you, Margaret."

"And I love you, Anna."

* * *

Robert's first few hours in Halifax were spent with staff at the bank. It was early afternoon on Friday before he was able to visit Margaret. He paused at the front door for a few moments. At last, he could visit Margaret alone in her home without sneaking about. He rang the bell.

"Mr. Fraser, come in. Margaret is in the study. "Oh, here she comes now."

Robert began to walk toward Margaret. Before he could say a word, she held out her hands to grasp his. "At last, you're here." The smell of his cologne was calming. "Come to the study. Anna's with me."

Robert stopped dead at the doorway. A pale young woman

he'd never met was wearing a black dress with a handkerchief pressed against her nose. Clearly, she'd been crying.

"Robert, this is my friend, Anna Hopkins. Anna, Robert Fraser." Margaret took a deep breath and continued. "Anna's husband George recently passed away."

"Please accept my condolences, Mrs. Hopkins."

"Thank you. Call me Anna, please."

Robert looked at Margaret. "I'll come back later." He turned to leave.

"Anna will be staying with me for a while."

"Please sit down, Robert. I can read in the kitchen or in the garden." Anna smiled at Margaret, left the room and closed the door.

Alone in the room, Robert reached for Margaret's hand, drew her to him and took her face in his hands. "You are glowing." He kissed her gently. He wrapped his arms around her and whispered in her ear. "You are free."

Margaret lingered in his embrace without speaking then pulled away. "It doesn't seem real." She smiled.

"Perhaps this will change your mind." Robert took a small box from his pocket. "Will you marry me, Margaret?"

Margaret stared at the open box, a three-stone diamond ring set in rose gold glittered. "Yes."

Robert placed the ring on her finger and kissed her. "The world is beginning to right itself. Let's sit. How are you feeling or are you tired of being asked?"

"I'm well so says Doctor Lewis. By the way, I'm not going into confinement a few months from now. People will just have to look at me getting fatter!"

"I haven't been home to speak with Mother. How is your mother?"

Margaret's eyes filled. "She doesn't want to live and we can't change her mind. Your mother has been visiting, hosting friends for lunches with her. I'm so grateful for your mother's kindness. But Mama's stubborn."

"I'm so sorry. And Anna. What happened?"

"George was shot at the Citadel last Saturday. Someone was cleaning a weapon."

"With ammunition in it!"

"Anna is of the mind it wasn't an accident. James has been making quiet inquiries and tells me it wasn't intentional."

"So it's all very painful for her. Best you keep her here for a while. She shouldn't be alone too much with thoughts like that."

"She's managing better the past few days. She takes a carriage ride every afternoon." Margaret crossed her hands over her heart. "I'm so happy you're here. My heart is filled with joy. Do I have you for a week?"

"Yes, then I'm afraid you have to put up with me every day after November first."

Margaret jumped up. "Oh my goodness. Oh my heavens. Oh my." Then her hand went to her mouth. "Pass me the bowl on the desk." She turned her back and threw up then pulled a handkerchief from her pocket and wiped her mouth. "How very romantic of me."

"Come here, soon-to-be Mrs. Fraser."

* * *

On Friday friends and good food failed to bring any joy to Grace. Regena was so worried she decided not to visit Margaret.

* * *

Margaret left her engagement ring in its box on Saturday. On Sunday morning, she put it on and went downstairs for breakfast. Anna and Cookie weren't surprised and happy for her.

"I'm making the wedding cake."

"Thank you, Cookie. I'm sure it will be delicious."

Margaret wondered when a wedding date would be possible, let alone appropriate. Perhaps Robert's mother would have some advice.

After breakfast, Margaret and Anna went to church together.

Ignoring society's expectations, Margaret wore a royal blue dress with matching hat.

Robert resisted joining Margaret and Anna but consoled himself there would be many Sundays in their future. It was Margaret's day to express her independence. If anyone was watching, they would have seen a broad smile on his face. The woman he deeply loved would soon be his wife.

Anna declined Margaret's invitation to lunch with her mother and James, saying she was enjoying her afternoon carriage rides through the city and would have a sandwich at the house. As Margaret turned to step into the carriage she missed seeing the forlorn look on Anna's face.

* * *

Part of Robert's Sunday afternoon would be taken up by unfinished business at the bank. When the carriage arrived at the house, he asked the driver to include a drive past the wharf on the way to the bank.

"Right you are, sir. Water's a great draw for people, just lookin' at it or being on it."

As Robert gazed toward the water sparkling in the bright sunlight, he was struck by the sight of a woman dressed in black standing alone at the very edge of the wharf. "Driver, please stop."

"What's she doin', sir?"

"I don't know but let's wait and see."

"You thinkin' we need to go get 'er?"

"Maybe."

Eventually, the woman turned and walked away. *Anna!* Seeing Margaret before leaving for Montreal was a matter of life and death. He took the carriage to see Margaret.

* * *

"What's happened?"

At the end of Robert's story, Margaret's mouth fell open. "You think she's going to harm herself?"

"Well, she's certainly not enjoying carriage rides in the city."

"I'll speak with her during breakfast. Now for a long good-bye kiss."

CHAPTER
THIRTY-EIGHT

During breakfast Margaret suggested Anna spend the morning with her, pick-up her new dresses, stop at the wharf then return home for a lunch. Anna nodded her agreement without much enthusiasm.

Anna was clearly ill at ease standing on the pier and she said so. "Let's get away from here. I want to go somewhere else."

Margaret sensed an opportunity at hand. "Where would you like to go?"

Anna's reply was quick. "To the Citadel."

Margaret paused, thinking Anna might say something more. When she didn't, Margaret took the plunge. "Have you been going there lately, to the scene of George's death?"

"Yes."

"Do you think that's a good idea?"

"What do you mean?"

Margaret felt uncomfortable, straightened her skirts, shifted her reticule to her left arm. "I mean it likely doesn't help you begin to forget, heal."

Anna stiffened her back. "You don't have any right to tell me I should forget George."

Margaret reached for Anna's arm. Anna moved away.

"I'm not suggesting you forget George. I meant letting go of the idea he was murdered. I'm speaking as your friend."

Anna clenched her fists, her eyes narrowed. "Some friend." Then she turned away. "Let's go back."

Anna's lasting coldness was like standing in a snow storm. Margaret's stomach was clenched the entire carriage ride home.

* * *

All thoughts of Anna's problem ended when Margaret saw James sitting in the kitchen with Cookie. "It's Mama, isn't it?"

James nodded. "She's refusing to leave her room. Doctor Lewis is with her. You should come with me."

Margaret and James left the house while Anna remained standing in the hallway.

"Mrs. Hopkins, your lunch is ready."

When Anna didn't respond, Cookie took her hand and guided her to a chair. "You're very pale, Mrs. Hopkins. I'll sit with you."

Eventually, "My husband was murdered, Cookie." She kept her head down. "I'm very angry with the army and Margaret." She continued staring at the tablecloth.

"Why would you be angry with Mrs. Bishop?"

"Because she wants me to stop going on about someone killing George."

"What does the army say about your husband's death?"

"They say it was a terrible mistake. They're wrong."

With no clever reply, Cookie changed the topic. "When are you going home to England?"

"I'm not."

"Oh!"

* * *

By the time Margaret returned home late in the day Anna was resting in the study, having given more thought to her earlier behaviour.

"I'm sorry for being such a nasty person this morning. I am angry but it's not your fault." A weak smile crossed her face. "How is your mother?"

Margaret shook her head. "She has no will to live." She sighed heavily. "You sound stronger, more positive. I'm sure you'll feel better when you are home in England, surrounded by family."

"I've decided not to leave Halifax. George is here and I'm not going back to hear all the lectures I happily left behind."

Margaret was unsure how to react, except to say, "I see." which of course she didn't.

* * *

On Tuesday morning, Margaret ate breakfast and went to her mother's home unaware Anna had a plan for her own morning. Shortly after ten o'clock she presented herself at Samuel Fraser's office.

"Come in, Mrs. Hopkins. I am truly sorry to hear of your husband's death. How may I help you?"

"Simply put Mr. Fraser, I wish to remain in Halifax. While I believe the army may want to send me back to England, I believe I have an excellent reason to have them approve my stay."

"And what would that reason be?"

"George was killed by a fellow soldier. It has been judged an accident. However, I don't see it that way."

"Go on, Mrs. Hopkins."

"George is buried here. I want to stay here and continue my work. Would you be prepared to speak to the army, present my request and strongly suggest they do the decent thing?"

"Yes, I'm prepared to do so. Now, tell me the details of your case."

* * *

Late Tuesday evening, Margaret returned home disheartened and exhausted. Anna was reading in the study. It would be ill-mannered to go straight to bed. She took a deep breath and entered the study.

Anna lifted her head. "Any better?"

Margaret shook her head and dropped into a chair, placing her feet on the footstool.

"I'm so sorry."

"Thank you."

"I saw Samuel Fraser today."

Margaret raised her eyebrows.

"He's going to present my request to the army. George is here and I want to be here too."

Margaret opened her mouth but was cut off.

"I don't want to return to England. Some of my family were pleased to see the back of me when I left England and I don't want to see them. My mother labelled George as an entitled man from the privileged class having fun while ruining my reputation. My father wasn't as harsh. He supported my work, quite possibly thinking it would be a godsend when George dropped me. It wasn't long until the relatives joined mother's little club. I was invited but mostly ignored at family gatherings. I did a pretty good job of sticking up for myself and George but it really was not the happiest time in my life. Weekends at George's family home were a godsend. When George asked me to marry him, I could hardly wait to leave the village." She grinned. "So now you know the other reason why I want to stay."

"Thank you for telling me." Margaret stood up. "I have to sleep. See you in the morning." She kissed Anna's cheek on the way out.

* * *

Margaret spent Wednesday and Thursday with her mother, only going home for a bath and change of clothes. Anna's story made her think about her own family. She fondly remembered her own childhood with loving parents and a big brother who looked out for her well-being. She frowned. Family could also be troubling. For days after Thomas' death, she'd been unable to banish the thought that perhaps James was at the heart of

Thomas' death. In the end she abandoned the notion for lack of any real proof and her own well-being.

* * *

As the sun set on Thursday evening with her son and daughter by her side, Grace left her earthly home to be with her beloved husband. In death her face looked peaceful, almost happy. On Monday, Grace was laid to rest beside William following a wake at home and a well-attended church service.

After the service and interment, James helped Margaret into the carriage. "As much as it is sad for us, it is what she wanted. For that, we must be at peace."

* * *

The final few days of October went by quickly. Samuel read Grace's will on Wednesday. James insisted in signing off his owership of the house to Margaret. He looked toward Samuel. "I would like to leave the city in about two weeks. Are you able to complete the paperwork within that time?"

"Should not be a problem. Are you comfortable with this arrangement, Margaret?"

She nodded. The deaths, the house, James leaving. Her heart was broken. She cried, unable to speak for ever so long while James held one hand and Samuel the other. "What else do we have to do today?"

Samuel answered. "Nothing. James and I can take care of the paperwork tomorrow. Would both of you like to come for dinner with us this evening?"

"Margaret, I think we should accept. Yes?"

"Yes."

"Lovely. Regena and I will see you both in a couple of hours."

James saw Samuel to the door then returned to sit beside Margaret.

"By the way my dear brother, you will discover substantial funds in your bank account tomorrow. I will accept no argument."

"Margaret, Margaret, Margaret." He hugged her. "This will all work out fine. Robert will be here soon. You'll have your own home before the Bishop house is sold. Perhaps Anna could stay with you for a while, keep you company. I'm going to have a little rest before dinner. I suggest you do too."

"I'm not sure how I will get on without you."

"You're spunky, Margaret. I have no doubt you'll find a way." He kissed her on both cheeks. "Robert is a lucky man."

* * *

On Friday, Margaret intended to spend the day taking in the sweeping changes about to engulf her life. A series of visits changed it all.

The first visit to the Bishop house took place before ten o'clock. A stern-faced older man wearing a shabby suit pushed a large envelope toward Cookie. "Give this to the missus of the house. She has to get out by the end of the month." Before Cookie could respond he limped down the walk and scurried into a waiting carriage.

While the delivery was nasty, Margaret was relieved to be rid of her final link to Thomas.

The next visitor less than an hour later, was much better dressed and asked to speak privately with Mrs. Anna Hopkins. Cookie led him to the study and Margaret joined Cookie in the kitchen.

The army would not object to Anna's immigration application to remain in Halifax. The balding gentleman handed her an envelope containing a cheque to help with her move and a second as George's monthly pension payment.

The third visit just before noon was a woman Cookie cheerfully greeted by name. "Hazel, do come in. Cup of tea?"

"No. I won't be here long. Is Mrs. Bishop accepting visitors?"

"Of course. She's in the study. Follow me."

Margaret was surprised to see Hazel. She hoped the visit

would save her from an unpleasant task. "Come in. Please sit down."

Anna quietly excused herself.

"No thank you, Mrs. Bishop. My news is short. I have a position with a very good family. I'm working today so must leave right away. Good luck to you."

"Thank you Hazel, and to you too." Margaret mentally checked that task off her list with a big sigh.

In the early afternoon, while Anna was out for a walk, Angus Stewart introduced himself to Cookie. The stiff fall breeze had rearranged Angus' unruly locks, leaving them hanging over his brow. He pushed his glasses to the top of his head, taking the locks with them. "Is Mrs. Bishop available?"

"Come in, Mr. Stewart. One moment."

Cookie went to the study door.

Margaret looked up in surprise. "Again? Who is it this time?"

"A fella with unruly hair. He's carrying a package."

"Oh, yes. My diary. Bring him in."

"Lovely to see you again, Mrs. Bishop." Angus removed his glasses from his head and put them where they were intended. "With Mr. Bishop's death, you have no need of my services. I'm simply here to return your diary." He handed the package to Margaret.

Margaret pointed to a chair. "Please join me, Mr. Stewart and call me Margaret."

"Thank you. I read your observations and comments in your entries with great interest. You have a talent for capturing and immersing the reader with your words and insights. Are you a writer?"

"Heavens no but I devour books. I'm addicted to them."

"We are too. I should say, my wife Elizabeth and I are also book addicts."

"My friend Anna Hopkins writes for the newspaper. I imagine you have seen her work."

"Yes, of course." He removed his glasses, looked intently at

Margaret. "Have you ever thought of writing your story? It would be a captivating read, especially in these times with so many women struggling for their rights, specifically the vote."

* * *

James left the following week, amid a tearful farewell. "If the detective job in Toronto doesn't work, I'll head further west toward Edmonton."

"You do know you will always have a home with us."

"Of course."

"You better write to us, even if it's a postcard."

"I promise."

* * *

A week later, Margaret and Anna were comfortably settled in the former Bell family home where Robert was a daily visitor, undoubtedly raising the eyebrows of some neighbours. Occasionally, he stayed overnight and left early in the morning. He wasn't fooling anyone but he didn't care.

* * *

By Friday, October twenty-second, the wedding arrangements were complete.

Cookie was the only one with wedding jitters. She'd read Queen Victoria's wedding cake in 1840 was not the usual one-layer. It was several layers with elaborate white icing, made to get attention. In secret, she set about to outdo herself. And she succeeded. The cake was four tiers with white icing and sweet pea blossom decorations made with coloured icing.

The intimate family ceremony was held at the Fraser home on Saturday. An Anglican priest from St. George's officiated with Anna as maid of honour. Margaret wore a pale blue velvet gown with navy satin collar and cuffs and her mother's sapphire broach and earrings. Robert wore a black suit, white shirt and a silk, silver brocade vest with William's cravat and tie pin.

After everyone had a piece of wedding cake, Robert asked Cookie what she planned for the considerable remainder.

"I'm taking it to the children's orphanage tomorrow for their Sunday lunch dessert. Doctor and Mrs. Bell would heartily approve."

EPILOGUE

During the winter of 1896 Margaret and Anna were absorbed in their writing. Taking Angus' idea to heart, Margaret was writing her memoir, a story she intended to finish before the baby arrived. Anna's work with the newspaper exploded in a variety of directions, including suffragettes and the arts.

Without fail, Anna visited George every Saturday morning. She found strength and peace in his presence, regardless of the weather or her frame of mind.

Margaret and Anna attended suffragette meetings and supported the cause by speaking to prospective members and hosting meetings. It was challenging work with many detractors who openly opposed their ideas. Robert was happy to offer financial information to any women who had questions and Angus provided the same support with legal advice.

Despite the winter weather, Margaret and Anna managed to walk most days. By early April, Margaret referred to the walk as the daily waddle.

In May, Anna found her own two-bedroom home not far from Margaret and Robert. The second bedroom became her writing room which included a reading nook. Oliver, her ginger cat claimed her footstool until Maisie made him a cushion to fit on the window ledge.

Following a restless night in late May, Margaret was wakened by a gush of water. Robert, the sleeper who could snore through a thunder storm soon felt the insistent shaking from Margaret. He rushed down the hall to waken the midwife. Mrs. Kelly, a widow who worked with Doctor Lewis had begun staying in the house the previous week.

Auburn haired, blue eyed William Robert Fraser arrived four hours later.

RESOURCES

A number of sources were consulted during the writing of this fictional story. The following resources were particularly helpful:

Canada's Historic Places
Canadian Divorce Records (National Institute)
Canadian Railway Historical Association Inc.
    (Bulletin 17, Montreal April 15, 1954)
Canadian Theatre Encyclopedia - Canadian
    Theatre History
Halifax and Its People/1749-1999
Halifax Public Libraries
History of Nova Scotia (with special attention
    given to Communications and Transportation)
Journal of the Canadian Historical Association
Library and Archives Canada (City Scapes Halifax)
McGill Law Journal (https://lawjournal.mcgill.ca)
    pdf 7591703-carron
News Media Canada/Medias d'Info Canada
    (Canadian Journalism article from A History
    of Journalism in Canada by W.H. Kesterton,
    McClelland and Stewart Limited, 1967)
Nova Scotia Archives – Royal Engineers
Nova Scotia Court System (Nova Scotia Public
    Prosecution Service)
Revelstoke Railway Museum (Jim Cullen,
    Executive Director)
Serving Hard Time in Halifax (Halifax Magazine
    October 31, 2016 – Katie Ingram)
The Canadian Encyclopedia

pagemasterpublishing.ca/by/dianne-palovcik/

To order more copies of this book, find books by other
Canadian authors, or make inquiries about publishing
your own book, contact PageMaster at:

PageMaster Publication Services Inc.
11340-120 Street, Edmonton, AB T5G 0W5
books@pagemaster.ca
780-425-9303

catalogue and e-commerce store
PageMasterPublishing.ca/Shop

ABOUT THE AUTHOR

Dianne (Taylor) Palovcik began her writing career after retirement when she challenged herself to write a novel. Her work focuses on Canadian history, bringing it to life with relatable characters, strong storylines and detailed settings.

Dianne's successful debut novel, *In Trouble* is disturbing and illuminating fiction, a story of unwed mothers and forced adoption in Canada during the 1960's.

In Trouble was recognized by the Writers Guild of Alberta in 2020 with an in-depth interview of the author and her work.

Not All Widows Wear Black weaves an engaging Victorian tale complete with lies, revenge, murder and a touch of romance.

Dianne lives in Alberta, Canada. She is a graduate of Acadia University and completed studies at the University of Alberta, University of San Francisco and Lakeland College. When not writing, she enjoys time with family and friends, plays golf badly and travels with her husband.

Follow Dianne on Facebook: DiannePalovcikAuthor